ABOUT THE AUTHOR

Barbara Vine is Ruth Rendell, the bestselling crime novelist. She has written many novels, including *The Lake of Darkness*, *The Killing Doll*, *The Tree of Hands*, *Live Flesh*, *Heartstones* and *The Veiled One*. As Barbara Vine she is the author of *A Dark-Adapted Eye*, which received huge critical acclaim and won the Mystery Writers of America's Edgar Allan Poe Award; *A Fatal Inversion*, winner of the 1987 Crime Writers' Association Gold Dagger Award; *The House of Stairs*, winner of the Angel Award for Fiction; *Gallowglass*; *King Solomon's Carpet*, winner of the 1991 Crime Writers' Association Gold Dagger Award; *Asta's Book*, shortlisted for the 1993 *Sunday Express* Book of the Year Award; *No Night is Too Long*; and *The Brimstone Wedding*. All of these are published by Penguin. *Gallowglass*, *A Dark-Adapted Eye* and *A Fatal Inversion* have all been the basis of successful BBC television series.

Ruth Rendell is a Fellow of the Royal Society of Literature. In 1991 she was awarded the Crime Writers' Association Diamond Dagger for a lifetime's achievement in crime writing.

BARBARA VINE

———

THE HOUSE OF STAIRS

PENGUIN BOOKS

PENGUIN BOOKS

Published by the Penguin Group
Penguin Books Ltd, 27 Wrights Lane, London W8 5TZ, England
Penguin Books USA Inc., 375 Hudson Street, New York, New York 10014, USA
Penguin Books Australia Ltd, Ringwood, Victoria, Australia
Penguin Books Canada Ltd, 10 Alcorn Avenue, Toronto, Ontario, Canada M4V 3B2
Penguin Books (NZ) Ltd, 182–190 Wairau Road, Auckland 10, New Zealand

Penguin Books Ltd, Registered Offices: Harmondsworth, Middlesex, England

First published by Viking 1988
Published in Penguin Books 1989
11 13 15 17 19 20 18 16 14 12

Printed in England by Clays Ltd, St Ives plc

To David

1

The taxi-driver thought he had offended me. I pushed a five-pound note through the opening in the glass panel and said to stop and let me out. The lights were changing from red and as he pulled in to the side he said in a truculent way,

'I've a right to my own opinion.'

He had been talking about forcible sterilization of the unfit, a subject resulting from some newspaper controversy, and he was all for it, voraciously and passionately for it. I might have been offended, I especially might have been offended – if I had been listening, if I had taken in more than the gist of it.

'I didn't even hear you,' I said, realizing as I said it that this would only make things worse, and I risked the truth, though I knew it wouldn't help, 'I saw a woman I know, a woman I used to know. On the crossing. I have to see her.' Out on the pavement, I shouted back at him, 'Keep the change!'

'What change?' he said, though there was some, a reasonable tip. He was one of those men who think women are mad, or tell themselves women are mad, this being the only way to explain otherwise inexplicable behaviour, the only way to defend themselves against the threatening regiment. 'You want to get yourself seen to,' he shouted, and – who knows? – perhaps he was reverting to his original subject.

It wasn't malice that had made him set me down on the south side of the Green. It only seemed like it as I stood there, imprisoned by the flow, the running tide of traffic, that at the same time had the effect of a door constantly slamming in my face. All the while the lights remained at green Bell was slipping away farther and farther from me. The metal tide, the slamming door, bore a great exodus out of Wood Lane and the Uxbridge Road, from the West End by Holland Park Avenue, out of the West

Cross Route, and the emerald light pulled it on, summoned it to a swifter onslaught, a more tumultuous roar. It cut off my view of the Green on which she must now be – walking which way?

Through the taxi's windscreen I had seen her on this crossing. With her characteristic gliding walk unchanged, back straight, head held high as if she carried an amphora balanced on it, Bell had passed northwards from the Hammersmith side. I gasped, I know I did, I may even have let out a cry, which to my cab-driver had sounded like a protest at his words. She disappeared from my sight towards Holland Park so quickly that she might have been an hallucination. But I knew she wasn't. I knew that strange though it was to find her in this unlikely place, it had been Bell I saw and I had to follow her even after all these years and after all the terrible things.

Enforced waiting when you are in a desperate hurry, that is one of life's worst small stings. It didn't seem small to me then. I jogged up and down, bouncing on my feet, praying, begging the lights to change. And then I saw her again. Buses moved, a red wall of them, and I saw her again, crossing the green, a rapidly retreating figure, tall and erect and looking straight ahead of her. She was in black, all black, the kind of bunchy clustered clothes only the very tall and thin can wear, the waist that looks breakable contained by a wide black belt as if to keep it from snapping in two. From the first sight of her I had noticed something startlingly different. Her hair, which had been very fair, had changed colour. Although I could no longer make it out across the expanse of grass and paths as the figure of Bell grew smaller, I understood with a sense of shock, with a kind of hollow pang, that her hair was grey.

The lights changed and we streamed across in front of the impatient, barely stationary, waiting cars. Or fled in my case, fled on to the Green and across it in pursuit of Bell whom I could no longer see, who had disappeared. I knew of course where she had gone, into the tube station, down into the tube. A 50p ticket out of the machine and I was going down on the escalator, forced now to face alternatives and make a choice, the ancient but everlasting choice of which of two paths to take, in this case westwards or eastwards? Bell had been a Londoner once. Before she disappeared from all our lives into the limbo years, into no man's land,

8

the cloister fort et dure, she had been a Londoner who, in spite of sojourns in exile, boasted she would lose her way west of Ladbroke Grove or east of Aldgate. West of Ladbroke Grove (simply The Grove to her and all of us then) she had been this evening but visiting only, I thought. Somehow I knew she was going home.

So I turned to the platform going east and the train came in at the same time, but before I got into it I saw her again. She was a long way along the platform, walking towards the opening doors, and her hair was as grey as ashes. It was ash grey and done up like Cosette's had once been, done in the very precise style of hers, piled loosely on her head in the shape of a cottage loaf with a knot in the centre like a bun of dough, the way it had been when first Cosette came to the House of Stairs.

There was something dreadfully disturbing about this, so upsetting indeed that I felt a real need to sit down and rest, close my eyes and perhaps breathe deeply. But of course I dared not sit down. I had to station myself just inside the doors so that I could see Bell when she left the train and walked past my carriage to the way out. Or even briefly go out on to the platform at each station in case her exit took her the other way and I missed her. I was very afraid anyway that I was going to lose her, but not so preoccupied that I couldn't examine the situation as I stood close up against those doors. For the first time I wondered if Bell would want to see me and I wondered what we would say to each other, at least to begin with. I couldn't imagine that Bell blamed me, as for instance Cosette had blamed me. But would she expect me to blame *her*?

I was thinking along these lines when the train came into Holland Park. The doors opened and I leaned out, looking along the length of the train, but Bell didn't emerge. It was about half past seven by this time and although a lot of people were about, the crowds had gone. Doing what I was doing, or trying to do, would have been impossible in the rush hours. The next station would be Notting Hill Gate and I was almost certain Bell wouldn't alight there, for this was the station we had all of us used in those days, all of us that is except Cosette, who went everywhere by car or taxi. Bell, for all that she had loved these particular parts of west

9

London, wouldn't have been so insensitive as to choose a return to those streets and that tube station when she came out of prison.

There it was, I had said it, silently and to myself, in my own head, but I had uttered the word. Not cloister nor limbo nor no man's land, but prison. It made me feel weak, dizzy almost. And this thought was succeeded by another, very nearly equally tumultuous: I hadn't expected her to be free, I had thought another year at least, I am not prepared for this. Had I expected her ever to be freed? But I had to be prepared, I had to get out of the train in case I was wrong, in case Bell was not living here but only visiting and was obliged to use this station. I stood on the platform, watching for her, but again she did not appear.

She left the train at Queensway. I got out and followed her, certain now that I must catch up with her in the crowd that stopped to wait for the lift. But when the lift came it could accommodate only so many of the waiting passengers. I saw Bell get into it, her fine ashen head held high above all but two of the others, but had to take the second lift myself. However, before I did so, before the doors of the first lift closed, Bell turned to face this way and looked straight at me. I don't know whether she saw me or not, I have been puzzling about this but still I can't say, though I think she didn't. The lift doors closed and the lift rose up, bearing her away.

It was sunset when I came out into the Bayswater Road, the sky a pale red but tumbled with ranges of cloud that were rust-coloured and crimson and nearly black. The skies of cities are so much finer than anything you see in the country and London has the best of them, though I know Americans would make that claim for New York and I will gladly give it second place. T. H. Huxley used to look down Oxford Street at sunset and see apocalyptic visions, and that evening I too seemed to see wonderful configurations above the Park and Kensington Palace Gardens, great swollen masses of cloud stained with the colours of ochre and dried blood, dividing in the wind to lay bare little limpid lakes of palest blue, closing again in vaporous surges dark as coal. But Bell I couldn't see, Bell I had lost.

I walked back and looked up Queensway. I looked along the Bayswater Road in both directions. There was a tall woman in black a long way ahead, walking westwards, and I think even then I knew in my heart it wasn't Bell, though her waist was small and her hair was grey. I deceived myself because what else was I to do? Go home empty-handed and empty-hearted? I should have to do that sooner or later, but not now, not yet. And the moment the woman had turned out of the Bayswater Road into St Petersburgh Place my conviction that it was Bell, it must be Bell, returned – for how could she have escaped and hidden herself so fast? – and I pursued more eagerly, up St Petersburgh Place, past the synagogue and St Matthew's, along Moscow Road and into Pembridge Square, across Pembridge Villas. By then, of course, we were nearer Notting Hill Gate tube station than Queensway and I was telling myself that Bell deliberately avoided it, took this long way round to her home because it was as hard for her as it was for me, or harder, to face the old associations.

I lost her somewhere this side of the Portobello Road. I say 'somewhere this side' as if I didn't know the place like the palm of my own hand, as if I could have been indifferent to any inch of it, forgotten any yard of it. It was in Ledbury Road that I lost her and found her again on the corner of the Portobello Road where she had met a friend and stopped to talk. And then I saw it wasn't Bell, as that part of me which would recognize her blindfold had always known. It was an older woman than Bell, who would now be forty-five, that I had been following and the girl she was talking to on the corner was a small dumpy blonde, her shrill laughter echoing in that empty ugly glamorous street. I walked on past them and saw the red sky was no longer red but a wild stormy grey of heavy jostling clouds and black with thunder over Kensal Town.

Few people were in the streets. It had been different when first I came here nearly twenty years ago and all the youth of England was on fire, and most it seemed to me, in Notting Hill. Now there were cars instead, cars which swallowed up the people and transported them in protective capsules. The houses here have gardens and in May they are full of blossoming trees so that the place smells of engine oil and hawthorn, honeysuckle and petrol fumes. It was French cigarettes it smelt of in Cosette's day, any old cigarettes come to that, French and English and Russian and Passing Clouds even, and marijuana in the Electric Cinema. I walked along, not the way I had come, but further south than that, along Chepstow Villas, and I knew where I was going, there is no possibility I can claim I was tending that way by chance, that I didn't know Archangel Place lay in that direction.

But it was of Bell that I was thinking as I walked, wondering who there was that I could find to lead me to her; who would know. My certainty remained that she had been going home, was very likely home by now. It was the sight of me from the lift at Queensway station which had sent her hurrying, hiding even. She had only to slip inside the entrance of the Coburg Hotel or even into Bayswater tube station, just a few yards along Queensway, to have eluded me. And of course she didn't live in Notting Hill, but somewhere in Bayswater. There must be someone I could find who would tell me where. But that she should have wanted to elude me . . .? I who never walk anywhere if I can help it had been walking fast and running in pursuit of the real and the false Bell and my legs began to ache.

It is inescapable always the feeling that this may be it, this time it is no ordinary tiredness but the early warning itself, and the usual unease touched me, the usual quiver of panic. I am not old enough yet to be out of danger, I am still within the limit. But oh, what a bore it all is, how dreary and repetitive and simply boring after all these years, yet how can something be a bore and a terror at one and the same time? I have told no one, ever, but Bell and Cosette. Well, Cosette knew already, naturally she did. Does Bell remember? When she saw me in the station did she remember then and wonder if it had caught me yet or passed me by and left me safe?

I told myself, as I always do, your legs ache because you're not fit (the muscle in your chin jumps because you are tired, carelessness made you drop that glass) and I thought what a fool I was to go out in high heels, in pointed shoes that pinched my toes. It scarcely helped, nothing helps except the ache, the tic, the weakness, going away. I thought I would hail the next taxi that came round one of those narrow leafy corners, out of a crescent or a terrace, for this region of West Eleven is a tight-knit confusion, a labyrinth of alleys and mewses, blown fields and flowerful closes, green pleasure and grey grief.

No taxi came and I was fooling myself when I said I would have taken it if it had. I had come to the narrow lane that leads into the mews and thence into Archangel Place, a lane which, for all its overhanging tree branches and dense jostling hedges, could never be in the country. Slates, polished by the passage of town shoes and their friction, pave it, and there is privet in the hedge and catalpa among the trees. It smells of a city, of staleness and use, and underfoot is dust rather than earth. Between the mews and the street stands the church called St Michael the Archangel, Victorian Byzantine, unchanged, not closed and boarded up, not transformed by one of those vaguely blasphemous conversions into a block of flats, but just the same and with its doors flung wide to show the archangel in the sanctuary with his outspread wings.

I paused on the corner, bending down to rub the muscles in my calves, then looked up and stood up, stood there looking down the narrow, straight and rather short street. From there the House of Stairs also appeared unaltered. But it was dusk now, the long London summer dusk, gloomy and cool, and changes might be hidden. Slowly and deliberately, as if out for a stroll, I walked down on the opposite side. On summer evenings when Cosette lived there people used to sit on doorsteps and when it was hot sunbathe stretched out on the flat roofs of porches. But Archangel Place has come up in the world and I suspect that behind the varied façades, Dutch, Victorian Baroque, neo-Gothic, Bayswater Palladian, are rank upon rank of neat flats that are called 'luxury conversions', with close carpeting and false ceilings and double glazing. It was soon clear to me that number fifteen was such a one, for where Cosette had a twisted wrought-iron bellpull is a row of entryphone buzzers with printed cards above each one.

How could I have had the bizarre idea that Bell's name might be on one of them? It was this at any rate that made me cross the road and look. The House of Stairs has become six flats, from basement to attic every floor economically used by occupants with Greek names and Arab names, a Frenchman by the sound of him, an Indian, a woman who might be German-Jewish or just an American, but no Bell. Of course not. The colour of the house had changed. From the corner of the street this had not been discernible, but now it was, this new, doubtful shade that might be quite different in broad day from what the lamplight showed me, a darkish buff. When Cosette bought it the house was painted the dull green of a cabbage leaf but the stonework remained its natural cream colour, as it still is now. The windows, five sets of them above ground level and one below, you can see for yourself in Ruskin's *The Stones of Venice*, the plate that shows the arch masonry in the Broletto of Como. Whether the architect went there to see for himself or simply copied these windows from Ruskin's drawing I don't know, but they are very faithful renderings, each consisting of three arches with a knot like a clove-hitch half-way up the two double shafts which are surmounted by Corinthian capitals. You can get a better idea from the picture.

There were lights on in these windows and not all the curtains were drawn. I retreated across the road and stood under one of the plane trees that line the street. It was shedding from its dying flowers the pale fluffy stuff that Perpetua used to say gave her hay fever. The new owners or the builders had changed the front door which when Cosette lived there would also have been to Ruskin's taste, having a pointed arch and its woodwork ornamented with ears of corn and oak leaves enclosed by fillets. The new one was a neo-Georgian monstrosity and the arched top of the architrave had been filled in with a pane of ruby-coloured stained glass. But no one had changed the garden – the front garden, that is, for the back was invisible from where I stood.

It is a very small area of garden, between the pavement and the deep recess that separates it from the basement window. What always made back and front gardens remarkable was that they were grey gardens of grey flowers and grey foliage, cinerarias and sea holly, rabbit's ears, lavandula lanata, the silver dwarf lavender, lychnis coronaria with leaves like felt, cardoons that are sisters of the globe artichoke, artemisia with its filigree foliage, ballotas and senecios. I who knew nothing of gardening learnt the names of all the plants in Cosette's garden. Jimmy the gardener taught me, was delighted to find someone who cared enough to learn, and those names have stuck with me. Did Jimmy still come? He used to say that lanata was frail and would scarcely survive without his care. The plants looked thriving to me and the pale silver irises were in full bloom, their papery petals gleaming in the greenish lamplight.

Without being able to see it, aware that I couldn't have borne to see it, I knew that the back garden would be different, would have undergone some tremendous change. Whoever had the house after Cosette, and after I refused it, must have known, must have been discreetly told and have decided to accept the facts and live with them. But along with this decision would have come a need to alter the garden, change the positions of things, perhaps plant trim box bushes and sharp-pointed conifers, bright-coloured flowers. All this would be designed to exorcise the ghosts that some say derive from the energy left behind after an event of violent terror.

I tried to see between the houses, to make my eyes penetrate brick wall and high hedge, black, nearly solid, masses of evergreen foliage. But if the eucalypt had still been there its thready branches with fine pointed grey leaves would by now far exceed in height the hollies and the laurel, for gum trees, as Jimmy once told me, grow tall quickly. If it were still there it might even by now have reached close to that high window. It wasn't there, it couldn't be, and before I turned my eyes away I imagined its felling and its fall, the powerful medicinal scent that must have come from its dying leaves and severed trunk.

There are two balconies only on the façade of the House of Stairs, on the windows of the drawing-room and principal-bed-room floors, and they are copies of the balconies on the Ca' Lanier, bulbous at the base, somewhat basket-like. This disciple of Ruskin was not averse to a hotch-potch of styles. As I stood there the central window on the drawing-room floor opened and a man came out on to the balcony to take in a plant in a pot. He didn't look in my direction but down at his plant and, re-entering, swept aside the curtain to afford me a glimpse of a gold-lit interior, mainly a tiny twinkling chandelier and a dark red wall no more than ten feet inside the window, hung with mirrors and pictures in white frames. It was a shock of a physical kind, clutching at the centre of my body. And yet of course I knew the drawing room must have been sub-divided; must, for it had been thirty feet deep, now comprise the whole flat. The curtain fell and the window was closed once more. I had a sudden vivid memory of returning from some time away, some visit to Thornham perhaps, and of climbing the first flight of stairs to open the drawing-room door and seeing Cosette seated there at the table, her head at once turning towards me, that radiant smile transforming her wistful face, her arms out as she rose to receive me into her unfailing welcoming embrace.

'Darling, did you have a good time? You don't know how we've all missed you!'

A gift for me there would be from that clutter on the table, a homecoming present carefully chosen, the strawberry pincushion perhaps or one of the gemstone eggs. And she would have wrapped it in paper as beautiful as William Morris fabric, tied it with satin ribbon, perfuming it as she did so by chance contact with her own skin, her own dress . . .

My eyes were tightly shut. Involuntarily I had closed them when the tenant or owner of the first-floor flat allowed me a sight of his living room, and I conjured up Cosette where the red wall now was. I opened my eyes, took a last look at the changed, re-ordered, spoiled house and turned away. It was dark by then and as I began walking towards Pembridge Villas, refusing for some melodramatic reason to look back, a taxi came out of one of the mewses and I got into it. Leaning back against the slippery upholstery, I felt curiously tired and worn. You will think I had forgotten all about Bell, but she had only temporarily been pushed out of my mind by remembering Cosette and by all the other emotions the House of Stairs awakened. What I had truly forgotten was the pain in my legs and this had gone, I was reprieved, the bore and the terror would be gone for a week or two.

Of Bell I now thought in a new mood of tranquillity. Perhaps it was all for the best that I had lost her, that there had been no confrontation. Again I wondered if she had seen me over the heads of those people in the lift and again I couldn't make up my mind. Had she fled from me or, innocent of my presence behind her, left the station and gone directly into one of the Queensway shops? It might even be, and this was disturbing, that, emerging, she had followed me, unaware of who I was. Or indifferent? That too had to be faced.

Perhaps she would want to know no one from those old days

but start afresh with new friends and new interests, and that (as I now decided must be the case) was borne out by her living in Bayswater or Paddington, areas of London I believed she had never lived in before.

But all this made no difference to my decision to find her. I would find where she was and how she lived and what she now called herself, and obtain a sight of her, even if I took it no further than that. My heart sank a little when I contemplated the prison years, insofar as I could imagine them, the waste of life, the loss of youth. And then, just as I had had a kind of vision of Cosette at that drawing-room table, loaded as it always was with books and flowers, sheets of paper and sewing things, the telephone, glasses for seeing through and glasses for drinking from, photographs and postcards and letters in their envelopes, so I seemed to see Bell as she was almost the first time I ever saw her, walking into the hall at Thornham to tell us that her husband had shot himself.

2

I was fourteen when they told me. They were right, they had to tell me, but perhaps they could have waited a few more years. What harm would it have done to wait four years? I wasn't likely to have married in those four years, I wasn't likely to have had a baby.

Those were the words I used to Bell when I told her this story. She is the only one I have ever told, for Elsa doesn't know, even my ex-husband Robin doesn't know. I confided it all to Bell on one dark winter's day in the House of Stairs, not up in the room with the long window, but sitting on the stairs drinking wine.

It wasn't that my mother's illness was apparent. They weren't even sure she was ill, not physically that is. Mental changes, which is how the books describe her condition, could be attributed to many causes or to none in particular. But they had set fourteen as the age and they stuck to it and told me, not on the birthday itself, which is what happens to the heroes and heroines of romance initiated into family rituals and family secrets on some pre-set coming of age, but two months later, on a wet Sunday afternoon. They must have known it would frighten me and make me unhappy. But did they understand what a shock it was? Did they realize they would make me feel as much set apart from the rest of humanity as if I had a hump on my back or was destined to grow seven feet tall?

I understood then why I was an only child, though not why I had been born at all. For a while I reproached them for giving me birth, for being irresponsible when even then they knew the facts. And for a while, a long while, I no longer wanted them as parents, I no longer wanted to know them. The rapid progress of my mother's illness made no difference. There is no time in our lives when we are so conspicuously without mercy as in adolescence. I turned from them and their secret, her distorted genes, his watch-ful eyes and suspenseful waiting for the appearance of signs, to someone who was kind and didn't cause me pain. I turned to Cosette.

Of course I had known Cosette all my life. She was married to my mother's cousin Douglas Kingsley and because we are a small family – naturally, we are – the few of us in London gravitated towards each other. Besides, they lived near us or near enough, a walk away if you didn't mind long walks and I can't have done in those days. Their house was in Wellgarth Avenue, which is Hampstead – almost Golders Green. It faced the ponds and Wild-wood Road, a thirties Tudor place, huge for two people, which was meant to resemble, but didn't quite, a timbered country farm-house. When people told Douglas that Garth Manor was very large for just two people he used to reply simply and not in the least offensively, 'The size of a man's home doesn't depend on the size of his family. It's a matter of his status and position in the world. It reflects his achievement.'

Douglas was an achiever. He was a rich man. Every morning he was driven down to the City in his dark green Rolls-Royce to join the queue of cars, even then, in the fifties and sixties, rolling ponderously down Rosslyn Hill. He sat in the back going through the papers in his briefcase, studying them through the thick lenses of glasses in dark solid frames, while his driver contended with the traffic. Douglas had iron-grey hair and an iron-grey jowl and the shade of his suits always matched hair and jowl, though some-times with a thin dark-red or thin dark-green stripe running verti-cally through the cloth. He and Cosette led a life of deep yet open and frank upper middle classness. When I was older and more interested in observing these things I used to think it was as if Douglas had at some earlier stage of his life compiled a long list or even a book of upper-middle-class manners and pursuits and chosen from them as a life's guide those of the more stolid sort, those in most frequent popular usage and those most likely to win reactionary or conventional commendation.

All this was reflected in the magazines that lay on Cosette's coffee table, *The Tatler*, *The Lady*, *Country Life*, in the food they ate – I have never anywhere else known such an enormous consumption of smoked salmon – the clothes from Burberry, Aquascutum and the Scotch House, his Rolls-Royce, her Volvo, their holidays in Antibes and Lucerne and later, as the sixties began, in the West Indies. But at fourteen I didn't of course see it like this, though I couldn't help being aware of their wealth. If I thought about it at all, I saw this lifestyle as the choice of both of them, willingly and happily entered into. It was only later that I began to understand that their way of living was Douglas's choice, not Cosette's.

I began going to see her in those summer holidays after my parents told me of my inheritance. She had invited me while on one of her visits to our house. I was a child still, but she talked to me as to a contemporary, she always did this to everyone, in her smiling, vague, abstracted way.

'Come over next week, darling, and tell me what to do about my garden.'

'I don't know anything about gardens.' I must have said it sullenly, for I was always sullen then.

'My lilies are coming out, but they're not happy and it seems a shame, because they have such lovely names. Gleaming Daylight and Golden Dawn and Precious Bane. It says in the catalogue, "thriving in all garden soils, tolerant of both moisture and drought, they can be grown in full sun or partial shade . . ." but I must say I haven't found it so.'

I just looked at her, bored, not responsive. I had always liked Cosette because she took notice of me and never fussed or inquired, but on that day I hated all the world. The world had been injuring me without my knowing it for fourteen years and I had a lot of revenge to take on it.

'We won't have to do anything,' said Cosette, evidently seeing the offer of idleness as a great inducement. 'I mean we won't have to dig or plant or get our hands dirty. We'll just sit and drink things and make plans.'

They had told her I had been told and she was being tender with me. After a while she wanted my company for myself and kindness didn't come into it. But at that time I was just a young relative who had been given a terrible burden to bear and whom she felt she could uniquely help. Cosette was like that. She welcomed me to Garth Manor and we sat outside that first time on the kind of garden furniture the other people I knew didn't have, chintz-upholstered sofas that swung gently under canopies, cane chairs with high backs that Cosette called 'peacocks'.

'Because they are supposed to look like the Peacock Throne but without all the jewels and everything. I wanted to have a pair of peacocks to strut up and down here – imagine the cock bird's lovely tail! But Douglas didn't think it would be a good idea.'

'Why didn't he?' I said, already resentful of him on her behalf, already seeing him as an oppressive, even dictatorial, husband.

'They screech. I didn't know that or of course I wouldn't have suggested it. They screech regularly at dawn, you could set your clock by them.'

There was a glass-topped table of white rattan, sheltered by a big white sunshade. Perpetua brought us strawberries dipped in chocolate and lemonade made out of real lemons in glasses that by some magical means had been coated with actual frost. Cosette smoked cigarettes in a long tortoiseshell holder. She told me how much she liked my name. She would have called a daughter of her own by it if she had ever had a daughter. It was she who told me how it was that Elizabeth became a perennially popular name in England. Since then, though not at the time of course, I have often thought of the trouble she must have been to, gathering this information and a great deal more, just to please me and put me at my ease.

'Because if you say it over and over to yourself, darling, it really is quite a strange-sounding name, isn't it? It's just as strange as any other from the Old Testament, Mehetabel or Hephsibah or Shulamith, and any of them might have got to be as fashionable as Elizabeth if a queen had been called by them. Elizabeth became popular because of Elizabeth I and she was called Elizabeth because of her great-grandmother Elizabeth Woodville, that Edward IV married – so you see! Before that it was as rare as those others.'

'Cosette must be very rare,' I said.

'It means "little thing", it's what my mother always called me and it stuck. Unfortunately, I'm not a little thing any more. I'll tell you my real name, it's Cora – isn't that awful? You must

21

promise never to tell anyone. I had to say it for everyone to hear when I got married, but never, never since.'

I wondered why Douglas hadn't given her an engagement ring and a wedding ring made of something superior to silver, not knowing then that the element was platinum, the latest fashion when Cosette was married. The big diamonds looked sombre in their dark grey setting. At that time Cosette's only excursion into cosmetics was to paint her nails, and these were the bright reddish-pink of one of the clumps of lilies. The gesture she made when she pointed was peculiarly graceful, and somehow swan-like – only that is absurd. Swans don't point. But we think of them as moving with a slow fluidity, a delicate poise, and this too was Cosette.

The flowerbed she indicated was shaped like a crescent moon and the lilies in it looked perfect to me with their red flowers and yellow flowers and flowers snow-white printed with a coffee smudge. The gardener had planted them and ever since tended them. Cosette might direct operations here and in the house, but I never saw her perform with her own hands any domestic task. I never heard anyone, not even my father who was rather carping, call her lazy, and yet lazy she was with an unruffled, easy idleness. She had a tremendous capacity for doing absolutely nothing, though her sewing was exquisite and she could draw and paint, but she preferred to sit for hours in quietude, not reading, without a pen or needle in her hand, her face gentle and serene in repose. For in those days, and she must have been rather older than I am now, something over forty, the sadness I have spoken of had not come into her expression. Simone de Beauvoir, in some memoir, laments age which causes the face to droop and therefore take on a sad look. It was this sagging of the facial muscles which later gave Cosette an almost tragical appearance, except when she smiled.

To me, then, she was old, so old as almost to seem of a different species. Unimaginable that I might live to be as old as that – and unlikely too, as I sometimes thought with bitterness. She was then a large fair woman, overweight, fat even, though in those days she never showed signs of minding about her weight. Her eyes were a pale greyish-blue that seemed to look at you uncertainly, with a wistful and perhaps timid regard. For there was shyness in Cosette as well as confident generosity.

'You think my hemerocallis is quite happy there then, darling?' she said. The names of plants presented her with no difficulty. She might never plant them or pull out the weeds that threatened them but she knew exactly what each one was called. I said nothing, but that did not deter her. 'I suppose I'm being unduly impatient, expecting great things when the poor dears have only been there six months.'

Even I, young as I was, miserable as I was, couldn't help smiling at the notion of Cosette as an impatient person. Her tranquillity was the essence of her. In her company, because of this almost oriental placidity, I – and others – inevitably felt eased of burdens, curiously enfolded by a sweet meditative calm. It made you think in a strange way of its opposite, of the restless briskness so many women of one's mother's generation had and which made people of my age feel nervous and inadequate. She was always the same and always there, always interested, always with nothing better to do.

I soon began visiting her three times a week at least, then staying overnight. I was at school in Hampstead Garden Suburb and it was easy to explain that it was far more convenient for me to live at Cosette's during the week than to go home to Cricklewood. Or that was how I did explain it, an explanation which would sound absurd to anyone aware of the distance between the Henrietta Barnett and Cricklewood Lane. Only the existence and frequent presence of Douglas stopped me attempting to live at Garth Manor. Everyone knows couples of whom one is congenial, the other unsympathetic. For me the return home of Douglas each evening, heralded by the sound of the Rolls's wheels on the gravel drive, cast a blight over the companionship I enjoyed with his wife. He was so male, so stiffly elderly, so stockbroker-ish, much of his talk incomprehensible, and he seemed, without actually asking for it, to require a measure of grave silence in his house while he was in it. And at the weekends he was there all the time.

Cosette changed not at all in her husband's company. She was the same sweet, smiling, calm yet effusive creature, the same woman whose great gift was as a listener. To his accounts of deals and negotiations she would listen with the same rapt attention that she gave to my own outpourings, the retailing of my dreams, visions, frustrations and resentments. And she really listened. It was not that she closed off her mind and wandered in thought to other regions. I marvelled at the intelligent replies she made to his mysterious diatribes and looked with suspicion and lack of comprehension when, getting up from her chair to move swan-like across the room, she allowed one plump white hand to rest softly against the side of his face. When she did this he would always turn his face into it and kiss the palm. This caused me a furious embarrassment. I know now that I didn't want Cosette to have any life of her own, any private life, that was not directly concerned with making mine easier and happier.

She didn't mention the terror and the bore but waited for me to do so. Cosette seldom raised subjects or showed curiosity. I spoke of it – it burst out of me in a passion rather – after a neighbour of hers, a woman called Dawn Castle, had been in the garden with us on a warm October day when the lily flowers were dead and gone and it was the late dahlias that Cosette and I were admiring. Dawn Castle was always talking about her children, what a worry they were, the youngest had just been expelled from school, something like that, and another one had failed an exam. She finished, as she always did, with the old cliché.

'Still, I suppose I wouldn't be without them.'

It never occurred to me that this often-repeated remark might be hurtful to Cosette. I saw it only as profoundly silly and said rudely, 'Why not if they worry you so much?'

She looked shocked, as well she might. 'One day you'll have a baby of your own and then you'll feel differently.'

'I shall never have a baby, never.'

I had spoken very abruptly, and I felt Cosette's eyes on me.

'I'd like a pound for every girl who has told me that,' said Mrs Castle with her hard little laugh, and after that she went home, being one of those people who are only at ease in an atmosphere of small talk and are quickly frightened away by what they call 'unpleasantness'. Cosette said, 'That was fierce.'

'It's cruel,' I said. 'People ought to think before they speak. If she doesn't know about me surely she knows about you, she knows Douglas is my mother's cousin.'

'In my experience no one ever remembers about other people's family relationships.'

'Cosette,' I said. 'Cosette, is that why you never had any children? Didn't you want children?'

She had a way of smiling in reply to a question she intended not to answer in words. It was a slow, mysterious smile that overspread her face, vague and gentle, but it somehow always put an end to further probing. I got it into my head then, for no reason, that Douglas had married Cosette without telling her of his inheritance. There was no foundation for this belief, you understand; I read it or thought I read it in her rueful eyes, in a kind of resignation. Adolescents do that, weave impossible romances around the lives of their older friends. I taught myself to believe Douglas had deceived Cosette, denied her children when it was too late for her to retreat, had attempted to compensate by showering her with opulence. That winter they went to Trinidad and I went home, where I found myself watching my mother in an almost clinical way. One day she dropped a wineglass and I screamed. My father came up to me and smacked my face.

It was a light slap, not painful, but I received it as an assault.

'Never do that again,' he said.

'And you never do that again to me.'

'You had better learn to control yourself. I have had to. In our position you have to.'

'Our position? What position? You've got one position and I've got another. I'm the one people are going to scream about, not you.'

Strong stuff for a fifteen-year-old. In the spring I went back to Cosette and Garth Manor from where I could walk to school across the Heath Extension and where I had in my large bedroom with its view of the woodlands of North End such luxuries as my own television and electric blanket and bedside phone. Though I must say, in my own defence, that it was not these things which attracted me. Why do young girls, at this particular stage of their development, enjoy the company of an older woman? I should like to think it wasn't stark narcissism on my part, it wasn't that

25

Cosette, very nearly thirty years my senior, presented no competition, or that my own good looks showed up more delightfully by contrast to her ageing face and body. For as ageing I certainly saw her, aged in fact, past hope as a woman and sexual being. The truth was that I had made Cosette into another mother for myself, the mother I had chosen, not had thrust upon me, the mother who listened and who had infinite time to spare, was prodigal with a flattery I believed and still believe sincere.

In those days she never seemed to mind being taken for my mother. That came later, in Archangel Place, when though she might not express it aloud, the pain she felt and a kind of humiliation at the frequent assumption made that I (or Bell or Birgitte or Fay) was her daughter, showed in her eyes and the wry twist of her mouth. But Mrs Kingsley of the Townswomen's Guild, the Wellgarth Residents' Association, school governor, purveyor of Meals on Wheels and occasional volunteer social worker, had no such vanities. Sometimes, in the holidays or on Saturdays, we would go shopping together and in Simpson's or Swan and Edgar, then still dominating the corner between Piccadilly and Regent Street at the Circus, an assistant would sometimes refer to me as her daughter. The same thing happened in the restaurants we dropped into for the cups of coffee Cosette seemed to need every half hour in order to survive.

'That would suit your daughter,' said an assistant in the Burlington Arcade, and across Cosette's face would come an almost adoring look of appreciation and pleasure.

'Yes, that would suit you wonderfully, Elizabeth. Why not try it on?' And then, as happened so often, 'Why not have it?' which meant she would buy it for me.

I had no impression then that she wanted to appear younger than she was. But would I have had, at fifteen? She dressed in suits which she had made by a tailor, an unheard-of thing today, and something which was old-fashioned even then. They were formal suits, 'costumes' made of cloth very like that which Douglas himself wore, with square shoulders and box-pleated skirts, the kind of garments least suited to someone of Cosette's type. She should have worn floaty dresses, cloaks and draperies. Later on, of course, she did, and not always to happy effect. On the shopping expeditions it was underwear she bought for herself, cruel ineffective girdles and slips of shiny pastel satin, clumping lace-up shoes with two-inch heels, blouses with big bows at the neck to show between the lapels of those worsted suit jackets.

As I grew older I, who had never judged Cosette, but loved her in a simple unquestioning way, became critical of her appearance. I never put this into words, or at least not into words I uttered to her. Sometimes, though, I am afraid I would make these comments to my friends and there would be giggling in corners. Cosette was one of those people whom others laugh at secretly, behind their backs. How cruel that it should be so, how painful! I wince as I form the words. But I am trying to tell the whole truth and it was true that when I brought a friend home (you see how I was then thinking of Garth Manor as 'home') and Cosette appeared, flushed and hot perhaps, untidy as she often was, that bird's nest of greying gold hair a mass of fluff and strands, collapsing and shedding pins, the hem of a silk blouse escaping from the waistband of a tailored skirt too tight over her jutting stomach – then we would glance at each other and giggle with sweet soft contempt.

Quite often, and especially when Douglas was away on a business trip, Cosette would take me and the friend out to dinner in Hampstead. First, though, a preening session took place in her huge and sumptuous bedroom (white four-poster with organza covered tester, curtains festooned and window seat cushioned, dressing-table with organza petticoat and triptych mirrors) and there in her admiring presence we tried on, like little girls, the clothes Cosette no longer wore, her fur capes and stoles and scarves, belts and artificial flowers and jewels, I always taking care never verbally to admire, for I knew from experience what the result would be. But my friend, out of ignorance or concupiscence, exclaimed, 'Oh, I love it! Isn't it lovely? Doesn't it look nice on me?'

And Cosette would say, 'It's yours.'

It was among these treasures of Cosette's that I first saw the bloodstone. It was a ring, the dark green stone flecked with red jasper embedded in a setting of densely woven gold strands. A ring for a strong hand with long fingers, Cosette said it was, and when she put it on it looked clumsy on her very feminine hand with the shiny pink nails.

'It belonged to Douglas's mother,' she said. I knew what had become of Douglas's mother and the cause of her premature death, but said nothing. I only smiled, the smile that grows stiff as the lips are held unwillingly stretched. 'She was born in March,' said Cosette, 'and heliotrope is the birthstone for March.'

'I thought heliotrope was a flower,' said my friend.

And Cosette smiled and said, 'Heliotrope is anything that turns to face the sun.'

I may not have been as kind to her as she was to me but I loved her, I always loved her. The nastiness of adolescence is ironed out as the senior teens are reached and, just as I now regret with a kind of agony the lack of compassion I had for my mother, so then I looked back with shame on my laughter and contempt. I was able to feel relief that Cosette had never known. For she asked nothing from those she loved except to be able to trust them. Perhaps that is not nothing, perhaps it is a great deal. I don't know, I can't say. She only wanted to feel she could surrender herself, her heart and mind, into the loved person's keeping and be safe there, not be betrayed. Years later, when I saw a college production of *The Maid's Tragedy*, two lines especially struck me, reminding me of her: 'Those have most power to hurt us, that we love. We lay our sleeping lives within their arms.'

Douglas she could trust. Whatever earlier doubts about that I had manufactured, he had never deceived her. He had loved her and made her safe and in exchange she had only to accept the way of life he had imposed on her: the neighbours to dinner and dinner with the neighbours, meetings of the Wellgarth Society in her dining room, Perpetua coming daily to clean, Maggie to cook, and Jimmy to weed the lilies, a view of North End in one direction and the Heath Extension in the other, inexhaustible money and unending placidity, Dawn Castle running in to drop platitudes from clacking lips, a surrogate child and six bedrooms. Of course it was not unending, nothing is. Cosette was fond of a story supposedly about the dying Buddha and I often heard her tell it in that soft unhurried voice.

'His disciples came to him and said, "Master, we can't bear to lose you, how can we live when you've left us? At least give us some word of comfort to help us after you have gone." And the Buddha said, "It changes." '

I used to smile because nothing ever changed for Cosette. Or so it seemed in those years while I lived most of the time with her and Douglas, her life an unvarying round of small, pleasant tasks, the high spots those holidays in conventionally exotic places, her excitements the dressmaker's delivery of a new evening gown for some livery-company dinner or, I selfishly flattered myself, my own satisfactory A-level results. It changes, but in some lives change is a long time coming.

One autumn morning, when the traffic was particularly heavy in Hampstead and the Rolls-Royce stationary in the queue above Belsize Park station, Douglas looked up from the document he had been reading, laid his head back against the seat and died.

The driver knew nothing about it. Douglas was not in the habit of talking to him unless something untoward happened and a traffic jam would not qualify as that. He had heard a sigh from the back of the car and a sound like throat-clearing, which was later how they were able to pinpoint the time at which death came. When they were down in the City, in Lombard Street, the driver came round to open the door and saw him reclining there with his head back as if asleep. He touched him and the skin of his face already felt unnaturally cool.

Douglas was fifty-three and therefore had almost certainly passed the time when his inheritance could have appeared in him. His death had nothing to do with this particular hereditary disease, for it was quick and merciful, not the long drawn-out torture that awaited my mother. Some kind of vascular catastrophe had wrecked his heart. The doctor told Cosette it happened so fast he would have known nothing about it.

3

They stood in the rain, Cosette and her brothers and their wives, a reception line of mourners under black umbrellas. Douglas, naturally, had had no brothers or sisters. We shook hands with the brothers and sisters-in-law and kissed Cosette on her cheek. I saw everyone else do this, so I did it too. I was there at Golders Green Crematorium with my father, my mother being past going to funerals by that time, or indeed going anywhere. A great many relatives of Cosette's were pointed out to me, but there was only one member of Douglas's family there apart from myself, his and my cousin Lily, an unmarried civil servant, who at the age of fifty was so deliriously happy at realizing she must now have escaped the scourge that even on an occasion like this she could scarcely suppress bubbling high spirits. She came up to my father and laid a hand on his arm.

'Tell me, how is poor Rosemary?'

No one ever asked a man after the health of his dying wife in more cheerful tones. Me she eyed with unconcealed speculation, for she knew, none better, that you can't get it unless one of your parents has it, that if the parent who carries the gene reaches fifty without it, you too will never get it.

Perpetua, who was there with a grown-up son, had told me when I called to see Cosette that she had screamed and sobbed at the news of Douglas's death, had wept hysterically and threatened to kill herself. When I saw her she was crying. I was no longer staying at Garth Manor even part of the time, for by then I was twenty and away at college. If you are at university in Regent's Park you will scarcely live in Golders Green if you can help it. But I rushed to Cosette as soon as I heard Douglas was dead, yet once there hardly knew how to comfort this woman who had nothing to say and who cried without ceasing. I come from a family that makes almost a fetish of not showing emotion and although I would have liked to be able to show it myself, I didn't know how. A friend that I envied – it was that same friend who had benefited from admiring Cosette's jewellery, a girl whose name was Elsa and whom naturally we called Lioness – used to tell me that throughout her childhood her parents shouted and raved at each other, all barriers down, all claws bared, but at least they showed their feelings. From this she believed she had derived the ability to show her own.

So I watched Cosette warily as the tears streamed down her cheeks, without an idea of what to say or do. And a week later her face was still red and her eyes still swollen. Standing there under her elder brother's umbrella, wreaths and crosses of dripping flowers at her feet, she looked as if she had been crying until the moment she entered the crematorium chapel, to stop abruptly only when Douglas's coffin disappeared and was consigned to the fire. She was in deepest black. Her suit was not one of those timeless tailor-mades, but dated from the period of the New Look, post-war, contemporaneous with my own birth, a long flared skirt which I suspect she could only have got into with the zip undone, a jacket with a peplum. I think she must have bought it for the funeral of her own mother, who had died about that time. It smelt of mothballs. Cosette, who was a rich woman, who had inherited from Douglas something in the region of a million, a huge sum in 1967, had not thought to buy a new suit for her husband's funeral. She disliked black, Perpetua told me later, and refused to waste money on something she would never wear again.

This was the first thing about Cosette that ever surprised me. It was the forerunner of many surprises.

There was speculation as to what she would do now. I have since learnt that relatives and neighbours are invariably ready with advice for a woman in her situation, while never suggesting the kind of things they would want to do themselves. The courses they propose always seem designed to keep the subject out of mischief.

No one less likely to get into mischief than Cosette could be imagined. She was forty-nine, but she looked older. Her hair was iron-grey. Her face was drawn and haggard, but she had put on weight, being a woman who ate for comfort. It was Easter and I went to stay with her. Once there, I made up my mind I would follow the example she had set me and be a good listener. I would listen and let her talk about Douglas and her life with him, for some intuition told me she would want to do this, that it would be a catharsis. My intuition was wrong. Bemused, looking slovenly and distracted, breaking off pieces of chocolate and putting them absently into her mouth, she asked me in a vague way what I had been doing, what my plans were.

'I want to know about you,' I said.

She responded with that mysterious smile, slightly shaking her head. It was as if to say her affairs were not important. I read into her look and her gentle insistence on my talking and her listening, an abnegation of a future, as plain as an utterance that her life was over, all that remained a slow decline to old age and death. And this attitude seemed supported by the visitors who came in a constant stream, relatives and friends, the usual widow's advisers with their glib counsel to move to 'a little place by the sea', a country cottage, a 'nice flat' in the Suburb.

'Not too big,' Dawn Castle said. 'Something compact for just you on your own. You won't want to wear yourself out keeping the place clean.'

Perpetua was even at that moment using the vacuum cleaner out in the hall, which made me think Mrs Castle must be deaf or else (more likely) one who never gave a second's thought to the sense of what she said. Cosette's brother Leonard suggested she move nearer him and his wife. They lived in Sevenoaks. A small house or bungalow near Sevenoaks, preferably a bungalow, said his wife, because as Cosette grew older she wouldn't want to climb stairs. She might not be able to climb stairs, this woman hinted darkly, watching Cosette helping herself from a biscuit tin. The other brother lived in one of those huge barrack-like blocks of flats in St John's Wood, an enormous place with four bedrooms he always called an apartment.

'There's a compact little one-bedroom apartment just come on the market in Roderick Court.' He added persuasively, 'It's on the ground floor, so you wouldn't even have to use the lift,' as if

Cosette would soon be too decrepit to step across a hallway and press a button.

She listened and said she would think about it. I never once heard her protest when they treated her as if she were on the threshold of senility. Of course women were older then than they are now, even twenty years ago they were. Middle-age then began at forty, but today at nearer fifty. The women's movement has had something to do with this change by altering the significance of beauty. It is no longer vested in youthful bloom, it is no longer even an essential part of attractiveness and attractiveness itself no more the essence of female existence. Cosette had never worked for her living, she had never even worked in the home, her life had been very near that of the concubine, and for twenty-eight years she had been the comfort and support of Douglas, his to be loved or left, to await his homecoming and listen while he talked. They would have been shocked, those callers with their advice, if they had heard this put into words, but they all knew it in their hearts. With Douglas's death Cosette's usefulness was over, just as the harem woman's is over when her lord dies.

She made no promises. Cosette hardly ever rejected any suggestion categorically, but she had her own kind of stubbornness. A refusal to study orders to view, to telephone estate agents, to be shepherded around show houses, is just as much a refusal when indicated by a smiling shake of the head as by an outright no. She was listening more and speaking less then that at any time I could remember. Grief had stricken her dumb, I thought, but later I came to understand she was silent because she had so much on her mind. She had so much to think about, and it was not her past with Douglas. She was making up her mind how to manage what she had set her heart on.

Men call to visit widows in the hope of getting into bed with them. Widows are ready, widows are grateful. Men who have been married for twenty years to the widow's best friend, apparently faithful husbands who have scarcely up till then ever called the widow by her Christian name, turn up sheepishly and make a pass at her in the kitchen while she is putting the tea-bags in the pot. Or so I have heard.

If this happened to Cosette it wasn't while I was staying there. Perhaps my presence put them off. The only possibilities anyway were Dawn Castle's husband Roger and the president of the Wellgarth Society. I have a photograph of Cosette taken in the garden that summer, and it looks like the kind of thing women's magazines use of some reader who wants advice on her appearance. On the opposite page is the same woman after the depilator and hairdresser and make-up artist, and plastic surgeon maybe also, have been at work. I can produce that photograph of Cosette too.

But reclining on the swinging seat, under the floral canopy, she looks blowsy, with her features taking on a blurred look and her hair hanging in disordered loops, lipstick apparently applied in a dark, mirrorless room, sunglasses hanging round her neck on what looks like a piece of elastic. She wears a dress like a cotton tent. At least she had abandoned the tailored suits, perhaps she could no longer get into them, the only change she seemed to have made in her appearance or way of living. For she still sat on her board of governors, went to meetings of the society, had the neighbours to dine and went to dine with them, they making a point of inviting her as if conferring on her enormous favours. No one, however, she later told me, went so far as to produce an unattached man for her. She was fifty, her birthday was that August, and we were living through a period of the cult of youth.

The notion of Cosette having a man friend, a lover, to me was grotesque. For that you had to be young. You might not have to be exactly good-looking, but you had to be attractive in some indefinable way or somehow charming, young and not fat. I had no idea I might be insulting Cosette in having these thoughts about her; I would never have had them at all, I would have supposed attracting a man was alien to her wishes as adopting a child or beginning a career might be, had Dawn Castle not said to me, 'The only thing for poor Cosette would be to marry again.'

Like a Victorian, I was shocked. 'Douglas has only been dead six months.'

'Oh, my dear, it's a well-known fact that if people are going to marry again they do it within two years.'

'Cosette would never want to marry again.'

'That's what you think, but you're young. Someone who's been married that length of time, of course she wants to be married.'

That conversation I remembered when a year later or less Cosette, alone with me, said in a burst of frankness,

'You're always hearing of men being womanizers. I'd like to be a manizer. Do you know what I'd like, Elizabeth? I'd like to be thirty again and steal everybody's husbands,' and she laughed a soft, hopeless, bitter laugh.

But there was no hint of this on the fiftieth birthday she quietly celebrated with a dinner in a restaurant to which she invited my father and me, her brother Oliver and his wife Adele. The Sevenoaks brother was away on holiday. In the taxi back to North End I was alone with her; she cried for Douglas and I put my arms round her, thinking of what Dawn had said, the absurdity of it.

In this house where I live in Hammersmith, in Macduff Street, are things which Cosette gave me. There are probably more things Cosette gave me than came from any other single source, certainly more than any other person ever gave me. For a long time they reminded me of her so sharply, with such pain, that I put them all away so as never to see them, but things changed, as things do – 'It changes,' said Cosette – and I got them out again and spread them about, in the living room, in the bedroom, in the room where I work. This is a little house, mid-Victorian, in a terrace. There is a garden which I am thankful to say is small, a box enclosed by walls like all the other gardens in this street and the next street, so that looking down on them from a helicopter would be like looking into a grocer's box when all the tins have been taken out. The two cats come and go over the walls, never venturing out into the front where the Great West Road threatens, not even knowing it is there or that it is possible for cats to go near it.

The three eggs Cosette gave me, one of chrysolite, one of agate, one of amethyst quartz, sit together in a round glass bowl on the living-room window sill. I had once had an idea of collecting gemstone eggs, but never collected more than these three. On the bookcase is Hans Andersen's Little Mermaid in Royal Copenhagen porcelain, a copy of the one in Copenhagen, which Cosette gave me for my twenty-fifth birthday. It comes in the category of disappointing things, she said, the things that are so much smaller and more insignificant than we expect.

'The Mona Lisa,' Mervyn said, and Gary said, 'The Commons Chamber, a little green box.'

'Niagara Falls,' I said, 'especially now they can turn them off.'

'The Central Criminal Court,' said Marcus.

We all looked at him.

'The Old Bailey, to you,' he said. 'Inside. It's little, it's not imposing. You expect something much grander.'

Strange, aren't they, these remarks of appositeness, of light-hearted, mild cleverness, uttered without thought that they might have an awful appropriateness, with no knowledge of the long shadows they cast before them?

'When were you at the Old Bailey, Mark?' Cosette asked him, and she looked so concerned that we laughed. Well, Bell didn't laugh, but the rest of us did. I think Bell had stopped laughing by this time. Mark said a friend of his who was a journalist, a crime reporter, had got him in. It was a manslaughter case, a man had killed his girlfriend.

'I thought it would be awe-inspiring,' said Mark. 'I wasn't exactly disappointed. I kept thinking about people being there on criminal charges and how it would make them feel less frightened, not more.'

'And would that be a good thing?'

Bell stared intently at him. 'Of course it would be a good thing,' he said. 'Of course it would.'

In the room where I work is a pen jar made of agate, a hollowed-out lump of red and purple and brown and green striped stone, which Cosette brought back from a holiday in Scotland and in it, among the pens, is a curious paper-knife whose handle, also striped in those colours but somehow a different kind of stripes, Cosette swore was carved out of a heather root. Or a bundle of compressed heather stalks or a fossilized heather root, something like that. In this room too are a cigarette-lighter with a blue-and-white Wedgwood base that Cosette gave me because she had it and I saw it and said I liked it. The old, generous, 'It's yours' response, that savours of the lavish hospitality of some clan chief-tain or head of an emirate. On a table in the corner is the old manual typewriter on which I wrote my first book at Archangel Place. This machine, a Remington, had belonged to Douglas. When I said I meant to write a book Cosette got a room ready for me, without telling me in advance, she just got it ready for me, she and Perpetua, and led me up there, showing it to me proudly, the desk she had bought in the Portobello Road, the swivel chair, the sofa for 'resting between chapters, darling,' and on the desk the ream of paper, the agate jar full of sharpened pencils, ballpoint pens, the heather-root paper-knife and Douglas's typewriter.

I no longer use it. I use an electronic one, not having yet moved on to a word-processor. Douglas's waits there for when I run out of cassettes for the electronic one, or it breaks down, or for the power cuts that seldom come, though they were frequent enough in the Archangel Place days. The bookcases in this house contain a lot of books Cosette gave me. A complete *Remembrance of Things Past*, a complete *A Dance to the Music of Time*, the complete novels of Evelyn Waugh. A whole set of the novels of Henry James, with *The Wings of the Dove* present, showing no sign of special wear, bearing no marks of time or pressure or pain. But why should it? It was not this copy in tooled blue leather, stamped with gold print, which Bell picked up and looked at, idly turning the pages, inquiring of me indifferently what it was about, Bell who never read anything more demanding than the *Evening News* or a fortune-teller's manual.

The Complete Works of Kipling, the Macmillan red-leather edition, tooled in gold. How Cosette loved sequences and sets! They enabled her to spend more money, be more giving, to overwhelm with a multiplicity of gifts. A dictionary of obscure quotations, a dictionary of psychology, a dictionary of modern Greek which Cosette bought me one Christmas, being unable to get a classical Greek one. And I was cross, I remember, I wasn't grateful or even resigned.

'But I told you,' I said, 'I told you over and over. I said not to get modern Greek. I told you not to get anything at all. What am I going to do with a dictionary of modern Greek?'

And poor Cosette said humbly, 'I'll get you the one you want. I've ordered it. They're going to get it in for me, they're going to get it next week. You'll have two that way. Wouldn't you like to have two Greek dictionaries?'

I stand here in my room looking at the dictionaries and at the sets and novel sequences. I look at my pictures, the water-colours my father gave me from our old house when he moved, the Fulvio Roiter poster of the Venice Carnival, the Mondriaan reproduction and the Klee reproduction – and I look at the space where I tried hanging the Bronzino but couldn't, couldn't face the sight of it. Douglas's typewriter is dusty and should be covered up, but there is no cover for it, the cover was lost long ago, probably while Cosette was still living at Garth Manor – pretentious, absurd name; if ever there was an instance of belonging in a category of disappointing things, this was it! – or lost in the move. On the desk, which is not the one Cosette bought in the Portobello Road, I have a London telephone directory and a list of numbers, not in London, that I wrote down from other directories while I was in the public library this morning. The London directory is an old one, but Cosette Kingsley isn't in it. I don't know why I look for her name, for something so impossible, but I do.

The Castles' number I have found, at the same old address in Wellgarth Avenue. It would be useless to phone them anyway, they won't know. But I could ask them for Diana's number, I could ask them where she is now, if she has married. I don't want to speak to them, that is the truth of it, I don't want to have to parry their innocent inquiries or offers of help. Fay's number is written on the piece of paper and so is Ivor Sitwell's. Fay lives in Chester and Ivor in Frome, in a kind of farming commune I gather, a place where they grow organic vegetables. I couldn't find the dancers' number, there was no number either for Llanos or Reed. There is only one Admetus in the phone book, initials M. W., but it must be Walter and he must have moved from Fulham up to Cholmeley Crescent in Highgate. But why should any of them know the whereabouts of Bell, whom they have no reason to care about, whom they may hate?

Also on the piece of paper is Elsa the Lioness's number, not because she lives outside London, but because she is ex-directory and I have had a succession of secret, closely guarded numbers of hers written down in my personal phone-book for years. The latest is on the paper now because it seemed more convenient to have all the numbers together. I have not seen her or spoken to her for a while, a month or two, but it is not the first time months have elapsed without our seeing or speaking, and when I do get to speak to her it will be all right, there will be no reproaches or accusations or grumbles, I know that. The Lioness has been married and divorced and married again and now lives on her own in a flat in Maida Vale. I dial her number but get no answer.

Her cousins, Esmond and Felicity, with whom we used to stay, she and I, live outside the area covered by London phone directories. Or they did and probably still do. I find it hard to imagine anyone willingly leaving that house. But then, of course, people leave houses unwillingly, they leave because they must, as Walter Admetus may have done, because they cannot afford them any more, or find them impossible for physical reasons, because of their staircases and steps up to the front door, their different levels, long passages, heavy doors. I should know that if anyone does. I should know. Then I remember that these cousins had a *pied-à-terre* in London, a studio in Chelsea they hardly ever used, the address of which I don't know, have never known, but in this case that doesn't matter because these cousins have a name so odd, so unique even, that in any phone book in the entire world anybody named Thinnesse is going to be one of them or closely related to them.

It is quite hard to pronounce correctly, that is to pronounce with both those middle n's separately enunciated as Esmond and Felicity always did. 'Thinnis' is the best other people usually attain to. I find their Chelsea number in the phone-book and dial it and, miracle of miracles, someone actually answers. It is not really a miracle at all, it is only what I should have expected. I knew their children must be in their early twenties by now, must be of an age when people are desperate to find accommodation in London away from parents, hostels, tiny furnished rooms. Perhaps I am not very happy admitting to myself that those Thinnesse babies who were three and six when I first went with Elsa to Thornham Hall are now grown up, are of an age to be taken by shop assistants and waiters for my children, just as once I was taken for Cosette's child.

It was the girl who answered my call, the girl Miranda. It is amusing to think that if this girl reads Beatrix Potter to her children it will be because I read Beatrix Potter to her when she was six. Of course we do not mention the Beatrix Potter sessions in the bedroom whose window overlooked the garden of Bell's cottage. She has forgotten them and I have forgotten everything about them except that they took place and that once, while reading *The Tale of Samuel Whiskers*, I saw Bell come out into the garden and peg ragged-looking, greyish washing out on a clothesline.

She tells me, this girl Miranda Thinnesse, that her parents still live at Thornham Hall and she gives me their number, a number which I wouldn't have been able to find in the directory for Outer East London and West Essex (or whatever it is called) because it has recently been changed to deter an anonymous phone-caller who said obscene things to Felicity. For all she knows, since she can't remember ever having heard the name Elizabeth Vetch, I might be the obscene phone-caller myself.

I can't bring myself to speak Bell's name to her. As she talks about her parents and her brother and the first her brother has just taken at Cambridge, I tell myself she will never have heard of Bell, her parents will have forgotten Bell. And then she says, what did I want to ask her parents? Did I just want to have a chat? Or was it something about that woman who killed someone – what was she called? Christine something?

'Christabel Sanger,' I say, and my voice sounds all right, sounds quite normal, as it might if I were speaking any other name, any name at all. And I say it again, to hear myself say it. 'Christabel Sanger,' and then, 'but we called her Bell, everyone called her Bell.'

'Did you want to talk to my mother about her?'

I sound remote, almost indifferent, or I think I do. 'I want to ask your mother if she knows where she is living.'

'Well, all I can tell you is she phoned my mother. She'd just come out of prison, an open prison I think, and she phoned home. I don't know why. It was a while ago now, I mean weeks. I think she phoned a lot of people. My mother could tell you more. Now you've got the number why don't you phone my mother?'

I say I will and thank her and say goodbye. It is strange what it does to me, this confirmation that Bell is back amongst us, that therefore it really was Bell I saw. It makes me feel a little sick, nauseous, no longer looking forward to the dinner I am being taken out to. Weeks ago she had phoned Felicity Thinnesse and 'a lot of people', but she hadn't phoned me. Me she had fled from along the streets of Notting Hill, had hidden from to elude me, had seen and stared at without smiling, seemingly without recognition. Or had not seen, had never seen, had not eluded, had merely gone into a shop outside Queensway station to buy a paper or a pack of cigarettes or a flower. Me she had perhaps tried to phone, had dialled my number many times, while I was away. For I have been away, was away first in Italy and then for a week staying with my father, who lives in a bungalow at Worthing now, the kind of bungalow they wanted Cosette to buy when she first became a widow.

I have gone upstairs into my bedroom to change my clothes, telling myself that I have no time now to speak to Felicity, telling myself that when I do speak to Felicity she will want to know all kinds of things I may not want to talk to her about. She may, for instance, ask me about Marcus, or even something about what the set-up was in Archangel Place just before Bell did what she did. She may invite me to Thornham Hall, and I am not sure whether or not I want to accept such an invitation. Probably I don't. Or suggest a meeting when next she and Esmond come to London. I move about my bedroom opening cupboard doors, opening drawers, looking at the phone extension and deciding to postpone the making of this call until tomorrow morning. Now I have in my hand a pincushion Cosette made me. It is in the shape of a strawberry and made of red silk, with the seeds on the strawberry's satiny outside embroidered in pale yellow thread. The pincushion is heart-shaped and fatly padded and it has never been used for the purpose it was designed for because I have been afraid to spoil the texture of the silk.

The cameo brooch in the jewel box was one of her birthday presents to me. The face in profile on it, carved from rosy-cream, strawberry-cream, coral is like Bell's, a classic profile, high of forehead, straight of nose, the upper lip short, the mouth full, the chin of perfect depth, and the hair, loops and tendrils of it

41

arranged in careless Regency fashion, disarrayed and tumbling, ringleted and tangled, is Bell's hair. I was taken by Cosette to choose this cameo and chose it because the face was Bell's, wore it expecting everyone to notice, to comment, to say, 'The girl on your brooch looks just like Bell,' but only Cosette noticed, only Cosette remarked on it.

I shall wear it tonight, going out with this man I haven't known very long, but like well enough. He is taking me to Leith's, something I have known for days and dreaded. How could I go to Notting Hill, the taxi perhaps passing the end of Archangel Place? How could I, in company, revisit those streets which were once my world, where everything that ever happened to me happened? All is changed and I no longer feel like this. I have been there, I have been back, following Bell. I am even excited. And I know the excitement does not stem from the prospect of sitting in a taxi with Timothy, eating dinner with Timothy, but because, up there, where Kensington Park Road meets Kensington Park Gardens or Ladbroke Square, I may see Bell again.

Tonight may be the night I shall find her.

4

After my mother was dead I went home to live with my father. I hated it and he hated it and both of us, I think now, saw it as our duty, I to be there and he to take me in. The arrangement endured only from the end of June until the end of September, my long vacation. He returned to work long before September came, before August came, I spending my days with Elsa and at Garth Manor with Cosette. Near the end of it my father suggested I go away for a holiday, without thinking perhaps that there was no desirable foreign place to which I could get a package he would pay for at such short notice. Most of the people I knew had already filled up the minibuses and Bedford trucks making for Turkey and India. His dreadful suggestion that he and I should together have a few days in Colwyn Bay caused his voice to falter with dismay even as he was making it. I compromised and went for a week with Elsa to her relations in Essex.

She used to talk of these relations, an aunt, a cousin and his wife and their two children, and somehow gave me the impression that it was north Essex where they lived, the Stour Valley, Constable Country, or the marshes, Great Expectations land. Or that was how I received it, which is nearer to the truth. Essex is a big county. When we set off towards the Central Line tube, I thought at first this was merely the first leg of our journey, that we should change trains at Liverpool Street, but no, Elsa bought a ticket for herself and a ticket for me to Debden, which is getting on for as far as the line goes. A huge council estate lay outside the station and my disappointment was bitter.

Elsa laughed and said, 'Wait a little, said the thorn tree,' a very nearly incomprehensible remark which was a favourite of hers and had something to do with Africa and the lioness personality she cultivated at that time.

Esmond Thinnesse came to meet us in a Morris Minor Estate car. He was older than I had expected, fair-haired with glasses and, fortunately with that name, extremely thin. Felicity was thin too and so was his mother, Elsa's Aunt Lois, and I used to wonder if there had ever been a fat Thinnesse and if so what misery and humiliation had he or she suffered. Or did Thinnesses keep themselves thin by rigorous diet and exercise and mortification of the flesh? There was no sign of this while Elsa and I were there, large, lavish meals being provided and partaken of enthusiastically by everyone. And no one was made to go out for healthful country walks.

For country it was, as deep I am sure as that to be found on the other side of Chelmsford. The Morris Minor took us no more than two miles away from the Debden Estate, but the little red-brick terraces stopped and the straight white dual carriageway stopped, and the shiny opal-green roof of the factory where they make notes for the Bank of England disappeared behind the trees, and the lanes became narrow and winding, the hedges high, the river Roding running between willows and alders. Thornham Hall had no place in the category of disappointing things. It was a real hall, with fifteen bedrooms and a library and a morning room. I sometimes used to think about those houses, so many of them, Jane Austen puts her people in and describes as 'new-built, modern'. Thornham was one such, about 170 years old when first I went there, austere, elegant, square, a balustrade running round its shallow roof, wide bays on either side of its flat, porchless front door. It stands on an eminence commanding a view of the winding Roding, of Epping and the villages, someone of incredible foresight having planted a screen of scotch pines and Wellingtonias, six trees deep, to conceal the houses for East End of London overspill no less-inspired person could have imagined ever being built. Now, I suppose, Thornham also has a view of the M25 motorway cleaving a long white wound through the meadows.

Its own estate, with vestiges of the feudal, stood near to it: stables, a cottage or two, a farm with barns at the foot of the hill. And there were huge trees, horse chestnuts and limes, fan-shaped screens of elms that must be gone by now, felled by the disease that changed the face of the countryside. I had never before stayed

44

in a house of this size and eminence, have not done so since. It was almost in the class of houses you are taken round on conducted tours. Esmond's father, a merchant banker, had bought it just before the Second World War, so in no sense was it a family home, he being really the first generation of Thinnesses to live there.

Today, in similar circumstances, I think we girls would have called his mother by her first name, but then she was Aunt Lois to Elsa and Lady Thinnesse to me. Her husband, Sir Esmond, had been rewarded with a knighthood for some particular merchant-banking service two years before he died. To me she was very old, though I suppose no more than in her late sixties. A rather carping though good-natured woman, she lamented the changes in her environment, notably, obsessively, the building of the Debden Estate. These moans dominated her conversation and went along with an often repeated regret that Sir Esmond, on their marriage, hadn't bought a house farther out in the countryside. She would ask me, or anyone else who happened to be with her, why he had failed to foresee that the London County Council, as it was then called, would take over some of the most beautiful pastoral land in the Home Counties for their 'slum clearance'. I was unused to such reactionary talk and her terms shocked me. She gave the impression that her marriage, at least from about 1950, had been permanently soured by her disillusionment over Sir Esmond's lack of prevision.

Also staying in the house was a friend of hers, an old woman called Mrs Dunne, who came from another, more rural part of Essex, and who was worried about proposals to extend the capacity and area of Stanstead Airport. No conservationist except where her own immediate interests were involved, Lady Thinnesse showed a bored indifference to poor Mrs Dunne's anxieties and wound up any discussion of Stanstead with the advice to her friend to move.

'It isn't as if you had a big house, Julia. You aren't trapped like I am.'

Felicity Thinnesse, who was a tease and liked showing up in company the follies and insensitivities of her mother-in-law and her mother-in-law's guests, used to enjoy what she called 'winding up' this old woman in front of us. In fact I think Mrs Dunne

45

liked it, had no idea Felicity was anything but serious, and rather appreciated attention from 'the younger generation'. Julia Dunne had once been a Master of Foxhounds and such had been her life and the narrow circle she had always moved in that she had no notion there were people existing – at any rate middle-class people in England – who might consider blood sports cruel or degrading. At the same time she loved animals. Certain horses had played a more important part in her life than her husband had, as far as I could tell. She had once had a pet fox which she had reared from a cub when its mother had been killed by the hounds.

'Didn't you ever think of that as being a bit odd?' Felicity asked her, innocently interested, 'I mean, hunting foxes and keeping a fox as a pet?'

'Oh, no, dear. I was very careful about that. I always shut him up in the stables when the hunt came by,' said Mrs Dunne.

Grave-faced, Felicity said she found it hard to understand this new disapproval of the keeping of battery hens when it was obvious they were safest while in those boxes. No fox could get them there. Julia Dunne was enchanted by this defence of factory farming. You could see she was storing it up for future use. Later Felicity told me that back home in north Essex Mrs Dunne used to crouch behind hedges with a stout stick in her hand, ready to club down any rabbit that might start eating the plants in her flowerbeds.

Felicity found the presence of her mother-in-law as a permanent resident and her mother-in-law's friends as temporary ones a cross to bear. Life was a laughing matter to her, sometimes a sick joke, and she demanded amusement, entertainment, as her daily food. Her husband was a quiet, dull, rather clever man, religious in a conventional Anglican way. Just as Lady Thinnesse usually had someone staying so did Felicity, but Felicity demanded more of her guests, far more; she expected wit and stories and even contributions such as young ladies made at Victorian parties, she expected visitors to play or sing or recite something. And she expected us to take part in the quizzes she set and the debates she instituted in the evenings and which would continue long into the nights. Elsa told me that on a previous visit, just before the Act of Parliament which made homosexuality legal between consenting adults in private, Felicity had organized a debate that 'this House will abolish outrageous laws that purport to interfere in the private sexual behaviour of adults'. Lady Thinnesse had had some other old woman guest with her and this person had immediately said that if this kind of thing were to be discussed it would be 'above her head' and she would go to her room. Lady Thinnesse had soon followed her. The debate had gone on until three in the morning, only breaking up when one of the children was heard crying upstairs.

On that occasion, Elsa said, the people from the cottage had come up for the evening and had taken part. They were friends of Felicity. Silas Sanger had in fact been an old boyfriend of Felicity's, they had parted on the best of terms, Felicity to be courted by, become engaged to, eventually marry Esmond Thinnesse, Silas Sanger to live with and later marry (or not marry, as Lady Thinnesse appeared to believe) Christabel. He was a painter, but not the sort who ever made much or any money by his painting, not the sort of 'artist' that Lady Thinnesse had known and approved of in her younger days. He had had nowhere to live, had been through some kind of breakdown, and Felicity had persuaded Esmond to let him and his wife, or non-wife, live in one of the cottages near the house, the one that was in the better state of repair.

There he continued to paint, feverishly sometimes, at others sporadically, gloomily, from time to time doing nothing, lying on his bed all day, suffering what Felicity rather inaccurately called a dark night of the soul. He was a ferociously heavy drinker and the substances he drank were bizarre. What Christabel did no one seemed to know, at any rate no one said, and she appeared as something of a mystery. These people were due to come up to the house for dinner – a dinner that would be cooked by a woman who cycled over from Abridge – and remain to join in the debate, scheduled to be on the subject: 'This House deplores the present divorce law and would make divorce possible between consenting parties after two years' separation'. Such a provision was, of course, to become law in 1973. I couldn't imagine there would be any dissenting voices, unless Lady Thinnesse and Julia Dunne consented to take part, which they had already declared with shudders to be out of the question, and I was surprised when Esmond said in his mild way that as an Anglican he must disapprove of any kind of divorce in any circumstances. Did Felicity remember that gently uttered but decisive statement when she ran away to Cosette's?

The painter's wife I had already seen. Reading to Miranda, the two of us sitting on the window seat in her bedroom, I could see the garden below and around us, the fans of high elms full of chattering starlings, the small meadow with the two horses and the big meadow shorn of its barley crop, the giant conifers that hid so much, that were always, at any time of the day, black silhouettes. I could see all this without raising my head and it was all curiously like what I was reading, all like the illustrations to *Samuel Whiskers*, the same sleepy windless pastoral, the same birds going to rest, the same sky of very high, small myriad clouds. To the right, on the slope of the hillside, stood Silas Sanger's cottage and its garden, a fenced plot of shaggy grass with nothing in it but two clothes posts with a length of dark-grey rope sagging between them. The cottage and its surroundings had an air of neglect. If Beatrix Potter had drawn it and been faithful to its true appearance, she would have used it as an illustration of the home of some villain of her animal world, a fox perhaps, or Bad Mouse. Curtains there still were at the window, but these were torn or coming down or, in the case of those at one downstairs window, apparently refusing to be drawn back, had been looped to either side of the frame with what looked from my vantage point like string.

Out of this hovel and into this small wilderness, as the sun was setting and those tiny clouds coloured with pink, came a tall girl too thin and too decorative to be one of Millet's peasants but having an air about her of some Fragonard woman. This was in the carriage of her elegant head with its crown of soft, fair, untidy piled-up hair, in the length of her narrow neck, in the bunching of her clothes, a long full underskirt, an overskirt clenched in at the waist with a scarf wound round and round, a low-necked blouse, a jacket over it of thin clinging stuff, the sleeves rolled up, a ribbon or two hanging in streamers, the whole in a variety of tones of brownish-pinkish-dusty-beige. No such personage ever entered the pages of Beatrix Potter. She carried a tray, not a basket, an ordinary tea tray laden with wet washing, which she proceeded to peg out on the clothesline.

I paused in my reading and said to Miranda, 'Who's that?'

On all fours she clambered over me. 'That's Bell.'

'She lives there with the painter?' Lady Thinnesse's view had almost unconsciously communicated itself to me.

'Silas is Mr Sanger and Bell is Mrs Sanger. Her washing looks as if it hasn't been washed, don't you think?'

It was all the same sort of light grey and there were big holes in something that might have been a pillowcase. I said it didn't look very clean, only to be reprimanded by Miranda.

'I'm not supposed to say that and especially you're not because you're grown up. Mummy says it's despicable to say things about people's washing being dirty. Go on reading, please.'

The girl in the garden, the girl called Bell, pegged her clothes out on the line with a kind of weary indifference. You could see her heart was not in it. Her whole stance, her attitude, the way she held her body, spoke of something worse than boredom, of encroaching despair. I had the impression those wet clothes had been lying about all day and at last, at an absurd time to hang out washing, at the close of the day, when the sun was setting, she had forced herself to drag the pile of it out here and rid herself of it, committing it to whatever fate awaited it from the dews of night. The tray empty, the line filled, she stood with the tray held loosely against her, stretched to her full height, gazing down into the valley, raising one hand to shade her eyes from the red sun's glare in a pose so Fragonard-like that she might have learned it by studying a reproduction in a magazine. But somehow I sensed she had no idea she was observed. Miranda reminded me once more that I was supposed to be reading to her and I reluctantly drew away my eyes.

The debate party was two days after this and in the event neither of the Sangers came to it. There was a phone in their cottage, according to Miranda, but they had had it cut off or it had been cut off due to non-payment of the bill. A note was put through the letter-box of the Hall rather late in the afternoon, certainly after the time the cook from Abridge had already arrived. Felicity read it aloud to us with a kind of exasperated resignation. She wasn't cross, she was amused – disappointed but amused by the way Bell did things like this.

' "Felicity: Sorry, we aren't going to come. I am not equal to it. Yours, Bell." She's proud of always saying what she means, not telling social lies – well, not any lies really.'

Felicity smiled at us, flinging out palm-upwards the hand that was not holding the note. She truly believed Bell never told lies, that Bell told the truth on principle no matter what the cost or how much moral courage was required. She believed this and we, hearing her tone and seeing her expression, believed too. Thus do utterly false testimonials of character and probity spread.

'She'd hurt someone badly rather than lie to them,' said Felicity. 'She'd involve herself in endless trouble. It's admirable in a way, you have to admire it.'

Yes, we had to admire it and did. I am not at all sure that Lady Thinnesse and Mrs Dunne admired it. They had looked at the small, torn, dirty piece of paper, written on in pencil, and then glanced at each other and Lady Thinnesse said, 'What does she mean, she isn't equal to it? Isn't she well? Does she mean she isn't up to it? Your debates can be rather strenuous, Felicity.'

'Living with Silas can't be any bed of roses,' was all Felicity said.

I was disappointed. I had looked forward to meeting the Fragonard woman who carried her washing about on a tray and hung it on the line at dusk.

'Wait a little, said the thorn tree,' said Elsa.

'That's all very well,' I said, 'but we've only got two more days here. Can't we go and call on her?'

'I don't think we could do that, I really don't. He is rather strange, Silas Sanger. Rude, you know, and often drunk. He wouldn't ask one in if he was in one of his moods, and he mostly is. In a mood, I mean. He doesn't like anyone much except Felicity – he adores her.'

'Doesn't he like this Bell?'

'I've only seen them together once,' said Elsa, 'and he didn't take any notice of her at all, not any notice. He didn't speak one word to her.'

'Are they married?' It was more important in 1968 than it became soon after that.

'Frankly, I wouldn't think so.'

The debate was postponed and we went home without meeting Bell or Silas Sanger, Elsa promising to take me there again soon. This I didn't take very seriously. I knew I should have to spend the Christmas holiday with my father. Or try somehow to manoeuvre my father to spend Christmas at Cosette's. For Cosette was still at Garth Manor, withdrawn, quiet, grieving it seemed, and apparently unable to make up her mind whether or not to move. Then she told me she meant to take the holiday she and Douglas had intended to spend together in Barbados. It was arranged for Christmas and the New Year, she had never cancelled those arrangements, and she would go. This announcement was curious in that it was a preparation for another announcement she was to make as soon as she returned, something far more momentous, something to stun us all. In the meantime I could comment to Elsa and to Dawn Castle's daughter Diana how very odd it was of Cosette to return to the hotel on Barbados where she and Douglas had stayed twice before, to return there alone and a widow, anticipating the pain and bitter nostalgia surely such a revisiting must evoke.

I thought I was condemned to sharing my father's Christmas and then he told me, with apparent insouciance, that he had been invited to spend it with my mother's cousin, that Cousin Lily who had been in such high spirits at Douglas's funeral. And he wanted to go, he was looking forward to it. I hadn't been asked, he said, but he would inquire if he could bring me. This was spoken in such tone of gloom and grudging unwillingness that I almost laughed out loud. Please don't, I said, please don't trouble, you'll have a great time without me, you'll be better on your own. He gave me a sidelong look, he asked if I thought it would be all right. And then I understood he felt he was doing a daring thing, a thing likely to give rise to gossip, for my father belonged in that generation, the last perhaps to think this way, who believed there was something improper and even scandalous in sleeping under the same roof alone with a member of the opposite sex. Times had changed, I said, no one would care. He seemed disappointed.

Thus I was free to go to Thornham Hall with the Lioness.

Two memorable things happened that Christmas. The first was Felicity's quiz.

Felicity was apparently as famous for her quizzes as her debates. She composed them herself, using the *Encyclopaedia Britannica*, *Brewer's Dictionary of Phrase and Fable*, Steinberg's *Dictionary of British History* and the *Oxford Dictionary of Quotations*. The quiz forms were typed by her and she did as many carbons as the typewriter would take, this being before the days of ubiquitous photocopying. We were to undertake this particular quiz on the day after Boxing Day, 27 December.

The Thinnesses' house was full. Mrs Dunne was there and Lady Thinnesse had also invited an ancient brigadier and his wife. He had risen to this rank during the First, not the Second, World War, which gives some idea of how very old he was. Felicity had her sister and her sister's husband and their twins and a friend called Paula she had been at college with and the friend's daughter and every day local people from Chigwell or Abridge or Epping came as well. On the day in question there might be as many as fifteen of us doing the quiz, the children being excluded. No mention was made of the Sangers, Silas and Bell, and I concluded they hadn't been asked. I concluded more than that, that a coolness now existed between the Thinnesses and the Sangers, and this was confirmed by Jeremy Thinnesse, aged three.

'My daddy wants Mr Sanger to go away and live in another house.'

'Really?' said the Lioness. 'Why would that be?'

'It's despicable,' said Miranda loftily, 'to wheedle information out of children who are too young and innocent to know better, Mummy says.'

It was not clear whether she referred to Elsa's conduct or possibly Silas Sanger's, but it had the effect she aimed at, that of stopping the conversation. No more inquiries were made. I found myself often looking in the direction of the cottage, but saw no one. The clothesline had gone and the two posts and the place looked unoccupied. Whether Silas and Bell celebrated Christmas I didn't know and don't know to this day, their life inside there was a mystery, their ways secret and surely wildly unconventional. Sometimes smoke could be seen rising from the cottage chimney and this fretted Lady Thinnesse, who seemed to think the house would catch fire.

After lunch on 27 December we all sat down in the hall to do the quiz Felicity had prepared, our twenty questions typed on two sheets of paper, foolscap size. This room, rather than the drawing room, was chosen because the latter being enormous took a great deal of heating and the weather was very cold. The hall at Thornham is itself very large, with the two-branched staircase mounting to a gallery at the back of it, but this area can be closed off with double doors, making a cosy chamber at the front where the fireplace is. A big fire of logs had been lighted and chairs and two sofas drawn up in three hundred degrees of a circle round it.

Thornham Hall has no porch and there is no inner lobby or vestibule, so draughts tend to come in round the front door. The long windows on either side of it rattled in the wind, but it was warm enough round the fire. Lady Thinnesse wore only a thin silk dress and seemed to take it as an insult to her household arrangements that Mrs Dunne had a shawl round her shoulders and Felicity's sister had put on fur-lined boots. I remember precisely where I was sitting in the circle: on the right-hand side of the fireplace and directly facing the front door. Felicity's brother-in-law sat on one side of me and her college friend on the other. It had been tacitly arranged that the old people should have their seats nearest to the fire, and between the college friend Paula and the fireplace were sitting the ancient brigadier, the ancient brigadier's wife and Mrs Dunne, with Lady Thinnesse and an old couple from Abridge facing them. The children were all up at the other end of the hall playing with their Christmas presents and warmed by a portable electric radiator.

Felicity handed out the papers, our names written on the top of them. I think it was at this point that I began questioning what I was doing, what we were doing, taking part in an examination we were not obliged to sit, giving up our leisure to an absurd general-knowledge test, vying with each other in a pointless contest. And for what? For what? A quarter bottle of brandy was the first prize and a box of chocolates the second. The force of one woman's personality dictated our obedience. No one had considered demurring, though those old ladies certainly must have feared failure and humiliation, that, in Bell's curious phrase, they would not be 'equal to it'.

Felicity had a chair at that point of the circle furthest from the fireplace, directly facing the fire, where for a few moments she had ensconced herself between her husband and Elsa the Lioness. To that chair she never returned, but stood watching us as we turned our eyes to our papers, a tall, strongly built yet slender dark woman, Juno-faced with massy black hair and the faintest black down on her upper lip, miniskirted as was the fashion, though not a fashion designed for a woman as strapping as she. Thirty minutes we could have, she said, precisely half an hour, the maximum possible score fifty points. Then she went over to the children, turning on lights as she passed the switch.

It was three-thirty but already dusk. The red light from the fire had been inadequate to see by. Some of the contestants were already writing, but I did what I had been taught to do and read through the questions on the paper before I began. I don't remember all the questions, only the first and the fifth. The first inquired what were Germinal, Brumaire and Fructidor and what did they have in common? I think the second question was something to do with architecture, the third with Second World War battles and the fourth with Shakespeare. The fifth question required contestants to explain what were Pott's disease, Klinefelter's syndrome and Huntington's chorea.

It gave me a shock, I felt the blood rush into my face, and that everyone must see that crimson blush. Inescapably, paranoiacally, I thought it was deliberately set for me, geared for me, designed as some kind of mockery of me. At the same time almost, or immediately afterwards, I knew of course that it couldn't be, that Felicity was not a cruel or vindictive woman, and moreover she didn't know, couldn't know, no one knew but my father and his Cousin Lily and my mother's doctor and Cosette. Elsa the Lioness didn't know. There was nothing to show, nothing in my appearance, my face, eyes, bodily movements. I had even been told (and my mirror told me) I was good to look at, beautiful even. If it was there waiting for me as it had waited for my mother, my grandmother, her father, it lurked silently in my central nervous system, hidden, static, resting, biding its time.

I looked up to meet the eyes I expected to see fixed on me, but all of them were looking at their papers with varying degrees of comprehension, lack of comprehension, pleasure, dismay. Most of them were writing. My eyes returned to the paper. Huntington's chorea. The words stood out of the rest of the text as if executed in boldface. My hands were shaking, the hand that held the pencil and the hand which, trying to grip the sheets of paper, failed and trembled as if Huntington's had already struck, had sent its first tremors down the nerves.

For once, of course, when experiencing trembling or lack of coordination or ordinary failure of manual dexterity, I had no real fear that this was the onset of Huntington's, I knew it was the effect of shock. But I told myself that I must exercise control, I must behave as if nothing had happened. And after all nothing had happened, everything was the same as before I read the questions on the paper, nothing had changed. 'Huntington's chorea' were words I repeated to myself if not every day of my life, almost as often. But for all these reassurances, trying to steady my still-shaking right hand, I found myself quite unable to answer the questions, unable to write a word. I knew, for instance, that Germinal, Brumaire and Fructidor were months in the French Revolutionary calendar, knew even (because I had had occasion to look this up not long before) that these names had been invented by Gilbert Romme, but when I brought the pen to the paper my hand felt paralysed. I tried to read the remaining questions but the print danced before my eyes, and when I forced myself to eye the lines of type as coolly as I could, the sense of what was there failed entirely to communicate itself to my brain.

It was almost funny. I didn't see it at all like that then, but later on, much later, I did. I saw it as an extreme irony that I, whom Felicity had certainly picked along with Elsa and Paula and her brother-in-law Rupert as her white hopes, her high scorers, would end up with a blank exam paper while the brigadier's wife, a self-confessed ignoramus, would certainly have answered three or four questions correctly. And this had happened to me not through simple exam nerves or drinking too much wine at lunch but solely as a result of the emotive, almost occult power, of a question composed by Felicity with a view only to demonstrating the superiority of intellect of those she saw as her own personal friends over her mother-in-law's cronies.

I looked up. I met Elsa's eye and she winked at me. She had been busily writing away and I could see she had a good chance of winning the brandy. I was wondering what to do, whether to admit to a sudden onset of blankness of mind or, more deceitfully, feign illness and escape upstairs to my room. I was wondering this and at the same time letting my gaze wander vaguely about the room, from Felicity kneeling on the carpet and helping her nephews build a fort from plastic bricks, to the tall, over-dressed, candle-laden Christmas tree in the corner diagonally opposite the fire, to the two long windows and the unrelieved misty dusk outside, back to Elsa feverishly scribbling, her head bent and her lower lip caught under her upper teeth. The room was silent but for an occasional crackling from the fire, a clearing of the throat from Felicity's sister, who had a cold. Even the children, raptly attentive to new toys, made no noise.

I had decided. I would stay there and face it out. What did it matter? People are made happy by such defeats of others. I had turned the papers over, so that the name would no longer leap black-lettered out at me, was reaching out to return my pencil to the box of pencils on the low table where the triumphant Elsa, her quiz completed, had already returned hers, when the front door flew open to let in a gust of wind and Bell Sanger.

The front door at Thornham was locked only at night. I expect things are different today. Then it was always unlocked and everyone knew it, but still Bell's eruption into the hall was a shock. The wind blew the papers the contestants were holding and actually blew Lady Thinnesse's quiz out of her hand and straight into the flames of the fire. She jumped up with a little shriek. Bell stood there, on the rug, in fact some kind of animal skin, just inside the door, her clothes and hair blown by the wind, a wild woman with staring eyes. Felicity got up from her knees and said rather crossly, 'For God's sake, shut the door.'

And Bell did. She reached behind her and pushed the door

56

which slammed. The whole house seemed to shake. Bell said, 'Would someone come please? Silas has shot himself.'

Someone said, 'My God,' but I have never known who it was, one of the men. Esmond got up, pushed his chair aside to let himself out of the circle, and took a few steps towards her. Bell didn't wait for him to speak.

'He was drunk,' she said. 'He was playing one of his games. He shot himself. I think he's dead.' She hesitated, looking at us all with a kind of dawning dismay, realizing who we were, as if we were the last people she would want to communicate this to, to share this with. But what could she do? What choice had she? We were there, we were the only people, it was unavoidable. 'He was playing,' she said, addressing these words to Felicity. 'You know what I mean,' and, incredibly, it seemed that Felicity did.

She nodded, one hand going up to her mouth. Esmond said, 'Felicity, phone Dr Thompson, will you? And perhaps the police, yes, we have to phone the police.'

Felicity said, 'Christ, what a thing! What a thing!' She seemed to realize she was surrounded by staring children. 'Come with me, all of you,' and she scooped children up, putting each arm round two or three of them.

My eyes met Bell's. She looked at me, I thought, as if I might be the only one there she could like, who might have some sort of affinity with her. Or that is how I took it, how I received her steady, aghast, long, grey-eyed stare. Esmond opened the front door and held it for Bell to precede him out into the dark. I got up and followed them.

5

Stiletto fatalis, far from being some sort of weapon, is the Latin name for the flaw worm, an agricultural pest. The entomologist who devised it must have had a sense of humour. There were posters in the Thornham village shop warning farmers to beware of this creature, and Felicity got hold of the name and made a tremendous joke of it. That Christmas, at any rate before the shooting of Silas Sanger, she was always talking about *stiletto fatalis*. If she had included a question on it in her quiz everyone would have been able to give the right answer. Stiletto heels were in fashion that winter and at parties, especially in houses with woodblock floors, you were given little plastic heel caps to keep the spike heels from making stab marks. All the floors at Thornham Hall were of wood, scattered with small carpets and large rugs. Felicity always examined the shoes of newcomers and gave a verdict on them, whether they could be classed as *stiletto fatalis* or not.

This aspect of her, which I thought I had forgotten, which I hadn't thought of for fifteen or sixteen years, the last time I saw her, comes back to me in the morning as I am making up my mind to phone her. I remember *stiletto fatalis* and how it and all its successors had given place, by the time Felicity was taking refuge at Cosette's, to a new conversational obsession with Selevin's mouse. Nothing much had evidently occurred in Felicity's life since then if she was, as it appeared, still married to Esmond, still chatelaine of Thornham, no longer perhaps much resembling the dramatic intense girl in a mini-skirt who had confided in Cosette evening after evening. I regard the piece of paper on which I have written down the number Felicity's daughter gave me. I dial it. For last night, though I went to Leith's, though I got the taxi to drop me on the corner of Pembridge Road and walked the rest of the way, I didn't see Bell, of course I didn't.

Felicity answers the phone herself, using as soon as she knows who it is, her unchanged characteristic greeting.

'Hallo, there!'

I once heard Esmond introduce himself to some newcomer as 'There', saying his wife had re-christened him. She sounds just the same and as if the last time we spoke was a couple of weeks ago. There is no marvelling that I haven't been in touch before, am in touch now, am still alive, and there are no reproaches. She doesn't even say what a surprise it is. I have no recollection of her being so wrapped up in her children twenty years ago or when she abandoned them for nine months to the care of their father and grandmother. But now she talks of them. She talks of them immediately she has been through the polite requirement of asking how I am, taking my 'How is everyone?' *au pied de la lettre* and telling me all about Miranda's amazing job with BBC television and Jeremy's history first. She even follows this up with genius's mother's cliché number one:

'And do you know we despaired of him, he didn't do a stroke of work!'

I let her go on a bit, then tell her I have spoken to Miranda.

'Oh, did you manage to catch her? What a relief! You've actually taken a load off my mind. I haven't spoken to her for days, you know what they're like, so elusive and of course quite indifferent to one's very real terrors. It's a simple relief just to know she's around and in possession of her faculties, answering the phone and so forth. And now tell me all about you.'

That can easily be avoided. 'Miranda told me you'd spoken to Bell Sanger. I thought you might give me her address.'

A silence. Then the voice changes, becoming stagey. 'Oh, my dear, I don't have it. I have a phone number. Do you remember those wonderful London phone exchanges, Ambassador and Primrose and Flaxman? So easy to remember. This is six-two-four something. What on earth would six-two-four have been?'

'Maida. It's Maida Vale and Kilburn.' So that is where Bell lives. I feel a little bit faint; I am breathless to know more, afraid we shall be cut off, that I shall never learn those four remaining digits. 'Six-two-four what?'

And I am right to be afraid, my fear is justified, for she has it written down somewhere but just where she can't remember.

'You know the size of this house, Elizabeth!'

'How was she?' I say, unable to keep this back, unable to contain it. 'How was Bell? Did she seem – well, not happy, no – resigned?'

But Felicity isn't going to answer this, perhaps has no opinion on it. She was, and no doubt is, a self-absorbed woman, interested not in the feelings of others but only in her own feelings about them. 'I wish I could have seen you to have a good talk when all that happened,' she says. 'After the trial, ideally. I had such a lot of things to tell you, inside stuff really. I mean there was such a lot I knew about Silas, personal, intimate things, though of course she was always a mystery. But you disappeared and one does have some reticence. Running you to earth wasn't really on. Oh dear, that does remind me! Do you remember that awful old woman I used to wind up about fox hunting? My mother-in-law's still alive, can you believe it? Eighty-six and sound as a bell – O God, you wanted Bell Sanger's number, didn't you? Look, I'll have to find it and call you back.'

'I would very much like you to do that, Felicity.'

'Of course I will. I'm going to ask you something and if you think it's too awful of me just don't answer. Don't put the phone down but don't answer, you don't have to. Now then. Did it ever cross your mind Bell might have shot Silas herself?'

I do reply. I say in a silly, faint, mealy-mouthed sort of way, 'Not then.'

'Well, no, not then of course. But at the time of the trial? I mean when all those other things about Bell's past came out. It did mine, I can tell you. And I knew all about his games. I knew all about what he got up to and his drinking and I still thought Bell might have shot him. Oh, Elizabeth, I wish we could meet and really talk this through. I mean it's fascinating, don't you think? Are you ever down this neck of the woods?' Mercifully, she goes on without waiting for an answer, 'No, I don't suppose you are. We shall have to meet in London sometime. We still have the flat, but of course you know that if you've talked to Miranda. Look, I'll call you back without fail and give you that number and then we can fix something. I can't promise when but it'll be today absolutely without fail. Goodbye till later. We'll speak again soon.'

She has always had that power of exhausting those she is with or just talking to. With some people it may be enjoyable, but it is also a wearisome battle to be in their company. And there are others, like Cosette, who revive their companions, revitalize them, leave them feeling restored and content simply by their own attentive listening and ability to ask the right small questions at the right time. When I got home from Thornham after the death of Silas Sanger – and Elsa and I were peremptorily dispatched by Lady Thinnesse on the following day – I gave an account of all of it to Cosette. And she listened, she was interested, she seemed really to want to know. By that time Elsa and I together with Paula and Felicity's sister had been amply regaled by Felicity on the subject of Silas's games.

Silas had two guns, a twelve-bore shotgun and a Colt revolver, which he claimed to have bought from a stallholder in the Portobello Road market, a man who sold silver. He had a passion for guns, which was not easy to gratify in this country where to collect guns and have the appropriate licence and so forth you have to be a respectable person with no criminal record and one who doesn't mind visits from the police. Silas, of course, had no gun licence. Felicity told us he used to play Russian roulette with the Colt and that was the least of his games.

'They don't kill themselves, those people, but they don't care for their lives the way the rest of us do. They do reckless things, they tempt fate.' I thought she looked wistful, as if she rather hankered after being that kind of person herself. 'You know how Carmen goes to the most dangerous places, sets herself out to get the dangerous men?' We didn't know. I at least had never heard *Carmen* then, not even on records. 'And at the end she doesn't have to get herself killed, she can easily avoid it, but she's too proud to avoid it and anyway, what else is there for her?'

Was Felicity saying Silas was like that? And if you take the analogy with *Carmen* as far as she took it, to the end of the last act, what was she implying?

She said Silas liked to play firing squads. It was never quite clear whether she had been the partner in these games or had only heard of them. If she had been I could understand she might not want the rather strait-laced High Anglican Esmond Thinnesse to know about it, and therefore could not risk telling us. What she did tell us was that Silas would get his woman, in this case presumably Bell, to gag him and tie him up, he having previously loaded one of the guns, the Colt or the shotgun. She wouldn't be told which one was loaded. She was to choose one and shoot him as a member of a firing party might do. Of course neither Bell nor her predecessors were good shots; he had taught them the basics of handling a gun and that was all. Felicity said that after her affair with Silas came to an end she met him once with his arm in a sling and he said he had been shot. She concluded some woman had picked the right (or the wrong) gun, but the shot had gone a bit wide.

He never shot animals or birds, that didn't interest him, and he was a vegetarian. Another one of his games was to get his girls to shoot at a target with the aim of improving their marksmanship, and just as whoever it was – and I believe at least once it was Felicity herself – took aim and fired, dash across in front of the target. He liked the naked terror, the loss of control, the screams.

'But was it something like this he had been doing that last time?' said Cosette.

'I don't know. I don't think anyone knows.'

'This girl called Bell must know.'

'If she does I don't think she'll tell.'

We walked across to the cottage, Esmond, Bell and I, through the wind and darkness. Can it really have been so dark at four o'clock even in December? I remember it as dark and the shock I felt at seeing the cottage in darkness, at observing that Bell had left no lights on. She had not at any rate locked the front door but left it on the latch as the front door to Thornham Hall was always left. We went in and lights were switched on and there was Silas Sanger lying dead on the floor.

I think it was at this point Esmond realized I was there. You see, no one had spoken a word since we came out of the Hall. Esmond realized and turned to me and said something about it not being right for me to be there, for me to see such things. But by then it was much too late. I had seen and Esmond had seen and he had gone very pale.

It might have been worse. I remember thinking that. Silas's face was intact. He had shot himself through the neck, severing, it later transpired, the spinal cord. He lay in a lake of blood and his face reminded me of paintings I had seen – they are legion – of John the Baptist, or rather the head of John the Baptist, in a dish of blood, being held by Salome. His face was a translucent greenish-white, white-lipped, the red-brown curly hair and beard and moustache looking very soft and somehow young. I thought I could look at this dead man with detachment, with simple interested curiosity, and I had no feelings of nausea, no physical revulsion. Or so I thought until my knees sank earthwards and a terrible faintness overcame me. I don't think the others saw. I sat down and breathed deeply, my eyes closed, and heard Esmond say, 'What happened?'

'He'd been playing with the Colt. It's there on the floor, in the – in the blood. He said he was going to fire it once, out of the window. To see what happened. He meant to see if you'd come out, I think.' When Felicity, later, was telling us about Silas's games she also told us that his indiscriminate letting off of the Colt and the shotgun was the reason for the quarrel between him and the Thinnesses. Esmond had been horrified, had had no idea of Silas's propensities. Silas must go and at once. The difficulty was that he and Bell had nowhere to go. And now she had nowhere to go. 'I went upstairs then,' she said. 'The bugger didn't fire out of the window. He was playing Russian roulette instead.'

She was very calm. It was despair, perhaps. She sat down on the only other chair in the room, looked at me and performed that action known as casting up the eyes, a curiously inadequate gesture in the circumstances. It suggested not so much shock or grief as exasperation. That day she was dressed in assorted garments of browns and greys – Bell's clothes were never like other people's, though a few years later they were to become wildly fashionable in the alternative mode – and the bundled layers were caught in at her thin, stalk-like waist by what looked like a luggage strap. There was blood on her left sleeve.

She said to Esmond, 'Cover him up!'

Esmond looked round the room for something to serve the purpose. It was a sparsely furnished, squalid little room with linoleum on the floor and cut-off pieces of carpet serving as rugs, two upright chairs and a horsehair sofa, a gate-leg table with a broken leg propped up on a flowerpot and bookshelves made of planks resting on bricks. A shawl, hand-crocheted in shades of mud and granite, obviously Bell's, was draped over the back of the sofa and this Esmond covered the body with, an action for which the police later reprimanded him. But everything felt better; the atmosphere didn't exactly lighten, yet it was like a sigh of relief. It was possible to keep one's eyes open, to breathe, now that face and that awful neck were hidden.

'You had better come back to the house,' Esmond said to Bell. 'You had better let Elizabeth take you back. I'll stay here.'

'I'm staying here,' she said.

I went back alone and in a few minutes the police came. Cosette, when I told her all this, asked me what Bell was like to look at and then what age she was. She had become, I noticed, very interested in other women's ages.

'Like an actress in a Bergman film.'

Cosette, dating herself, revealing the preoccupations of her own youth, mistook my meaning. 'Ah, yes. *Intermezzo. Casablanca.*'

'Ingmar,' I said. It was the era of the director. No one any longer knew the names of stars. 'Like a Swedish actress, tall and thin and with a long neck but very soft features, a little straight nose and full lips, big eyes. Masses of sort of dusty fair hair. About, I don't know, twenty-five?'

'As young as that?' said Cosette.

I thought she meant Bell was very young to have experienced so much, and perhaps she did. But it was from this time, I believe, that Cosette's obsession with age began to grow. It was as if she had slept away her life, or most of it, and had woken up in a panic to find it gone and irrevocable. The sad, wistful look came into her face. It had nothing to do with her grief over Douglas and not much to do with the sagging of facial muscles, which came later. It was a change wrought in her by that awakening. I think she saw Bell in her mind's eye and thought that to be twenty-five again and tall and beautiful would be worth any amount of suffering and tragedy and poverty and deprivation. But of course I don't know what she thought, I can only guess, I can only hazard ideas about her in the light of what happened later.

'And they sent you home next day?' she said.

'Well, you can understand that. We must have been in the way. They sent everyone home and took Bell into the house and I think they were very nice to her.'

'There would have to be an inquest, wouldn't there?'

'I don't know. Perhaps. Yes, of course there would. She told us what happened, you know, later on. She wouldn't stay in the room with him when he started playing with the gun. She went upstairs and sat in the room where all his paintings were. It must have been very cold, it was icy in that cottage, and there were only oil stoves heating it. He had been drinking, the stuff he usually drank, cheap wine with methylated spirits in it. She told us in a very matter of fact way. And the thing was she told all of us, I mean Elsa and Paula and Felicity's sister and brother-in-law, that didn't seem to bother her, the fact that we were strangers.

'She sat up there, looking at his paintings. Apparently she had some idea his paintings might be saleable; I mean, in the sort of way he would have scorned. Some of the landscapes she thought she could take down to the local pub and ask them if they'd hang them in the bar to see if any of the customers would pay five pounds for one of them. It seems they were desperately poor – to the extent of not getting enough to eat, only he always had his wine. Anyway, she was sitting up there thinking like this when she heard the Colt fired, she heard a shot. It wasn't specially unusual, that, but what followed was. She heard a sort of gurgle, an awful sound, she said, between a groan and a gurgle. So she went down and she found him and if he wasn't dead thirty seconds before, he was by the time she got there.'

Not a very credible story, was it? But I believed it then and Cosette believed it. Cosette wasn't the sort of person to ask the question Elsa asked me some months later: why couldn't Bell have got a job if they were so poor? Jobs were to be had then, it was different from now. But I never knew Bell to keep a job of any kind, then or later or ever. A very strange thing happened to make employment for her not essential: a few hours before Silas died his father had died of heart disease. He wasn't a rich man and he had no savings, but he owned the house he lived in and though he had made no will, he was a widower and Silas his only child. It came automatically to Bell, for Silas and Bell had been married, she was as much his wife as Felicity was Esmond's. She sold the house for £10,000 and this sum, when invested, brought her just enough to live on, just enough to scrape by on without working, to hang on by the skin of her teeth.

All this was in the future. I knew nothing of it when I was relating my story to Cosette. I awaited a verdict from her, a summing-up. I meant to receive it, discuss her conclusions, then (on the grounds that it would be good for my psyche) if my mood could be rightly established, confide in her question number five of Felicity's quiz and confess my foolish tremors, my spontaneous terror. I was so entirely accustomed, you see, to Cosette as listener, Cosette as recipient. When Cosette talked about herself it was almost an affront. As, instead of pronouncing on the probable fate of Bell or the curious cerebral processes of a man who played firing squads with his wife, she now did:

'I have bought a house.'

It was hardly an astounding act but only what everyone expected her to do sooner or later. I looked inquiringly.

'I made an offer for it before I went to Barbados.'

She could have a very childlike look sometimes, the look of a child who expects to be reprimanded. I asked her where this house was.

'It's in London.' She lived in London already. I waited. 'It's in Notting Hill. You'll like it, it's a big tall house on five floors with a staircase of 106 stairs. I counted. I call it the House of Stairs.'

I must have looked rather blankly at her. It all seemed to be out of character, so unlike Cosette, whose two weeks in the heat had reddened her skin but done nothing to reduce her weight. One of her cotton tents enveloped her. The chignon her hair was done up in was very like Bell's but on her not Fragonard-like, only untidy. The flesh-tinted transparent rims of her glasses had been mended with a piece of sticking plaster. All I could think of was, how was she going to manage climbing all those stairs?

66

'You won't have so far to come to see me,' she said.

'Notting Hill?' I said. It was still, at any rate the northern and western parts of it, a slummy, shabby, dirty and dangerous area of London. The street carnival, an annual event that had begun a few years before, led to trouble, recalling the violence of the riots of the fifties. I asked her why she wanted to live there.

She said naïvely, 'It's in the best part. It's Bohemian.'

'Why do you want somewhere so big?'

'I don't suppose I shall be on my own – much. People will come.' She was looking at me anxiously now, doubtfully, in need of reassurance. 'Don't you think people will come?'

What people? Dawn Castle and her husband? Elderly Maurice Bailey, president of the Wellgarth Society? Her brothers? 'Well, I suppose. If you invite them. They all expect you to live in a flat or a bungalow.'

'There are a lot of young people in that part of London,' said Cosette.

It seemed irrelevant. 'But what will you do?' I said.

'Live,' said Cosette, smiling, and then, perhaps because she thought that sounded pretentious. 'I mean I will just live there and – and see.'

It is absurd the way I am waiting for Felicity to phone. I am waiting with the breathless anticipation of someone expecting a call from an unreliable lover. What will happen if she phones while I am out? Will she call back again? I dare not take the risk so cannot go out. This should be a good opportunity to get on with the book I am currently writing, and I might with truth say that I have at least sat in front of my typewriter all day, or on and off all day. And the sheet in the typewriter is not blank. No doubt though what is on it is rubbish and will all have to be done again. It and its contents, its theme and plot and personages, fail to distract my thoughts from Bell. And when I abandon it, though still sitting there, looking from Cosette's agate jar and the curious heather-root paper-knife to Douglas's old Remington on which my first books were typed – with such enthusiasm, with such excitement – when I turn my attention from it and try to think instead of my first visit to Archangel Place when Cosette took me there on a bitter day in February, concentration is impossible and this too fails. Remembering the House of Stairs as it was that day, the yawning icy rooms that seemed to branch off that winding trunk of staircase like leaves from a twisted bough, goes no further than remembering this, evokes no consequent memories of acts and activities, of the changes that came, of the people that came, of Cosette's 'salon'. Bell alone occupied my thoughts. I remember her in those early days, or rather, I remember what I heard of her, what Elsa and Felicity told me of her, for she vanished from any scenes of mine for more than a year.

But then, after Silas had been covered up with that shawl (a shawl Bell later calmly went on wearing) I went back to the house and left them there, Bell and Esmond Thinnesse. And after a long while, several hours, after the police had been and a doctor, and all sorts of adjuncts of the police, Esmond brought Bell back to the house and she walked into the drawing room where we all were. It was almost palpable in the air, the embarrassment everyone felt, everyone that is but me and Felicity, who doesn't know what embarrassment is, and Elsa. I could tell the others were wondering what they were to talk about, how the rest of the evening was to be passed, now Bell was among them. But their difficulty was momentary. She stood there and said in a voice of cold disdain, a voice that made nonsense of what she said, 'I am sorry to be the cause of so much trouble.'

An odd thing to say, wasn't it? Surely poor dead Silas was the cause, he and what he had done? She said it and immediately turned and went upstairs. Felicity was later obliged to go after her and ask her if she wanted anything, a drink, for instance, or something to eat, a share in the supper of cold Christmas leftovers we were all picking at downstairs. Bell refused everything. Next day the police were back, talking to her, and after being closeted with one of them for a long time in Esmond's study, she walked in among us.

She was all in black. But I later came to know she often was, it had nothing to do with mourning for Silas. I had never seen anyone like her, never before encountered that air of indifferent confidence and tragic poise. Sorry for her, pity for her, I never felt, though perhaps I ought to have felt it. After all, she was a widow, she had lost her husband only the day before in the most appalling circumstances of violence and horror. I felt only admiration, the kind of hero worship I had not had for anyone since I had a crush on the music mistress some seven years before. What I would have liked was for the two of us to go away somewhere and talk. I would have liked to be with her, alone with her, to talk and learn about her and tell her about me.

Of course this was impossible. Elsa and I were going back to London, were due to be driven to Debden tube station by Esmond in about half an hour's time. Felicity's sister and her husband and children had already gone by car, taking Paula and her daughter with them. Bell came close up to the chair where Felicity was sitting with the little boy Jeremy on her lap. She laid her hands lightly on the back of the chair, holding her head high, that mass of untidy fair hair, hair the colour of tarnished brass, plaited and tied up on top of her head with a piece of string. Without looking at Felicity, looking at the plaster mouldings on the ceiling, the cornice, the elaborately pelmeted tops of the windows, she asked if she could remain at Thornham a little longer.

'Not in the house. In the cottage. Just until I find somewhere.'

Felicity was beginning to say, 'But, my dear, of course, of course you must, I wouldn't dream . . .' when Bell said, 'I know Esmond doesn't like me. I know you don't any of you like me.' Did I imagine her roving glance coming to rest for a moment on me and the slightest change, a softening, in her expresson, as if she made an exception of me? 'But I have,' she said, 'nowhere else to go.'

She had a reputation for being honest. On the way to the station Esmond said to us, 'It's true I don't much like her. Frankly, I didn't like him. But one can say for Bell that she's a totally honest person. She is incapable of deceit.'

It is interesting how such reputations are built. They come about through confusing the two kinds of truth-telling: the declaration of opinion and principle and the recounting of history. Bell always expressed her feelings about things, her beliefs, with frank openness. It wasn't in her, for the sake, say, of politeness or social ease, to say she was pleased about something when she wasn't or that she liked something or someone when she didn't, or that she didn't mind when she did mind. And because of this, because of this well-known honesty of hers, it was assumed – no, taken for granted – that she also told the straightforward transparent truth about what she had done, what her past was, what had happened. I came to know, and it was a hard lesson, that Bell was in fact one of the world's grand liars, who tell lies from choice and, I think, for pure pleasure.

On that occasion she told Felicity she had nowhere to go and Felicity, first denying for all she was worth the plain truth that no one at Thornham much liked Bell, offered her the cottage rent-free for as long as she might want it. Bell nodded and said thanks in that laconic way of hers that she could make sound as if she had little to be grateful for.

'What shall I do about the blood?' she said.

Felicity nearly screamed. She put her hand over her mouth. Jeremy was staring, big-eyed, mouth open.

'Someone will have to clean it up.'

'The police will see to that, Bell,' Esmond said. 'You can leave that to the police.'

That was the last time I saw her, as I have said, for two years. Elsa told me that she had no relatives to take her in. Her parents were dead. She had no profession, was trained for nothing, her life since she was nineteen had been the wretched sharing of Silas Sanger's poverty and the homes he had contrived for them, a cottage that was no more than a hut on an estate in the Highlands of Scotland, a room in south London, a coachhouse loft in Leytonstone, finally this cottage of the Thinnesses. The knowledge that she was to inherit Silas's father's house took her away from Thornham and translated her to that house, first to live in it, then to sell it and realize from the sale a skimpy income. She moved out of the orbit of Esmond and Felicity and such lesser moons as Elsa and Paula who circled about them, and for quite a long time was lost among the unnumbered galaxies that made up the youth of London in the late 1960s.

It occurs to me as I wait for the phone to ring that it is possible Bell herself will still phone me. When the phone does ring it may not be Felicity, whose voice I longed for, but Bell, who would be much the greater prize. In moments of stress, when alone, I always talk aloud to myself. Does everyone? Do you?

'Are you mad?' I say aloud to myself. 'Are you mad to care like this, to need like this? What do you want and what do you need after so long, after receiving so little, after knowing everything? Are you mad?'

But I don't pursue that one. Madness is something we don't speak of lightly, frivolously, in our family, for madness of a kind we are also heirs to, the schizoid delusions associated with our inheritance. I don't pursue it and, strangely, when it gets late, too late for anyone reasonably to phone, much too late for Felicity, I feel a curious unexpected lightening of the heart.

6

Of the figures who come into our dreams, according to the Jungians, the only ones whose identity we can be certain of are ourselves. When I first read of this I wanted hotly to deny it, for hadn't I often encountered Bell in my dreams? And Cosette and even, once or twice, Mark? But I came to see that they were not in fact themselves, but only figments that exhibited aspects of those people, that often metamorphosed, changing into unknown personages or half-forgotten acquaintances or even animals. Why this should be, taking into account how little we really know of those who are closest to us, is no mystery, but a warning not to be hasty with our assumptions about the nature of others or complacent about our knowledge of the human heart.

So it wasn't Felicity I dreamed about last night but only someone who looked and sounded like Felicity, and that not for long; someone who, once she had led me into the grey garden in Archangel Place, turned her head and showed me a changed face, the face of someone I can't name but connect with that time, a face I find it hard to say was a man's or a woman's. Before that happened we had been in the House of Stairs together, and from Cosette's table Felicity had picked up the sheets of paper on which her quiz was typed. Some were untouched, some half-completed. She said, as I never remember her saying at the time, as I would remember if it had happened, 'That woman is such a fool, she has identified Huntington's chorea as a geography book. I suppose she thinks the Isles of Langerhans are off its coast.'

Freud's dream theory has been much ridiculed. But no one disputes the wisdom of his suggestion that in trying to understand our dreams we should write accounts of them as soon as we wake up, keeping pencil and paper beside the bed for this purpose. Felicity's remark didn't pain me in the dream as it would have

72

done had I been conscious and she real. I was amused by it in the dream, and hastened to write it down. Then I reflected on the rest of the dream, how she and I had gone outside where the plants in the grey garden were taller and more luxuriant than I remember them, where even the flowers were not yellow or white but a metallic, silvery grey. We stood looking up at the back of the house, a tall house of five storeys and a basement, but not as tall as in the dream, in which it had become a tower whose pointed top was half-obscured by the lowering London sky.

But the windows were the same. These wide apertures, one on each of the four middle floors, pairs of glazed french doors really, opened on to narrow balconies with low plaster walls. But on the basement floor and on the top the windows were simply long narrow sashes. It wasn't Mark who came out on to the fourth-floor balcony from the room that was once mine, it wasn't Bell or Cosette. The figure who stood up there leaning perilously over the wall was a child's, a child I didn't recognize but that Felicity knew, that Felicity or the possessor of the changed face she turned to me recognized as one of her own. She began shouting at the child to be careful, to go back.

'Go back, go back, you'll fall!'

And now I am reading my account of this dream along with Felicity's remark, which no longer seems so brilliant to me, so witty, as it did at first. Written on the paper too is Bell's phone number which she gave me when she phoned me this morning, accosting me with her cheerful, 'Hallo, there!'

I asked her what I had not been able to bring myself to ask her yesterday. (How much joy do we miss through cowardice?) I asked her why Bell had phoned her.

'Oh, Elizabeth, I thought you knew. Didn't I say? She wanted your number.'

Joy, indeed. Immediately I reproached myself for feeling such a surge of happiness. I should know better, I should have learned something in all those years, after so many friendships, a marriage and other loves.

'Didn't you give it to her?' I realized as soon as I said this that there was no reason why she would have known it. It is a long time since we have spoken, though something to Felicity's credit

73

perhaps that it doesn't feel long, that she, maddening woman though she is, has that quality of taking up the reins of friendship and driving merrily along as if no lapse of years had ever been. 'No, you couldn't have. I'm in the phone book in my married name. My publishers wouldn't give my number.'

'I didn't try them. Frankly, I thought Bell would be the last person you'd want to be in touch with. After all that happened.'

I realize now, after some hours have passed, that she thinks I was in love with Mark. Maybe others thought so too. That, they suppose, is what accounted for my unhappiness and my withdrawal. I contemplate this number that begins with the three digits six-two-four, the Maida number, but I do nothing more with it, I only look. Strangely, the last thing I need to do at this moment is dial it, speak to Bell. I am so supremely content to know she wanted mine, that her sole purpose in phoning Felicity was to ask for my number, that I feel no need to proceed further – yet. I feel, sitting here in my workroom in front of the typewriter, rather as I felt on the very few occasions in the House of Stairs when I smoked the cigarettes Bell passed to me at the window's edge: at peace, serene, there is no tomorrow or if there is it is of no significance, there is only the everlasting, delicious, tranquil now.

In which to recall Cosette seems to come naturally.

She didn't mean to live alone in the House of Stairs. She was going to have Auntie with her and Dawn Castle's daughter Diana.

If I haven't mentioned Auntie before it isn't because she was unknown to me or played a small part in Cosette's life, but because it is so hard to know what to say about her. She was a cipher, a little old woman who seemed without character or opinions, almost without tastes, who seemed to dislike nothing yet enjoy nothing. I have never known her christian name. Cosette always called her 'Auntie', though she wasn't her aunt but I think her mother's cousin. We – I mean the crowd of the young – were supposed to call her Mrs Miller, but no one ever did for long and she became 'Auntie' to us too. To her we were all 'dear', because our names eluded her memory, even Cosette's.

Two or three years earlier Auntie had been living in a miserable room in a run-down part of London. Somewhere in Kensal Rise

I believe it was. She was being harassed by a landlord who wanted the house vacated so that he could sell it, and was plagued too by the four-man jazz band who occupied the top floor. Cosette had always looked after her, paid her some sort of allowance, had her shopping done, taken her out. She and Douglas rescued Auntie and bought her a tiny one-room flat near them in Golders Green. From this flat Cosette removed her and carried her off to Notting Hill.

She gave no reason for doing so. Auntie had seemed quite happy where she was, though it was always hard to make any sort of assessment of the state of her emotions, and if Cosette could have gone from Golders Green to Kensal Rise to tend to her she could probably have made the journey equally often in reverse. It may have been a simple act of kindness. I shouldn't express surprise at Cosette's kindness, which was so frequent as not to be remarked, and yet I came to believe there was another motive. I came to see that Auntie was needed in the House of Stairs for her role in the attempted recapture of Cosette's youth.

Her presence had no effect on me one way or the other. It was different with Diana Castle. My reactions to her being asked to live there, given a room there, were I am afraid those of jealousy and resentment. You have to understand that, without being fully aware of it then, I had replaced my mother with Cosette – and this not just since my mother's death but long, long before. Of course I should have known that Diana's being there didn't exclude my being there, that I was always welcome, that there would always be a place for me, that Cosette took it for granted and supposed I did too, that her home was my home whenever I chose to make it so.

I sulked a little. I had my degree and I wandered about Europe, meeting nomadic people like myself, thinking of the books I meant to write. The first of these was in fact written in Cosette's house, but not yet, not then. Instead, I went off to do a year's post-graduate teacher training, something I have been glad of since, but which was undertaken as a result of the injury I felt Cosette had done to me, a result of sulking.

The House of Stairs I had seen once or twice and had responded to it in a way which might have been more justly expected from my own father, say, or Mrs Maurice Bailey. I saw it as big, old, dirty and cold, the stairs a curse and a handicap, the arrangement of the rooms – the kitchen was in the basement, all the best living and sleeping space loftily high up – seemingly designed to be as inconvenient as could be, the steep staircase and windows dangerous. The second time I saw it Cosette had moved in, had been in three weeks, but the furniture still stood about where the removers had stuck it, the crates of books and china and glass remained unpacked, the windows uncurtained and the phone not yet connected.

But the third time I went there all was changed. I had been away and Cosette had been busy, though this is the wrong word to use about someone so gently and contentedly indolent. Others had been busy on her behalf: Perpetua who still came to her, travelling down each day on the 28 bus, Jimmy the gardener and handyman, a troop of carpet fitters and curtain hangers. The rooms hadn't been re-painted, that was something she refused to have done, and their faint faded shabbiness suited them, keeping them from a glossy *Homes and Gardens* look, though there was never much danger of this *chez* Cosette. But the windows had been festooned with curtains in slub silk and curtains in velvet, with Roman blinds and Austrian blinds and Chinese bead curtains that were mêlées of rainbows when they moved and showed pastoral pictures, remote and oriental, when they hung still. I don't think Cosette any longer knew there were such colours as brown, as beige, as fawn, as grey. The house gleamed with rich blues and reds and purples, with emerald green, with dazzling white. And in her own wardrobe gone were the tailored suits and gone the cotton tents in tablecloth patterns. That day when I came in, when I used the key she had sent me and mounted the stairs, carpeted now in blood red, came to the top and found her seated at her table, she was in yellow silk on which blossomed white daisies and red roses and sprays of green fern. And that was by no means the only change in her.

She put out her arms and without a word I went to her and into that embrace and we hugged each other. Being sent the key had touched me, had moved me near to tears, the trust it implied. I hugged Cosette and felt her warmth and smelt her scent and felt the new thinness of her under the slippery silk.

'I've been on a diet.'

'I can see,' I said.

'The doctor told me to lose weight because of my blood pressure.'

It was a shy look she gave me, her eyes not meeting mine. I had a curious feeling that though she was telling the truth, it wasn't the whole truth. This wasn't her honest and entire motive for losing weight.

'You've done something to your hair.'

Cosette put up her hand to the reddish-brown coiffure. 'First of all they tint it to your natural colour and then every time you have it done,' she said confidingly, 'they tint it a slightly paler colour until you end up nearly blonde. That way all the grey gets sort of absorbed and doesn't show.'

'Yes, I see,' I said.

Had that ever been her natural colour? Come to that, had it ever been anyone's natural colour?

'The hairdresser says it takes ten years off my age.'

I wasn't going to deny it, though I couldn't see it myself. The strange coppery colour made Cosette's face appear tired as the grey never had, and worse than that, her hair looked like a wig. I told her heartily that she looked very nice, it was all an improvement, and this seemed to make her happy. She said I must come and see upstairs, I must see 'my' room, and I half-expected her to jump out of her chair with a new lightness of step. But she was the same languid Cosette, apparently with all the time in the world at her disposal.

We climbed up, looking into the rooms as we went. Auntie was out in the garden, sitting in a deckchair, sleeping probably, so we looked into her room up on the next floor, a big room full of old lady's things, a strange radio from the forties in a polished wooden case, silver-paper pictures and a collage of sepia postcards, antimacassars on the two armchairs. A flypaper hung from the central light. I looked out of the window which, being at the back, was one of those glass-doors-opening-on-to-a-balcony arrangements. Among all that grey foliage the top of Auntie's head looked rather like a white chrysanthemum. She was sitting with her hands folded and her legs up and stretched out. If she had been doing anything, sewing for instance or even reading, I think I should have been very surprised. But she was doing nothing, just existing, basking in the mild autumn sun, the grey leaves all around her. Later I came to learn that the smoke-coloured tree which made dappled shadows was a eucalypt, but I didn't know it then, I didn't know the names of anything in that pale, ghost-like garden.

Cosette had allotted me a room on the floor above, but at the front. It had one of the Venetian bays. I have harped rather on windows, I see, as if I noticed them more than I noticed the proportions of the rooms and their sizes. Of course I didn't. It was what happened later that makes me think I must always have been more aware of the windows than of any other feature of the House of Stairs, even the staircase itself, aware not only of their size and shape but of the danger to which they exposed those inside them. The ones at the front were safe enough, with their deep sills or guarded by their graceful iron baskets, but at the back of the house – what careless architect had designed windows that were in fact glass doors out of which you stepped almost into the void, on to at any rate a narrow ridge of plaster with a low wall a child could have stepped over? And one at the top which, when open, was just a doorless doorway?

The room that was to be mine had a bed in it and crates and crates of unpacked articles. I began to wish I hadn't committed myself to that teacher-training course. For some reason, and this sort of attitude isn't typical of me, I wanted to start unpacking and arranging immediately. The sun was shining, the last sun before the winter came perhaps. On the balcony in a house opposite, an austere Parisian angular balcony very unlike the ones on this side, a woman was watering geraniums. There were more trees in the street than cars.

'You can come every weekend,' said Cosette.

Going downstairs, we met Diana Castle and a boy coming up. Their appearance had been heralded by the front door slamming and making the house shake, shivering on its spine of stairs. Diana kissed Cosette and to my surprise the boy did too. They went on up into the room that became known as the room of the 'Girl-in-

Residence'. Who coined the expression I don't know, perhaps Cosette herself. The door up there slammed too. Cosette smiled in a way I knew meant she was glad Diana could make herself at home in her house.

She said to me, 'I like the idea of having a girl living here. I'd like it to be you, but until it can be I'll have someone else. People do seem to like it here. I *am* pleased.'

Diana was supposed to look after Cosette a bit, do some shopping, clear up after parties, count and pack up the laundry, things like that, but not cleaning. Perpetua did the cleaning. But if Diana started off doing these tasks she soon gave it up, just as her successors did. With the best will in the world it is almost impossible to wash dishes, tidy up, go down to the shops, when someone (the someone you are doing it for and in lieu of rent) keeps telling you not to bother, to leave it, that it isn't important, but to sit down and talk to her instead. Already an enormous untidiness, a jumble-sale clutter, had begun to accumulate in the house around Cosette, covering the surfaces and lying in heaps on the floors. But it was a somehow pleasing disorder, it was the kind of delightful mess that puts visitors at ease.

A great deal of it was strewn across the large circular rosewood table at which Cosette had been sitting when I arrived, at which I was to learn she sat for a large part of every day. It was the reception point of her salon, the place from which she held court. I remembered this table from Wellgarth Avenue where, with two leaves inserted in its centre and twelve chairs around it, it had nearly filled the dining room. There it had been kept polished to an immaculate glassiness. This gloss was already dimmed, the surface already marked with white rings and dull rings, water spots, the indentations made by handwriting on thin paper without a pad beneath. And this somehow, of all the observable changes in Cosette's style of living, more than anything expressed to me the break she had made with the past, the revolution in her life.

And, of course, because this is the way with human beings, I felt a twinge of fear and more than a twinge of resentment. When we are young we want ourselves to change, but everyone and everything else to remain the same. She didn't mention Douglas.

79

Perhaps that wasn't unnatural, but by no oblique word or hint or adumbration did she refer to her loss or her widowed state. There was no photograph of him in the house that I could see or ever did see. Later that day we went into her bedroom, a lavish boudoir new-furnished with a big oval-shaped bed, a Hollywood-style dressing-table, the circular mirror surrounded by light bulbs, Chinese screens in ebony inlaid with mother-of-pearl. The rich-man's-bride furniture of Wellgarth Avenue, the honeymoon bed with its frilly white canopy, was distributed about the house, a piece here, a piece there, a couple of chairs for Auntie, the bed itself, stripped of its flounces, donated to the Girl-in-Residence. The silver-framed photographs Cosette now had were of me, of her St John's Wood brother and sister-in-law and a niece's wedding.

That evening people came, all of them young, students, hippies, I suppose. Someone must have set this influx in motion, started it off. Cosette can hardly have advertised or stood in the street crying the house's amenities like a barker. Perhaps Diana was the moving spirit behind it originally and her friends told their friends. I think even then I knew they came because it was free, what they got there, drink, at any rate tea and sometimes wine, food if they wanted it, unlimited cigarettes, talk or silence, and an offer if not of a bed of a floor to sleep on. But it was also because of Cosette herself, her capacity for loving. She should have had ten children.

These people came like the flies came to Auntie's flypaper, lured by the sweetness of the gum, but unlike those flies paying no penalty for their attraction. And Cosette sat at her table with the books on it and the phone-books, the sheets of paper, the empty cups and glasses, the phone and the radio, the dying flowers in the vase, her bulging handbag, glasses, cigarettes, powder compact and her nail varnish, but no biscuits or chocolates because she had to retain her new figure. For Cosette was looking for a lover.

I didn't know it then, I couldn't have guessed. To me she looked like these people's mother, an impossibly indulgent one of course, for what mother in the late sixties would have permitted a daughter to take a boyfriend off to bed or a son to roll a joint and as it was passed round, partake of it? These things Cosette not only allowed but seemed positively to promote with her all-permissive smile. Did she smile with greater warmth on those passive bearded boys, the silent one who sat with bent head over Kahlil Gibran or the frenetic one who for hours on end plucked tuneless vibrations from a guitar? If she did I would have attributed her smile to some other cause; I would never have guessed at a loneliness and an almost agonized longing that made her consider boys thirty years her junior as potential lovers. It was only later, at Christmas, when by a miracle we actually found ourselves alone together one evening, that she explained to me. It was then she talked about being a 'manizer', about stealing husbands.

'If I was thirty again, Lizzie. I'd been married for eleven years when I was thirty. I'd never worked, you know. Lots of girls didn't in the thirties, it wasn't just married women who didn't. Girls stayed at home with their mothers till they got married and you were lucky if you got married young, the younger the better. You never heard any of that talk you hear now about waiting to get married till you're older, about having to be mature and all that. I was envied, everyone thought I was fortunate to be engaged at eighteen and married at nineteen – really, I was the envy of all. It seems mad now, it's all changed.'

'Do you wish you hadn't?' The conversation made me feel a little uncomfortable.

'In the climate of the times what else could I have done?'

'I suppose it was what sociologists call a culture-specific,' said I, being clever.

She lifted her shoulders, said very quietly, looking down, 'I ate my cake and now I want to have it.'

Even I, at twenty-one, knew better than to tell her she wasn't thirty any more and never could be again. She leaned forward and looked hard at me, then placed her fingertips on her cheekbones, raising the facial tissues until the lines on either side of her mouth disappeared and the jawbone was defined. I had no clue as to what she was doing, although I knew she was waiting for some comment from me. I looked up and then down, feeling my eyes flicker, feeling the embarrassment the young do feel when the old exhibit desires discordant with their years. I didn't know what Cosette meant, only that it seemed to involve a loss of dignity. She took her hands down, letting her face sag once more.

'I've got a lot of money,' she said. 'I'm rich. I think I should be able to do what I like with it within reason, don't you?'

'Sure,' I said on firmer ground. She led me back to the quick-sands.

'Lots of middle-aged women find men to love them. A woman in her late forties isn't what a woman would have been when I got married. My father used to say that you were middle-aged at thirty-five and elderly at fifty. That sounds absurd to you, doesn't it?'

Not specially. It sounded about right. Knowing Cosette was already past fifty I said I thought she looked very nice, lovely, I loved the way she looked, and I meant all that. I did love her tired, gentle face, made haggard by the dieting, her still plump, unused hands with their pink polished nails, her dry reddish hair which the hairdresser, true to his promise, was gradually bleaching to a rosy blonde, her dress of midnight-blue lace. It didn't occur to me to tell her what she wanted to hear, the only thing she wanted to hear; it didn't occur to me that she would have been delighted if, for instance, I had said she looked awful or ugly but young, if I had said I hated her hair, her dress, the colour of her lipstick, yet reluctantly admitted how young she looked for her age. I would gladly have lied if I had only thought of it.

Soon after that Auntie came into the room. She invariably knocked before coming in, though Cosette tried very hard to stop her doing this. There was a chair she always sat in, far from the table, near the window, a rather stiff and upright wing chair upholstered in Cosette's favourite red velvet. Cosette always fussed around her, making her comfortable, looking in vain for the Girl-in-Residence – still Diana Castle, who was of course out somewhere – to fetch a small sherry or a cup of tea. In this particular instance I fetched Auntie's drink and when I came back with it a crowd had arrived, five people whose combined ages probably added up to a hundred, and whom Cosette was in the process of presenting in a measured and formal way to her old second cousin.

'This is Gary, Auntie, this is Mervyn, Peter, Fay, this is Sarah, Auntie. I want you all to meet my Auntie.'

It must have made her young in their eyes, you see. Elderly people, even middle-aged people, don't have aunts. There was exploitation in it but no cruelty, no harm. It was scarcely comparable, say, to the conduct of those Spanish Habsburgs who kept dwarfs at court the better to show off their own height and looks. Auntie suffered no loss of dignity, no humiliation. She looked well on it, this court-dwarf role; she, ironically enough, actually did look younger than when I had seen her last. Placid, complaisant, almost totally silent, she sat in her wing chair at the window, not looking out into the night, for the red velvet curtains were drawn, but staring as if mesmerized at the soft, cherry-coloured folds.

When I saw Cosette again, a month later, she had had her face lifted, and, newly done, it was purple and yellow with bruises so that poor Cosette looked as if she had been in a fist fight. By Easter all these efforts had had their effect and the man who called himself Ivor Sitwell was her lover.

7

It was he who, indirectly, led me back to Bell, or who brought Bell back into my life, though that was a while ahead. At first there seemed no possible good that could proceed from that source. I remember the shock I felt at finding him in the House of Stairs, the self-control I had to exert to stop myself telling Cosette exactly what I thought of him.

She hadn't told me about him in advance. But this was at first unnoticeable, because after a fashion she had achieved her salon and there were always people coming and going, the red stair-carpet was already showing signs of wear. Some had even moved in to occupy the empty bedrooms and on your way to Cosette in the drawing room it wasn't unusual when passing the ground-floor rooms to see beyond an open doorway four or five unknown people sitting on the carpet in a circle with a candle in the middle and someone playing a sitar or ocarina.

Cosette herself had submitted to, or enthusiastically taken up, the sixties' candle craze. (It came in useful for those seasons of power cuts a few years later.) Though there was a light on the stairs, in the drawing room the gloom was pierced only by candle flames. Candles stood in the pair of iron and bronze candelabra she had bought in the King's Road, and in saucers too and even the screwtop lids of jars. I could just make out the shape of Auntie, in her red wing chair but facing into the room, and the shadowy candlelit forms of several others sprawled on floor cushions or seated at the round table. The huge ornate chandelier hung unlit but faintly luminous in its thickening drapery of cobwebs, a ghostly object growing out of darkness.

I knew better than to comment on Cosette's new face in that company – in any company. I liked the old one better, but I wasn't a lover and Ivor Sitwell had never seen the old one. Somewhat egg-like and with less expression, tautly pulled and faintly polished, the new face broke into the old smile. I was reassured. I kissed the smoothed-out skin and it felt the same as the old crumpled skin, or perhaps I mean there was the same smell, the sophisticated flowers of Patou's Joy. Cosette's hair had nearly reached the desired shade. It was the colour of dry sand. On the third finger of her right hand she was wearing the bloodstone ring. It had become very fashionable but it still didn't suit her.

People were introduced, but I forget their names. If Ivor alone was introduced by his Christian and last names that, perhaps, was only because his surname was a distinguished one, at any rate one that someone like me was bound to notice if not remark out loud on. For the sake of suspense I might keep this a secret but I won't. A long time afterwards I found out that Ivor was not 'a' Sitwell, was not connected with the family and Sitwell was not even his real name. He had picked it himself when he shook the dust off his feet of his parents' semi-detached house in Northampton. One of the Sitwells – Sacheverell, I think it was – had happened to live in the manor house of a village not far away.

Ivor was a poet. Cosette told me so when she told me his name. She also told me his poetry was wonderful and she would show me some of it next day. He was a thin, unhealthy-looking man with a bony sallow face and very long brown hair. Most young men were wearing their hair long then but Ivor wasn't very young, he was getting on for forty, and he had a bald spot on the top of his head. He said, 'Hi', which was what everybody said then, which if you still say it brands you a child of the sixties, but Ivor murmured it without looking up from the book with which he was preoccupied. I say 'preoccupied' and not 'reading' because he was standing up, looking down at the book which was open on the table. It was one of those books which are collections of the best work of some photographer, interesting enough if the photographs are of people but boring (to me) if they are merely of artefacts. These photographs were of objects in incongruous juxtaposition to each other and Ivor Sitwell was staring with a look of rapture at the picture of two empty milk bottles, the milk scum still clinging to their insides, standing next to a dead fish in a birdcage.

He was one of those people who have made up their minds

which members of the company are worth bothering about and which are not. I was not and Auntie was not and, with the exception of the prettiest girl, the people on the floor cushions were not. It was Cosette he spoke to. 'That sensuous, tender curve,' he said, indicating the side of one of the milk bottles with a dirty finger, 'don't you find that almost unbearably exciting?'

Cosette smiled at him and agreed. 'Yes, it's lovely, darling.' I knew that smile. It indicated only a sympathy with the inquirer, a desire to please, to be kind.

'Lovely, yes, but doesn't it make your juices flow?'

I thought I detected a movement from Auntie, a start of astonishment, but then I saw that she was fast asleep, she had jerked in her sleep. Ivor picked up the book and set it in Cosette's lap. She was to look, she was to study it. He stood behind her instructing her, holding the candle. It was soon after this that the candle grease spilt. People used to think Cosette clumsy, probably because she did things slowly, but in fact she never was, she was manually dextrous, delicately so. She reached up the hand with the green and red ring on it and Ivor made to thrust the candle into it. Perhaps it was not for this reason she raised her hand, perhaps it was to take his, but whatever it was, between them they dropped the candle on to the open book, letting fall before it went out a long stream of grease.

'You clumsy cow,' Ivor shouted. 'Look what you've done!'

That was when I knew he was her lover.

A mere visitor to the house wouldn't have spoken like that. Of course it was indefensible in Ivor to do so and I wasn't yet used to his ways. But Auntie must have been, up to a point. His voice woke her up and I saw her sleepy old eyes fix themselves on him in a kind of innocent bewilderment. The people on the floor took no notice and nor did the two at the table who were setting out the Tarot. Cosette said, 'Oh, darling, I'm terribly sorry. I can't think what made me do that.'

Ivor was holding the book up close to his face. 'Do you know what I sometimes think? I sometimes think you've got one of those nervous diseases, Parkinson's maybe, something like that.'

Inwardly, I trembled. How could I not? Cosette caught my eye, as she would, she must, when such things were said. I knew her look of anguish and the faint swift shake of her head were for me, but he took them as a reinforcement of her apology.

'A normal woman wouldn't be so awkward, even a woman in the throes of the menopause.'

Auntie got up, gathered together her book, her bag, her glasses, and began making her way to the door. I had never before known her signify disapproval of anything and perhaps she wasn't disapproving, perhaps she was only tired. Cosette, of course, intercepted her with a strained fluttery, 'Are you all right, Auntie? Can I get you anything?'

'No, thank you, dear. I'm off to bed.'

The door closed the way Auntie always closed it, extremely, exaggeratedly slowly, with the faintest whisper of a click, as if the house were full of sleeping invalids. I sat at the table, watching them, Cosette and Ivor. She was telling him in her most soothing tone that she would replace the book, she would buy him another copy tomorrow. I didn't know then that the one damaged by candle grease had been her gift, as was almost everything portable Ivor possessed, including the clothes he stood up in. If this didn't of course justify her spoiling it, it did make his abuse the more outrageous. But I sat there dwelling on my discovery, the revelation that had been made to me. I was shocked.

My reaction, I suppose, was close to that of a child who finds out that its mother is having a love affair. The foundations of life are shaken, security slips from under one's feet, is pulled away. Did it make a difference that this lover of Cosette's was such an odious person? Perhaps, but not entirely. Anyone in that position would have been shocking, for the position itself was shocking. Cosette might have told me she would like to be a 'manizer', to be thirty again and steal husbands, but I supposed there was a natural gulf fixed between wishes and reality. Naïvely, I believed the slimming and the hair dyeing and the face-lifting undirected to any other end but her own self-esteem. A curtain was lifted and I looked out into a world for which I felt distaste, a world where those I thought of as old had desires and excitements to 'make juices flow'.

She never told me he was her lover in so many words. And certainly he never said he was. His attitude was one I had never

87

seen before but have since. She was thirteen years his senior and therefore had no rights, no claim upon him, and he no obligations of fidelity or the duty even of courtesy. In other words, she was lucky to get him and he had the right to use her as he chose and get out of her what he could. A while later, when he had decided I was worth taking a little notice of, not so much due to my daughterly role in Cosette's life as to the fact that I was young and good-looking, he remarked to me in one of his pensive moods, 'You see, I have no sweetheart at present, no one to make music with.'

Cosette, supposedly, didn't count. Yet they shared a bed, the big new oval bed in Cosette's bedroom. I even saw them together in it. One morning a man came to the front door delivering a piece of furniture I was sure had been mistakenly sent; it seemed very unlike Cosette's taste, the old taste or the new. Cosette, of course, was still asleep. Like her young guests she so much wanted to resemble, in this new life she slept late and was seldom up before noon. I went upstairs, up the four flights to the second floor, and knocked diffidently upon her door. I was actually shrinking at what seemed to me the enormity of what I was doing, the intrusion.

But Cosette, of course, wasn't sorry to see me. Had she even feigned sleep so that I was obliged, when I had knocked repeatedly, to open the door and go inside? She was gratified that I should see her with her young lover, in a situation to prove their sexual involvement. He lay on his front, bundled up in bedclothes, a selfish man who grabs the sheet and blankets to himself, his bald head showing. Her hair, which she had formerly been in the habit of pinning up overnight, flowed loose on to her shoulders. She wore a nightgown designed for a young mistress, black lace and thin straps.

'Don't make a noise, darling. We mustn't wake Ivor.' Her finger to her lips, she climbed with exaggerated care out of bed.

He turned over, snorting as he did so. I felt quite shaken by the sight, by this encounter. Sometimes, in the past, as adolescents do, I had tried to imagine Cosette and Douglas in bed together. And I had succeeded in imagining the two of them engaged in the sexual act, a love-making carried out in a stately way with the minimum of movement, without speech, in darkness, to their

88

mutual, quiet, unexpressed satisfaction. It is only recently, in the past couple of years, that I have come to understand this is the way most children imagine their parents making love.

To envisage Cosette and Ivor together – this was harder, this was to be shied away from. And I was too old to indulge that kind of curiosity. I pictured Ivor as merely servicing Cosette and with less enthusiasm than an animal at stud, but I may have been wrong. In the light of what happened later with another man I may have been quite wrong. Ivor may not have been in love with Cosette, may have been waiting for some young 'sweetheart' to come along, but he could still have been attracted by her. That languor can be very attractive, that slow sweet gentleness, that air of issuing invitations to love in idleness. And no doubt the pains Cosette had taken with her appearance had paid off. I alone still saw her as she had been before the transformation, stout, grey-haired, in her tailored suits. I alone saw her as a mother.

Nor was she in love with him. At the time I couldn't face so bleak a notion, but now I know she wanted a man of her own, a man to show off to others, a man to go about with, perhaps too a man to sleep with. Strange that I could accept such a concept quite naturally when it applied to my contemporaries, to myself, to Diana Castle, say. Diana and Fay, the pretty floor-cushion girl Ivor flirted with, had taken full advantage of sixties morality to sleep with anyone they fancied. Love didn't come into it. Why should it? They had discovered it isn't necessary to love someone in order to enjoy yourself with him. And that was all right, I understood that, I felt the same. But that Cosette might feel the same – that was too much for me, that was something I didn't want to confront. I know now that while Cosette had loved Douglas dearly, had been a good and faithful wife to him and mourned his death with great bitterness, she was only in love once in her life, and that was neither with Douglas nor Ivor.

I wish, I really do wish, I could say something in Ivor Sitwell's favour, could have found in him some redeeming feature. It would have reconciled me to his presence in the House of Stairs, it would have gone some way to explaining Cosette's unaccountable partiality. He was ugly and mean-spirited, ungrateful and rude, as discourteous to Auntie as he was to Diana and me, capable of caressing Fay in Cosette's presence and then walking up to Cosette and asking her for money in front of all of us. He did nothing to help in the house and used Perpetua as if she were a servant in a Victorian household. Perhaps he was a good poet. I can't say, I don't know. Cosette had shown me, as she promised, a volume of his verses. They had been published but had he, as I was sure at the time, paid to have them published? Or, rather, got some woman, some predecessor of Cosette's, to pay for their publication?

These verses weren't bad in the way Patience Strong is bad. They weren't doggerel, they didn't express stale emotion in clichés. That I found them incomprehensible is nothing against them. I might not do so now if I were ever able to get hold of any examples of them. After all, people in the sixties found Pinter incomprehensible and fraught with *non sequiturs*. Once or twice, in the evenings, Cosette read them aloud to whoever might be there. It was only while she was reading his poetry that I ever saw Ivor look at her in a lover-like way, look at her, that is, with neither indifference nor anger.

That spring I stayed with Cosette for several weeks. I had teaching practice to do as part of my course and had, by a lucky chance, been sent to a school in North Kensington. Times have changed, but even then it was a rough area, shabby and sordid by day and dangerous by night. The children, then as now, were a mixed lot and in order to teach them satisfactorily one should really have been proficient in Gujarati and Bengali. But it had the great advantage of being within walking distance of Archangel Place.

In the evenings Cosette used often to take us all out to dinner. Perhaps the truth was that Ivor didn't specially want to spend time alone with her. They hardly ever went out alone. Instead Cosette would gather up whoever happened to be around, myself and Fay who had become the Girl-in-Residence – Diana having gone off to Cornwall to live with her boyfriend – the boy with the sitar and the boy with the ocarina, Perpetua's brother, an Irishman from County Leix who had come to London to seek his fortune and been given a room in Archangel Place, 'just until you find somewhere, darling'. And, of course, Ivor. We always went to expensive, exclusive places: the Marco Polo in the King's Road, San

Frediano's, The Pheasantry, the Villa dei Cesari. On the few occasions Cosette found herself dining at the Hungry Horse in the Fulham Road she thought she was slumming.

She had brought the big old Volvo with her from Wellgarth Avenue and she left it parked in the street. It was still possible to do this at that time in the little streets of Notting Hill. An old-fashioned woman in some ways, she never drove the car herself when Ivor was with her but handed the keys to him before we left the house. He was a terrible driver. Already the Volvo, which Cosette's years of slow, skilful driving had left unscathed, was scarred and marked and chipped and one of the rear lamps smashed. To drive eastwards to the Edgware Road and then south along Park Lane is neither the easiest nor the shortest way to get to Chelsea, but it was the way that Ivor took. Perhaps he took it in order to drive along Moscow Road and give himself the opportunity of pointing out to all of us the house in which Edith Sitwell had once had a flat. 'Cousin' Edith, he called her. To other Sitwells he referred in a similarly familiar way, speaking of 'Sachie' and 'Georgie'. I didn't then know that he had absolutely no right to claim this relationship. Interested, I even asked him if he had any special memories or anecdotes to relate of the celebrated three. He then told several tales which I later came across pretty well word for word in Osbert Sitwell's *Laughter in the Next Room*.

It showed me one thing. That if you wanted to put Ivor in a good mood you either had to praise his poetry or ask him about these people we all believed were his relatives. Nothing else would do it. We went to the Marco Polo that evening, as we often did then, and it was there that I received, without knowing it at the time, news of Bell.

Chinese restaurants were not common then as they are now. At least, good ones were not. It felt very grand to sit round a table big enough to accommodate us all and fiddle about with the dishes that make up what was then a rarity for London, Peking duck. I sat between Dominic and a boy called Mervyn, and on the other side of Dominic was Fay and on the other side of her, Ivor. I sat there enjoying it but thinking how strange it all was, recalling the decorous dinner parties at which Cosette and Douglas had entertained her relations and the Wellgarth neighbours. Some of those people had occasionally called at Archangel Place and their astonishment, expressed in wandering eyes, hesitant inquiries, was greater than mine. They were older and more set in their ways. They thought Cosette had gone mad.

Eating at the Marco Polo, or wherever it might be, produced the same sort of astonishment in some of Cosette's young guests. You could see they wondered what it was all about, why Cosette did it, and in the case of some of them, what price were they going to have to pay? This was specially evident in the Irishman, youngest of Perpetua's large family of siblings. Dominic had come to London to find work and when his sister told him she had found a place for him to stay, must have expected a miserable room in a comfortless house, an exigent landlady, a shabby neighbourhood. He could scarcely believe his luck or overcome his terrible suspicions. Like the streetwise beggar picked out of an alley to attend the rich man's feast, he seemed always on the watch for the reckoning. Sooner or later Cosette's motive must emerge. What was surely some gross and elaborate practical joke would end in his humiliation, or else she was mistaken in him, believed him other than he was, and when she discovered the truth, that he was a labourer by necessity not inclination, poor and nearly illiterate, accustomed to a diet of fried bread and chips at his mother's kitchen table, she would expose him and fling him out of doors.

Or so I suppose. This is what his expression told me, for at that time he never spoke except to say thank you, and later on when I might have asked him, I didn't. His wild beautiful dark face was anxious in repose, marvellous when he smiled, as he did whenever he was spoken to, his eyes, the bluest I have ever seen, positively glowing with gratitude and apprehension. On the other hand, the boy called Mervyn was out to get what he could. I think Fay was too. I think it now, though at the time I never quite believed in people actually and purposefully having an attitude of this sort. I thought it was something come upon in old novels whose authors were not conversant with the subtleties of human nature. I had never read Balzac. I hadn't yet begun reading Henry James.

So when I saw Fay raise and lower her long eyelashes at Ivor Sitwell, stretch her bare arms behind her head to lift her breasts, smile at him and whisper something indecent and provocative, having apparently waited for the moment Cosette left us to go to the bathroom, I thought it done in innocence and by chance. And these factors of accident and random acts I thought operating again when she later turned her back on him and concentrated on Cosette, pinning up Cosette's back hair that was flopping out of its pins, complimenting her on her perfume, sniffing with eyes closed as if ravished by it, going off to find a waiter and demand a jug of water because Cosette had asked for it. Mervyn had different methods: eating and drinking as much as he could get, far more than any reasonable person would want to eat and drink – Cosette always asked for the bill and paid it without a word, with scarcely more than a glance at it -- remarking that he had run out of cigarettes, observing loudly and often how much he liked the jacket some man on the other side of the restaurant was wearing or how he had always longed for a certain kind of pen or cigarette lighter. I believed it all artless, but I learned.

At Cosette's table, whether at home or in a restaurant, there was always excess, too much food, too much wine, a bottle or two left half-empty, cigarettes stubbed out half-smoked, cigarettes left in packets on the cloth, liqueurs left in glasses, chocolates on dishes. If Gary, the boy who played the various exotic musical instruments was there, he would gather up all these leftovers and put them into a carrier bag he kept with him for this purpose. For all I know this may have been the first doggy bag to make its appearance in London. As well as the bag, Gary carried a Tupperware box to put beansprouts and noodles in, including those that other people had left on their plates.

It was a few days after this that I first witnessed this spooning up of leftovers, and saw him, green in the face after drinking four glasses of kirsch, stagger to the bathroom to be sick. On this occasion Ivor burned the five-pound note to show his contempt for money.

'Can you let me have a fiver?'

Cosette didn't hesitate. The banknote, worth so comparatively little now, would then have paid a week's rent of a better room than Dominic could have afforded. Ivor took it out of her fingers. He had been discoursing on the wealth of 'his' family and how happy he was that, due to some legal mix-up, none of it had come the way of the particular branch to which he belonged. He talked about money corrupting and about selfishness. I have since then noticed that it is only deeply selfish people who point out the selfishness of others. Earlier that day, it appeared, he had proposed that Cosette should back the founding of a poetry magazine of which he would be editor. She hadn't refused outright, only said it would be hard for her to lay hands on such a large sum at short notice.

'Now why do you suppose we refer to people who oppose innovations in the arts as Philistines?' he asked us, still holding up the banknote in his fingertips.

No one answered him, no one knew or cared.

'Possibly because no documents in the Philistine language are extant,' Ivor said. 'Equally possibly because the Philistines long held a monopoly in smithing iron, their only known skill.' He looked at Cosette, drawing towards him with his free hand the candle a waiter had just lit. 'But how did the use of the term in its modern sense arise?'

Cosette was very tolerant, very easy-going, so well able to conceal hurt that you might think she scarcely felt it. Betrayal was what she feared and Ivor, who had presumably made her no promises, given her no guarantees, couldn't betray her. But she liked things to be pleasant, she was one who poured oil on troubled waters.

'You've just told us how, Ivor,' she said. 'It's very interesting. I didn't know that.'

'The use of the term for people deficient in liberal culture and whose chief interests are material was first applied by German students in the nineteenth century to those who hadn't been to a university. People like you.' He might equally have said people like himself, since his claims to have been to Oxford, or indeed any seat of learning after he left Northampton High School at the age of sixteen, were without foundation. The information about Philistines I later discovered he had purposefully mugged up in advance. Cosette didn't in the least mind these insults, having no inflated image of her own intellect, indeed very much underestimating it. He too saw this, he saw he had misjudged his victim and her vulnerable area, and now, unerringly, he aimed at her tender place. 'Not that I blame you for that, you can't help it. You were born too soon.' He said to the rest of us, 'Women of her age just weren't allowed higher education.' And leaning foward, he thrust the folded note into the candle flame and lit his cigarette with it. 'Naturally their chief interests would be material, but there's no harm in showing them how' – pause – 'little' – pause – 'these' – pause – 'things matter.'

His efforts were largely wasted, for I think it was only I who saw Cosette's deep blush. The others were too busy watching, like animals hypnotized by headlights, the consumption in flames of the five-pound note. All except Gary who, in an agony at the wicked waste of it, actually making a wailing sound, lunged forward and tried to snatch the burning paper from Ivor's hand. All across the restaurant people were looking. Ivor was laughing, holding in his fingers the burnt fragments of paper, snuffling smoke out through his nostrils. I looked to see if the strip of metal, allegedly embedded in every genuine banknote, had survived the fire, but could see only rags of dark brown ash. It seemed to me in that moment, as Fay leant back, resting her head against Ivor's shoulder, crying, 'Oh, magnificent, magnificent!' as Gary with tears on his cheeks sulkily shovelled leftovers into his plastic box and Dominic, thunderstruck, murmured, 'Holy Mary and Joseph,' it seemed to me then that I saw in Cosette's face the flash of fear that says, 'What am I doing here, what have I got myself into?' I think so, but I could be mistaken.

She paid the bill, as always, with the merest glance at it. She added her usual excessive tip. We walked out into the King's Road and Ivor suggested we all go on to some drinking club he knew in South Kensington, a place called the Drayton. Cosette had a headache and I could see she was being overtaken by pain. Under the harsh acid lights, dressed in the bright colours she now favoured – that night a red silk skirt and red silk sleeveless jerkin over a flowered blouse – she looked old and tired. The 'lifting' had done little to prevent a droop at the corners of her mouth. It wasn't for me to resist going to this club, no one would have taken any notice if I had, and besides I wanted to go on there, I was young, I wanted to live. At that time I was passing through one of those phases of recklessness that perhaps come to everyone over whom hangs the sword of a fatal disease that may strike next month or next year or tomorrow.

Cosette wouldn't have considered refusing. She had taken on the role of youth and she must play the part in all its aspects. But she was unable to fake enthusiasm, and Ivor saw this at once, he was sensitive in his way; he saw that she was tired and in pain and not able to disguise it, able only to acquiesce. It was one of the things about her that made him angry, her complaisance, which I think he saw as a rich woman's indifference. If you have that much money you need scarcely trouble yourself about anything or make yourself interesting, you need merely be supine. I think he saw it this way. He was consumed with envy, with covetousness for her money, and would without a doubt have married her for it. Someone had told Bell who told me later that he couldn't marry because he was already married to a Catholic woman who wouldn't give him a divorce. And this was a couple of years before the new, easy, divorce law came in.

He was angry and anger always made him vindictive or silky. That night he was silky. In the car on the way to Drayton Gardens he began talking about women, about the types of women he admired. For some reason he least admired the type in which I belong, small, slender, dark, brown-skinned. By the time we were in the club, which Cosette was obliged to join and pay a membership fee, for no one could be found to support Ivor's claim to membership, he was describing this type in detail as anathema to him. Since I disliked him so much I was rather amused, and I was touched to see how Dominic resented it on my behalf.

Fay's looks were the kind he most appreciated.

'Tall and not too thin,' he said, 'lots of very light hair but not yellow hair, never yellow. Grey eyes, large grey eyes, and a little short nose and a sensuous mouth.'

The ironical thing was that though he was describing Fay and looking at Fay, he was also describing Cosette, or the way Cosette had tried, and with some success, to re-make herself. She saw this, if no one else did, and it revived her. Her eyes brightened, she smiled a little. Not, I think, because she much cared what Ivor said, she was passing beyond caring what he said or did, his days were numbered, but because he was after all a man talking about a woman like her, talking of her as desirable, placing her by definition in a stage of youth.

Fay enjoyed it too. Fay thought she was being individually praised and perhaps knew she was being flattered, for she wasn't very tall and her nose turned up. We were all sitting round a table, drinking a mixture called Singapore Sling, and a girl had come on to the little stage to sing Edith Piaf songs in what Ivor said was very bad French. It sounded all right to me and I said so. He cast me one of his poisonous looks, so ridiculous as to arouse derisive laughter. I had never laughed at him before. Had I been a coward and did I now sense his star was setting? Perhaps. Anyway, I started to laugh and after a while Dominic laughed too, tentatively at first, then with uninhibited uproarious mirth. Ivor watched the girl leave the stage.

'I've met her,' he said coldly. 'I met her in a friend's house at a party and the most beautiful woman I've ever seen was there. She rents a room from my friends.' He warmed to this. I thought he was making it up. I was sure he was as his vindictiveness increased. 'She would make any woman in this room look a clapped-out old slag.' Cosette grew still, stricken. He had shocked Fay, whose face had become a joke-mask of drunken incredulity. A kind of hysterical giggling afflicted me and it took all the control I had to suppress it.

'A daughter of the gods,' said Ivor, 'divinely tall and most divinely fair.'

'Did you make that up yourself?' said Mervyn, awe-struck.

'Of course I didn't, you stupid arsehole. I'm a real poet. I tell you, she has that face I've described, only she has it to perfection, as if all the others' – he looked at Fay – 'were just bad copies, as if they were waxworks. A Scandinavian face, the face of a Viking maid – "a face to lose youth for, to occupy age with the dream of, meet death with" – and I didn't write that either.' I realized he was terribly drunk, but weren't we all, except Cosette? Something was striking a chord in my consciousness and there came back to me a conversation Cosette and I had once had. I looked at her to see if she remembered, but saw in her tired face only pain and perhaps regret, as if there had come into her mind a memory of peace and of lilies in a garden and her high-powered, dull husband.

'You could imagine her in *Smiles of a Summer Night*,' said Ivor. 'You could imagine her in Strindberg.'

I said suddenly, 'What's her name?'

He was too taken aback by the abruptness of it to attempt cleverness. 'Christine Something. They call her Chris. Why?'

'Nothing,' I said. 'It's not the same one,' for I had forgotten Bell's name was Christabel; I had forgotten it entirely.

They were dancing now to the dull tuneless jungle beat of rock. Gary had fallen asleep with his head on the table. Mervyn was doing a kind of solo caper as if for the edification of the band. Perhaps because Cosette sat staring at the art nouveau wall panels with what looked more like indifference than despair, Fay put out one hand to Ivor, fearful that he would refuse her. But instead of refusing he got up and with his arm round her walked precariously up the length of glassy floor.

I said to Dominic, 'Come and dance.'

8

Something over a hundred years ago George Huntington described a disease which he had observed affected families in New England. These people were descendants of seventeenth-century immigrants from the Suffolk village of Bures. I have heard that an ancestor of mine, from far, far back, was a Bures woman.

There is a test you can have now to determine whether or not you will fall victim to Huntington's. It is very complicated and involves not only taking a sample of one's own blood but also that of a number of one's relatives, at least seven. I haven't got seven living relatives on the appropriate side of the family. They have all died of Huntington's.

Once there were quite a lot of us. My grandmother had six children. Her own father had died aged thirty-five, not of Huntington's but of poliomyelitis, then known as infantile paralysis. Her mother vaguely remembered her mother-in-law afflicted with what she mistakenly called St Vitus's Dance which made her limbs jerk and her hands fly out, but she didn't know it was hereditary, she didn't know her own husband would have succumbed to it had he lived. She didn't know her children might inherit it. Three did. My grandmother's choreic movements began soon after her sixth child was born, soon after her thirtieth birthday. Of her six children each had a fifty-fifty chance of succumbing to it. That is the genetic ratio, neither more nor less. If one of your parents had it, you are fifty per cent likely to have it and fifty per cent unlikely to have it. If neither of your parents had it you can't have it. My mother showed the first symptoms, inconsistent behaviour and malaise, when she was thirty-six. One of her sisters had died of diphtheria as a child. Would she have developed it? Two others did, a brother and a sister, and both died before her. The other sisters never had children, never even married, they dared not, though in fact neither of them have developed it and both are still alive. They alone are alive, though if the test had been in existence twenty years ago probably enough could have been mustered to supply blood for me: Douglas, who was the son of my afflicted grandmother's afflicted sister, Cousin Lily descended from my grandmother's other afflicted sister, my mother, her sisters, one dying, insane uncle – well, it would have been a near thing but maybe sufficient could have been found.

And if they had, if the test had existed, if I had dared take it, if it had shown negative, would it have made a difference to my life? Would I have done more and done less and done differently? Would I have had children, written other, better things? What is the use of talking about it? It didn't exist and now that it does there aren't enough people left and I am balanced on the final ridge – only two or three more years and I shall know for good or ill, I shall know for ever.

I wrote my first three books in Cosette's house. The first one I wrote on Douglas's old typewriter in the room at the top of the house with the window that had no real balcony and where there could be no noise above my head to disturb me. It was written rapidly and badly and with the maximum injected sensation and violence and crude sex. I couldn't blame Ivor Sitwell for saying some time later, 'Still churning them out, are you, Elizabeth?'

But all this was a way ahead. I was going to be a teacher. I was going to write a thesis on Henry James. And Ivor was still living with Cosette and sharing her bed and insulting her and trying to squeeze money out of her for his poetry magazine. Over this she proved exceptionally stubborn. There was a stubborn side to Cosette and, surprisingly, a businesswoman side. It must have rubbed off on her from Douglas. At any rate, she wanted to see figures and estimates and meet the people who would be involved with Ivor in this venture before she was prepared to do what she called 'come across'. Two others were concerned. One of them was a woman, now married, Ivor said had once been his 'sweet-heart' and who had written a libretto for a musical that had actually been performed somewhere in America in theatre-in-the-round. The other, who had some connection with *Private Eye*, was called

Walter Admetus, and it was in his house that the woman who had so enchanted Ivor, the woman called Chris or Christine, rented a room.

I don't know why I behaved the way I did, I don't know why I suddenly became devious. I had already made up my mind the beautiful woman couldn't be Bell, having got it into my head that 'my' Bell was really Isabel, and yet Ivor's description tallied with her so closely, matched her feature for feature, colouring for colouring. I could easily have asked Elsa the Lioness whom I often saw, who was a regular visitor to the House of Stairs, to find out from the Thinnesses if Bell Sanger was still in their cottage. Come to that, I could have rung up Felicity Thinnesse myself. We had encountered each other once or twice since that Christmas, we had all met at a party at Elsa's. If I didn't do this I think it was because I wanted to enjoy a shock of recognition, I wanted some rapture of the heart. I think it was that but I don't know. Certain it is that although I had seen her so little my emotions were already involved with Bell and her life.

So when Cosette suggested that Walter Admetus and the woman he lived with were invited to dinner in Archangel Place, I opposed it. She suggested it to me first, we were alone with no one there but Auntie, and this was a piece of luck – or so it seemed, so fatefully it seemed – for if Ivor had been there he would have jumped at the chance, as he always did, of getting something, anything, out of Cosette for himself or anyone connected with him. I have often wondered since then what would have happened if Cosette had refused me, if when I said it would be better to phone Admetus and suggest a meeting at his house, then later if she liked him he could be asked to dinner, if then she had rejected this idea, as with her hospitable ideas she well might have done, she all too well might have done. Would I have made my way alone to the northern reaches of Gloucester Place where Admetus lived to seek out Bell? I don't think so. It would have been hard, it would have required a brashness I don't possess and never did. I would have left it, I would have forgotten Bell – and Cosette would never have been granted bliss nor had her life broken nor come with the rest of us to the high window with the narrow ledge.

'I don't think I could do that, darling,' Cosette said. 'I couldn't invite us to someone's house – ' and, doubtfully, ' – could I?'

It was so funny coming from her, to whose house everyone invited themselves, that even Auntie laughed. She caught my eye and daringly, fearful of giving offence, she laughed her old woman's thin, throaty laugh.

'I don't mind phoning him,' I said. 'I'll say I'm your secretary.'

'Oh, no,' said Cosette, shocked. 'Then he'll expect the sort of person who would have a secretary. I suspect he's very Bohemian.'

This archaic term would have earned Ivor Sitwell's ridicule and the incomprehension of the other inhabitants of the house. But I was used to it, it had been one of Douglas's words. 'If he's Bohemian,' I said, 'he won't mind us inviting ourselves.'

Only then did Cosette catch on. 'Do you mean you'd come with me, Elizabeth?' There was something touching in the way she spoke, that she who conferred so much love and largesse should also be shy, be fearful of intruding, be inordinately grateful that I would spare the time to give her my company. 'That would be very kind of you.' Her face took on the look it wore when she was making plans of generosity, a mischievousness, an almost youthful anticipation. 'We could take him some nice wine. Or Madeira – should we take him a bottle of Madeira?'

I did my best to persuade her that it would look very odd indeed to take presents of wine to someone with whom she might never be on more than a business footing, someone in any case who would be offering her a glass of lemonade, since Cosette herself rarely drank. She looked doubtful. It went against the grain with her not to be giving; instead to be, as she saw it, taking. But in fact she was to give and take nothing, beyond that lemonade, for the magazine never came into being. The libretto woman disappeared to South America and Ivor went off with Fay. Of course he intended to come back, as Fay also intended. Because Cosette was kind and generous, because she never lost her temper or sulked, because she seemed endlessly forgiving, people who were not very percipient thought her gullible. They thought her foolish and ripe to be deceived.

Ivor told her he was going to Northampton to see his mother who was ill. Fay just went without a word. I believe they borrowed a room in Putney which belonged to someone they knew who had gone away on holiday. Cosette, taking Auntie out for a drive, saw them lying in each other's arms in Richmond Park. She showed a side of her character which I had not suspected if I call it vindictiveness, but if I call it something else, not spite, not revenge, but a horror of being betrayed, then I had always known of it.

She had her man from Golders Green come in – Jimmy the faithful handyman who had done all these odd jobs for her in Wellgarth Avenue and now came to Archangel Place – to change the locks and have new keys cut. However, if she didn't change her phone number this was because she hardly ever answered the phone herself. I used to think that if she got anything out of having a houseful of freeloaders it was that there was always someone to answer the phone, an operation she very much flinched from. Mervyn, whom I had never suspected of having a particular dislike for Ivor, took intense pleasure in telling him when he phoned that Cosette had 'given orders' he wasn't to be admitted. Cosette was horrified when she heard about this, but by then Mervyn, and Gary too, had had enormous fun telling Ivor Cosette 'knew all about him', had 'an important friend at Scotland Yard' and was at that moment 'with her solicitor'. Ivor, supposedly, took this to mean that among other things his deception about his family origins had been rumbled, though in fact none of us then suspected he was not as much a Sitwell as the late Sir Osbert himself, whose funeral the year before he claimed to have been invited to.

But before all this happened Cosette and I went to Walter Admetus's house, having arranged to meet Ivor there. We went in the big, old, dusty navy-blue Volvo which gobbled up petrol and which it was Gary's job, never performed, to clean in lieu of rent. Its interior was like an extension of the House of Stairs, being full of Cosette-style clutter, full and half-full and empty cigarette packets, bottles and sprays of Joy, boxes of pink tissues, new novels with torn dust-jackets, shoes to be worn for driving and shoes to be put on after driving, and all those parcels to be taken somewhere that never got there, laundry and dry cleaning and things to be sewn and things to be mended. I felt excited and my excitement communicated itself to Cosette who took it for anxiety that she shouldn't be gulled or lured into parting foolishly with her money.

'When I'm in danger of not being prudent,' she said gravely, 'I think of Douglas. I remember how he worked hard to make all this money for me and it does restrain me.' It was the first time for many months I had heard her mention him.

Elegant-appearing Georgian houses can be just as much tips inside as anywhere else, a fact which was new to me then. Fifteen Archangel Place, though untidy, was not squalid, thanks to the efforts of Perpetua. Walter Admetus's house was. It looked as if it had never been cleaned and it smelt. The upholstery on the furniture was greasy, or rather encrusted with some kind of sticky deposit, the accumulation of years, to which animal hairs adhered, in places as thickly as the pile on a fur. The smell was of fried onions or sweat – which smell much the same – of clogged sink waste-pipes and of old dog and sick cat, though we saw neither animal while we were there. Even Cosette, the least fussy of women, hesitated a little before sitting down on the spot indicated, a stained, hairy sofa cushion on which a blowfly crawled.

Walter Admetus is the only man I have ever known actually to introduce his girlfriend as his mistress. He was a courtly person, with a small, pointed and prominent beard, the kind of beard that turns up and sticks out, and she was very prettily dressed in early Laura Ashley with shiny hair and a pink hair-ribbon. It was a mystery how people could come out of that place and yet be so spruce and groomed.

'Admetus,' he said, holding out his hand and close to clicking his heels. He behaved like some German or Scandinavian aristocrat, though he is as English as I am. 'May I introduce my mistress, Eva Faulkner?'

I was wearing the cameo brooch Cosette had given me for my twenty-first birthday, the one with the head of a girl on it that looks like Bell. I found myself fidgeting with this brooch as I sat rigidly on the sticky filthy velvet of my chair seat, watching Cosette hand over the bottle of red Graves she must have secreted in one of her always huge handbags. It had occurred to me for the first time that Bell simply might not appear, most probably wouldn't appear, might not be at home, and even if she was in was only a lodger here, not a friend. I wondered what I should do. Walter Admetus took the bottle with extravagant expressions of gratitude. His manners were at any rate a far cry from those of Ivor. He insisted on pouring glasses of the wine immediately, although it was very much the sort of stuff to be uncorked in advance, stood about at room temperature and served with food.

'I'm afraid I haven't anything for you and your daughter to eat,' he said.

Cosette winced. I said quickly that I wasn't her daughter. Admetus made things worse by saying with extreme cloying courtesy that no doubt Cosette wished I were. Cosette's face was fixed in that gentle, dreamy smile she could hold for several minutes without relaxing her mouth or blinking her eyes. There seemed absolutely nothing to say. We had arrived rather late, so by now Ivor was very late. The sun poured through the dirty windows, making bars of dull yellow light in which dust motes swarmed like insects. It fell on Eva Faulkner like a purposely directed spotlight and she sat silent and bored, reminding me of the description in *Antony and Cleopatra* of Octavia as a statue, not a breather. I began to realize that I had made a mistake in not telling Cosette that I expected Admetus's lodger to be Bell, for how could I now ask Admetus about her without revealing my duplicity?

I also began to doubt once more. What had I really to go on? A description that I had perhaps distorted in my own mind to suit my wishes and a name I had no real reason to connect with Bell. Cosette had begun a conversation, stilted and very much of the small talk kind, on the amenities of the neighbourhood. Rigid in her sun bath, Eva Faulkner made no replies, gave no sign of having heard, but it seemed just the kind of exchange of pleasantries to appeal to Admetus, who responded with a positive eulogy of the backwoods of Notting Hill, so that you wondered why he didn't immediately move there. His beard wagged and his eyebrows worked up and down and his hands waved like fans. I began to feel angry, we had been there three-quarters of an hour, and I was about to say to Cosette we shouldn't wait, it was hopeless, Ivor wasn't coming, when I heard the front door open and Ivor's voice.

It was disquieting to observe Cosette's reaction to the sound of

Ivor's voice in those days. Her expression would become one of resignation, even of stoicism. I couldn't distinguish the words, nor did I speculate as to whom he might be speaking or, come to that, how he happened to possess a key to this house. I was only wondering if he would break the apparent rule of a lifetime and apologize.

The door to the room opened and he came in with Bell. Typical of him was the way he pushed his way in first and left her to follow.

I don't know if she recognized me, remembered me or if Ivor, who immediately began telling us how he had encountered her in the street outside, had already told her who would be there when they reached the house. I could have asked but I didn't, I never did. She looked at me and said very calmly, 'Hallo, Lizzie,' as if we had last seen each other the day before.

She was all in black – like James's Milly Theale. I never saw her in any but dark or dull or muted shades except the time I made her put on the dress of 'wasted' red like the one the girl wears in the Bronzino painting. This was before the antique-clothes cult, before the knitted-cotton revolution, before long skirts. Bell's clothes had probably been bought at a jumble sale, the long, narrow, black wool skirt with box pleats front and back, the man's black cotton shirt, its sleeves rolled up, its waist defined by a black 'locknit' scarf tied round and round, the rope of black and brown wooden beads. Her fine, thin ankles, the long shaft of the Achilles tendons, just showed below the hem of the skirt. Her feet, brown and long-toed, were in Greek rope sandals. It looked as if she had tied her hair on top of her head with a bit of picture cord. Tendrils of it hung alongside her cheeks and down the long straight nape of her neck, hair that was the colour of pale unvarnished wood, but leaving the high smooth forehead bare. She held her head aloft, poised as she always did, as if balancing on it a heavy vessel full of liquid.

A great deal of marvelling now took place on the part of Cosette, Admetus and Ivor – though not of Eva Faulkner, who apparently took all such coincidences as a matter of course – that Bell and I already knew each other. Once Admetus had gone through the elaborate process of introducing Bell to Cosette, only he called it 'having the honour to present', Ivor began praising Bell's beauty in her presence, walking round her, his head on one side, pointing out with a curved index finger each exceptional feature, as if she were an item on sale in a slave market.

'Look at that chin, look at those dear little ears like shells, and that skin. Have you ever seen such a carriage? A plumb line could pass through her from the crown of her head to the soles of her feet.'

The pointing finger just brushed Bell's neck. She didn't recoil. She said quite slowly, almost casually, but absolutely without amusement, 'Take your hands off me, you ugly bastard.'

She was frank and open, you see, honest they said, she always spoke her mind. Cosette gasped. Admetus gave a nervous titter. To my extreme pleasure I saw that Ivor had gone quite white. Bell said to me, 'Come up and see where I live.'

I didn't hesitate. I left the room with her. Therefore I never knew what actually happened at the tripartite discussion between Cosette, Ivor and Admetus. I know only that Cosette never handed over any money for the founding of the magazine and Ivor was soon to depart, though we went on seeing Admetus, he became a friend and visitor to the House of Stairs, and for a little while, after Eva had left him, I even wondered if he might become Ivor's successor with Cosette. That was before Marcus of course, that was before the coming of Marcus put all other men, any other man, out of the question.

So I went upstairs with Bell and she showed me the little room where she lived, where she had been living ever since she sold the house she inherited from Silas Sanger's father. There was very little in it apart from the bed and a table and a chair, for Bell, then and perhaps now too, has no feeling for domestic comforts or for the appearances of her home. But Silas's paintings were there, canvases stacked against the walls.

'I take them with me wherever I go,' she said. 'He was a really shitty painter, but that doesn't mean a thing. One day there's a chance he'll be recognized and then I'll have an exhibition and sell them for huge sums.'

She spoke to me as if we were old friends. She spoke of Silas without emotion, coolly, practically, as if she were a gallery owner and he a painter she had discovered and invested in. I was awed, remembering the dead man, the blood on the floor and on her.

'Did you stay long with Felicity?' I asked her.

'Two months, one week and two days,' she said. 'Then I went and lived in the house the old man left until I sold it.'

Another question. I asked her a lot of questions that afternoon, though none of the ones I ought to have asked, none of the vital questions. 'What do you do? I mean for a living. What do you work at?'

'I don't.' She looked pleased to be able to say that. 'I don't work at all and I never shall. I'm *never* going to work.'

'Then you're rich?'

Her eyes opened wide. They are sea-grey, her eyes, and very large and clear. 'I'm not, I'm not rich. But I hate working. I've got just enough to exist on without working if I live in a hole like this.' She had a way of dismissing subjects when she had had enough of them, turning her head quickly from side to side, lifting her shoulders, changing on to a new topic. 'Who's that shit I came in with? I've seen him here before.'

'He's a man who lives with my friend you were introduced to.'

'That's a relief. I thought maybe he lived with you.' Too bad if he did. It hadn't stopped her calling him a shit. 'What a turd,' she said. 'Isn't he a bit young for her?'

'A bit stupid for her,' I said. 'A bit ugly and selfish and bloody. I don't know about young,' and, untruthfully, 'I never thought of that.'

She laughed. 'I shall have to see what I can find out about him.'

It was the first time I'd heard her laugh, and it was a surprisingly deep, rich, gurgling sound. Her pale face glowed and she was beautiful. I found her exciting in a disturbing way, a soul-shaking way, without knowing in the least what I wanted of her. That we should be friends? That we should meet and talk and be together? And what did she want? Not of me, but of life? I know now, of course I do, I have known for a long time, but I didn't know then. It mystified me, later on it did, it puzzled me that someone young and beautiful and healthy and intelligent should be content to live in that mean little room in that dirty house, she and all her sparse worldly goods contained in a space twelve feet by twelve, with no job, no career, no prospects, no apparent aims. She was a childless widow of twenty-seven, skilled at nothing, trained for nothing but more beautiful than any model whose photograph graced magazine covers, who dressed in rags, who – I discovered this a while later – had no lover and scarcely a friend.

Of course she was waiting, looking about her, biding her time. That was what she wanted of life. We opened her window on to the white sky, the plane tree with its branches on which pink-bronze pigeons perched, its thread-like twigs and fine silky leaves hanging still in the windless air. We leant out on to the broad windowsill. So many of my memories of Bell concern windows, sashes, casements, glass and draughts and drops, but there was no draught that summer's day. The air smelt fresh from Regent's Park, it smelt like the air of a spoiled countryside. Bell took a tobacco tin from a drawer in the table and, without asking me, taking things for granted, began to roll a joint. It was the first time for me. She showed me how to draw in the smoke and hold it in my lungs until my head began to swim and curiously to expand, and with the exhalation feel the arrival of a deep, tomorrow-less peace.

That September Cosette and I went to Italy together. She had meant to go with Ivor, but by that time Ivor had gone.

'You come,' she said to me. 'I'd rather it was you than him anyway. Really. I was dreading going with him.'

I had seen Bell a few times. She had been to visit me at the House of Stairs and we had gone to the cinema together, to the old Electric Cinema in the Portobello Road, and I would have liked her to come to Italy with us.

'I've only once been to a foreign country,' she had said to me, 'and that was to France with Silas. We were at a place called Wissant which is so near it's practically England.'

It made me marvel that someone young and fit preferred to forgo so many pleasures rather than work. Bell had enough to live on but not enough for holidays. One word to Cosette and she would have been invited to join us, her fares and hotel bills paid as a matter of course, for it was taken for granted that any friend of mine partook of Cosette's largesse just as I did. That was the reason why I couldn't say the word. I couldn't even mention that Bell had scarcely been abroad or had no holiday plans this year. I even had to go further and, against the grain as it was, say to Cosette, 'Bell never wants to leave London. She's got to make up for those years she was with Silas out in the sticks.'

In Florence, at the Uffizi, hangs Bronzino's portrait of Lucrezia Panciatichi. This is the painting most critics have agreed inspired the one Henry James describes in *The Wings of the Dove* as hanging in 'the great gilded historic chamber' at Matcham and calls 'the pale personage on the wall'. It resembles, of course, the doomed Milly Theale in her 'eyes of other days, her full lips, her long neck . . .' With its 'face almost livid in hue, yet handsome in sadness and crowned with a mass of hair, rolled back and high', it also profoundly resembled Bell.

I wish I could remember whether I saw it there on my first visit to Florence when I went to Italy with Cosette. We must have gone into the Uffizi. I have certainly seen the portrait on subsequent visits but it is no use, try as I will, I can't remember whether I saw it that time. It was a print of that portrait which, walking along the Arno with Cosette, near the Trinità bridge, I saw in a shop window. Cosette was struck by the resemblance – remember that only Cosette saw the similarity between Bell's face and that on my cameo – and standing in front of the print, said that we should buy it.

I concealed my enthusiasm. Although I knew how sensitive to the wishes and secrets of others Cosette was, how she would readily have fallen in with any plan of mine concerning the fate of the picture, I somehow imagined it framed in stainless steel by the 'little man' in Kensington Park Road, hung on the drawing room wall and pointed out to all comers.

'A postcard then,' Cosette said. 'Do you know, I have a dress very much like that somewhere that I had made for the Chelsea Arts Ball. I was supposed to be Lady Jane Grey. I wonder if I could still get into it?'

But Cosette couldn't find a postcard of Lucrezia Panciatichi. Next morning, while she was still asleep, I went out on my own and bought the print of Bronzino's painting which I carried home secretly and for a long while kept in a hiding place.

9

I was standing in front of my small version of this portrait when Bell phoned.

For a long time the print lay in a drawer of that desk Cosette bought me. I had it framed as soon as I could afford things like that and hung it in my bedroom. If Cosette ever saw it she didn't remark on it. A little while before the murder I took it down and put it away once more, but I never considered ridding myself of it and it travelled with me, first to the flat I had on Primrose Hill when the House of Stairs was sold, then to Hampstead where it again hung on the wall, out to Cambridge for a year or two during my brief marriage, back to London and this Hammersmith house. Though telling myself I am not superstitious, I nevertheless came to associate displaying it on a wall with the coming of bad things.

All the bad things but one thing have happened to me, yet I have put the picture back in the drawer. But three days ago, in the study here, I took the framed Roiter poster down from the wall and hung up the Bronzino in its stead. It is many years since I have looked at it and I seemed to see among its reds and blacks and golds things I have never observed before, the fact for instance that Lucrezia, though well bejewelled, wears only a single ring and that with a very dark stone in it which may even be a bloodstone. Her hair, whatever Henry James may say, is not really red but a very pale copper colour. Of course, he speaks only of a Bronzino, of a pale red-headed lady in red, not of this specific portrait and he would have known very well how many people sat for Bronzino, that this Florentine Mannerist was as distinguished a portraitist as a painter of allegories. Looking at the picture, I was reminded of course not only of Bell herself but of other aspects of our life when Cosette had the House of Stairs, of Bell's interest in *The Wings of the Dove*, of her surprising request to hear the plot of it, of the conspiracy.

In a moment, I thought, I will make that phone call. I will call that number on the six-two-four exchange and put an end to the fearful impasse I have been in this past week, for it is nearly a week now, put an end to procrastination and doubt and persuading myself it is too early or too late to phone, that she is bound to be out, that it is too soon, that it is not soon enough, that tomorrow is the best, destined, most appropriate, day. Lucrezia was returning my regard with her calm, reposeful look – not 'handsome in sadness', surely, not 'livid' – was meeting my eyes with her own large, limpid eyes so that I now saw a resemblance there not only to Bell but also to the young Cosette of early photographs, when the phone rang.

It never crossed my mind it would be Bell. But although all she said, when I had given the number, was 'Hallo', I was in no doubt even for a second who it was. My silence was due to the stupefaction of shock, a shock I felt even though I was prepared, even though I had seen her and knew she had asked for me.

'It's Bell.'

'I know,' I said. 'Oh, I know.' I sat down, feeling a sudden great tiredness. It was a few seconds before I realized I had closed my eyes. 'I saw you,' I said. 'I followed you but you disappeared.'

Bell was never one for explanations if she didn't want to make them, never one to apologize. It was much later I learned that Felicity Thinnesse had rung her up and told her I wanted to be in touch with her.

'Will you come and see me?' she said.

Which is why I am here facing her now across a room which is very like the room in Walter Admetus's house where I was first alone with her. There is a bed with a dirty white cotton cover and a table and a wicker chair and a couple of suitcases as well as two tea-chests. It is a warm spring day and Bell has opened the window, but no fresh breeze from Regent's Park penetrates here, there are no plane trees outside and no Georgian terraces. This house is squeezed up against a railway bridge, crushed so close as to be absurd, all light surely excluded from its front bays, while the back rooms, of which this is one, overlook a scrapyard. Bell tells me that when she was first released from the open prison where she served the final year of her sentence, she was obliged to live in a hostel. Then her probation officer found this room for her. This woman has also found her a job. It is due to start next week and is in a shop where the owner has of necessity been told who and what she is.

'I don't know if I shall be equal to it,' she says, but whether this is because she has scarcely had a job before or because the job is in, of all places, Westbourne Grove, I don't know and she doesn't say. She is very changed in appearance, though still slender and straight with that high-held head on her long neck. Her hair is iron-grey and coarsened by its greying. A tracery of lines lies on her face as if a cobweb had been spread there, and I remember what James said about the portrait in relation to Milly Theale as 'a face . . . that must, before fading with time, have had a family resemblance to her own'.

She wears black, a skirt and a sort of tunic that seems to be no more than a length of material with a hole cut for her neck and the sides sewn up, sandals, no stockings. Her legs have become very thin. I haven't touched her yet, I haven't shaken her hand or kissed her. Shock prevails, and pity and wonder. Will I ever get used to her? Will I ever be able to say calmly to myself, this is Bell?

When I came to the door and she answered it and brought me up here, when the door was shut, she remembered. All these years she has remembered. And she said to me, 'Are you out of the wood yet?'

I was immensely grateful to her. It seemed the greatest kindness, more than any valuable gift.

'Coming to the edge,' I said.

She nodded. I haven't yet seen her smile. 'I often thought about it,' she said. 'I used to wonder.'

She sleeps a lot. She told me she couldn't sleep in prison and since she has been out – over two months had passed before she got up the nerve to phone Felicity – she has slept all night and half the days. 'That's why I mayn't be equal to this job.'

'I don't work at all and I never shall,' she had once said to me, 'I'm never going to work again.'

113

On the evening I saw her she had been to see the therapist in Shepherds Bush she goes to for her counselling. On the way back she got out of the tube to look at the shop where she is destined to work, vanishing into a tobacconist's in Queensway as I emerged. For while the rest of us gave up cigarettes in the seventies, Bell still smokes. Living on social security, she goes without food to buy cigarettes. Her clothes smell of them and her hair and this room, just as they must have done in Admetus's house, only we all smelt of smoke then, so none of us noticed it.

'Do you mind if I sleep for a while?' she asks me. 'You can stay if you like, or go. I know where you are now and you know where I am.'

But as she stretches out on the bed under the open window, as she curls up and lays one hand under the pillow, she reaches out with the other and takes mine. Like a sick person or a child she means me to hold her hand while she sleeps.

When we came back from Italy, Cosette and I, Bell had moved away from Admetus's house and disappeared. She had gone, leaving no forwarding address, no message for me. To this day I don't know where she went and I no longer care, it no longer matters. Perhaps she was with a man – or a woman – or the simple truth may have been that she could no longer afford the rent Admetus asked.

Somehow, though, I knew she would reappear and find me, that out of the blue or by some other kind of coincidence we would confront each other again. And yet, apart from Felicity, I knew no one who could be called a friend of Bell's, I had never then heard her speak of any friend, or, come to that, of mother, father, siblings, any relatives. She had been married, been widowed, had never worked, always spoke her mind with what seemed like transparent honesty, and that was all I knew of her. Whereas, so thoroughly already had I confided in her, that she knew all about me, my family and, yes, my horrible inheritance, my dead mother, my special regard for Cosette and hers for me, and even the affair, though I am afraid I called it a relationship in those days, I was having with Dominic.

I shouldn't have done it, I know that now. It was one thing to flirt with him, to dance with him, quite another, when we all reached home in the small hours after that dinner at the Marco Polo and that visit to Ivor's club, to go up to his room with him almost as a matter of course. I fancied him, you see. He was so beautiful. It not only didn't seem important then that he was Perpetua's brother, a country boy nearly illiterate, naïve, lacking in almost any kind of sophistication; I also didn't even think about it. I must have known he was a devout Catholic, too. Hadn't I seen him go off to mass every Sunday, every Day of Obligation? I didn't think of that either. I made him my lover because he was slim and tall and straight, because he had the bluest eyes I ever saw and the silkiest raven's-wing hair (the kind that turns grey before any other kind) and a face like one of El Greco's young clerics. Also, and this is more excusable, because of the terror and the bore, because of the thing that hung over me, so that I believed I must take everything I wanted, do everything, live, before an end was put to living for ever.

We were drunk that first time. We didn't talk. But in the morning we made love again and afterwards he said, 'How can someone like you love me?'

I felt a little chill, for I didn't love him, but I didn't understand then either. I didn't understand his simplicity, that from his innocence and his strict life, he believed not only that a woman would sleep with a man solely if she loved him, but also that this man would be the one she had chosen for ever, to be her life partner, almost as though human beings were as monogamous as certain birds who, imprinted in early youth with the image of a mate, remain exclusively bonded to this one for always. Instead, I asked him what he meant. Humble, shy, without self-confidence, his attitude of mind entirely at odds with his splendid, even arrogant, looks, he said that I was clever, educated (had 'been to college' was what he said), was of a 'different class'.

'I'm just an ordinary working fellow,' he said in that voice that was like the *Playboy of the Western World*, that was like Christy Mahon's.

'What,' said I with incredible insensitivity, 'does any of that matter?'

Later on I made him read that bit out of Synge about the holy

115

bishops straining the bars of paradise to catch a glimpse of Helen of Troy, and her walking abroad with a nosegay in her golden shawl. Only he couldn't read it very well, he stumbled over the words, and I had to help him. Oh, I have been too fond of literature one way and another, and produced too little of it myself!

So when I came back to the House of Stairs there was Dominic waiting for me like a husband, calling me 'dear' and telling me he had changed the sheets on the bed for my homecoming. And my heart sank as had begun to happen whenever he came home to me or I to him, for I had wanted a sensuous tumultuous adventure lasting a few weeks and he, it grew ever more obvious, wanted an exclusive lifetime's partnership. Cosette, romantic and with that Wife of Bath side to her, who had rather encouraged our affair in the beginning as she would have encouraged almost any affair, especially one between the young and good-looking, now saw it all.

'The next thing will be he'll want you to marry him,' she said. 'In Brompton Oratory, I expect, or even the Cathedral.'

'I thought it was women who clung and men who wanted to be off,' I almost wailed. 'How can someone look like Don Giovanni and have the soul of a milkman?'

'You can't judge a sausage by its overcoat,' said Cosette.

She had shifted her enthusiasm from my sex life to my career, or at any rate to my immediate project. The idea that I should write a book in her house was delicious to Cosette. What kind of book hardly mattered. Almost without critical judgement, she came close to worshipping anything made by someone she was fond of. Thus, Diana's typing was the fastest and most accurate in London, Gary was the world's greatest virtuoso of the sitar, and the section of the Underground tunnel dug out by Dominic was the best bit. To her the only flaw in my writing project was my insisting on having a job as well, though working in an after-school-hours play-centre wasn't much of a job, and if I am honest about it I shall have to admit it brought me in enough to live on only because I lived rent-free.

The writing room was created in secret during the two or three hours I spent at work in the early evening. It was almost the only room in the house vacant at that time, Gary and Mervyn having one each, Dominic his and I mine – I had never consented to move in permanently with him – Cosette with her grand chamber and Birgitte the new Girl-in-Residence, a real au pair girl this time, in Fay's old room. The top floor of attics, where the high, balconyless window was, remained unfurnished, a depository for cardboard crates and tea-chests. The room Cosette and Perpetua prepared for me was directly below this one, its window having one of those narrow balconies without a railing which overlooked the grey garden.

A quiet woman with an intense devotion to Cosette, Perpetua would have probably done anything she asked, did in fact put herself out tremendously for her, travelling all that distance daily by bus and cleaning up after a troop of careless, untidy people. Otherwise I doubt if she would have consented to carry furniture upstairs for my benefit, lay carpet and hang curtains for me. She saw what everyone but poor Dominic now saw, that I had been using him and was not in the least in love. And twenty years his senior, a sister grown up before he was born, she resented it as a mother might. Her resentment took the curious form of her ceasing to use my Christian name when she spoke to me. How I was to recall this later when the woman who failed to use my name meant so much, so infinitely much, more to me!

Instead of, 'Coffee's ready, Elizabeth,' she would say, 'There's coffee if you want it,' or, calling upstairs, 'Are you there?' and waiting until the appropriate voice answered.

The desk was delivered and the typewriter unearthed and dictionaries placed in a new bookcase. I stood and admired, was effusive in my gratitude. Cosette, a good as well as a generous giver, took a simple, innocent pleasure in being thanked and enjoyed an enthusiastic reception of her gifts. It was then that I said how much I should like a dictionary of classical Greek (which I intended to teach myself and later did) and then that Cosette promised me one for Christmas, failing, producing instead a modern Greek dictionary, and earning from me those unkind reproaches I am for ever ashamed of having made.

So that winter, the winter that was the bridge from the sixties into the seventies, I sat down to write my novel, beginning on a glorious day at the end of October when it was as hot as midsummer. With the example of Henry James before me, knowing James as thoroughly as I did, I might have at least tried to write something that was an examination of the human heart, but I didn't. I wanted money, I was after the fast buck, the quick return, because I was an inheritor of Huntington's chorea and I had to live now while I could, I had to have it all now. So I embarked on a cheap, sexy, romantic adventure story about people of the kind I had never met and set in places I had never been to but could mug up well enough for my purposes from travel books and other people's novels. That is the sort of book I have been writing ever since.

Cosette treated my endeavours with reverence. In her eyes I had become almost overnight an 'artist' and she had the attitude the French have towards those who create, almost irrespective of what they create. My work must be looked on by others as the most important activity going on in the house, they must creep up the stairs, forbear to play their records and musical instruments, lower their voices, and never, never interrupt me by coming to my door. Naturally, after a while, this discipline slackened and the old hub-bub returned, but Cosette herself never changed, continuing to treat me in this area of my life in a way appropriate to a Balzac, say, or at any rate Graham Greene.

One afternoon, when I had been writing for most of the day and was nearly due to go off to my play-centre job, I had a phone call from Felicity Thinnesse. She sounded excited and distrait.

'I got your number from Elsa. The woman whose house you're living in, she takes paying guests, doesn't she?'

I was unreasonably incensed. Poor Felicity of course had asked me in good faith, probably like most people being unable to imagine anyone giving board and lodging to a host of freeloaders like Gary and Mervyn and Fay and Birgitte.

'Why do you ask?'

'I've left Esmond. Well, I will have left him when I've found somewhere to go. I have to find a room.'

I don't know why I thought of the children. I remembered Miranda repeating her mother's strictures on right behaviour. 'For three of you?' I said doubtfully.

'I can't cope with Jeremy and Miranda. They'll stay with

118

Esmond. Then,' Felicity added very oddly, 'he won't have so much to make a fuss about.'

I told her I would ask Cosette, promising to call her back 'before Esmond gets home or after he's gone out to the Conservative Association'.

I found Cosette in the drawing room accompanied only by Auntie and Maurice Bailey from Wellgarth Avenue. Now he was a widower he used to spend a lot of time pottering about in Harrods and the big Kensington High Street stores, and at teatime he would take a taxi through the park and look in on Cosette for half an hour. The purpose of these visits seemed to make comments on the wretchedness of Cosette's lifestyle by contrast to what she might have had. Therefore the question I had to ask Cosette only served to inflame him further. I made it in his presence because I knew, or thought I knew then, that Cosette rather enjoyed what Felicity would have called 'winding him up'.

'Another sponger,' he said. 'This place must be notorious as the local doss-house.'

Auntie, enjoying it, looked timidly from one to the other of them. Cosette appeared rather splendid in a totally unsuitable blue brocade caftan. Since the departure of Ivor Sitwell she had been wearing less make-up and had regained some of her lost weight, so that she looked younger and quite well and flourishing. Her hair was by then a very pale golden blonde. I told her, quoting Wilde, that at the loss of Ivor it had turned quite gold from grief, and she liked this so much that she repeated it to everyone. Now, mildly to rile Maurice Bailey, she began to enthuse over the coming of Felicity.

'Of course you must tell her she can come here, darling. How awful to be obliged to stay with a man because you've nowhere to go; can you imagine?'

'I'll call her back then, shall I?'

'Yes, do that, and tell her she'll be most welcome. I don't know where we'll put her, one of the rooms at the top, I suppose. Perpetua will organize that, you know how marvellous she is. Don't look at me like that, Maurice.' She put one of her beautiful hands out to him, lightly touching his jacket sleeve. Unused all her life, Cosette's hands were still girlish, plump and white, taper-fingered, with nails like blanched almonds, heavily be-ringed. 'Maurice,' she cajoled. 'Haven't you a smile for me? Felicity will pay me rent, you know, or at least she'll make it up in kind. There'll be all sorts of little jobs for her to do.'

As there were for Mervyn and Gary, who had long since ceased to carry out their functions of floor-polishing and car-cleaning; as there were for Birgitte, the Danish au pair who, perfectly willing to work for her living when first she arrived, had rapidly been persuaded by her employer that there was nothing for her to do, told it was a shame for someone so young and pretty not to have a good time while she could and why not enjoy herself in Carnaby Street and down the King's Road?

So Felicity came a few days later. Subdued and chastened at first, fearful that Esmond would find out where she was and come after her, she took to Cosette immediately and poured out her heart to her. A tête-à-tête was virtually impossible, there were always too many people around for that, people used to follow Cosette into her bedroom at some ungodly hour of the morning, at three or four, and continue their conversations or their musical renderings sitting on her bed. But Felicity, undeterred, would commandeer Cosette, corner her and talk, sometimes sprawling at her feet with her head in Cosette's lap, sometimes opposite her at the table, leaning forward, gazing into her eyes, and snatches of what she said would reach the rest of us, or those who cared to listen, isolated words and phrases: 'my bloody husband', 'his old bitch of a mother', 'prison', 'buried alive', 'living death', 'frustration', 'pain', 'misery'.

At that period there were living in the House of Stairs: Cosette, myself, Dominic, Mervyn, Gary, Birgitte, Mervyn's girlfriend Mimi, Auntie and now Felicity. Nine people. At Christmas Diana Castle and the man she lived with came up to stay for the holiday and stayed on for several weeks. That made eleven. Those two were obliged to bed down in sleeping-bags on the floor of the top front room. Cosette, of course, was prepared to buy a bed to accommodate her visitors, except that no one, not least the shop delivery people, could be found willing to carry it up a hundred stairs. Even Perpetua rebelled, saying darkly that any more lifting would give her a prolapse.

She and Dominic had transported a convertible sofa-bed upstairs for Felicity, for which service they each got extravagant praise and a fiver from Cosette. The room was the one above what Cosette called my 'sanctum' and Felicity, when she arrived, was very politely requested to be 'as quiet as a mouse' during the sacred hours of ten till three, while I was working. It had once been for a maid or maids and was a shabby chamber with sloping ceiling, very different from the rooms on the lower floors. By the look of the walls and woodwork, no one had painted it since the house was built. Cosette was all for getting Gary to paint it before Felicity moved in and gave him some sort of extravagant payment in advance, but in fact it was a long time before he got around to the painting and by then Felicity had gone back to Esmond and her children.

A few days in the House of Stairs and of confiding in Cosette set her up splendidly and she was soon her old self, teasing, fascinated by everything, censorious, dispensing useless, inconsequential information, contemptuous of the slower-witted. I was invited up to her room to look at the view and pronounce on whether the dome she could see was Whiteley's or the Greek Orthodox Church. That window was alarming when you stood close up to it and looked out. Even worse when you looked down through the sheer drop of forty feet or so to the garden, its grey-leaved plants sodden with rain or nipped by frost. Directly below the window was an area paved with York stone that Cosette called the terrace and Perpetua the patio. Somehow the window would have been less frightening if there had been lawn beneath it or a flowerbed.

Felicity said she had been out of the window on to the narrow ledge. You have to understand that this was a window, not a glass door or pair of doors, but coming very low down, to no more than six inches or so from the floor, a sash window which could be opened to create an aperture four feet deep either at the top or the bottom. Outside, Felicity said, on the stone or ashlar or whatever it was surrounding the window frame, there were deep holes, each with a trickle mark of iron stain under it, to which, she was sure, the bars of some kind of cage or grille had once been attached. It was long gone by Cosette's time. We speculated as to why the foot of the window should be so close to the floor and Felicity suggested, rightly no doubt, that at some time the floor had been raised. For sound-proofing? To make a greater space between the floor of this room and the ceiling of the room below? Because the maids, rising early, might have disturbed a sleeper in the 'sanctum'?

'No one ever opened their windows in those days,' Felicity said very sweepingly, and lingering with relish over the word, 'so there wouldn't have been any risk of defenestration.'

I don't believe I had come across the word before. 'Haven't you ever heard of the Defenestration of Prague?' said Felicity. 'I expect that was when it was first used. "Defenestratio" would be the Latin, you know. It was in the Thirty Years War. Some Protestants threw two Catholic bishops out of a window in Prague, but they weren't really hurt, they fell into the moat.'

'You mugged that up for one of your quizzes,' I said.

'I'll tell you what, Elizabeth, I never did another quiz after the one we couldn't finish because that woman Bell Sanger came in telling us Silas was shot. It put me right off.'

'I never heard what happened at the inquest,' I said.

'Suicide while the balance of his mind was disturbed. It was more the balance of the gun, if you ask me. He'd been playing Russian roulette.'

'I don't exactly know what you do in Russian roulette,' I said.

'It's something White Russian officers used to play to alleviate boredom,' she said, true to form. 'You've got six chambers in the revolver, you see, and you put a bullet in just one, so in theory you've got one chance in six of killing yourself, which makes the odds pretty high. But if the chamber's perfectly balanced the weight of the bullet will generally carry it to the bottom, so the chances of surviving are a lot greater than you'd expect. That's why they say Russian roulette cheats death.'

'Only Silas's gun wasn't perfectly balanced,' I said.

'That's what they said at the inquest, but I don't know, I thought it was jolly fishy. Silas was mad about guns, he was always messing about with guns, he really knew about them.'

'Maybe he wanted to die.'

'Maybe he did, poor Silas. If he'd lived another day he'd have known he'd inherited his father's house and have had something to live on.'

I didn't tell her I already knew that. She opened the window, raising the sash from the bottom, and we looked down the long drop, I crouching on the floor for safety's sake, Felicity, who had no fear at all of heights, standing there in her miniskirt, her long long legs in red tights, glancing idly down as anyone else might at an object dropped on the pavement. The cold drove us back and we shut the window once more on the flurry of sleet the wind carried.

10

Once I would have held Bell's hand until she woke, I would have held it the night through. Even though my fingers were numb I would have held it. But not now. Once I would have been fearful she would never phone, no matter what promises she made, but now I knew she would. It changes, as Cosette said. She slept, relieved I think that she had found me and that I was willing to speak to her, visit her, know her. I extricated my hand, touched her cheek lightly with my finger, and went home.

In the spring I went with Dominic to one of the performances given by a company that called itself Global Experience. I had an idea that poor Dominic would find the whole thing incomprehensible and even frightening and that was why I wanted him with me. Unforgivable this was, shamefully unkind. For what Global Experience put on was the ultimate in audience participation. Dressed in cheesecloth robes which were conspicuous for being without buttons or zips, the company danced and mimed, took partners from out of the onlookers and each pair then stood or sat gravely face-to-face, experiencing each other by touch, stroking arms and shoulders and hair, but being quite prudishly careful to avoid erogenous zones. Objects were also examined by each couple together, with a view supposedly to seeing them in a new light, and I remember I and my partner (not of course Dominic) going into raptures over the texture, colour and scent of a very ordinary and rather battered Jaffa orange.

It was months since I had seen Bell, but she was in the audience at Global Experience that night. For some reason, perhaps because stroking a stranger and exploring an orange demand great concentration, I didn't see her until afterwards, when Dominic and I were in the theatre's cafeteria, called Food of Love, drinking apple juice and eating sticks of raw carrot and celery. We were just about to leave, poor Dominic by then bewildered to the point of being seriously upset, when I saw Bell sitting at a table in the far corner with two other girls and two men.

One of these men was very much like her to look at, darker but with the same sort of features, the same straight carriage and graceful way of moving. Before I reached the table and said hallo to her he had got up and gone to the bar or food counter.

'Is that your brother?' I said.

She turned to look at him, hesitated, nodded. 'Yes. Yes, it is. Good-looking, isn't he?'

'He's like you.'

'You could say that. D'you fancy him then? Shall I see what I can do?'

'I'm with someone,' I said, 'and I do have to go.' And then I said, 'I wish you'd come round, I'd love to see you.'

That was my first sight of Mark. Perhaps it was true that I fancied him, that I admired him desirously at that first encounter, briefly, for a matter of seconds. Any woman would have. And Dominic took it upon himself to be jealous, accusing me of only going to Global Experience for the opportunities he said it gave for wanton behaviour. His words, not mine. He was an Irishman, after all, and though often silent, never inarticulate. I forgot Mark within minutes, hardly supposing I would ever see him again, naturally having no prevision of the part he was to play in all our lives. It was Bell alone I held in my mind, hoping she would come.

A week or so later she did. There was a crowd of us in the drawing room with Cosette: Diana Castle and her boyfriend, who were back again, Mervyn and Mimi, Dominic, Birgitte and Felicity. Mervyn and Mimi were one of those couples who can't keep their hands off each other for five minutes. You seemed to come upon them all over the house – it was almost as if they could be in two or even three places at once – standing on a bend in the stairs kissing, lying mouth to mouth and hip to hip on a sofa or someone else's bed, just inside an open door, with hands on each other's shoulders, gazing into eyes. Cosette, true to form, had seemed to like it at first, but by then most of us, for various reasons, resented Mervyn and Mimi. They served to show us what we all lacked. I would have liked someone to love me, but not Dominic. Dominic wanted me and no one else. Diana and her boyfriend were on bad terms, they quarrelled all the time. And Cosette, poor Cosette, was no nearer finding the lover she longed for than she had ever been. As for Felicity, she was dying for a love affair but afraid to have one, 'woefully out of practice', was how she put it to me, scared all the time Esmond would come and haul her off before she had had a chance to make up for all those years of repression. That evening she was talking to us about Selevin's mouse. This had been quite funny at first and Cosette, particularly, had been enchanted.

'It's a Russian rodent that lives in the desert, and can you imagine, it was only discovered in 1939. I mean, think of them, millions of them probably, little fat animals with grey fur, all living in the deserts in Russia, and no one knowing they were there. They only come out at night, you see. The really amazing thing about Selevin's mouse is that it can't stand more than a few min-utes' exposure to the sun without becoming ill.'

'I don't believe it, Felicity,' Cosette said. 'You're making it up.'

'I swear before God,' said Felicity with unnecessary melodrama, 'I can prove everything I've said. Look it up in the *Encyclopaedia Britannica*. That's all you have to do, look it up.'

'We haven't got *Britannica*.'

'You can go to the library in the morning and look it up.'

'I do believe you really, darling, only it seems so odd. I think it's lovely really. I think it's enchanting. The poor little loves being ill when the sun shines.'

This had been a day or two before. Felicity, however, went on and on about it, she couldn't leave it alone. When Auntie had admitted the day before to not feeling very well, Felicity said that, like Selevin's mouse, she must have been out in the sun. Someone, Gary I think, happened to mention he was an only child, where-upon Felicity said he was like Selevin's mouse, the only member of the family *Seleviniidae*. To her it was all uproariously funny. Dominic sat there eyeing her uneasily, having an unfounded notion that all this was being done to mock him.

That was the evening Cosette was wearing the bloodstone. I had seen it on her finger only once before. This time she must have put it on to match her rather grand and dramatic new dress, a long-skirted robe of dark green shot silk which showed a red or green gleam according to the way the light caught it. The ring still seemed too heavy for her hand, but it no longer looked out of place. In candlelight – and Felicity was going about lighting candles – the red in it glittered like sparks against the deep green of the chalcedony.

'Haematite,' Felicity said, picking up Cosette's hand to look at it.

Cosette said gently, 'No, heliotrope, I believe, Felicity. I think that's the term in – what do you call it? Petrology?'

Felicity wouldn't have that. 'Oh, no, absolutely not. It's from the Greek for blood as in haemorrhage, haemophilia and so on. "Haema", meaning blood and "tite", stone.'

'Yes, but not this stone, darling, that's quite another kind, a sort of red rock.' Cosette was right, as it happens, I looked it up next day, but she didn't insist, she wasn't the kind to insist, having a horror of seeming superior to anyone. She was quite capable of apologizing for being right, just as she was of spending much of her time (as Henry James has it) making excuses for obnoxious acts she had not committed. Afflicted by no such scruples, Felicity was going on in her didactic way about Greek and the ignorance of people now they seldom learned it any more, going on much as she did about the lifestyle of the Russian dormouse, when the doorbell rang.

'That will be Walter,' Cosette said.

It was the sort of time we often saw Admetus, around nine-thirty in the evening. I went to the window. It was the end of April and not really dark. If I appeared on the balcony the courtly Admetus could be relied on to strike an attitude, to step back, place his hand on his heart and declare that this window was the east and Juliet the sun. For some reason I liked the idea of that. It came to me in that moment that if Admetus and I were to get something going, it would free me from Dominic. I opened the french windows, stepped out on to the balcony and, looking down over the Ca' Lanier railing, saw Bell looking up. The lamplight shone on her pale hair. She was in black, but with that mud-and-granite-coloured shawl wrapped tightly round her, the shawl I had

127

last seen draped by Esmond over Silas Sanger's dead body. I swear it was the same, I recognized it at once.

Bell came upstairs with me and, seeing Felicity as soon as the drawing room door was opened, receiving her rather surprised, 'Hallo, there!', seemed thunderstruck.

'What are you doing here?'

'Thanks very much,' said Felicity. 'I suppose I can be here as much as you can.'

'Is Esmond here too?'

Nobody answered her. Mervyn and Mimi were lying locked in each other's arms on the carpet in a corner. Dominic had picked up some musical instrument of Gary's and sat disconsolately plucking the same note over and over on a string. With a glance at the couple on the floor, Bell lifted her thin straight shoulders, loosened the shawl, looping it over her arms. Rather to my surprise, she went up to Cosette, shook hands with her and asked her how she was. But no more time was to be wasted. She had come to see me and, being Bell, made no bones about it.

'Can we go up to your room?'

For some reason I took it that she meant the room I wrote in rather than my bedroom. On the stairs – there were 106, remember, to the top, ninety-five to my writing room – she said, 'They're all on the make, aren't they? Getting what they can out of her? Does she know?'

'I don't think she minds,' I said.

'I should mind those two wanking around on the floor. I'd throw them out.'

'Cosette would never do that.'

Bell never read a book. I don't think she had read a book since she left school, whenever and wherever that had been, but if there were books lying about she would pick them up and scrutinize them in a wondering, curious sort of way, as someone else might examine an ornament. We lit cigarettes and she walked about the room looking at everything, astonished that I was writing a novel, glancing at *The Princess Casamassima*, which I was currently reading, picking up a couple of works of reference that lay on my desk, surveying the dictionaries Cosette had provided, at last turning

128

her back on literature and its mysteries, back to me and to reality, which was what she understood.

'I suppose Felicity has left Esmond. When they had rows she always said she would leave him before she was thirty-five. He'll come for her though, you'll see, and she'll go back to him.'

I couldn't go along with that. Felicity was adamant that she would never go back. Even if she never saw her children again she wouldn't go back. She had even found herself a waitress's job at a café in Shepherds Bush. I had yet to learn that when it came to human behaviour Bell was almost always right. She knew people and how they were likely to react. Not being addicted to literature, scarcely knowing that literature existed, she had not had her perception suppressed under its narcosis or her assessments of human nature distorted by its false reality.

'She's going to divorce him,' I said.

'Esmond will never let himself be divorced.'

'Under this new law,' I said, 'he won't have much choice. She can do it without his consent after five years.'

Bell didn't answer directly. She had lit another cigarette from the stub of the first, was sitting on the floor with her back against the wall. Comfort never meant much to her. 'Who knows where we'll all be in five years?' she said.

It was pouring with rain when the time came for her to go. I suggested she stay the night, though in the present state of overcrowding that would have meant another sleeping-bag. But she wouldn't stay, though it was nearly midnight. Nor would she tell me where she was living. That is to put it rather too strongly, for of course she didn't actually refuse to tell me, just as I didn't ask her outright. I asked her for her phone number and she said she didn't have a phone. But she had walked, she told me when she first came, to Archangel Place. Now Bell was a great walker, unlike me, and it would have been nothing out of the way for her to undertake three or four miles, which gave a pretty wide radius for her to be living within.

'You aren't going to walk back?' And I added, 'To wherever it is?'

'Sort of that way.' She waved in a vague north-easterly direction. 'I could get a cab, only in my budget I don't allow for cabs.'

We would phone for a cab, I said. Cosette was always phoning for cabs.

'Then she'll pay for it. I don't want that.'

I was struck by this, a very rare attitude for anyone in Cosette's orbit to take. There was a purity about Bell, I thought, a rectitude. She gave me one of her cool smiles. All she wanted, she said, was for me to lend her a mac or a raincoat or even just an umbrella. And that was how we came to go into my bedroom.

Descending, we encountered on the third-floor landing, standing within an alcove like a pair of statues in the half-dark, Venus and Adonis perhaps, Mervyn and Mimi locked together. I opened the door of my bedroom, having forgotten for the moment what hung on the wall facing us. The light came on and Bell, entering, looked straight at the Bronzino. She approached it slowly, stood silent in front of it while I grubbed around in the cupboard for something to cover her. Then, 'That's me,' she said.

I prevaricated. 'It was painted about 400 years before you were born.'

'It's still me. Where did you get it? Did you put it there because it looks like me?'

'Yes,' I said.

I held out my thin, silky black raincoat for her to put her arms into. She drew it round her, shawl and all, her back still to me. I had never closed the door, it still stood ajar. From downstairs came the weird plucked notes of the sitar. Bell took my face in her hands and kissed my mouth. It was a mouth-to-mouth kiss, but it might just have been received and interpreted as a woman saluting another woman in friendship and affection, except that it lingered rather long and I thought – I was not quite certain but I did think so – I felt the tip of her tongue touch the rim of my upper lip. The sound of a door opening downstairs and the volume of the sitar music increasing parted us. In a little while, after she was gone, I would begin to tremble but not then, not then. I said, very lightly, 'There's an umbrella down in the hall. You mustn't get wet.'

But she changed her mind about the taxi, one happening to come cruising along Archangel Place as we splashed out into the wet windy dark. I hadn't a key and I let the door close behind me so that Cosette had to come down and let me in.

'Darling, you're cold,' she said. 'You're shivering.'

Until they came and took her away I never lost Bell again after that. Let me correct that and say she never went off again and disappeared.

A lot of things happened that summer. My book was accepted by a publisher. Felicity found a lover. Cosette gave the first of her big parties. Birgitte left and went home to Odense. Mervyn and Mimi departed to set up house together in a caravan.

Cosette said she never had any doubt I would find a publisher. She had read the typescript and went about telling everyone, to my mild embarrassment, what a wonderful book it was. A sort of cross between *Gone With the Wind* and *Murder on the Orient Express*, she said, without irony and intending high praise. She wasn't, in fact, far wrong. Now, I thought, having received a much bigger advance than I expected, I should be able to get down to my critical work on Henry James. That was before I had really looked at my contract and seen my publishers had an option on my next work of fiction, which they had been led to expect within twelve months. I hadn't known until then that in life there are traps in which one gets caught where one is obliged to pedal round and round in a squirrel cage.

Birgitte had been caught shoplifting in the food hall at Harrods. It can't have been because she didn't get enough to eat at home, but perhaps for some neurotic or compulsive reason. If meals were irregular in the House of Stairs and mostly you had to get what you wanted for yourself, the fridge and the larder were overflowing with food, splendid food of the luxury kind, out-of-season vegetables, salmon and pheasant and caviar and paté and profiteroles and cream and strawberries. Cosette was in the habit of taking Auntie out for drives, and while they were out they always went shopping. Birgitte had gone into the food hall carrying two empty Harrods carriers. With incredible naivety she must have believed they would therefore think she had paid for what she had in them. She had helped herself to tins of biscuits and boxes of chocolates and a jar of some sort of candied fruit before she was caught. It made me wonder if she had got the idea from Gary's habit of filling bags with leftover food in the restaurants Cosette took us to dine in. He too was gone by July, off like so many others at that time on the golden road to India. And Mervyn had departed for his caravan, no longer able to endure, he told us, any company but that of Mimi and hers too in isolation. We were missing two bottles of brandy and six of claret after he left, but I said nothing about it to Cosette, though I think she knew.

Felicity's lover was called Harvey something. He was one of those tallish, thinnish, thirty-ish men with dark shaggy hair and moustache and beard, in much-worn crew-neck sweater and patched jeans, who thronged the streets of west London then and still throng them today. He hardly spoke and was shy, being more Auntie's type, one would have thought, than Felicity's. I never heard how she met him or witnessed his introduction to the house. He just appeared in her company. One day she was alone and the next Harvey was with her, sitting beside her holding hands. To be fair to her, she had probably asked Cosette if he could stay, could move in with her that is. It just happens that I didn't hear her ask.

You could see she was very proud to have secured a man of her own. She was like Cosette had been when she first landed Ivor Sitwell. I remarked on this to Bell as we sat side by side on one of the flights of stairs at Cosette's party. Bell was very dressed-up, wearing a feather boa and artificial pink roses with a dress of black crêpe de Chine and lace, bought for seven and sixpence at a jumble sale at St Mary The Boltons. It was then that she told me about Ivor not being a real Sitwell, though she seemed to have no actual idea what a real Sitwell was.

'Brothers and a sister who were writers, Eva said.' For it was Eva Faulkner, Admetus's standoffish ex-girlfriend, who had spilt the beans. 'She's well rid of him,' she said of Cosette. 'Do you think she'd like someone else?'

'She'd like someone she could love and who would love her. Wouldn't we all?'

Bell gave me a strange, sidelong look. She didn't reply. Perhaps she thought I didn't expect a reply, or more likely because she herself did not come into the category I spoke of. There had been no repetition of that kiss. We were cool, friendly, chain-smoking, with a bottle of wine between us on the stairs, half a French stick and a piece of Brie. We sat there commenting on the guests who came up and down, who sat five stairs below us, who congregated on the landing beneath.

Dawn Castle and her husband had come, out of place but determined to enjoy themselves. Even Maurice Bailey had come. He spent the evening in the dining room talking to Auntie. Walter Admetus was there with a new woman – so much for my ideas of seducing him – and Fay, long forgiven by Cosette, there with a new man. A pair of ballet dancers, Cosette's latest acquisition, had arrived early. They were husband and wife. Perdita Reed was as beautiful as Bell but in a different way, tiny, white-skinned, with classic ballerina looks, the raven hair drawn back and centre-parted. She had been approaching international fame when she fell in love with a dancer from Madrid. Apparently she wanted him to appear in everything she was in, it might be thought to the detriment of her career. I overheard Fay's new man say something slighting about Cosette, and if Luis Llanos gave no reply beyond a smile, he didn't spring to her defence either. Though inhabiting a borrowed flat in Hampstead, though grandly and gorgeously dressed, they were poor and needy.

A lot of people at that party, as Bell pointed out, were there for the purpose of freeloading. 'Everyone comes here,' she said, 'on the gravy train to Cadgeville.'

It reminded me of *The Great Gatsby*, the bit about all the world and its mistress going to Gatsby's house and where the young ladies are saying nasty things about him while picking his roses and drinking his champagne. Of course it didn't remind Bell of any such thing, she never having heard of Fitzgerald, or almost any other novelist, come to that. Sometimes I think it would have been better for everyone if I never had, if it had been history or political economy I had read at university.

Caterers had done the food but everyone was left to help themselves. They were left to help themselves to drink too because this was Cosette's way, she who seldom drank more than half a glass of wine, but it was a mistake. A lot of them were well away by ten-thirty. It was at about that time too that the sweet reek of marijuana crept up the stairs from somewhere down below. Auntie followed it up, carrying with her all the things old ladies take to bed with them, a book and glasses and a handbag and a knitting bag. To my surprise Bell jumped up and gave her an arm. Auntie had been rather dragging at the banister, her face grey with a kind of tired bewilderment, and Cosette, watching her from the landing below, seemed about to follow and help her. I had never seen Bell do anything like that before, I had never seen her take a scrap of notice of Auntie before. She seemed to know which room was hers though, for she opened the door and escorted Auntie in, saying, 'Good-night, Mrs Miller,' and telling her to sleep well.

We went downstairs in pursuit of what Bell succinctly called 'dope'. The landing on the drawing-room floor was more spacious than the others and there stood on it at one side a scroll-ended sofa and at the other a kind of day-bed with no back but vertical sides. I once possessed a postcard photograph of Proust seated on just such a day-bed which so enraptured Cosette that, at enormous expense, she got an antique dealer in Kensington Church Street to find this one for her. Seated on it now were Felicity and Harvey who, perhaps following Mervyn and Mimi's example, were kissing and nuzzling and fondling each other. Admetus was sitting on the sofa opposite, drinking brandy, his girlfriend stretched out with her head in his lap.

People sat on stairs all the way down, most of them drunk and a lot of them engaged in what I once heard Ivor pompously define as 'the preliminaries to sexual congress'. Maurice Bailey had had enough of it and was going home. Having donned his summer hat of white straw, he was shaking hands with Cosette just inside the front door and telling her in a very repressive way not to over-tire herself.

For a little while Bell and I joined the circle of smokers in the dining room, passing round the joint speared on a hatpin with a marcasite rose on it, which must have belonged to Cosette, if not to Auntie. The doors to the garden were open. It was a warm soft night and a big orange moon was slowly rising behind the roofs and spires of Notting Dale. But the light it shed was mysteriously pale. As it rose, revealing itself like a large, glowing, not quite spherical, fruit, a light breeze came with it, ruffling all the grey foliage and making the leaves of the eucalypt shake with a soft rattle. A group stood watching it and commenting on this moonrise with extravagant admiration. There were a lot of people around at that time who raved about nature, about almost any natural phenomenon, about a common flowering weed even, and they were always those who were entirely ignorant of natural history. Over in the corner, on the stone seat, behind which the macleaya grew tall with its bluish vine-like leaves and feathery orange blossom, Gary and Fay were supervising a friend of theirs who had embarked on an acid trip. They had given him the LSD in a spoonful of jam, and now that it was too late, though nothing had so far happened, he had remembered a good reason for not experimenting with hallucinogens.

'I'm a phobiac,' I heard him say nervously. 'I have arachnophobia. Suppose I start seeing spiders. I might see spiders on me. I'll go mad if I get spiders on me.'

Dominic, somehow isolated in this crowd, stood watching them with the unhappy near-disbelief of a crypto-Christian at a Roman orgy. When he saw me his expression changed from incredulous dismay to reproach. I knew he would soon be leaving, that his sister had found a room for him in Kilburn in the next street to where she lived, and, coward that I was, I hoped to avoid a showdown, an explanation, telling myself it was an ugly rather than a dignified parting that I feared. So I looked quickly away, I turned away, and taking Bell by the arm, was leading her back into the house when two things happened simultaneously. The clock on the tower of St Michael the Archangel at the end of the street struck midnight and the doorbell rang.

It didn't just ring, it rang insistently, as if whoever it was had put finger to bell and kept it there, pressing hard. I thought it was more guests arriving, or rather gatecrashers, for as many of the people there were uninvited as invited. How could you tell, when Cosette had said to Gary and Fay and Dominic, to Felicity and Harvey and even the ballet dancers, to ask anyone they liked?

'Most likely the neighbours complaining,' said Bell.

But it wasn't the neighbours or gatecrashers. It was Esmond Thinnesse.

Neither Bell nor I let him in, but we were the first people he saw that he knew, indeed, apart from his wife, the only people there that he knew, for by then Elsa the Lioness had married and gone to live in France. He had been thin before, but now he was much thinner. He had an ascetic, even priestly, look. In fact, that was essentially the way he did look, like some monk long subjected to a severe discipline or fast. I remembered he was supposed to be particularly religious, and now his face had the rapt, trance-like look of a holy martyr in a Renaissance painting. Or so it appeared in the mixed moonlight and candlelight which was the hallway's only illumination.

He said to me, 'I've come for my wife. Where is she?'

Someone behind me gave a nervous giggle. I was momentarily stunned. It was the oddness of it that astounded me, that a man as conventional and in many ways old-fashioned as Esmond should for any purpose whatever come like this to a stranger's house without warning in the middle of the night. He seemed to sense what was passing through my mind, for he said, 'I have been in London all day on business. I have the motor with me. Finding myself at Marble Arch, I had an impulse to come here. It seemed the best way.' He spoke rather remotely, like one who has suffered such terrible unhappiness that it has drained him of all emotion. Or perhaps like someone who has done as his faith adjured him to do and cast his burdens upon God. 'We can't,' he added in the same tone, 'go on like this.'

I was beginning to say, 'She's upstairs somewhere . . .' but Bell was quicker and, recalling no doubt what Felicity had been doing upstairs, was half-way up the first flight before I had finished my sentence. Esmond followed her and I him, a crocodile of people following me, all of them somehow sensing melodrama, growing bored with the party, wanting a new stage for it, a climax or at least a diversion. But a curious silence fell, at any rate on the stairs and that first landing where faces appeared over the curve in the banisters. Above, of course, the hubbub continued, augmented at that moment by music from the record player in Gary's room on the second floor where someone had put on, at full volume, a Rolling Stones record.

Bell, in any case, was too late. Not knowing what all this signified or who had arrived, Felicity and Harvey, having long before this gravitated from the day-bed to a real bed, came out of

Cosette's bedroom carrying empty wine glasses and in a state of extreme dishevelment. Felicity persisted in wearing her mini-skirts, though the fashion for them was past, and the one she had on, of black leather, had its zip undone. Her long dark hair hung loose over her shoulders, and her face -- she always made up heavily -- was like a painter's palette at the end of a hard day's work. Harvey had his arm round her shoulders, his hand scooping up and squeezing her left breast as if he were trying to express milk from it.

Cosette whispered to me, 'Who is he?'

'Her husband.'

'Oh dear. It's all like the worst excesses of the Roman Empire, isn't it?'

Felicity screamed when she saw Esmond.

I said afterwards to someone, Cosette I think it was, that it must have been dreadful for him, her screaming like that. He must surely then have remembered moments of passion and tenderness between them, perhaps those first moments of love beginning or the time when the sight of him, far from causing her to scream and hide her head in another man's arms, brought her running to him with joy. But his face showed nothing of this. He said, 'Felicity, I want you to come home with me. Come with me now and we can be home in an hour.'

You could see Harvey didn't want any part in this. Felicity was clinging on to him, but he wasn't holding her. He whispered something to her and then actually began backing away. She lifted her head from his chest and turned slowly round, cringing, with her shoulders hunched. People were coming down the upward flight now. I don't think Esmond was aware of them, I don't think he was really aware of anyone but himself and Felicity and perhaps a few vague, scarcely human, presences, a faceless chorus in a tragedy.

'Come with me now, please,' he said. 'This has gone on long enough.'

I thought he would say something about the children, but he didn't. He simply repeated his request to her. The landing was still lit only by candles and moonlight but now Esmond, who had never been in the house before, put out one hand and pressed the light switch as if he had been doing so in this particular place every night for years. A kind of chandelier of metal branches bearing spheres of etched glass hung there and the light it gave was so bright that Cosette avoided having it on. When the brilliance flooded us all, making people blink and showing up their untidy hair and crumpled clothes, Felicity gave another cry, but this time it was a piteous, yielding sound. Esmond approached her, putting out his hand. She hesitated. She said, incredibly, 'What about all my things?'

I wouldn't have been surprised if someone had laughed, but there was utter silence except for Mick Jagger upstairs. Bell's and mine were the only names of those present that Esmond knew and he said, without looking at us, without taking his eyes from Felicity, 'Elizabeth or Bell will send them on.'

She took his hand and went with him. They passed me and went down the stairs. On her face was a look of total defeat. Her freedom had lasted nine months, and I should think it was a matter of doubt whether she had enjoyed it. Esmond spoke not a word to anyone and nor did she. The front door closed quietly behind them and I heard a car start.

I had a note from her two or three weeks later, thanking me for sending the two packages of her clothes, and after about a year, or a year and a bit, she phoned to invite Cosette and me to Thornham for Christmas. For various reasons, though rather touched at being invited, we refused. Later on Elsa told me Esmond had bought the flat at the World's End, very much the 'in' place to live at that date, to afford Felicity a kind of bolt-hole. I heard about her, but I never heard from her nor spoke to her until two weeks ago.

The party began to break up after they left. That kind of thing casts a blight on merry-making, in much the same way as a ghost might, coming to the table and sitting down in an empty chair. We never saw Harvey again. Though he had been living in the House of Stairs, sleeping with Felicity in her room on the top floor, he must have had somewhere else to go, for he disappeared along with the crowd that went when the dancers went.

Only Gary and Fay and their phobiac friend remained, still out in the garden, still on the stone seat, and looking now in the moonlight like a group of statuary on a fountain after the water has been turned off. Arms round each other, heads lolling, they sprawled in attitudes of abandonment, even the acid-freak in a peaceful, stupefied doze. Bell and I looked down at them from the dangerous window of the top room, the room which had been Felicity's. I had conducted her there, offering her the bed, when she said it was too late for her to go home. We opened the lower sash and leaned out, lying on our stomachs for safety's sake. The sky was clear but no stars were visible. Cosette's garden had become a tip of empty bottles and broken glasses and cigarette ends and heels of loaves.

'I don't understand why people get married,' said I, who was to do so myself three or four years afterwards.

'Women get married to have someone to keep them,' Bell said quite seriously. 'They get married to be safe.'

'Felicity's got a degree, she could get a job. Why does she need someone to keep her?'

Bell laughed a little at that, a small, dry laugh. 'You know my feelings about that. Not everyone's into working the way you are, as you could see by the gang here tonight.'

Emboldened by the night and her niceness, I asked her why she got married. Why had she married Silas?

She was at art school, she told me, Leicester College of Art, and she met Silas there. He was her supervisor, she a first-year student. They got married because she was pregnant, but afterwards he made her have an abortion. Then Silas got the sack, or got warned he would get the sack, or something like that, on account of his propensity for doing dangerous things with firearms, so he left and tried to live by his painting alone.

'So you didn't marry to have someone keep you,' I said.

'Yes, I did. Partly. I knew he'd got an old dad who was ill and who'd leave him something. As a matter of fact, I thought it was more than it was. But I wasn't far wrong, was I? I did get it and it does keep me – just.'

We said good-night soon after that and I went down to my own room, congratulating myself on having at last found out something of Bell's history. I had no idea then – naturally I didn't, believing her, as everyone did, as Esmond Thinnesse had once said he did, because of her honest and direct manner, to be totally truthful – that most of what she told me at the window that night was false. The important bits – none of those were true. When people tell lies about the past, they nearly always distort it to flatter themselves. That is why they lie. The truth isn't glamorous enough, it doesn't make them into the exciting, experienced, successful people they wish to appear. Bell was unique. She invented a past that showed her in an unsympathetic light.

I think she rejected the truth out of mere caprice.

11

In Venezuela there is a village where half the population has Huntington's chorea. Such a high incidence is brought about by the inbreeding in this remote place where the poor people until recently have been quite ignorant about the hereditary nature of their sickness and have intermarried regardless of a parent's disease and the disease of a partner's parent. In their lakeside village they also thought Huntington's – though not knowing it by this name – exclusive to their locality and were amazed when told it was worldwide.

I have been reading all this in today's paper and can't help wondering if Felicity has read it too. Unless she has changed greatly, it is right up her street, just the thing to regale her family with the way she used to regale us with Selevin's mouse and *Stiletto fatalis* and the Defenestration of Prague. But she may have embarked on it long before today, for the newspapers and television and magazines have been full of Huntington's lately, Huntington's has become a fashionable disease, displacing multiple sclerosis and even schizophrenia in the public's curiosity. I glanced at the piece again before I got ready to go and meet Bell, at the photographs of the poor bewildered people, and re-read the paragraph at the end of the article about the test that can now be done and the counselling for potential victims that can be sought.

If the sixties were the age of the sexual revolution and the seventies of the destruction of our environment, the eighties are the decade of the support group and the counsellor. I doubt if there is any problem, physical or mental, confronting modern man and woman, for which counselling can't be obtained. If I had been able to talk to a counsellor in the sixties, would the course of my life have been different? Who knows? As it was I did so much of what I did in the expectation of grotesque paralysis and encroaching death: writing for financial gain my bad, sensational, insensitive books, so as to live and enjoy the present; making love with whom I chose, often promiscuously, on the dubious ground of not missing anything; marrying, criminally, dishonestly, in the hope of pretending none of it was true, and giving a false reason for my refusal to have a child. And then, of course, there was Bell . . .

It sounds insane, but can you believe me when I say, half-truthfully, more than half, that if Huntington's had come, at least it would all have been justified, at least I could say, I acted in the fearful expectation of this and I was justified? I was right not to have a child, I was right not to give birth to another being with a fifty-fifty chance of Huntington's. I was right to produce twenty-five sexy, romantic, sensational adventure books in seventeen years, so that I could live those years in comfort. I was right not to struggle half-starved and alone in a rented room creating the literature I know I could have created and on the dream of its being published one day in the sweet or paralysed by-and-by. (Though in fact the gain was never as great as at first I anticipated, I never made a fortune, or achieved great success or fame, as perhaps writers don't, even the purveyors of adventure and passion and crime, unless they write from the heart.)

I shall be forty next week and as Bell said I am very likely out of the wood. To speak, as I am sometimes inclined to do, with the truest deepest pessimism, I have made a mess of my life for nothing. But it is useless to brood on it, pitifully absurd to maunder like this. I have been to meet Bell, as I hinted just now, I have been to meet her after her first day at the shop in Westbourne Grove.

It wasn't that I much wanted to. Nor did she ask me, though she rang up the morning after I left her sleeping to remind me rather dolefully of when she was starting and where the shop was. I went because I thought I ought to. A poor woman who has passed years in prison – the least an old friend can do is keep an eye on her, give her some kind of support until she adjusts to her new world. Anyone who has loved passionately and now feels an obligation to the object of her love, that where desire once impelled, duty now dictates, will know how I felt. For that renewal of excitement, of passionate need, which I experienced when I pursued

Bell on the tube train and through the streets, that was ephemeral after all, was a false fire, and now what I feel is more a wariness and a dread of something I can't define.

She was surprised to see me but very pleased. How ecstatically grateful I would once have been for those signs of pleasure, the lighting up of her whole face, her hands stretched out to me! Once, of course, I wouldn't have been late but waiting for her to come out ten minutes before the shop was due to close. As it was, the phone rang as I was leaving and then I found one of the cats on the front doorstep, a place neither of them is supposed to know exists, and had to stop to put him inside, so when I met Bell it was on the corner of Ledbury Road, I having raced down from Westbourne Park station.

I spotted her before she saw me and it seemed to me that she was walking aimlessly, and if she was making for Notting Hill Gate, in the wrong direction. But before I spoke to her I understood, or thought I understood. She was avoiding Archangel Place. The extent or depth of this I didn't realize until she said simply, 'I can't exactly remember where it is.'

You would think that anyone who had done such things and known such things, would have the place where they happened indelibly printed on the memory, so no matter what was forgotten that could never be forgotten. There would be a map in the mind, a street plan with fearful corners and ominous landmarks and signposts that warned what to shy away from. But, 'I think something has gone wrong with my memory,' said Bell. 'I expect I could find it in the London guide. Anyway, it's all changed round here.'

It hadn't – much. Apart from some smartening up, nothing had changed in this immediate vicinity. Together we walked westwards, towards Ladbroke Grove.

'How was it?' I said.

'The shop? I don't know if I shall be equal to it.' Bell laughed the laugh that was always dry and faint but has now become ghostly, a whispered giggle at the far end of a passage in the dark. 'She doesn't like me handling money, you can tell that. I nearly told her it wasn't for helping myself from the till I got sent to prison for.'

143

'Perhaps you had better not say that.'

'Oh, I won't. I am not so open as I used to be, I can tell you.'

I had no clear idea of where we were making for. It seemed that, considering our separate destinations, we were both going in the wrong direction. And then it came to me both that Ladbroke Grove station would do for me as well as Westbourne Park and that Bell intended to come home with me. What else had I had in mind? A cup of tea in a café and then dispatching her back to Kilburn? She was a ghost, I thought, and not only in her laugh. We always think of ghosts as pale, as white and glimmering, and Bell has faded, has bleached to pallor, her skin and her hair and even her eyes, vague now, leached of their colours. Only her clothes remain deepest black. I wonder what has become of the shawl she wore the first time she came to Cosette's and which once covered Silas's body?

She smoked as she walked, by the station going into a tobacconist's to buy more cigarettes. In the train she fell briefly asleep but revived once we were home and walked about my house, admiring it. The cats homed in on her, loving her for some reason, clambering over her and the ash-scattered folds of her bundled black cotton. I fear the reason may be that they love anyone who smells strongly, no matter what of, and Bell reeks of stale cigarette smoke, she smells like something raked out of the ashes of a fire. She is sleeping again now, her long pale hands hanging over the arms of the chair like empty sleeves.

I am sitting opposite her with a glass of gin and dry vermouth in my hand. Bell has only sipped hers and her cigarette has burnt itself out in the ashtray. It seems strange to me that though we have been talking for the best part of two hours she has never once mentioned Cosette, or for that matter, Mark. But perhaps that isn't so strange.

Cosette and I had refused Felicity's invitation but Bell accepted, spent Christmas at Thornham and reported back to me that everything was just the same as before Felicity ran away. Even the children seemed unaffected by her long absence, and Miranda was still quoting, with proud sententiousness, her mother's opinions.

'My mummy says it's revolting to eat quails' eggs,' or 'My mummy says only old ladies wear stockings.'

The party was run on the same lines as those of the one the year Silas died. Only there was no quiz on the day after Boxing Day. There was no quiz at all. But the same people were there, more or less. At any rate, old Julia Dunne was there and the ancient brigadier and his wife and Rosalind and Rupert, Felicity's sister and brother-in-law. And Lady Thinnesse, of course, was there, behaving towards Felicity exactly as she had always done. On Bell's last evening Felicity organized a debate, the subject being the possible reintroduction of capital punishment, in which, Bell said Esmond stood up stoutly for the noes and Mrs Dunne became quite rejuvenated and vociferous for the yesses.

One of the things I liked so very much about Bell, I mean one of the definable things, was that she was quite as interested in people as I was. She was the only person I have ever known who really wanted to get inside people's heads and know how they worked and the only person who could talk about other people for hours on end without getting bored or tired. Without any tutelage or training, she had a fine grasp of human psychology. I learnt a lot about people from Bell, though I never had the wisdom to put any of it in my books, preferring to use stereotypes for my characters. And of course she had, has, will always have, a wonderful imagination.

By this time I had found out why she hadn't wanted me to know where she was living or to go there. It was her mother's flat in Harlesden. Bell often said how she didn't really think of anywhere west of Ladbroke Grove or east of the City as being London at all, so I could understand her detestation of West Ten and all its subdivisions. Besides, it was her mother herself. She said she wanted to be totally open about it now she was on the subject and the truth was she would have been ashamed for me to meet her mother.

'If you saw her in the street you'd think she was an old bag-lady. She doesn't even keep herself clean. She's an old cockney' – and here Bell laughed her dry laugh – 'who carts her false teeth about with her in a tobacco tin.'

'She can't be that old,' I said.

'She's old to be my mother. She was a lot over forty when I

was born. The thing was, when I left Admetus's place I hadn't anywhere to go but to her. She's not well anyway. She needs someone with her and there's no one but me.'

I hesitated. Still, why not say it? 'But you've a brother, haven't you? I've seen your brother; I saw him at that Global Experience thing.'

She laughed. It must have been at the memory of those dotty happenings. 'Oh, Marcus, yes.'

'Is that what he's called?' I was enchanted by his name. A person couldn't be that bad, I suggested, who would call her children Marcus and Christabel.

'She probably wasn't as bad then but she's very bad now.'

I told her she couldn't live with her mother for the rest of her life, meaning her mother's life.

'Don't you worry, I won't,' said Bell.

Soon after that conversation I remembered Elsa the Lioness telling me just after the death of Silas that Bell had nowhere to go and no relatives to take her in. Her parents were dead. But since she was so ashamed of her mother, wishing to keep her existence a secret from most people, no doubt she would have said she was dead. It seemed reasonable enough. How strange and sad that she should so detest her mother and I so love mine – well, my adoptive mother. For that was the year, or the spring, Cosette was ill. In fact, she wasn't really ill at all, she had a scare and gave me a scare, but because I loved her so much I magnified it out of all proportion. I was sure that because she was having uterine haemorrhages she must be dying of cancer and I confided my worries to Bell.

'When will you know what she's got?'

'In about a week,' I said.

I imagined losing her, I imagined her own fear of death. I talked to Bell about it, about Cosette's long, half-asleep life, and the chance that had come at last, too late perhaps, for her to live. How terrible if freedom, so short-lived, not even surely enjoyed, should so quickly end in death! Bell listened, calmly attentive. Sometimes she looked as if love was something she didn't quite understand and, lips parted, head held slightly on one side, was considering

146

it as a subject for possible research. But I am not sure if I thought like that then, if I was as wise as that then.

Cosette went into hospital, it was the Harley Street Clinic, and they scraped something from the inside of her womb and found she had a benign polyp which they removed. I think – no, I know – Cosette was proud of all this. You see, it made her seem young. It made her seem as if she still had active reproductive organs and when I went in to see her along with the crowds of other people who gathered round her bed, I was embarrassed by her talk. I was embarrassed when she said to Dawn Castle and Perpetua that they hadn't 'taken anything away', that her insides were still in 'working order', they hadn't made her sterile. Because of this I said not a word to other people, not even to Bell, telling myself that because the worry was past so must any interest in Cosette's condition.

We welcomed her home with flowers and a feast. We put flowers in the drawing room and flowers in her bedroom and in the big jardinière that stood at the top of the first flight of stairs. Bell helped me fetch the flowers and arrange them and she helped me lay the table in the dining room and shop for food. It was Cosette's money, of course, for she had an account at the delicatessen and an account at the florist's, and because she was always more or less on a diet, she ate less than anyone, but as she would have said, it was the thought that counted. She looked tired when she came home and rather bemused. It occurred to me – too late – that someone ought to have gone to fetch her in her own car, not left her to be brought back by an unknown minicab driver. But I wasn't able to drive then and as for Gary and Fay and the acid-freak Rimmon (his real name was Peter) who had come to live in the house without invitation, none of them offered or were even at home when Cosette left the clinic.

People of Cosette's kind, generous, selfless, patient, dispro-portionately grateful for any little thing that may be done for them, these people are always used, taken advantage of and neglected. Nineteenth-century fiction is full of them and this had led us to believe that they and their fate are the invention of novelists. But they exist, to endow others and be trodden on by those who owe them the most. All of which makes Cosette's subsequent life and eventual fate the more bizarre. Her life to come and her fate were what no one could have expected, they seemed a contradiction and a defiance of the rules that say, such a woman will never find passionate disinterested love, tragedy, violent death and final irony, but only exploitation and disillusionment.

None of us young ones had given much thought to Auntie while Cosette was away. It is only now, looking back, that I understand she must have seen Cosette almost in the light of a protector. She was so mouselike, so quiet and creeping, that even to Bell and me with our never-satisfied hunger to know what went on in people's heads, our constant examination of personality, she seemed a person without feelings, certainly a person not worth wasting conjecture on. That she might be afraid in Cosette's absence, afraid of us all with our habits acquired in a revolution she had never understood, of our youth and our music, our comings and goings and our sexual freedom, never crossed our minds.

Perpetua, of course, was sometimes there. Jimmy the gardener would always put his head round the door with a word for her. But Cosette's old friends from Wellgarth days, though visiting the clinic, never thought of visiting Auntie. Bell had been kind to her on the night of the party, but if she paid her any particular attention while Cosette was away, I wasn't aware of it. Did anyone actually speak to the old woman while Cosette wasn't there to speak to her? As I try to imagine the drawing room as it was without Cosette I also see it without Auntie and this makes me sure Auntie kept to her own room most of the time, hiding herself from us and the challenges and dangers and shocks we offered, longing surely for Cosette's return. And when Cosette walked into the drawing room Auntie had taken care to be there. For once she showed emotion, getting up from the red velvet chair and coming to Cosette with her arms out.

'Why didn't you come to see me?' Cosette asked her when the embrace was done.

Auntie had no answer, perhaps didn't care to say the means were not at her disposal, that none of us had offered to take her or even call a taxi and direct the driver. She could only shake her head and frown mysteriously, in the way old people do when they want to keep their needs and shortcomings a secret from the young.

We all assembled in the dining room for the meal, Cosette and Auntie, Bell and I, Gary who had just come back from India, and Fay and Rimmon. It was a small party for the House of Stairs, no one having come to take the place of Mervyn or of Felicity and Harvey. There was no longer any Girl-in-Residence, a function as empty and free of duties as being a Gold Stick or Steward of the Chiltern Hundreds, but still a role with a room that no one filled. Cosette had tried to persuade the ballet dancers to take over the top floor as their home but they, naturally, were reluctant to give up rent-free occupancy of the Hampstead flat whose owner, with luck, might never come back from South Africa. A girl called Audrey, who was a cousin of Admetus's new girlfriend, had said she might take up the vacant post and vacant room. I don't think she quite believed she could have that large second-floor room for nothing and live there without performing any services beyond talking and listening and making cups of coffee, and that was making her hesitate. Cosette talked wistfully about this during the meal.

We finished eating and, as usual, got up without thought of clearing the table or washing up. Perpetua wouldn't be there next day and it was Bell who said in a very uncharacteristic, housewifely way that she and I should do the dishes.

'Oh, leave it till the morning,' said Cosette, not at all uncharacteristically.

'I shan't be here in the morning.'

'But, darling, I thought you were living here now!'

She sounded not just polite. She sounded appalled that the number of her household was therefore even smaller than she had supposed.

'Bell has to live with her mother,' I said. 'For the present anyway.'

'I'm sure we've room for your mother too. Look at all the room we've got!'

Of course this was absurd. Cosette could be absurd, her liberality taken to ridiculous lengths, and to insensitive lengths too. Even supposing Bell's mother was very different from the grotesque description I had been given, why should she want to give up her home and come to live in a strange woman's house? Bell gave her dry chuckle.

'I'll bear your kind offer in mind, Cosette.'

No kind offer had been made, of course, only an assumption. But now the idea was in her head, Cosette wanted Bell. Not in the Girl-in-Residence's room, that was reserved for Audrey, but why not in the top room above the place where I worked if she wanted some privacy? We even had to go up there and look at it, the lot of us, though Auntie disappeared into her own domain on the way. Cosette, sitting on the bed that had been Felicity's, breathless from all that climbing, apologized for the room, its location up 106 stairs, its slanted ceiling, its dangerous window.

'I'll have bars put on that window. I'll have a kind of cage made to make it safe.'

She never did. Because Gary said how awful it would be, you would feel you were in prison? Or because Bell said not to do that for her, she couldn't leave her mother's house in Harlesden at present? Apparently, though, she was well able to leave her mother for a night or two, for she stayed and slept up there and next day, when I came home from the play-centre, told me that she had met an old friend of her mother's who might just be willing to come and share her house.

It was not that evening but a week or so later that I dressed her up in Cosette's gown of 'wasted' red. I had forgotten those remarks of Cosette's, when she first saw the Bronzino reproduction, about still possessing somewhere a dress that looked like Lucrezia Panciatichi's. But Cosette had been invited to Glyndebourne by the Castles and it was still obligatory then to wear a long evening dress when you went to hear opera there. Very seldom did anyone take Cosette out. I was happy that the Castles had thought of this, even though I knew it was done to show Cosette a contrast to the House of Stairs. At a party Cosette gave for Admetus's fortieth birthday, I had chanced to hear Dawn's husband murmur to his wife, 'I wonder if she knows the life she gave up for this circus is still going on?'

The Glyndebourne evening was two months off but Cosette took it into her head she must root out a suitable dress to wear, or in default of this, buy a new one. It reminded me of the old days at Garth Manor where Elsa and I used to try on Cosette's jewellery and she would say when either of us admired something particularly, 'It's yours!'

'Have it, have it,' was what she kept saying to me if I lingered a little over some thirties 'frock' or post-war floor-length creation. But I laughed at her and shook my head. What did I want with a shawl-neck dress in powder-blue rayon crêpe or a black ballerina skirt with bead embroidery? Then we came upon the Bronzino gown and it was very much like the one in the painting. Lucrezia's low-cut neckline is of course filled in with gold lace and the lower parts of her sleeves are of a rich, ruffled black satin, but otherwise the dress was the same, tight bodice, puffed sleeves, full skirt, and all made of silk the colour of a ripe Victoria plum.

'Have it,' said Cosette. 'You'll be doing me a favour, darling. I'm such a hoarder, can't bring myself to throw things away.'

Bell was in her rusty, dusty black. Looking at her now, as she sleeps in my armchair, I can see no difference between what she wears today and what she wore on that momentous, tremendous, wonderful day, when she arrived at the House of Stairs in the early evening, except that, because it was March and cold, she had a black cape on and the shawl wrapped round her. Cosette was taking us out to eat and Rimmon and Gary were coming too. I don't remember where we went, though it may have been that Russian place down in Brompton. Later events must have obscured my memory of such things as restaurants and food and drinks.

The house was nearly empty. Auntie, who would never eat out in the evening, had long gone to bed. Gary and Rimmon had gone off to see a friend in Battersea and if it seems strange to me now to hear of people going out visiting at eleven-thirty at night, it didn't then. I don't know where Fay was, staying perhaps with her new lover, an Indian who kept a sordid hotel, a kind of house of call, near Paddington Station. Bell and Cosette and I were alone and Cosette, at only midnight, talked of going to bed. She easily got tired, debilitated still from her not very serious operation.

'Though it isn't a delightful prospect,' she said, embarrassing me, 'getting into that great big bed on one's own. Sometimes I pull down one of the pillows and hug that.'

'I want you to put the dress on,' I said to Bell.

At first she wouldn't. She said it was silly, her hair was wrong and she hadn't any jewellery. But as she stood there looking at the picture, the idea grew on her. It would take a little while, she said, for she would have to braid her hair and wind it round her head, and I mustn't be there, I must come back when it was done. I gave her the cameo that was herself and fastened it to a string of pearls, for it is a necklace rather like this that Lucrezia wears.

While she was changing I went down to Cosette's room. Cosette, in a Hollywood thirties bedjacket with white feathers on it, was sitting up in bed reading my book, which had been published the week before. She had already read it in manuscript and proof, but she swore it would be different because I had dedicated it to her. I now had to listen to a lot of extravagant praise of what I knew even then was worthless trash; it made me wince, and serve me right.

In her bed with its piled satin-covered cushions and its pink pillows, its pink silk and white lace counterpane all covered with magazines and tissues and pairs of glasses, white telephone, telephone directories, address-book, writing paper, fountain pen, Cosette, rising from befeathered fluffiness, scented with Patou's Joy, looked much younger in the flattering pink lamplight, looked almost girlish. Since the coming of Ivor Sitwell she had abandoned the plastering of her skin with greasy cream at night and the pinning up of her hair and these exercises had never been resumed after he left. Her hair, now a silvery-gold, lay smoothly on her plump white shoulders. The lines on her face scarcely showed, and the sad look, which came now that the tissues had begun to droop once more, gave her an appearance of wistfulness, not age. And those words someone speaks of Cleopatra at the end of the play came into my mind, that 'she would catch another Antony in her strong toil of grace'. Or I think they did, they should have done, but could I really have had such foresight?

We were talking about the book, I with reluctance, for I should like to have taken the money and forgotten it, Cosette with enthusiasm, when the door opened and Bell came in. Or Lucrezia

Panciatichi came in – or Milly Theale. She was wearing the pearls and the cameo and had found a gold chain of mine as well and a string of beads to wind round her braided coronet of hair. The red dress was loose on her, but you couldn't see that from the front, she having skilfully pinned it down the back and at the waist. Her skin had that very pale luminous brownness that gives Lucrezia her glowing look. Instead of smiling at our delight – Cosette actually clapped – she stood gravely between the Chinese screens, then sank softly into the high-backed chair and became entirely the portrait, her left hand closing over the carved arm, her right holding open the little leather-covered book she had brought with her.

Cosette wanted to take a photograph of her. She even got up and started poking about the room in a fruitless hunt for flashbulbs. I think she did take some sort of picture in the end, a picture that we all knew would never come out. Though she couldn't find the flashbulbs, she found the bloodstone. She tried the ring on Bell's hand, but Bell's fingers were very long and slender. It was too big for the third finger and had to go on the middle one. Bell sat there, curiously serene, not laughing at Cosette's efforts, not even smiling. It was as if Lucrezia or Milly had entered into her, infecting her with an old-fashioned placidity. After a while, when Cosette was back in bed, Bell joined in the conversation, idle midnight talk it was, about fashions and how uncomfortable it must have been to dress like that all the time, but she didn't smoke while she had the red dress on. My cigarettes were on the green-room-style dressing-table with its mirror ringed by light bulbs, but Bell didn't take one.

Cosette was tired and falling asleep. It wasn't in her nature to say she wanted to sleep now, to shoo us away. She nodded off, smiled, shook herself, her head dropped again. We took pity on her and left, turning out all the lights at the door. Bell slipped the ring off her finger and left it on the dressing-table.

It was a black night, starless and with no moon. I was aware of the quietness of the house, for at this time there would usually still be music coming from somewhere, the murmur of voices, the sound of languid laughter. That night there was a deep silence, and even the perpetual hum of distant traffic seemed hushed. For a long time the light bulbs on the staircase had needed replacing, a job for Perpetua if only she had known it needed to be done, but she was never there after dark. As our ancestors had done, we took candles to light us to bed.

But Bell in the red dress had come down from my room in the dark, guided by the light from the doorway above and the doorway below. On the stairs she took my hand in hers and led me. The long stiff skirt of the dress rustled as we made our way up. In my room the light was soft and dim, coming from the bedlamp. The painted Lucrezia looked down at the living Lucrezia. I thought – but not then, next day – how strange it was, how infinitely mysterious it would have been to that cinquecento girl if she could have imagined, while she sat to Bronzino in all her beauty and finery, the picture he made reproduced and the copy, no less brilliant and true, hanging in the room where two women, one of them surely herself, entered each other's arms and made love.

Bell pushed the door closed with her toe, a naked toe that had not previously made itself visible under the red silk. Oh, there was such a silence! No words, no sound of breath, after our mouths parted and our eyelids half closed, then like a roar in the quiet, the rustle of cascading silk and the tinkle of gold and stones, as the dress fell and the jewels fell. A shivering and a rapture of silky skins touching, and we moved into the pool of light shed by that single lamp on to the bed.

12

Today is Sunday. I never write on Sundays and Bell hasn't to go
to work in the shop. It is time for us to talk. By whose decree? It
was a decision we both seemed to reach simultaneously, as if each
knew at the same point that the time had come and there was
nothing else left to do.

Working in the shop wears her out. She falls asleep as soon as
she gets home, and by 'home' I mean my house, for it is here that
she has returned every day. On the second evening and the third,
when she woke up at about ten, I had a taxi take her home to
Kilburn and the house under the railway arch. But it seemed a
cruelty, perhaps because she was so malleable and so meek, allow-
ing her arms to be pushed into the sleeves of the old black coat
she wears, letting herself be led out to the waiting cab, lifting her
face to be kissed on a cold cheek. So on Friday I made up the bed
in the spare room for her and there she has been sleeping, fourteen,
fifteen, hours at a stretch.

And all this sleeping, the cumulative effect of it, has at last
refreshed her so that when she came down this morning, smoking
her first cigarette of the day, she seemed less ghostly, more
present, younger and fresher looking, even managing to smile.
And when the bigger, friendlier cat climbed on to her lap, she
began stroking him instead of pushing him listlessly away. Facing
each other later on, we came to this joint decision. We must talk.
The things that had been waiting so long for utterance must now
be said. It was only on which things should take precedence over
which other things that we differed. I believe it was Felicity's
phone call as much as anything which directed the turn our talking
took. Yesterday evening, quite early in the evening, while Bell lay
upstairs sleeping and I was sitting in the study reading for the

fourth or fifth time *The Spoils of Poynton*, she phoned from the World's End flat.

I had truly supposed I should never hear from her again. All that about our meeting in London, about our having unanswered questions to discuss, I had taken as so much flannel, the stuff of small talk. But no, she meant it. Here it was, Saturday night, and she and Esmond up in town planning to eat at a little French restaurant round the corner when she suddenly thought – 'Why not ask Elizabeth to join us? We did actually book a table for four but of course the chances of Miranda and Jeremy actually wanting to eat with us were pretty well nil from the start.'

There was something attractive about it. What is she like now? What is he like? What, above all, are they like together? As she spoke I could again hear her scream when she saw Esmond come up Cosette's stairs, I could see her turn her face away into Harvey's shoulder. But I had Bell to think of, Bell who slept because I was there, a reassuring presence downstairs. I lied to Felicity, I told her I had already arranged to go out. My refusal seemed not to distress her.

'Some other time then,' she said, and then, incredibly, so that I had to suppress my laughter. 'As a matter of fact it's our wedding anniversary, so perhaps Esmond wouldn't have liked it.'

'I should think not.'

'I'll ring you again, I shan't let you go as easily as that. Did you ever hear from Bell Sanger?' Poor Bell has acquired a permanent surname in Felicity's speech. This sets her apart, puts her outside the friends category in which she may no longer be allowed a place.

Why did I lie again? For the usual reason for all our lying. It makes things easier. 'No,' I said. 'Oh, no.'

'What did she want?' Bell asked me when I told her about the call. Through her half-sleep, half-waking, she heard the phone ringing or dreamed she heard it.

'Me to go out with them.'

She jumped up and the poor cat shot off her lap. 'She isn't coming here!'

'She isn't. Don't worry. But would that be so bad? You've spoken to her.'

Touchingly, she said, 'Only to find out about you.'

But Felicity's name brought her into an area of her past that isn't the part I want to know about. These revelations, the ones she made this morning, are not those I longed to hear. At least she has begun, though. She has begun to reveal.

'Has she said anything to you about Silas?'

I asked her carefully, 'What sort of thing?'

'Anything. Has she mentioned him? I can see in your face she has. Did she ask you if you ever thought I might have been responsible for Silas's death?'

What was the use of denying it? I nodded, pursing my lips, as if perhaps it was too bad, too awe-inspiring, for speech.

'No one mentioned it at my trial, did they? Did you notice? The prosecution didn't even say I'd had a husband who killed himself. But all that stuff about me as a child came out, all that. And I'd forgotten it, did you realize that? I'd forgotten everything about it. I had to think for a moment who Susan was. It might have been some other person, some other twelve-year-old they were talking about. But that's why I got such a long sentence. Isn't it terrible to go to prison for all those years for something you've forgotten? They found it out, all the dirt, but they never found out about Silas, or if they did they never questioned that he shot himself, even though by then they knew what I was.'

She took another cigarette and lit it, shaking the match too slowly to extinguish the flame, having to drop it burning into the ashtray. 'I did kill him,' she said. 'Well, isn't it obvious, knowing what we all know?'

'You're making it up, Bell,' I said.

'Why would I? Haven't I got crimes enough and notoriety enough? Why would I make it up?'

'Why did you ever make anything up?' I said, and I know I said it bitterly.

'To make things work better, of course. To make them go the way I wanted them to. Do you know anything about Russian roulette?'

'Only that you use a revolver, put a bullet in only one of the chambers and then spin it round. Felicity told us that much.' I was reluctant to talk about it. It is an unpleasant feeling to think you may be encouraging someone in her lying. It marks you as a dupe. 'I never thought about it again,' I said. 'I wasn't interested.'

'Not even when you met me again? Didn't you wonder?'

'I thought I was living in a society where people might commit suicide but not where they killed each other.'

She laughed her distant dry laugh. 'In Russian roulette,' she said, 'what do you think the odds are? Come on, don't look so – pained. You know most of the things I did, you ought to be tougher. You know now you were living in a society where one person anyway was capable of killing. So what do you think the odds are, using a revolver with a six-chamber cylinder?'

'They must be five to one.'

'Oh, no. That's the mistake most people make. Because, you see, in a well-balanced gun, if you are loading only one cartridge, when you spin the cylinder the chamber with the cartridge in it will be heavier and will naturally tend to fall to the bottom. So the odds are much much higher than five to one, perhaps, if you know just how to spin, as much as a hundred to one.'

This seemed to echo something I'd heard before; but: 'What has all this to do with Silas?' I said.

'Silas taught it to me.'

'Among other things he taught you, I suppose. At art school. Before he got you pregnant and married you and you had your miscarriage.'

'Is that what I told you?'

'Oh, Bell, don't you even remember?' I realized I was carping pointlessly. It was hardly cruel, since she showed no sign of suffering, seemed almost to enjoy my sarcastic reminder of one of her prime lies. But it was useless and it was too late, she would never see. 'What exactly did Silas teach you?'

'About spinning the cylinder and the heaviest chamber falling to the bottom. And then he said if you got a lead bullet, a blank but not a cartridge, a solid lead bullet, and loaded it into one of the other chambers, that would be quite an interesting situation. Because now when you spun the cylinder that one would fall to the bottom, not the one with the cartridge in. If you calculated which chamber would be brought into line with the barrel when the chamber with the lead bullet fell to the bottom, say the one next but one to it on the left, you could load a cartridge into that chamber. Or if the cartridge was already in the revolver you could calculate which chamber to put the lead in to bring the cartridge into line with the barrel.'

'Would you say that again, slowly,' I said.

She said it again. She offered to draw it.

'No, don't bother. I can see it without that. But barring mistakes or unless, say, the revolver wasn't well-balanced, it wouldn't be a matter of odds then, it would be a certainty.'

She nodded. 'Yes.'

I looked up at her. Her face had the impassivity of Lucrezia Panciatichi's, bland and composed, Lucrezia aged but still Lucrezia. 'I don't understand what you did,' I said.

'Silas put a cartridge into one of the chambers and he left the revolver and went to get a drink – you know that filth he used to drink, wine with meths in it, one part purple meths to two parts red wine. While he wasn't there I put the lead bullet into the next chamber but one.'

There was silence. Bell took another cigarette and held it between her lips unlit for a moment. She reached for the Wedgwood lighter Cosette gave me, watching me speculatively.

'The police would have found it,' I said.

'I took it out after Silas was dead and before I went over to the Hall.'

I didn't know whether to believe her or not. All that stuff about well-balanced revolvers and the heaviest chamber falling to the bottom – how would I know if it is true or false? I know nothing of guns. I know no one I could ask. Would a man load a gun and then just lay it down somewhere while he went to get a drink? He might, if he were Silas Sanger. For one thing, he might have had a lot to drink already. I couldn't believe it but I could see Bell doing it just the same. Oh, I could see her.

'Accepting that you did, which I don't accept, why did you?'

'I was so pissed off with him, I was so bored; he was driving me insane. He married me to get a slave and that's what I was, a slave and a drudge, a thing to use, a servant to serve. When he married me I was grateful, I thought that was the life, ten times better than anything I could expect with what was behind me. I didn't know anyone else, my mother and father wouldn't have me near them, I hadn't seen them for seven years, I hadn't any friends. I only knew social workers and one or two kids from the home. You know all that, it all came out in court. I thought I was lucky to get a life with Silas, but I learned, I did a lot of growing up and learning in my six years of married life.'

'There's such a thing as divorce,' I said.

The look she gave me brought it back, that sidelong calculating look brought back to me my old delusion that money meant nothing to Bell, that she was uninterested in material things. But I am no longer deluded, that went long ago, I just remember with wonder and self-disgust the faith I had in the purity of her aims. 'His old father was dying, wasn't he? And he was rich. Well, he wasn't as rich as Silas boasted, but his house was worth a bit. I knew what Silas would do with it, he'd told me often enough. Go and live in bloody Java and paint. He'd been there, he liked the climate. That's why we were hanging on at Thornham, even though Esmond wanted us out. We were waiting for his old dad to die so that Silas could flog the house and go to bloody Java like some old French painter he was always wanking on about.'

'Gauguin,' I said, 'and it was Tahiti.'

She took no notice. She always hated those interjections of mine, what she called 'boring bits of culture'. 'He didn't care whether I came or not. But if I didn't he said he wasn't going to keep me. I could go out to work. He'd kept me for six years, what did I expect? So when the telegram came saying his father was dead I didn't show it to him. I kept it to myself and put the lead bullet in the revolver.'

'You can't send telegrams any more,' I said stupidly. 'Well, you can but they won't get there any faster than letters.' Had there been a telegram sent up to Thornham? It was possible but who would remember now? 'I don't believe any of it, Bell,' I said.

'Suit yourself.'

'I can believe you wanted him dead.'

'What's the difference?'

'There is a difference.'

'I wasn't there when he did it,' she said. 'I was upstairs like I said. He wouldn't have known anything about it or if he did for a

160

split second he'd have thought his time had come, the way you must be sort of expecting your time to come when you play Russian roulette.' She picked up the little cat and began stroking him, long hands pushing hard down the length of his body the way he loves. 'His liver had gone rotten anyway. He wouldn't have lived long. One glass of that red muck of his and he'd be staggering. His liver couldn't handle it any more, he was going yellow all over. God, I hated him.' Another cigarette, and the little cat flinching from the lighter flame. 'Felicity saw the telegram come, you see.'

'What do you mean, Bell?'

She didn't answer at once. 'If Silas had died before his father I wouldn't have got the house, I was only his daughter-in-law. At any rate I'd have had to fight for it. But once he was dead it was sort of automatically Silas's. Only as soon as Silas could get his hands on it he was going to be off to Java. And he mightn't even have bothered to take me. Why would he? He was as sick of me as I was of him.' She drew on that cigarette then and puffed the smoke out through her nostrils as if there was a fire inside her face. 'You'd finished lunch,' she said, 'and Felicity was upstairs fetching the quiz papers that were in her bedroom. She looked out of the window and saw the boy come up on his bike. I don't think she made the connection for quite a long time, not till just before I was going to leave in April. She got me talking about the old man and his death – I was moving into his house, you know. She just said, "But didn't you get a wire an hour or so before it happened?" I didn't know what she meant at first. Have you ever heard a telegram called a wire?'

'Only in books,' I said.

'Sorting that one out gave me a chance to think. I told her the boy had come to the wrong house but I could tell she didn't believe me. Funny, at my trial I thought she might be a witness. And then I thought that if I got off they'd get me back again on another charge, on killing Silas, and Felicity would be there ballsing on about that telegram.' She sighed, looking at her fingers that were beginning to turn yellow with nicotine. 'Have you still got that picture?'

'What picture, Bell?' Though I knew, of course I knew.

'The one of the girl in the red dress that whoever it was wrote a book about?'

Not the same words, but the same kind of words, the same lack of comprehension, the same wonder. The wonder to me is that she can speak of it after the part it played, the role it had.

'It's in the study,' I said.

'I haven't been in there yet,' she said, and then, 'Can we go out? I should like to go down to the river and go in a pub. Could we find a pub and eat there? Isn't there a pub where some guy wrote the words to "Rule Britannia"?'

'James Thomson and it's The Dove. How did you know?'

'You once told me,' she said.

We didn't talk about it but we each made assumptions. Or so I suppose. I made assumptions and all Bell's behaviour showed that she must have done so too and that they were of the same kind. But there was no talk of why.

I would have told anyone who asked me that I was heterosexual. I had only, till then, had affairs with men. A few men. Several. I would like to say I didn't count their number, that it wasn't in that sort of light that I looked on them and back at them, but it wouldn't be true, for that is a number we all know. After Dominic, there was a man at my publisher's, an editor, though not my editor, and for one night there was Gary, just once. We weren't drunk or high on anything, we just happened to be alone together in the house, talking, experiencing a sudden mutual warmth, fellow-feeling, shared knowledge, all those things and being young. But it was something like that, something of the same kind only magnified a hundred times, that brought me and Bell together that silent night.

I have never wanted any other woman before or since. On the other hand, I never felt it was a shocking thing we did or wrong or perverse. It seemed natural. Homosexual men who have occasionally slept with women have told me it was enjoyable, they liked it, but they felt it wasn't the real thing. Doesn't Proust say somewhere that the homosexual man only sins when he sleeps with a woman? So afterwards I half-expected my love-making with Bell, though delightful, though immensely pleasurable, not to

162

be like the real thing. But my reaction was very different, for 'delightful' and 'pleasurable' were not words to be used, other hitherto undiscovered words had to be found, and as to the real thing, this was more real than whatever the real thing is. And so I come up against an inability to express my feelings, my desires and my fulfilments, a blankness like a sheet of dark water, a pool on which float dazzling mysterious memories and whispered words, a drowning place where the thin branch I clutch at is the recollection that I was in love. I was in love with Bell with the kind of fierce, jealous passion experienced by girls ten years younger than I was for someone they are at school with.

Psychologists would say – oh, I know what they would say – that I had been arrested in my sexual development by a shock, a trauma-making revelation. This there had certainly been, and perhaps the knowledge of my possible legacy of Huntington's did freeze me in some inverted phase. But it didn't feel like that, it felt like passion, it felt like being in love, it *was* being in love, it was the kind of thing you delude yourself that, if all goes well, will last a lifetime.

Things, of course, didn't all go well. When do they?

On a high and glorious plane it lasted a little while. The girl called Audrey had vanished, so Bell moved in and became the Girl-in-Residence. I have never known if Cosette knew but I tend to think she didn't. Cosette had an attitude towards lesbians characteristic of her generation: 'Don't leave me alone with her, darling. Whatever would I do if she made a pass at me?'

Did she then suppose that all heterosexual men she was alone with would make passes at her? Hoped it perhaps, poor Cosette. I never felt the hint of a recoil when I kissed her or saw her flinch when Bell came near her. No doubt she saw us only as 'best friends' and the jealousy in her that I observed was due to this, that Bell took me away from her and – incongruously perhaps, but who really understands people? – I took Bell away from her.

She was very alone that summer which was Bell's summer and mine, she must have been, though I was aware of it only afterwards. Being in love and having, at least supposedly, one's love returned, there is nothing like it for making one oblivious to the loneliness of others. I was a little dismayed, I am sorry to say a little fastidiously disapproving, when I understood Cosette was sometimes sleeping with Rimmon. She was fifty-five and he was twenty-seven, he had no money and she had a lot. If I didn't understand about loneliness I understood even less that in middle age the heyday in the blood does not always grow tame. Going to Glyndebourne with the Castles and taking Auntie for drives in Richmond Park were not enough for her.

Bell has never read any of my books. She has scarcely read any books by anyone. If I am to be very honest I will say that in a secret corner of myself I was glad she never read mine, for my books are not the way I talk, they don't reveal real emotion, real sensitivity, they are not about people in the way Bell and I talked about people. Anyone who knew me the way she knew me would, after reading them in the spirit in which Bell would necessarily have read them, be disillusioned about me and see me as a hypocrite. Useless to talk to someone so unacquainted with books as Bell is, of the dichotomy between the writer's art and the writer's life or, as she would have put it, other balls like that.

She was in my room just as I finished my stint of writing for that day. It was late summer, early autumn, and she was in white cheesecloth, a kind of robe with huge sleeves, the waist caught in to its tiny span by a belt of plaited leather. Above my head, while I typed the last of my requisite 2,000 words, I had listened to the movements she made prior to coming down to me, the closing of that window, the window which had never been protected by the promised cage, her footfalls muffled by the carpet, then touching the wood surround which did not at all muffle the clack-clack of Indian sandals, the door shutting, the creak of the 104th stair as she began to descend. These are the stuff of love's obsessiveness, in which I was up to my neck.

She never read a book, as I have said. But she would walk about picking books up and examining them. I have said that too. It is such a strong image in memory. I was still intending to write my paper on Henry James, between books I would write it, and eventually I did. It was *The Awkward Age* that Bell picked up off my desk, a copy from the library in Porchester Road, and, looking at it with interest, feeling the texture of it, assessing the number of its pages, reading its spine, rather than even glancing at its text, said, 'Is this the one that's about the girl that looks like me?'

'No, that's *The Wings of the Dove*.' I found my copy and gave it to her, taking the other book out of her hand and kissing her hand, holding it against my face. She was so touchable, Bell, her skin sweet-smelling, like a child's. We stood close together for a moment, the sides of our bodies pressing. 'It's the painting that looks like the girl and you look like the painting.' She turned her face into mine, smiling close to my cheek, said in that light way she had, teasing, incredulous, 'When did he write it, this guy you're so keen on?'

I had a shot at it, but was a year out, '1901.'

'I don't see how she can be in a painting you say was painted in fifteen hundred and something if he didn't write it till 1901.' She was looking at *The Wings of the Dove* now, and if there was ever a novel to daunt the non-novel reader, the dipper into magazines, the desultory scanner of newsprint, this is it. The pages of text scarcely broken into paragraphs, uninterrupted by dialogue, as she viewed them with increasing dismay, brought such a look of horror to her face that, stepping back to get a clearer look at her, I burst out laughing.

'What's it about?' she said. 'It doesn't even make sense, it might be in a foreign language.'

So, sitting there cross-legged on the floor, Bell dropping to sit beside me and be close to me but still with the book in her hand, still disbelievingly turning its pages, I told her the plot of *The Wings of the Dove*. That was all I ever did, all. It wasn't even the only or the first novel plot I had told her, for I remember some weeks before she had wanted me to go with her to the Electric Cinema where they were showing *The Wanderer*, which is the film version of *Le Grand Meaulnes*, and I had given her a kind of précis of that too. But Milly Theale remained in her memory, Milly Theale and Merton Densher and Kate Croy, though I don't believe I ever told her their names. That wasn't necessary, the plot was enough, the melodramatic central spring of the novel which James somehow makes not sensational but subtle, tenuous, like life. I suppose it was the painting that anchored her to it, the

Bronzino that looked like her and which poor doomed Milly Theale looked like.

She said slowly, wonderingly, 'What a clever idea!'

'James was clever. There's never been a cleverer novelist.'

'He could have fooled me,' she said, typically Bell, 'the way he goes wanking on.'

13

The first time Mark came to Archangel Place there were living in the House of Stairs Cosette and myself and Auntie, Gary and Fay, Rimmon and a Filipino friend of his and, of course, Bell. In the autumn of 1972 she had gone back to Harlesden for a while because of some crisis in her mother's household. I know now, and have known for years, that Bell had no widowed mother in Harlesden, that her own mother and father were living together in Southsea, attempting to put their unhappy foray into parenthood as far behind them as they could. But I didn't know it then. I believed Bell when she said she had to go 'home' to 'sort things out'.

Though an adept at self-delusion of many kinds, I have never deluded myself about the moods and climatic changes in love affairs. I know at once when something is going off the boil. That first tiny break in the lover's absorption, not rejection, nothing as plain as that, more an air of distraction, a vagueness, then the unavoidable painful observance that it is always the other now who is first to end an embrace, withdraw the tongue, harden and retract the lips, the other whose laughter ceases to be slow and conspiratorial and whose fingers no longer have all the time in the world at their tips. I am aware of these things, I don't delude myself that they are not there. Where the self-deception comes in is in my ability notwithstanding all this, to persuade myself of its being a phase, a stage in a progress, or a mere lapse.

Bell's passion for me, which I am sure, am still sure, in spite of everything, was once as real as mine for her, had begun to slacken its intensity. She became abstracted, withdrew herself a little. My second book was published, there was some press attention this time and talk of it as a candidate for an adventure-novelists' prize; American publication was assured, and I was busy with all this, but not so busy as to be unaware of Bell's absences, of some business she had that was private from me. What could she have to do that took her away from the House of Stairs so much? Where was she when occasionally she phoned me or Cosette to say she would be late, she was 'held up'? She did nothing – ever. In this way she rather resembled Cosette, as in so many others – and what does that say about Mark and about me?

Bell had no occupation, hobbies, interest. Her interest in people and their behaviour absorbed her. She liked to look at beautiful things, in shops and in exhibitions; not at clothes, though walking through fabric departments, stroking the more extravagant stuffs, gave her intense sensuous pleasure. Mark told me later she sometimes went to look at the crown jewels in the Tower. Was that what she was doing, in all those absences, looking at the people and the lavish artefacts in Bond Street? Stroking damask in Liberty's? Strolling round the V and A?

Then she went back to her mother's. There was an awful evening when we sat together in the grey garden, Cosette and Auntie and I, each feeling our peculiar individual loneliness, not even a warm evening, but humid and cool and smelling of soot and the leaves of the eucalypt. Anyone who looked over the high walls of brick and flint might have taken us for the representatives of three generations in one family, daughter, mother, grandmother, but no one looked over the walls. The sky was like white marble, the night long in arriving. Once, I remember, Cosette said, 'Why does no one come any more?'

That shy, half-fearful smile trembled on Auntie's lips. She seemed to understand less and less as time went on. Her bewilderment was of the kind that is afraid no sincerity remains, everything is becoming a joke, but a joke that to her is meaningless. In another way she was like one of those poor zoo animals that, accustomed to living in a group of their peers and in a particular habitat, are imprisoned in an alien one and alone. I went indoors, ostensibly to fetch a sweater and, mounting the stairs, hearing with the first of many twinges of pain my foot set the 104th creaking, entered Bell's room to hold one of her dark wraps to my face and smell her sweet child's smell. *The Wings of the Dove*, unread, never to be read of course, lay on a chair. I took it away downstairs.

Another time, when Auntie had gone off to bed, Cosette said to her reflection in the drawing-room mirror,

'Is this the form, she made her moan,
That won his praises night and morn?
And, Ah, she said, but I wake alone,
I sleep forgotten, I wake forlorn.'

I put my arms around her, I hugged her. How that would have flustered her had she known about Bell and me! But she laughed at Tennyson and herself.

'Isn't it dreadful? Ivor wrote better poetry than that. Well, marginally better. "My life is dreary, he cometh not, she said . . ." '

He cometh not . . . The inexpressible, absolute he, the nonpareil of he's she has waited for. She had been reading *Washington Square,* lent to her of course by me, and she identified with poor Catherine Sloper. Women are usually shy about admitting their need of a man. They deny this need, dismiss it; they could easily, they say, get themselves a lover, a husband, if they wanted one. But why go to so much trouble? Why bother? They are content as they are. Not Cosette. Frankly, she would declare it, not just to me but to almost any listener, to Perpetua, to Auntie, that she was sick for a man's love, a man's companionship. Her life was dreary, he cometh not, she said . . .

But two days later he did come. He arrived like the answer to a prayer, or like the answer one dreams of but doesn't expect to get. He arrived like the prince that some fairy messenger brings, and he wasn't even in disguise. Or not apparently so. It was Bell who brought him. There was no fanfare of trumpets. Very casually, she gave notice to Cosette of what was about to happen, announcing this event that was to prove so momentous in her usual offhand way. She had reappeared in the House of Stairs after an absence of two or three weeks – why do I say two or three weeks when I know the length of time precisely, when I know it was exactly eighteen days? – and sauntered into the drawing room as if she had never been away. She was wearing her white cheesecloth, carrying her cigarette packet and matches in her hand. I never saw Bell with a handbag. Us three, Cosette, Auntie and I, she glanced

at us as if we were equally casual acquaintances, people she toler-
ated in an indifferent good-humoured fashion.

'My brother's coming this evening. Is that all right?'

But Cosette spoke to her as if she were her daughter. 'Darling,
how can you ask? Of course it is. We all long to meet him.'

Mark – how can I describe him? He was simply the best-looking
man I have ever known and one of the nicest. Or so I thought for
a long time, marginally, at last, changing this view of him. He was
one of those people you at once feel at ease with, who are 'always
the same', without vanity or apparently the knowledge they have
anything to be vain about, clever and amusing without cruelty,
unfailingly kind, seductively charming without any of the slyness
or conscious affectation this implies. Yet when I look back on this
I see I have given an impression of someone quite unlike Mark,
for the point with him, I might even say the point *of* him, was his
naturalness, that all these most delightful possible attributes of a
young handsome man had come into being and coalesced by a
happy chance and he was not even aware that they were there.
Even the things he said seemed never the result of calculation but
the expression of a warm and gentle nature. Have I made him
sound like a fool? I don't think he was a fool, for a long time I
thought him intelligent, but that view too I revised. Let me say
only that Mark was exceptional to look at but intellectually
nothing out of the common way.

Older than Bell by several years, he was thirty-six that
winter. By then I had put him and Bell down as probably being
of Scandinavian origin, but Mark's looks were really more
of the Slavonic kind, the wide, high cheekbones, the nose that was
perfectly straight but rather short for a man's nose, the short upper
lip, the full but firm mouth. His skin was brown and his hair nut-
brown with a streak of silver running from one temple across the
crown. How Cosette came to love that silver streak, how important
it was to her!

She wasn't looking particularly nice that evening. Her hair
needed doing and the roots showed grey. Staying thin wasn't just
a losing battle with Cosette but a series of skirmishes in which
about fifty per cent of the time her side won. Necessarily, therefore, the other half of the time fat was the conqueror and he was

in the ascendant now, positively crowing his victory on the scales that morning. She had a silk caftan on, in a shade of light red that didn't suit her, and she had sprayed on too much Joy. Fay, on the other hand, with twenty-five years' advantage over her, was looking gorgeous. She went through phases, did Fay, times of indifferent, rather shabby looks when she would be washed-out and stringy, and times of glory, each dependent on the attention she paid herself. She must have been attentive lately, for she glowed under make-up as heavy but more skilfully applied than Felicity's had ever been, and instead of her usual jeans, she was in a skirt which showed off her legs and fine ankles. Perdita, the dancer, who had been left there by her husband while he went off to some charity performance, also presented an appearance with which Cosette couldn't have competed. She was always exquisite, like an exhibit in a little girl's glass case of dolls, waxen-faced, raspberry-fuchsia mouth, hair that might have been painted on with lamp black and a fine brush, every gesture learned and every pose rehearsed.

I mention competing because that was the impression they gave, those three women, when Mark walked in. Bell had gone out on to the balcony to check that it was he when the doorbell rang and then she went down to let him in. He was the only man and there were we five women. You could see at once what an impact he made. His grace as much as his looks did that. He was very thin and he walked like a dancer – imagine Nureyev entering a London drawing room incognito – or perhaps he walked like an actor, which is what he was. It would have been amusing, the reaction of those three, if it hadn't been sad, for in the few seconds before Mark went over to her and shook hands, you could see Cosette, bowed and humbled, retire from the contest. It was as if she took in for the first time without self-delusion the appearance of the other two, as if the shock of it struck and pained her, her fifty-five years and her weariness smote her, and she put out her hand to him with a half-smile in which was self-mockery and defeat.

It was not she whom he approached first. Mark was Mark and he knew what was due to the obviously eldest lady there. Auntie was the first of us he shook hands with, Auntie who was so accustomed to being ignored by pretty well everyone except Cosette –

you see how, even here, I said that we were five women, not six –
that she was too stunned to reply when he said how do you do to
her. Bell made no introductions, I should have been astounded
if she had, she simply waved a hand at him and said, 'This is
Marcus.'

He said quickly, almost apologetically, 'No – Mark, please.'

And of course I found out long afterwards that it was Bell, with
her fondness for pretentious fancy names, who had Latinized him.
Cosette told him who we all were. Something like this had happened the first time Walter Admetus came round, the first time
Luis Llanos did. The dancer had merely bestowed on all his
charm-laden smile and a 'Hi!' while Admetus went from person
to person, carefully enunciating names – 'How do you do, Gary?'
'How do you do, Mimi?' Mark said how do you do only to Auntie,
an individual hallo to all the rest of us. I saw no special glance of
admiration rest on Perdita or on Fay. Bell, too, was watching,
with the same passion for the finer points of human behaviour.

Mark didn't talk about himself and it was from Bell that I found
out what he did. He had a part in a radio serial, precarious work
since there were constant threats to kill off the character he played,
but it was more secure than his past, which was a history of tiny
parts in television drama, as a film extra and repertory work in
places such as Colchester or Gateshead. It took me just as long to
find out where he lived, in a studio flat in the neighbourhood of
Brook Green, and his age, and that he was single and had never
been married. But Mark was a listener, at any rate not one to fill
the conversation with his history and his opinions, and for a while
we knew of him only that he was charming and interesting and
'an addition to our circle', as Cosette put it in a kind of parody of
Victorian talk.

'Why have you kept him to yourself for so long, Bell?' Cosette
asked her when we were all down in the dining room, eating one
of those luxury cold meals the fridge disgorged.

She shrugged but she looked at him with the modest satisfaction
of someone who has brought unquestionably the most stunning
exhibit to the show. 'He could have come before. He knew it was
here.'

'Don't you believe her. She never said a word about all this.'

172

He put out a hand to encompass Cosette's art nouveau hanging lamp, the walls all laden with Flora Danica porcelain, the purple curtains not drawn but carelessly flung back to show the grey garden made yellow and shiny and glittering by shed lamplight and winter wet. Later he was to say he had always hated the House of Stairs, but there was no sign of that then. 'She never said a word about you, all of you. I just knew she had a room here and a friend.' His glance lighted on me charmingly, it seemed to me admiringly. 'For all I knew, it was another glory-hole like old Walter's tip where the cat fleas can be seen nightly, dancing on the carpet.'

'The origin of the term "entrechats" perhaps,' said Cosette with a smile at the dancer who, not understanding, returned her look with her usual one of wistful wonder.

Mark laughed. Cosette's gratitude for his amusement fairly blazed in her face. She wasn't sitting next to him, she would have thought it selfish to have placed this prize next to herself, but now that we had finished eating, though two just-opened bottles of wine remained, we followed one of our customs of changing places at table and Bell, who had been between Mark and me, got up and invited Cosette to take her chair. In my turn I moved to change with Fay, ostensibly to sit beside Gary who had come in just as the meal began, but really to be in a position to observe Cosette and Mark. I was afraid for her, I was already afraid.

They talked about Walter Admetus. Though he had been to his house to see Bell, he had never actually met Admetus, but he was far more familiar with the pieces he wrote for *Private Eye* and the *New Statesman* than Cosette was. With the kind of intellectual approach actors rarely have, he told Cosette what a good critic he thought Admetus was, how considered and searching, never going in for the cheap jibe for the sake of raising a laugh and at the expense of truth. Did Cosette know he had written a novel which had never received the attention it deserved? This, of course, led Cosette into fulsome praise of my own imperishable works. I was embarrassed, of course I was, but to my surprise I found Mark knew I was a writer, had in fact read my first book and the only good review I had ever had – almost the ònly review – and instead of Ivor Sitwell's sneering remarks or Admetus's manner of ignoring entirely that I had ever written or published anything, said, 'I sat up all night to finish your book, I had to know what happened. You deserved that prize.'

I muttered some sort of thanks. 'Did Bell tell you about it?'

If she had he would have answered directly, but, 'Oh, Bell's illiterate and proud of it,' he returned. 'And I'm not one of your readers who get your book out of the library and then expect you to go down on your knees to me for graciously borrowing it.'

This was so accurate I began to laugh. 'Did you actually pay down good money?'

'The best,' he said.

Cosette fell in love with him that evening. It happened as quickly as that. I was dismayed to see it, I watched aghast as, when we returned to the drawing room to drink, for some forgotten reason, champagne, she turned on him a look I had once seen on another face in very different circumstances. This had been when Cosette and I were together in Italy and into this café in Bologna came an itinerant musician with a guitar. There was a child in the café with her parents and older sister, a girl of about eight. She fell in love at first sight with the guitarist, following him in worshipful silence round the restaurant from table to table, watched with unconcealed amusement by her mother and father and the older girl. When he became aware of her attention he turned to her and performed only for her, seating her on a chair at a table alone, playing for her a grotesque pluck-plucking version of *Santa Lucia*, and receiving with evident kindly delight her gaze of adoration. Cosette, of an age to be that girl's grandmother, wore that look identically, as for a long moment when he brought her a glass of champagne she met his eyes with undisguised wonder and glory in her own.

It would pass, I thought, it *must* pass, it must be no more than a 'crush', an evening's infatuation that with nothing to feed on would die, would become for poor Cosette no more than a piece of nostalgia on which to look back with a, 'Do you remember that beautiful man who came here once and was so nice to us? I was madly in love with him for a whole week . . . !'

But she wasn't going to give that a chance to happen. She wasn't going to let him get away. Bell she rightly knew as evanescent, unreliable, an occasional 'disappearer'; one not to be trusted to bring her showpiece back again. And Cosette was aware of the invalidity of the vague invitation that postulates another visit 'sometime soon' or 'when you're passing'. Mark had to be summoned back for a specific occasion and he was: a party; she would give a party – for what? For Bell's birthday, her thirtieth it was going to be. This seemed tremendously young, of course, to Cosette, though I am less sure of how Bell felt about it. Not too happy to have this milestone advertised, I suspect.

'If I could be thirty again, I'd be a "manizer", I'd go about stealing everyone's husbands.'

I remembered that then. I remembered that when she invited Mark to Bell's birthday party, including Fay in the invitation, of course, and Perdita. Her face was radiant still. It was like the little Bologna girl's face in that there was no disguising her joy, as if she had seen no men before, never been married and had her two or three lovers, but had slept her youth away in the depths of a wood or wasted it in a nunnery, and like Miranda, cried, 'O brave new world, that has such people in't!'

That night, later, lying in bed beside Bell, I said to her, 'Cosette is going to fall in love with Mark.'

'She's in love with him already.'

'You saw that?' I said.

'Didn't you? Of course you did.'

'I wish there was something we could do to stop it.'

'Why? Why ever? Because you're afraid for her? But he'll be different, he won't be like that bastard Ivor Thing. Mark doesn't fuck women over.'

'I mean he won't feel the same as she does, he won't be able to return what she feels.'

'He'll be kind to her, though. That'll be the difference, you'll see what a difference that makes, he'll be so kind.'

'I'd rather he didn't get the chance,' I said.

'Would you? Cosette wouldn't.' She turned over, pulling herself away from me. 'I'm going to sleep now. Good-night.'

This morning we went shopping together, Bell and I, down to the supermarket where I buy food for my cats. As we waited in the queue at the check-out, I pointed out to her the pictures in bright gilt frames the supermarket offers for sale at £9.95 apiece. In one of them was represented a favourite subject of Silas Sanger's, an animal walking across a clearing in woodland, though this animal was a retriever in a sunlit grove, whereas Silas's would have been a bloody-jawed predator in a rain forest.

She thought of him too. 'Silas used to freak out when he saw things like that,' she said. 'They're obscene, they make me feel sick.'

'That's the Leicester Art College view, is it?' I said. I know I shouldn't make these scathing remarks to her every time we come near places in the past where she lied to me, but I can't help it. Still, I must, I must resist. She doesn't seem to care though, she takes it as if I have a right to try and settle scores, and perhaps I have.

'You know I was never there. It's a wonder you ever believed all that crap in the first place.'

'Curious as it may seem to you, people do tend to believe what they're told.'

Her laughter is as dry now as sticks crackling when they start to burn. We paid for the cat food and lugged it out and waited for a taxi. She hasn't after all found herself equal to that job in the shop in Westbourne Grove and has moved in with me, she lives with me now. Not that this has actually been said, not in those words, and rent is still being paid for that room under the railway arch. How she expresses it is that she is staying with me, but I know she means to remain. The irony of it amuses me greatly, for I remember how ecstatic I would once have been to have Bell living with me, to know Bell wanted to live with me – wanted it more than I wanted it. But such a state of affairs was unthinkable, unimaginable.

Now, frankly, I don't want it at all. I don't want Bell as some sort of temporary but long-term guest in my house. She is too much for me, her past is too much, the things she has done. I jib at that. Who wouldn't? It has made me nervous, all of it, it is causing me the kind of stress that always results in – well, you can guess what, can't you? In a tic, a twitching, a jumping of the muscles. The more I worry about it the worse it gets. This is not the way Huntington's begins, but I don't like it and I worry about it, I know I am still not too old.

My fortieth birthday has passed and gone. Bell and I went out to dinner and celebrated. We go out together a lot, several evenings a week, often to the cinema, for there have been so many good films lately, *Mona Lisa* and *A Room with a View* and *Prick Up Your Ears*. I haven't been to the cinema so much for years. And last week we went to see *Antony and Cleopatra* at the Olivier, the finest performance this century some say, and had our supper at the National Film Theatre by the river. Two rather good-looking women in early middle-age, people must think us, not sisters, too dissimilar for that, and not suburban neighbours either. No one could think Bell in her black layers, her different black textures all bunched and bundled and tied, anyone's suburban neighbour. She wears nothing but black now. Like Chekhov's Marya perhaps, she is in mourning for her life.

'What bollocks,' she said when I told her this. 'Half your trouble is you've read too many books.'

'You mean half *your* trouble is I've read too many books.'

You see, I want to get her to talk about Cosette and Mark. Sooner or later, if she fails to respond to all these hints, I shall have to say their names to her, talk about them myself, but I don't want to do that yet. No, that's not true. I'm afraid to mention them. When we got home the phone rang and it was Timothy. Do you remember Timothy, the man I was having dinner with in Leith's the day after I first saw Bell? He doesn't mean much to me, I am not in love with him or he with me, but he is a friend and I can't see him now, not at present. I can't ask people to meet Bell, I can't introduce her to them. They may not know who she is and what she has done, there is no need for them to know, but I know and it inhibits me.

Bell smoked all the way back in the taxi in spite of the driver's notice saying 'Thank you for not smoking'. She couldn't believe this wasn't a joke when she first read it. The driver coughed ostentatiously and when we got to my house said, 'I'd have put you out of my cab, only I've got old-fashioned ideas about what's due to ladies. Pity others aren't so considerate.'

I thought Bell might swear at him, but she didn't, she didn't say anything, hardly seemed to have heard. She walked up to the front door and waited for me to unlock it and when we were inside said, 'Shall I tell you how I really met Silas?'

'Suit yourself.'

'Come on,' she said, 'that's me, that's what I say. You're pinching my lines.'

I started laughing. 'Tell me how you really met Silas.'

'It was in the children's home. The home was a big house that was a sort of experimental unit – experimental fuck-up, actually. I mean they mixed up big kids with much younger ones and really little ones. It was supposed to be like a family, Christ. Give me my cigarettes, will you?

'They put me in there when I was sixteen. You know where I'd been and why. Well, they put me in there sort of secretly, it was all supposed to be very progressive, in tune with the changing times and all that, it was 1958, not a word to get into the newspapers. There wasn't much else in the way of media then. But they weren't progressive enough to think I ought to be at school. I went out to work and lived at the home and in the evenings I used to have to help put the little ones to bed. Yes, really, that was a laugh, wasn't it? I was dying to get away but I didn't know when I could, if I ever could, being me, whether it was eighteen or twenty-one then or what, or whether it was just another kind of prison. Well, it wasn't.

'Silas had a relation with a kid in care but they used to let the kid go home at the weekends. Sometimes it was Silas who brought her back. Felicity was his girlfriend then. She was at college and I reckon she thought it ever so wild and daring screwing around with a schizzy soak like Silas. OK, so I got him away from her and I really did get pregnant and the superintendent that ran the home made him say he'd marry me. They told him who I was and made it look like he'd done something really awful even touching me, like I was a leper, and now we'd both have leprosy but we'd have to have it together. I had a miscarriage on my wedding day. I started bleeding in the Registry Office.'

'Is that true, Bell?'

'Is what true?'

'All of it.'

178

'Of course it is. You said yourself even liars tell more truth than lies.'

The muscles were jumping in my neck and shoulders. I tried to control them, breathing deeply. 'Where was Mark then?' I said. 'What was Mark doing?'

She jumped up and ran out of the room, banging the door.

Mark came to the party Cosette gave for Bell's birthday. For some reason, it was a far more decorous affair than the one Esmond Thinnesse interrupted to take Felicity away. People got drunk, of course they did, and Rimmon went on one of his acid trips, but these had become habitual to him, were a weekly indulgence. As far as I remember no couple disappeared into a bedroom as Felicity and Harvey had on that previous occasion. I have sometimes thought that this party was less of a saturnalia than previous ones simply because Mark was there. Of course I am not implying that he had prudish views or that there was anything repressive or disapproving in the way he behaved. There was nothing like that. It was more that his presence seemed to make people feel that it was possible to have a good time socially without getting drunk or high or pawing others about, that conversation and being nice to fellow-guests was a reasonable, if out-dated, alternative. Of course I realize I'm making a pretty high-flown claim for Mark and maybe I'm quite wrong, maybe the party was the way it was because Admetus wasn't there and nor were Felicity nor Fay nor Gary.

Cosette urged Bell to invite her own friends. She was very anxious that Bell and Mark's mother should be invited and in fact wanted more than that. Because it was for Bell's birthday, she wanted Bell's mother asked round in advance, she wanted her actually to take some part in organizing the party. Bell invited no one. I can quite see why not now, but at the time it seemed strange to me. Apart from Mark, the guests were all Cosette's old gang, the usual Wellgarthians, Oliver and Adele and the ballet dancers and Perpetua with a lot of her family, including Dominic, and Mervyn and Mimi, and some neighbours from Archangel Mews.

At that party, for a birthday present, Cosette gave Bell the bloodstone ring. She said it suited Bell's hand much better than her own and she was right. Bell said thank you and looked at the ring on her finger and then up at Cosette, but without smiling or showing any special signs of pleasure. Almost anyone else would have kissed Cosette for that, thrown her arms round her and kissed her. I wasn't surprised when Bell didn't do this, but I was sorry. I was sorry too that she never wore the ring afterwards, or if she did it wasn't when she was with me. The next time I saw her and I think every time since then, her hands were bare.

Mark didn't stay till the small hours. He went home a little after midnight. Cosette pressed him to come back the following evening to dinner when they would talk about the party.

'I don't think I should come tomorrow,' he said.

There was something in the way he put it that made it far from a direct refusal. Cosette seized on this.

'If you mean you ought not to come because you've been here twice, that's nonsense, you know. Everyone else comes just as often as they want. We don't stand on ceremony here. Please come.'

He smiled at her. 'Just the same, I won't come tomorrow.'

I was angry with him. It seemed to me he was playing hard to get. Why follow these rules with a rich woman old enough, nearly old enough, to be his mother? It was unkind. Or it was deliberately making himself elusive, unattainable and therefore the more longed-for. He said no more. Cosette watched him go down the street, watched his long thin shadow the lamplight cast. She closed the door. We were alone in the hall, the party and the music still going on upstairs.

'I'd give everything I've got to have my youth back,' Cosette said. She said it in a fierce, intense whisper. 'I'd give all the future and take death at the end of it if I could have one year of being thirty.'

It was nearly a week before she heard from him again. In that week, what was she like? Sad, I suppose, just sad. She didn't talk about him, she didn't say anything, but you could imagine her thoughts. If only, they must have run, I could have been just a handful of years younger and he just a fraction older, if only we could have met with no more than five or six years between us – ah, then! As it is I can do nothing, I can't even phone him as I would Walter, say, or Maurice Bailey or some other man, I can't do it because of the way I feel, I can't face the humiliation of a refusal. So she must have thought. Sometimes I caught her looking at Bell as if there lay her only hope. Bell was the key to Mark. What questions could she answer, what histories give, what analyses of his past behaviour? But Cosette never asked, and I didn't ask either. It seemed to me – quite wrongly, of course, as I now know – that perfect confidence had existed between Bell and me and the coming of Mark spoiled it. I was afraid to ask and she was not willing to explain. It erected a barrier between us, or so I thought. In fact it did erect a barrier, it was through Mark that we began to be drawn apart, but not at all in the way I supposed.

14

There is a limit, said Henry James, to the impunity with which one can juggle with truth.

I could question that. He never knew Bell, he never knew the arch-juggler in the circus of the world. It is a strange thing the conclusions we draw not from the impressions we are given but from the impressions we take. I took it for granted Bell was experienced, sophisticated, richly travelled in all kinds of sexual regions, as street-wise as could be, as tough. Yet she never told me so. Did she act these things, or did I choose to see her as acting? Certainly she told me she had been at art school, had lovers long before she went there, grew up fatherless and with a strange mother who had been a concert singer. Her maiden name, of course, had been Mark's name, Henryson.

I reached a conclusion: life with Silas had compounded her distaste for men. Even while with him, married to him, she had turned to women as lovers, probably a series of women. And after he was dead and she was free she was able to indulge her love for her own sex. I thought it likely that this accounted, more than a need to be with her mother, for those absences of hers and that disappearance which took place soon after our meeting in Admetus's house. She had had a lover, a woman, to whom she was deeply committed but with whom she had finally broken in order to come to me. For, looking back over our life together and the multitude of things we had talked about, I could recall no mention of any man she was involved with except Silas, no mention indeed of any man at all except her brother Mark, and on the subject of him she was not communicative.

I thought we would never see him again, and I was surprised when I answered the phone to hear his voice. He recognized mine at once. Mark wasn't one of those people who, though they have met you, when they phone treat you, with their 'Can I speak to so-and-so?', like the secretary or the housekeeper. Mark called me by my name and asked me how I was and then sounded taken aback when I said Bell wasn't in.

'It isn't Bell I want. I hoped I could speak to Cosette.'

He had rung to ask her out to dinner. Just the two of them, not a party, just he and she because he thought it would be nice to entertain her for a change after he had twice been her guest. Her reaction wasn't at all what I expected. It wasn't what Bell expected either. I won't say I knew Bell by that time. In view of how tremendously I was deceived, that would be stupid, but I knew sides of her, I knew what it meant when she watched someone in that cold interested way of hers. She was making mental notes of their follies, how far they would go. Having seen Cosette – well, let me make no bones about it – having seen her simper at Mark and bridle and gaze with adoration, hang on his words and defer to his opinions, she was waiting for some fresh ridiculous display. Isn't it strange that I was beginning to understand that Bell disliked Cosette? Hardly anyone ever disliked Cosette, you see, it was nearly impossible, so I had discounted the signs I had seen before, only keeping in mind the kindnesses and politenesses Bell had rendered Cosette when first they met. Now I saw in Bell's eyes a mild scorn, and I saw disappointment that when Mark asked her out to dinner Cosette didn't get into a panic about what to wear, when to have her hair done, what to do about her face, and cry, oh, if she could only be a little bit younger!

You see, I think Cosette had given up the battle. Probably she had taken a good, hard, long look at herself in the glass and decided it was no use. *This man was too important for it to be any use.* Ivor Sitwell was one thing, the kind of man you had your face lifted for and dieted for and bought new clothes for, but only to get back into the running. Rimmon – well, what was he but what Bell called a snack-fuck, something to have between proper meals? There had been another man, I think, some pal of Admetus's, no more than a one-night stand. But Mark was the real thing and because he was the real thing it was no use. Better to have him as a friend, to have his respect, his delightful company, than make a guy of oneself, an over-scented, over-painted show, and thus earn his contempt.

'I am trying to teaching myself not to mind when the people in the restaurant take me for his mother,' she said to me. 'No, I'm doing better than that. I'm teaching myself to expect it and like it. I mean, I'd have loved to have a son like Mark. Imagine how different things would be for me now if I had a son like him.'

'You never liked it when I was taken for your daughter and he's ten or eleven years older than me.'

'I would like it now. I'm changing, I've got to. I'm going to grow old gracefully.'

The interesting thing was that she looked a lot nicer and a lot younger for not going in for all that make-up and rigid hairdressing. She wore her hair in a simple loose knot on the back of her head (the way Bell wears hers now), touched her face with a little soft colour, put on a plain, dark-green dress with the pearls that had been Douglas's last present to her. Handsome and dignified she looked and only a very unobservant person would have thought her old enough to be Mark's mother, unless she had mysteriously been reared in a society where girls get married at twelve.

Over-courteous in Admetus's way, obsequious and deferential, Mark never was. He had arranged to meet her at the restaurant, not call for her. And it was a little bistro in Queensway to which he was taking her, none of your *grande cuisine*. I didn't see her go or return. Bell and I were invited to Elsa's divorce 'thrash', the party she was giving to celebrate extricating herself from her French Catholic husband. Next morning, late because we had got home in the small hours, Mark was there in the drawing room with Cosette and Auntie, and he and Cosette, facing each other across the table, were engaged in animated conversation, their eyes fixed on each other's faces. I caught a sentence or two of it. Cosette was saying, 'But I don't know anything about Schoenberg,' and Mark rejoined, 'Neither do I – yet. We can learn. We can learn together.'

They – at any rate, Cosette – didn't seem too pleased to see Bell and me. Of course she put up a show of being pleased because she was like that, but I could tell. They went out soon after that, they were taking Auntie somewhere. It was Cosette's day for taking

Auntie for a drive and Mark had said he would come too. Auntie
went along obediently, in the rather zombie-like way she did most
things, just doing what she was told, but I fancied she looked
less bewildered. Mark was a person she could understand, not
curiously dressed or using words she had been taught it was a
crime to utter or smoking strange things or making discordant
music. And he talked to her, he didn't pretend she wasn't there.

I went out on to the balcony to watch them go, wondering if
Mark would drive the car, but he didn't, not that time at any rate.
He sat in the back.

'He must have stayed the night,' Bell said in the curious, unin-
flected tone she sometimes used.

'I'm certain he didn't.'

'Why not?'

'I just have a feeling he didn't. They would have been different,
Cosette would have been different.'

And it turned out the way I supposed. Bell asked Gary directly.
I thought it a strange thing to do, to ask him outright like that.
Gary never slept much, going to bed very late always and seldom
staying in bed much after seven. Mark had come in with Cosette
at eleven the previous evening, he said, stayed ten minutes, come
back at ten that morning. Gary had let him in himself.

'You sound like you're his wife's spies,' said Gary.

'He hasn't got a wife,' Bell said.

'Do you want to know if he kissed her good-night?'

'For Christ's sake!' I said, trying to put a stop to it. 'This is
Cosette we're talking about, *Cosette.*'

'So what?' he said, rather unexpectedly. 'The wine she drinks
is made of grapes.'

'Maybe, but he's not likely to drink the same wine, is he?'

Bell said slowly, 'I don't see why not, I really don't see why
not.'

'Cosette's well into her fifties. She doesn't expect it, she doesn't
dream of it.'

'I bet she *dreams* of it,' said Gary.

Mark was just a friend. How could it be otherwise? At least he
wasn't on the gravy train to Cadgeville. He took Cosette out to
meals or else he came to the House of Stairs when dinner was over.

Very occasionally, when all of us were taken out by Cosette, he would join us, but he behaved rather austerely at these dinner parties, drinking sparingly, eating cheaply. He didn't smoke, he didn't drink spirits. When he was present you could feel the lavish days were past, the days of green chartreuse and burnt banknotes.

I had got it into my head, on the strength of once having seen them together, that he and Bell were close. This seemed not to be true. It was plain, at any rate, that he didn't come to the house to see his sister. They took no more notice of each other than each did of Gary or the ballet dancers, less in fact, for Mark was always polite and pleasant to Cosette's friends. Bell was the only person I ever saw him apparently indifferent to. And he was more than indifferent to her, he was capable of ignoring her when she walked into the room. Sometimes I saw him look up, realize who it was that had come in, and look away again without a nod or a word. I don't know why, but somehow I thought this must be Bell's fault, this must be something Bell had done.

I asked him one day what she was like when she was a little girl. He smiled. 'I haven't the least idea.'

'You must have. You're her brother.'

In Cosette's presence, out of a compliment to Cosette supposedly, he often added unspecified years to his age. 'I'm so much older than Bell.' He made it sound as if the age gap was twenty rather than six and a half years. 'I was away at school.' It was plain he didn't want to talk about it.

That same day I looked up Henryson in the phone book. Mark was there at Brook Green, a Riverside number, but there was no Mrs Henryson in Harlesden. Why would there have been? I had never known Bell to phone her mother; no doubt she didn't have a phone. I was naïve, I was gullible. I believed in Bell, confusing frankness with honesty.

Her frankness has led her to talk to me about Silas and their life together. We have moved on. Not to Cosette or Mark, she reacts to their names like an animal when it hears a gun fired, but to herself and me.

'No, there weren't any women before you,' she said. 'There haven't been any since, come to that.'

'Am I hearing what I think I'm hearing?'

'I'm not a lesbian. Sometimes I've wished I was. There was a lot of that going on in prison.'

'Then why . . .?'

She said simply, 'Because you were.'

'Never, till you.'

Her dry laugh rattled in her throat. It is the kind of laugh that used to be called 'dirty', scathing, self-mocking.

'Something came over me,' she said, 'that night when I put the dress on. I thought you'd like it, and you did, didn't you?'

'Didn't *you*?'

'Oh, sure. I loved it, but it was never quite the real thing. Did you feel that?'

'No,' I said. 'It was the real thing for me. But I've heard other dabblers say what you say.'

'What do you mean, dabblers?'

'Queers trying it straight and straight people trying it queer.'

'Have I upset you, Lizzie?'

'You've given me a shock,' I said.

I couldn't look at her. I was wrong, wasn't I, about her having been as much in love with me as I with her? But this is the kind of thing which must often happen to certain people, finding out that a lover made love to them only to please them or to gain a particular end. It must happen to rich old women and rich old men, to ugly rich people. But I had been young and poor and some said good-looking . . .

'Were you ever in love with me?' It took me a good hour to work myself up to ask that question and when I asked it my voice sounded strange, hoarse and horribly anxious. 'I was in love with you. Were you with me?'

Something has softened her, the dreadful prison years supposedly. She takes pains not to hurt me too much. 'I don't know. I was very fond of you. I liked the sex. I liked the feeling of doing something – outrageous.'

Has she always been so grossly insensitive? Was she then, when we were together? She laid her hand on me. She touched my shoulder, my neck. I stopped myself jumping up, shrieking, the way Cosette said she would if any woman made an advance to her.

I just picked up the hand and threw it off, though not as fiercely as you would throw off an insect that fell on you out of a tree. I cast it away as Cosette once cast my hand off her arm.

'The last thing I want,' I said. 'I'm not sure what you're offering but I don't want any part of it. Not if you and I were the last people on earth and marooned somewhere.'

'That's all right then. I'm sure I don't. I don't mean you specially, not anyone, man or woman; it makes me shudder, the mere thought.'

As Mark's visits grew more frequent, as he came more to the house and he and Cosette went out more together, spending a lot of time in each other's company, so Bell and I grew apart. You must remember that I didn't know then what I know now, that she didn't love me, had never loved me, looked upon me – well, it is true, isn't it, it must be faced? – as a sort of perverse indulgence, a co-player in a naughty game. I thought she had loved me but that her love was passing, she was getting tired of me. Perhaps, anyway, that isn't much of an improvement on the truth. Never to have been loved – that is somehow more acceptable than being the kind of person a lover quickly tires of.

We talked less, too. The confiding stopped, the discussion of people in the house, the way they behaved, the things they said. It was Bell who stopped it. I would begin with a question as to why Gary had done such and such, what Cosette's brother Oliver had meant by some remark, and my answer would be a shrug or, 'Who cares?'

Cosette, rather late in the day, had bought a television set. Ostensibly, it was for Auntie. It wasn't in the drawing room, Cosette wouldn't have that, but in the front room on the ground floor, a place that had never before had any particular function except sometimes as a centre for musical or hallucinogenic rites. A sofa and chairs were set out in it and Cosette had bought a huge, gilt-framed mirror to hang on one wall. Bell spent a lot of time in there, watching television. It was as if the television was my victorious rival, drawing her away from me. She and Auntie, who had nothing else in common, who had scarcely spoken to each other, were now usually to be found down there in armchairs side by side, a sporadic, totally screen-focused conversation carried on between them.

'Shall I switch over to the other channel?'

'Yes, if you like. It's our serial tonight.'

Auntie was usually off to bed by ten. Bell stayed up watching until midnight or beyond, if there was any beyond. And I would lie in bed waiting for her, first hearing Cosette and Mark come in, Mark sometimes but by no means always coming up to the first floor for a drink or a last word with her, then the front door closing on him, then finally Bell's footsteps mounting the first flight and the second, but passing my door and going on up, up, up, to her room on the top.

My heart was sore. I had had my dreams and made absurd plans. Our affair, or whatever you liked to call it, couldn't of course go on, I knew that, but I had a romantic idea that a special bond would always be there, each of us as the years passed would be first with the other. And some ritual would come into being, we would for instance meet and make love once a year, we would always have a unique friendship, our secret closeness would enrich our lives and there would arise between us a special empathy so that, as separated twins are said to do, we would sense from a distance whenever the other was enjoying good fortune or in danger.

For this to happen there would have had to be something to alter things and wrench us apart. Cosette's moving, for instance, or illness afflicting me or Bell's mother needing her. Now I saw that there were other ways of parting a pair like us, evanescent, subtle things that took away the substance and left – nothing. For, as if we were true gays, we had always behaved with the utmost decorum in public. Homosexual couples invariably do, I have noticed, except in the society of others like themselves. When with straight people they never touch each other, exchange glances, or even sit side by side. So there were no changes for Bell and me to make in our social behaviour. We had never touched and caressed in the sight of Cosette and Auntie. Now we no longer did so by night, in private. I knew only that I had no human rival, for Bell hardly ever went out and never received or made phone calls. She watched television.

She said so little to me that spring and summer, whole weeks seemed to go by without a word from her, that I remember only one remark of any significance. We passed on the stairs. I was on my way to see my agent – to be told no one was interested in publishing my monograph on Henry James – and she had come up only from the hall where she had been to pick up the household's post from the front doormat. Bell had grown pale and sickly looking from never going out. The weather was warm, sultry, windless, but she preferred to be indoors, lying on her bed for hours on end up there, the dangerous window open to its fullest extent. And the dusty black she wore reminded me of the clothes of Middle Eastern women.

'I feel like escaping, but where would I go?'

I said, and immediately wished I hadn't, 'We could go away somewhere together. We could go for a holiday.'

She looked me hard in the eyes. 'I don't mean that at all.'

Sisters can be jealous of brothers – anyone can be jealous of anyone – and I thought it might be that she minded Mark's spending so much time with Cosette. Had Cosette separated them? Was that the event which had taken place since I first saw them together and had changed their relationship? I fancied Cosette might have taken a sister's place in Mark's life. His own sister had perhaps been cold, uninterested, no longer the comrade of earlier years, and Cosette had slipped into that role. Certainly there was no sign of her and Mark being anything to each other but friends. Mark, who after his first few visits seemed cast for Ivor Sitwell's part, had never stepped into it, but had rather retreated. And Cosette, who gave him at that same period so many languishing glances, who seemed set to fall deep into adoration, looked at him and spoke to him in the same tone she might use to Gary or Luis. The promise she had made, to teach herself that sexual love between them was impossible, to grow old gracefully, it appeared she was keeping. Her reward was his affection.

He liked her for herself. She was his dear, special friend. Or that was how it looked. Very likely, he was the son she had never had and she the sort of mother he would have liked to have. There are plenty who would see it in that light. Young men do have older women friends and go about with them in an apparently sexless relationship. Of course it is impossible to generalize and insensitive to try. They liked each other.

They went to concerts, presumably to learn about Schoenberg, as I had overheard Mark say they would. They went to the cinema. They took Auntie out for drives. Eating out as a way of life was becoming fashionable and they usually ate out together. Only sometimes would Cosette be assailed by guilt feelings that she was doing unfairly by the rest of us and then we would be gathered together into rather a formal dining-out group and shepherded off to the Marco Polo or even somewhere very grand like the Écu de France, on which occasions Mark would conspicuously not be present. It was very different from Wellgarth days and as different again from that early wild, decadent, chaotic time in the House of Stairs.

I remembered Cosette's dying Buddha story: 'It changes.'

Mark never stayed the night, though, not even in the spare room on the top floor next to Bell's. I was as sure as one can be of such a thing that he had never slept with Cosette, never even kissed her beyond putting his lips to her cheek. Had he even done that? Once he spoke of her to me. We were alone together, it was a rare event, and very short-lived. Bell had refused to go out, Gary was away somewhere, it was all too late for Auntie, but Mervyn was back, he and Mimi still together, though used to each other by now and as comfortable together as an old married couple. The two of them, Mark and Cosette and I were all dining out and Mervyn and Mimi were dancing. Cosette got up to go and pay the bill. It was a discreet way of doing this which she had learned, a way which made it seem as if there was no bill to be paid. Mark sat watching the dancers and I watched him. I have said he never cared what he wore, he was indifferent to clothes, but he was always decently dressed for the place he was in, and that night he was wearing grey flannel trousers and a jacket of some sort of loose-woven dark-blue stuff, far from new but not shabby either. Men were wearing their hair long then, but his was short by the standard of the time. He was very thin and this gave him a look of particular elegance. There is something sexually moving about a man's upper back when it is straight and the bones are barely covered with flesh. Mark had tremendously attractive shoulder blades. I was very aware of it at that moment as he leaned forward across the table, lifting his head. His hands were long and slender but not at all effeminate, the bones of the knuckles too prominent for that.

He turned his head and spoke to me.

'It seems so strange that all this time Cosette and I were both living in London and we never knew each other. It seems such a waste.'

'You can make up for it now,' I said, reflecting that it wasn't so long since Cosette had had a husband who I was sure wouldn't have welcomed Mark among the visitors to Garth Manor.

'We are making up for it.' He looked over his shoulder quickly. To try and find her in the crowd or to make sure she wasn't coming? Mark's eyes, the deep dark blue of lapis, had the clarity of water, but water that flows over a multitude of living things. 'I've never known anyone like her,' he said. 'She is the most wonderful person; she has everything.'

Except youth, I thought, and I thought he was going to say it. I thought he was going to say, with rue, that if only, if only, she had been a bit younger. He didn't. He pursued his theme.

'Every gift, every grace. It's rare to find a woman who's never bitchy. Cosette envies no one.' I would have taken issue with him there. She envied all the girls she met, only without vindictiveness. He made nonsense of my thoughts. 'Of course there's nothing she could be envious about.'

Cosette came back. I thought she looked tired and worn, the make-up she wore runnelled and smeared, her hair lank, and that red dress – the one she had been wearing when first she met him! But her face lit at the sight of Mark, lit as if there truly were a lamp of great brilliance inside her head and his smile had switched it on. He said, rather crossly for him, 'It's time you went home, you're tired. Come, let's go.'

'But, Mark, they're still dancing, and look, you can see they're enjoying themselves so much . . .'

She never called him darling. 'Darling' was for all the rest of us. But her face betrayed everything, the love in it at that moment was naked, stretching out its yearning arms. He said, 'They can either come now or get home by their own transport.'

She loved it, you could see that, she loved a man who would be masterful and put her wants first. Had anyone, even Douglas, done that before? But when we reached Archangel Place, Mervyn and Mimi naturally with us, willing to sacrifice any pleasure rather than pay a bus or tube fare, Mark came only as far as the hall where, in a curiously formal way, he placed Cosette in my charge, asking me with his usual simple courtesy please to see she went to bed now, that she had a good night's sleep. He would phone in the morning and see how she was.

He always did exactly what he said. If he said he would phone, he phoned. I happened to take the call, it was made a bit early for Cosette and she was still asleep. How, anyway, would he be cognisant of Cosette's retiring and rising habits? He seemed amused and strangely delighted – 'tickled to death' is the expression my father would have used – to hear she was still in bed. On no account must I wake her. Just tell her he had phoned to ask how she was.

'And give her your love?'

There was a pause. 'Whatever you think she'd like,' he said.

Cosette always listened to the radio serial he was in. He had quite a significant part in it and certainly could be heard at least three out of the five nights of the week it was on. She hadn't possessed a radio, but she bought one after she had known Mark for about a week. Alone, she would sit listening to his voice while Bell and Auntie stayed downstairs, preferring the television. I came into the room to hear him utter the last sentence of the episode. He had been in private conversation with the heroine and the words he had to speak struck me as immensely strange in the circumstances. They had a thrilling effect, and an embarrassing one too. It was disquieting, it was shiver-provoking, to hear Mark's voice say, 'You must know I love you. I've been in love with you for ten years, ever since we first met . . .'

This was the signal for music to swell, to break like a wave on a beach. There would be no more till tomorrow when that music would begin afresh. Cosette switched off her transistor and there was a deep silence, until into that silence, dully fragmenting it, came the thud-thud and mutter of Auntie's television from below.

You have to understand that Cosette didn't talk about herself, she wasn't always airing her feelings. The concerns of others seemed more important to her, formed more of the substance of her converse. I have told you of that vague mysterious smile she put on when asked questions she wasn't happy to answer. She was an adept at shifting interest from herself on to others. I believe she genuinely thought that in her sphere and at her age she was no longer an object to provoke interest or excite curiosity. But that evening, at that moment, when we had heard Mark's voice and she had abruptly cut the music off, I had a premonition confiding was to begin and revelations to be made.

Suddenly she said, her voice fierce – it was as if she clutched at me, though she hadn't moved and we were yards apart – 'I'm so much in love with him I think it will kill me.'

'Mark?' I said stupidly. Yet, was it so stupid? I had convinced myself by then that they were friends, the best of friends but only friends, that the desire for no more than friendship was hers as well as his.

'I didn't know what it was,' she said. 'I never had it for anyone before. No, not for Douglas, never, never, I didn't dream of it. Don't look like that, Lizzie. Why are you looking at me like that?'

'I'm sorry,' I said.

'I think of him day and night. When he's not with me I'm thinking of him and talking to him. I have these long imaginary conversations with him in my head. You needn't look like that, darling, so pitiful. You don't have to be sympathetic. It doesn't make me unhappy, it makes me happy. I've never been so happy in my life. Is there anything so blissful as being in love? I couldn't stand not being now, I should die.'

I didn't remind her that five minutes before she had said that being in love would kill her. Instead, prudently, I advised caution.

'You'd better go a bit easy.'

'Why? Why should I?'

I hesitated. I was remembering what Stendhal says somewhere about wishing he were in love, his longing for the bliss of that condition. Though she might be the ugliest kitchenmaid in Paris, that would be of no account provided he was in love with her and she returned his passion. I said, with care, 'Perhaps being in love isn't all that great if it isn't returned – I mean if the other person doesn't feel the same.'

Her reply shook me; I seemed to feel the floor beneath my feet quiver. Cosette was soft-voiced, but she almost shouted, 'Who says he doesn't feel the same?'

Her beseeching face, turned up to me, her hands curiously stretched out to supplicate, induced in me a chill and a nausea that were quite physical. 'Cosette . . .?'

'Cosette what?' she said. 'Is there any reason why I shouldn't be loved? Aren't I lovable?' Her face wasn't haggard then, it was young. It was as if, briefly, a young Cosette had crept out of the skin of age.

'I don't want you to be unhappy,' I said, the words wrenched out of me.

Her voice trembled. 'If I were a man and Mark a woman no one would think anything of me being fifteen years older.' Poor Cosette had entered her phase of reducing when she talked about it the span of years between them. After the same fashion she had taken to pointing out the silver streak in Mark's hair. 'Why does it matter so much the other way round? We live longer than men. Why do we have to be old for so much longer?'

In the years since then things have happened to redress that balance. Elsa married a man eleven years her junior and everyone said how lucky he was. I said to Cosette, lamely I'm afraid, 'Everyone can see how fond he is of you.'

'How I hate that word!'

I could think of nothing more to say, so I went over to her and hugged her. We held each other in a strong warm embrace which I can easily think myself back into now and feel again, which I can remember more readily than any of those love passages with Bell.

15

We have had two visitors, Bell and I. It is two weeks since she came to stay and in all that time, until yesterday, no one has come to the house. We have been alone together and every morning I have gone into my room and tried to write – that is, I have tried to write the novel I am supposed to be working on, a tale of international intrigue and sexual adventure in Vienna and Mauritius. I haven't written a word of it. All I write is this account or record or whatever you care to call it. What Bell does while I am in here I don't really know, but I hear her go out, so I suppose she walks, ranging the west London streets. Never since she has been here have I heard a word scorning suburbs or about my house being too far west for her.

But yesterday my father came. Twice a year he comes to London for a medical check-up. He has a pacemaker to regulate his heart and although he could easily and far more conveniently go for his examinations to a heart specialist in some hospital on the south coast, he has an idea in his head that everything in London must be better. Especially in Hammersmith, where the hospital enjoys a glamorous reputation in matters of the heart. He is spry and energetic for his seventy-three years, but London and its crowds confuse him and I always go to meet him at Waterloo and take him to the hospital. After his check-up he comes back here to stay the night.

It may seem strange, when Bell and I were so close, that he should know nothing of her, not even know until yesterday that she exists. But I wasn't called upon to give evidence at her trial, there were other witnesses to do that. And although he must have heard of her, for, briefly, every newspaper reader and television viewer heard of her, there is no reason for him to connect the sombre and austere woman in her mourning clothes, whom I introduce to him simply as Bell, with Christine Sanger. Did I tell you Christabel was another of her inventions, that instead of Christabel she was really Christine, that Ivor Sitwell in giving her that name was unwittingly correct? I am telling you now.

My father has changed. His tragedy he has put far behind him. If he knows that there is still time for his daughter to go the way his wife went, he never gives a sign of it. Sometimes he even talks of the distant future, *my* distant future, and with satisfaction of the good fortune that awaits me. For although he has, and has had for years, a woman friend a few years younger than himself, a widow living on the same senior citizens' estate, in the same street three bungalows away, he declines to marry again because thereby he would deprive me of my rightful inheritance. His bungalow and the few thousand pounds he has in unit trusts are destined for me, and it is in vain that I have told him over and over that I don't need them, that they are his to dispose of as he pleases, to leave to a wife if he likes.

He reverted to this subject, as he always does whenever we meet, while we were all watching television, during a commercial break. A banking advertisement set him off.

'It's all in my will, it's all set down in black and white,' he said. 'I've done that so that you don't have the fuss and bother of applying for Letters of Administration.'

'That's a long time off,' I said.

'Easy to say at your age and when you don't know what illness is. There's a chap I've seen at that hospital every time I've been there for the past three years, he always had his appointments the same day as me, a curious coincidence, really. Well, he was missing today and why do you think? He'd dropped down dead a month ago on his way on holiday to Ibiza, fell over and died in the duty-free shop.'

We turned our eyes back to the screen, Bell rather more slowly than my father and I. She had been watching him in wonder. I supposed it was his refusal to recognize my continued danger that she found astonishing, but perhaps it wasn't that, perhaps what he said recalled to her the evening she asked me about Cosette's will. I didn't inquire. When he went off to bed and for half an hour or so we were alone, I didn't ask her. I am not yet prepared to force a discussion of Cosette or of Mark. They must wait a little longer.

This morning I took him to catch his train. As I walked back along the street where I live I saw ahead of me a taxi stopped outside my house and a woman getting out of it. I didn't recognize her. She was a big dark woman, tall and heavily built, with one of those figures in which the stomach has become very prominent, jutting out nearly as protuberantly as the bosom. Her hair had been dyed raven black and dressed in such a bouffant way that it would have given the impression from a distance that she was wearing a wide-brimmed black silk hat. She paid the taxi-driver and turned to face my house, looking up at the roof and down to the little front garden in an appraising way as someone might who was surveying the place with a view to buying it. She opened the gate and began to walk up the path. My footstep behind her made her turn. I may have changed as much as she has, but she had the advantage over me, she knew that living in this house I was more likely to be Elizabeth Vetch than not. The voice I recognized, when she had spoken my name.

'Felicity,' I said.

I was at the typewriter in my working room in the House of Stairs, listening to Bell's movements above me, listening with pain to the closing of the door and the creak of the 104th stair, for I knew that what would happen was what always happened now. She would pass my door without slowing her pace. It was late summer, a weary dusty time, the London air stale and still. Below, in the grey garden, when I went as I now did to the window, I could see the top of Auntie's white chrysanthemum head in one of the deckchairs and, resting lightly back against the canvas of the other, Cosette's freshly blonded chignon on to which a silver eucalyptus leaf had fallen, seemingly pinned there like a hair ornament.

But this time, instead of passing my door, Bell's footsteps slowed. She must have stood there for a long moment – doing, thinking, what? Wondering perhaps about the enormity of what she planned to ask? I held my breath. Bell knocked on the door, causing me pain, more pain than I want to write about. She had never before knocked at the door of any room I was in. My whispered 'Come in' was so low I had to repeat it.

She entered the room without any awkwardness, unless to pause just inside the door and light a cigarette is to be awkward. If she felt she owed me some explanation for repudiating me, she never showed it. The paperback books on the desk and on the table were not those that had been there last time she was in my room. It was a long time since she had last been there. She picked up *What Maisie Knew*, turned it over, looking at it in the way one might look for an assay mark on a piece of silver. At the window she glanced downwards, no doubt to check that Cosette was still far away, still well out of earshot.

'I suppose,' she said brusquely, 'Cosette will leave everything she's got to you.'

'*What?*'

'In her will, I mean. You must know what I mean. When she dies this house and all her money will go to you.'

'I *don't* know. I don't suppose she has made a will. Why should she? She's not going to die.'

Bell went once more to the window. The casement was opened a little waỹ. She closed it, stood there with her back to the window. 'She's got cancer, hasn't she?'

'What gave you that idea?'

She didn't say anything and her silence spoke terrible things to me. I jumped up out of my chair.

'Who told you? Are you keeping something from me?'

'I don't know anything you don't. I thought they found cancer when they scraped her out or whatever they did.'

'They didn't find anything, she was perfectly clear. She's been for a check-up since and she was fine. She'll probably live for thirty years, she'll live longer than I will.'

Bell said slowly, as if she were thinking deeply and enormously, laying out options and rejecting them, biding her time, 'I see,' and again, 'I see.'

From that moment I date my anger with her, my distaste for her, my near-hatred of her. All those things are quite compatible with love, aren't they? I was angry with her because what she had said seemed to confirm my fears that she disliked Cosette, that

Cosette's generosity inspired no gratitude in her, that living on Cosette's bounty, rent-free, with heat and food freely provided, had provoked no affection, aroused no warmth. I said, speaking to her as I never had before, 'I was working and I'd like to get on. So would you mind going?'

After she had gone I couldn't work. I repeated to myself, carefully, word for word, all the things she had said, and though I read into them a suggestion that she expected and indeed wanted me to inherit Cosette's property, my anger wasn't cooled or my hurt less painful. I only saw her as inquiring in order to make sure of the future good fortune of her 'friend', under whose protective umbrella she meant to shelter. With luck, by playing her cards right, even when Cosette was dead a home here would be secured for her, an even freer and more spacious home in fact, with me as owner. I felt I was being used, perhaps had always been used to this end. Was it possible that Bell had got to know me, had then engineered our relationship into what it had been for those few months, solely because she saw me as a rich woman's adopted child and necessary heir?

Of course I was quite wrong. I was even flattering myself; I was attributing to myself an importance I didn't have. Bell's motive for asking those questions was outside the bounds of my imaginings. I heard her go down the stairs, down all the stairs to the bottom, and then I heard the front door close after her rather harder than usual. She had nearly slammed it. I used to wonder where she went, perhaps only to walk, or to visit those corners of London where the beautiful things are displayed, to range Kensington Church Street and the King's Road and Camden Passage. She was back again by six, watching television with Auntie, while Cosette, on the floor above, listened to Mark in his serial, the character he played newly married and just returned from his honeymoon.

That evening, an hour or two later, Auntie died.

I wasn't there, I wasn't in the house, my bitter anger against Bell having sent me to the telephone to ring up a man I had met a week before at a party, a man who had phoned since and left a message for me with Mervyn. His name was Robin Cairns and three years later I was to marry him, but I foresaw nothing like that then. He was just a useful person to keep thoughts of Bell away.

Auntie sat in the armchair next to Bell's and they watched an episode in a serial about policemen in San Francisco. At some point during the car chase up and down those switchback hills, while guns were firing and tyres bursting, rictus-faced men doubling up to clutch gunshot wounds, Auntie lay back against the cushion and died. It was a death not dissimilar to Douglas's. If we might all die so gently, so quietly! Bell saw her glasses fall off her nose, but since they were attached to a chain round her neck, they didn't fall far. She never took any particular notice of Auntie, and though I suppose she answered if Auntie spoke to her, it seemed she was herself never the instigator of an exchange, it was never she who was the first to remark on a programme or an actor.

Mark came at nine, but he didn't look into the room where Bell was, though the door was always left ajar. Mimi let him into the house and he went straight through the dining room into the garden to find Cosette. It was darker than dusk, for by then it was September, but it had been very hot that day, hot as July, and the heat still hung in the air. There must have been a strong pungent smell of eucalyptus out there, as always on warm nights. I know there was a moon, for Robin and I saw it and watched it rise, a smoky red harvest moon, unusually large and glowing, as we walked along Kensington Gore.

It was Mimi who told me what happened. She preceded Mark into the garden and went back to the corner where she had been lying beside Mervyn on a blanket spread out on the paving stones. They had been smoking, of all things, locust beans. Mervyn had heard that kids in Philadelphia hallucinate on them and had got someone to bring a bagful back from a trip to the United States. Like Rimmon, those two would smoke or chew anything they thought capable of changing their consciousness. They had even tried the eucalyptus leaves, though to no effect. Mimi saw Mark go up to Cosette and kiss her cheek, sit down in the chair facing hers across the white-painted iron table and heard him say something to her about the stars which were peculiarly visible that evening, bright punctures of light in the dark blue sky which often, in London, seems to cover and conceal them. Some constellation hung brilliantly above them and they were both look-ing up at it, their chairs pushed close together, their shoulders touching, Mark pointing with one lightly extended forefinger, when Bell came out into the garden.

She came across the paved area quickly, though not running, and went up to Cosette. I am sure there was no deliberate cruelty in the way she behaved. It was only thoughtlessness, only insensi-tivity. She had no feeling for Auntie and, on account of her eighty years and her reserve, scarcely considered her a human being. And I, perhaps wrongly, had once passed on to her my theory about Cosette's only having her there to seem young in contrast to Auntie's age. So she stood in front of Cosette and said, 'Auntie just died. She's dead.'

Bell, of course, was familiar with death. She had seen death of more frightening sorts, the death of Silas and that other death I haven't yet told you of, though I shall, I shall. Auntie's was a quiet affair compared to those, all in the day's work, something to be communicated much as one might retail a somewhat unexpected item from the television news.

Cosette gave a cry and put up her hand to cover her mouth. Mark turned on Bell and said roughly, 'What do you mean?'

'I just told you, Auntie's dead. She lay back and died while we were watching TV.'

'Are you absolutely unfeeling, coming out here and telling her like that?'

Mimi said Bell didn't care for this. It made her wince. She stepped back, frowning, holding her hands up to her head. I could imagine her doing that, I could see that gesture of hers, as if her mass of fair hair were a wig and she was holding it on in a high wind. Cosette, silent, turned her face to Mark. They had both stood up. Mimi didn't expect him to do what he did. She too had accepted he and Cosette were friends only, a son for a mother who had never had one, a mother for a son whose own was inadequate. Mark took her in his arms and held her and she put her arms round his neck and held him. They stood there very close, embracing for comfort, for solace, and Bell watched them.

When I came in about two hours later the doctor had been and gone, had certified Auntie truly dead. A massive stroke had killed her. He and Mark moved her and laid her body on the sofa lest rigor should set in before the undertaker came in the morning. The sofa was rather less than five feet long, but it was more than big enough to accommodate Auntie's small, shrunken body. I found Cosette desolate, not crying, not giving way to any transports of grief, but shattered with sadness, already shadowed by the guilt that was soon to oppress her. She had nothing to be guilty about. If Auntie had been a mother to her these past few years, she had been a good daughter. It was all of us who had neglected Auntie, treating her like a bit of furniture, who should have felt guilt, and of course none of us did. And for some reason, with very misplaced pity, Cosette was worried about Bell.

'Poor girl,' she said to me, 'I wouldn't have had that happen for the world. Imagine what it must have been for her, finding Auntie dead. I should have been there, I shouldn't have left her on her own.'

Useless to tell Cosette that for one thing she wasn't on her own and for another that Auntie adored television, that only exhaustion could drag her from it. I did tell her that the year during which Auntie had had television had probably been the happiest of her latter life, only to have Cosette retort that this made things worse, that she should have given Auntie television five years before.

Mark came in and told Cosette she ought to go to bed, there was nothing more to be done till the morning. She should go to bed and try to sleep and he would come back first thing in the morning. Cosette turned to him and said with a kind of artlessness, as innocent as a small girl, 'You're not going, are you? I somehow counted on your staying.'

It was then that I noticed, in spite of the shock and sorrow which had left tearmarks on her cheeks, how much younger she had begun to look. I mean, how much younger than, say, a year before. And I remembered what she had told me about loving Mark, about being in love, being killed with love, and I thought, killing or no, it's done this for her, it has taken the lines away and the shadows, it has made her eyes shine and her face glow, it's put a spark of youth back, I don't know how.

'Of course I'll stay if you want me to,' he said.

It stabbed me, the shock of it. I thought he meant with her, in her room, in her bed, and I didn't want that, I was afraid of it. It was important to me to go with them up the stairs to Cosette's door, to observe them. Bell, someone had told me, Mimi probably, had long ago gone to her room. Even she, Mervyn remarked, wouldn't keep on watching television over Auntie's dead body. I was hurt by that, struck by the unfairness of it, for he in that household had been no shining example of altruism.

Cosette took Mark's arm up the stairs. Not like an old woman might, though, more like a young girl who has received some injury. It astonished me that he wasn't even sure which of the doors was the one to her bedroom. She opened the door and stood there, said suddenly, 'I've this stupid feeling we shouldn't be leaving her alone down there.'

'It is stupid,' Mark said, but very gently.

'I'm sorry to be such a fool. Don't look so concerned for me, I shall sleep. I'm only sorry to say I shall sleep soundly.'

She drew herself away from him, took a step into the room, still holding his hand. Their hands clasped more tightly for a brief moment, then each let the other go free. I knew it was going to be all right. Mark said to me, 'There's a room I can sleep in at the top, isn't there?'

I nodded. 'Next to Bell. The right-hand door, Bell's is on the left.'

He didn't kiss Cosette. They looked at each other with a strange grave regard and he said, 'Good-night, Cosette.'

Her voice was very quiet. 'Good-night, dear Mark.'

It was a great relief to me, all of it. I watched him mount the next flight and pass out of sight on his way to the top. I knew it was all right then. Cosette slept in her own room and Bell in hers and Mark next door to her in the room that had been Felicity's and everything was as it should be. Or so I thought then.

I lay in bed having fantasies about their future, Mark and Cosette's. She would always have a special place in his life, a unique role. One day, of course, he would marry and she would suffer bitter pangs, but she would adjust, she would acclimatize, ultimately coming to love his wife too. I imagined her godmother to his children, an honoured matriarch in his home. Not to make myself out too great a fool, in fairness to myself, I must say here that I also imagined retailing this to Bell and Bell saying, in typical utterance, that it was all a load of shit.

Next day the undertaker did come and Perpetua came, commiserating with Cosette as perhaps no one else could, and something else bad happened. Mark lost his job. Or, rather, they decided to write out the character he played in the radio serial, to kill him off by the end of the following week. According to Bell – Mark never went into details himself – the actress who had the role of his wife had landed a Hollywood contract and the producer had decided the best way to handle this was to have them both die in an air crash.

Cosette listened to the last instalment he would ever be in. We listened to it together. With not too much verisimilitude the script had had the character Mark played offered a wonderful job (too wonderful for him to dream of refusing) in the Far East. In this final episode for Mark, his brother-in-law and parents-in-law were seeing him and his bride of two months off at Heathrow. The next day's would have the news of the air disaster brought to these relatives. We decided not to listen to it.

'Mark won't have any trouble in finding work,' Cosette said to me after she had switched the set off. 'He's such a marvellous actor.'

It might have been true, but from her it was no reliable testimonial. Everyone close to Cosette, whatever it might be that they did for a living, in her eyes did it to perfection. And, in some ways, no one had ever been as close as Mark, in the way of passionate love, that is. I agreed with her, I said I hoped so, but I wasn't really confident.

'He'll move on to television,' said Cosette. 'He's ready for that now, it's a step he ought to take.' She spoke as if Mark had never made his unsuccessful foray into this medium and as if a move now was entirely a matter for his own decision.

I expected her to have an enormous showy funeral for Auntie, partly as a remedy for guilt. But one of the interesting things about Cosette was her way of behaving unexpectedly. She would act in character for a long while, until you thought you knew her thoroughly, could predict any move she might make, then perform the startling. It was Bell who once pointed this out to me, during the conversations we had used to have about people and their ways. So, instead of announcing to the household that the funeral service would be at such and such a church and the cremation wherever it might be and the post-funerary food and drink at this or that particular hotel, Cosette only gave the necessary information quietly to me, and no doubt also to Mark. There was no fussing about what to wear, no lavish ordering of flowers. Cosette surprised me further when she said, 'Would you very much mind not saying anything to Bell?'

'You mean that the funeral is today?'

'I don't suppose she would want to come but I'd – well, I'd prefer her not to be there.'

I might have said there was no fear of that, but I didn't. It was the nearest Cosette ever got to intimating not so much that she didn't like Bell or found her uncongenial but rather that things about Bell deeply upset her. I promised not to mention it, but I think that by that time, a week or so after she had found Auntie dead, Bell had forgotten she had ever existed. Cosette and Mark and I went to the crematorium together. Her small cross of white chrysanthemums – a coincidence it must have been, their resemblance to Auntie's pretty white curly hair – lay alone on the coffin. There were no other flowers and no one else there – who else could there have been?

'The whole Archangel Place circus,' Mark whispered to me when I put this question to him. 'Very sensibly, Cosette didn't tell them.'

A bit of a nerve, I thought he had. Who was he to talk in that patronizing fashion about her friends when he was no more than one of them? Mark out of work had subtly shifted his position in my estimation. One of the reasons I had looked on him in a different light from the 'circus' was the fact that he worked, he supported himself. As the weeks passed and he found no work, refusing, as I understood from Cosette who was hotly indignant at the suggestion he should, any jobs outside acting, I found myself watching him with suspicion. I was waiting for him to borrow money from her (though I might not have known if he did), instigate once more the big dining-out parties which would include himself and for which as a matter of course Cosette paid, move in, and of course, at last, do the inevitable at this stage and sleep with her.

That autumn Cosette suddenly became far richer than before.

I haven't said much about Cosette's income, her fortune, rather giving the impression perhaps that she just possessed a lot of money. But it wasn't quite like that. Douglas had left all kinds of assets, including defunct companies which still however had stock exchange quotations, and a certain amount of apparently undesirable real estate. By that I mean it was in the form of land in outer suburbs with derelict industrial buildings on it, that sort of thing. One of these companies had already been bought out, the purchaser being in need of the stock exchange quotation, and paying something in the region of a halfpenny a share. That was just before decimal coinage came in at the beginning of 1971. Of course that didn't bring Cosette in much money, but the piece of land she owned did. She had forgotten she owned it, these few acres somewhere on the edge of south London. A firm of accountants administered everything for her and they were pleased to tell her that an enormous offer had been made for this land by a garage and petrol-station chain. A new road was going through and Cosette's old industrial site would abut on to it.

The precise figure I never knew. Perhaps Cosette didn't know it herself. It wasn't in her nature to be discreet and she broadcast the news of this 'windfall' as she called it to all the visitors to the house.

'Hundreds of thousands of pounds,' was the nearest she got to exactitude. 'It will make me a real millionairess.'

Bell was there to hear it and so was Mark – inevitably. I looked at her, expecting to meet eyes turned to meet mine as she calculated the benefits of staying friends with me, but she wasn't looking in my direction. She was looking at Cosette. It struck me then that, for one who prided herself on her powers of observation, she had made a curious mistake in supposing anyone who looked like Cosette to be suffering from cancer. For unhappy on one level as Cosette might be, guilty that is and really sorrowing for Auntie, missing her as one might miss a mother, on another level she was quite obviously rapturously happy and her happiness made her beautiful. People tend to eat less when they are in love and Cosette had got slimmer without effort. Her skin glowed, her hair shone. I don't suppose it's really possible for happiness to tighten up the muscles of the face, but that was the way it looked. I am sure Mark never went shopping for clothes with her, but since knowing him her dress sense had improved. It was a surprise to me what good legs she had, but I had never before seen her wear very fine denier stockings and plain high-heeled shoes. She had bought some simple dresses in silk or fine wool with which she had taken to wearing that jewellery that had been the envy of Elsa and me. She had become elegant – a word no one would have thought in the past of applying to Cosette. But of those who were assembled in the House of Stairs I alone remembered the stout, sturdy woman whose iron-grey hair matched her tailored suits.

Bell, who had been watching Cosette in silence while Mervyn made some hopeful remark about going out to celebrate, now got up, pushed her fingers through her tangled, tendrilled, bird's-nest hair, and announced that she would be going to Felicity's for the holiday, she would be going next day. And Cosette, as if to neutralize this cold tone with an extra warmth in her own voice, said, 'Oh, darling, we *shall* miss you. It has become quite a regular thing for you, going there for Christmas, hasn't it?'

Bell looked at her, lifting first her eyebrows, then her shoulders, her expression remote. As if someone walked over her grave? Or as if she had a strange prevision this would be the last time?

It wasn't, anyway, to invite either or both of us for Christmas, that Felicity came to visit me this morning. Even for her July would have been a little early. And Bell she will never want again, whatever her feelings about me may be. She was astonished to see Bell, so surprised that she actually jumped at the sight of her, recognizing her at once, with no difficulty. Before going into my living room, where I supposed rightly that Bell was, I tried to whisper a warning, to utter simply the three words that would be enough, 'Bell is there!' but Felicity, who has become far more overbearing and dictatorial, gave me no chance, walking rapidly ahead of me and remarking loudly about how sweet these little houses could be made, how delectable mine was, what wonders could be done with these former artisans' cottages. For Bell there was no escape, the artisan's means not having stretched to two exits from the living room.

Being on what Henry James calls almost irreconcilable terms with the printed page, Bell was watching television, some abysmal late-morning offering. The little cat lay in her lap, watching the big one who sprawled on top of the set. Or possibly watching the lion on the screen that slowly stalked a wildebeest. Bell still has that enviable poise. No jumping for her, no attempt at rising even. She looked at Felicity in a way that made me doubt for a moment if she knew who this was.

'My God,' said Felicity. 'Surprise, surprise.' How did I know, even then, that whatever it cost her, she wasn't going to utter Bell's name?

'Why?' Bell said. 'I talked to you on the phone. You knew I wanted to find Elizabeth.'

'Oh, true, true.' Felicity gave an unpleasant little laugh, a laugh I couldn't remember from the old days. 'When I said "surprise" I meant I was surprised on Elizabeth's behalf, not yours.' It was the kind of silky rudeness Cosette used to hate so much and it is from her I have derived my hatred of it. Felicity sat down, her skirt riding up, showing a lot of plump leg and black stocking top. It is horrible, for she isn't in the least like Cosette, never has been, but the way she dresses, showily and unsuitably, *coyly*, reminds me of Cosette's early efforts, between the departure from Wellgarth Avenue and the coming of Mark. 'I'm having lunch with a friend in Barnes,' she said to me. 'The taxi almost had to pass your door, so I thought, why not? I'll never get to see her if I wait for her to phone.'

A strange route for a taxi going from Glebe Place to Barnes to take. I didn't say so though. I was relieved she wouldn't expect to lunch here. 'I knew I'd catch you because you'd be doing your writing at this hour.' It was said with a fine, artless regard for the writer's self-imposed disciplines.

'You were wrong, weren't you?' said Bell, her first contribution, and a hard cold one. 'About her writing, I mean, not about you catching her.'

I explained about my father. It was something to say. I didn't know what to say with the two of them there, Bell seemingly so despairing of her life that she didn't care what she said, consequences being of no account to her, Felicity revengeful and disapproving of Bell's very existence. I was afraid Felicity would say something about Cosette, it seemed so obvious that she must, though I doubted if she would go so far as to refer to Mark. And now I noticed for the first time that she was carrying, along with her large black patent leather handbag and a pair of absurd white gloves, the early edition of the evening paper, the *Standard* which had been on the streets a couple of hours. I had already glanced at it while at the station, at the lead story which is that of the murder by a child of a child. With a dreadful feeling of heart-sinking I saw Felicity lay her handbag on the table, place her gloves beside it, so that this newspaper, though still folded, lay alone on her unattractively bulbous lap, the large bold print of two words only of the headline exposed, but the two words of greatest significance: 'child' and 'killed'.

Bell perhaps also saw it. I don't know if she did. Felicity said, 'Do you think we could possibly have the television off?'

Carrying the little cat, pendulous from her forearm as a muff might be, Bell got up and made the most offensive response to this request there is, not excluding refusing it. She turned the sound down to a low murmur. Felicity was unfolding her paper, I don't really know why, I can hardly imagine what she intended to say or do. To read that story? To ask Bell in her didactic way (teaching always, reverting always to the vocation she had missed) what comments she had on it? Listing, for I am sure she still lives in a world of quizzes, a catalogue of mini-monsters, adolescent and sub-teen assassins?

But Bell forestalled her. Still standing, still with the cat draped over her arm as if boneless, a stretchy rubber sling sheathed in sable fur, Bell said, 'It looks to me as if you've come a long way since you were sponging on Cosette and that ponce with the beard was screwing your brains out.'

I was more shocked to hear her speak Cosette's name than by the actual content of what she said. She had got back into the dangerous country, she had taken some terrible plunge, was swimming the river.

You could see it in her face, too, in the width of her eyes, the recoil, as if someone else had spoken those words. Felicity, of course, looked terribly offended. But she didn't jump up and leave the house in dudgeon. I think people very seldom behave quite like that. They like to have options left to them. In fact, she managed a breathy deprecating laugh.

'Sponging!' she said. 'Oh, dear, what a word! As if people, some of them not too far from here, didn't sponge on me year after year. Inevitably, that's your lot if you happen to be rather better off than the run of the mill.'

She got up then, taking care to display the entire front page of the paper and the headline: *Tyneside Victim Killed by Child, 10.* Then she dropped the paper on the seat of her chair. 'Oh, no, you keep it,' she said sweetly when I reminded her. I used rather to like Felicity, her enthusiams, her rebellions, her intensity, her passions. All that seems to be gone now. No doubt it was necessary, if she was going to live with Esmond at Thornham and have a modicum of contentment, to ditch all that. Perhaps it was a case of ditching it or going mad. Who knows? I saw her out and we made cool, careful farewells, with of course no added riders of meeting again.

I was afraid to go back in there, I was really afraid. But you can hardly avoid going into your own living room for the rest of your life. I braced myself, opened the door. The newspaper was on the floor by Bell's chair. The little cat sat on one edge of it washing his face. Bell had her head in her hands, the fingers plunged into her grey, wiry, coarse hair. I didn't know what to do. So I sat down and waited and said nothing and thought of the peaceful, quiet, reasonably industrious, life I had been leading before she came out of prison and I found her. Presently she took her hands down and looked at me and said in quite a normal, ordinary voice, 'Am I a psychopath? I suppose I must be, they all said I was. But I don't feel like that, I just feel like anyone else.' What she had said must have struck her as absurd or shallow, for she corrected herself. 'Or I think I do.'

16

Since Bell has been here I have got into the habit of looking at people and wondering which of them, if any, are like her. I mean, like her in that they have killed someone and been sent to prison for it, served their sentences and come out again. It is a new phenomenon. Murderers used to be hanged.

Now they are set free and come back to live among us. Or to exist. I look at people and I wonder. Think of the number of murders we read are committed each year. Give it ten years – Bell was exceptionally long incarcerated and that for a particular reason – and their perpetrators (as the police say) are out again, ordinary people looking like everyone else, having ordinary jobs, perhaps living next door. But that woman I find myself sitting opposite in the tube, she may have shot her lover. That man with his dark scowl, arms folded across a thickly muscled chest, leaning against a wall on a street corner, may have knifed someone in a street brawl. How many have smothered the baby in its cradle or helped the elderly encumbrance on its way? People like me and Felicity and Elsa know them and go on knowing them and learn to adjust. Yet you would think murder the one act no one could adjust to, no one could make allowances for.

She had asked me if I thought she was a psychopath – well, she had asked the question, of the air perhaps, or of God. I could only shake my head and say I didn't know. I have always understood psychopaths to enjoy tormenting animals. Having uttered her question and made her half-despairing remarks, Bell turned away from me and coaxed the little cat back to her. It jumped on to her lap and she began stroking it in the way it likes, long hard movements of the hands, strong enough to push it to a crouching position. Then, as it folded itself up and curled into the thick black bunches of her skirt, she let her hands rest with the softest and most caring of movements on its sleek back. I would never have associated tenderness with Bell. Sensuousness, passion, a kind of tragic grandeur, all those, but not tenderness. Yet she is tender with my cats, as wondering and appreciative and absorbed as some women are with babies.

'I was never with animals before,' she said, as if reading what I was thinking. 'I didn't know I liked them.'

'Admetus had a cat,' I said, 'with cat fleas,' and I remembered Mark, and Cosette's anxious witticism about the 'entrechat'. 'There were dogs at Thornham.'

'Big and loud and domineering like their bitch of an owner. She would have invited you down there if I hadn't been here.'

'I wouldn't have gone,' I said, and, 'What was it like that – that last Christmas?'

We used to talk of people, she and I, why someone said that at just that moment, why someone else did that particular thing, what their motive was, and wasn't it all strange? I see little sign that this still interests her. People have been too much for her and now she likes animals better.

'Just the same, only without the quiz,' she said. 'The same as the year before. It always *was* the same. I don't know why I went.'

'Don't you?'

She looked at me with a sort of cold stubbornness. Why should I talk if I don't want to, she may have been thinking, why should I explain? 'You went so that you shouldn't see those two together,' I said, 'so that you wouldn't be there when *it* happened.'

'You're as bad as me,' she jeered at me. 'You'll no more say their names than I will. Only I will, I will. Mark and Cosette – there!'

'All right,' I said. 'You needn't shout.'

'When *it* happened – you're like some mealy-mouthed old woman, like *her* auntie. Why don't you say what you mean, that I didn't want to be there the first time he fucked her? As if I cared. I only wanted him to get on with it. Christ, he was so slow, like some fellow in those old-time books you read. The truth is I thought he'd get on faster if I wasn't there.'

'It made no difference whether you were there or not.'

213

She shrugged. 'It doesn't hurt any more,' she said. 'None of it does, nothing does.'

'I want to know something. If nothing hurts you I can ask it.'

She looked at me, smiling now. 'Ask what you want. I don't have to answer.'

'Did you,' I said, choosing words with care, 'mean to kill Cosette? I mean, were you planning it even at that early stage?'

'I got it into my head she'd die naturally.'

'But when you knew she wouldn't, were you planning it then?'

It was so open, her response, a frank scoffing. 'Planning it? Making a sort of plot? You know I don't do that.'

'Oh, Bell,' I said. 'What was all your time at the House of Stairs but a plot?'

'I mean plan to kill someone. I do that' – she spoke quite proudly as if talking of some arduously acquired special skill – 'on the spur of the moment. Even Silas – I thought about it often but I was only planning for about five minutes. It's only when things get intolerable or I – I want something very, very much.'

She got up, carrying the little cat. The big one, which was still on top of the television set, she scooped up and hung over her other arm. It is something she has taken to doing when she goes up to her room, at bedtime or to rest. 'I don't want any lunch,' she said. 'I'm going to lie down.' She is such a curious figure in her black and with that crown of ashen hair, saved from appearing absurd by her tragic slenderness, the cats entwined round her arms like a boa of living fur.

Here, in my house in Macduff Street, she once again has the room above my work room. That is where my spare room happens to be. The difference, one of the differences, is that it happens to be sixteen stairs up, not 106. As I sit here at my desk I hear nothing but a single murmur of the bed springs when she lays herself down on the mattress, a sound like a heavy sigh. The cats will stay with her for a little while, then climb out of the window while she is asleep, get on to the slate roof of the kitchen and try to catch starlings. They are never there when she wakes up.

That last Christmas I missed the sound of her above me, the creak of the 104th stair as she came down, even the murmur of the television she had taken to watching alone now Auntie was gone. The house was full. Diana Castle had come with a new boyfriend, and Birgitte, though having left under a cloud, reappeared with a boy she said was her cousin. The dancers and Walter Admetus went home only to sleep. Cosette refused to allow any visitor to occupy Bell's room, she thought that wouldn't be right, so with Gary and Fay, Mervyn and Mimi and Rimmon as permanent residents, when her niece, Leonard's daughter, turned up, she had to sleep on the sofa in the television room. Rimmon, trying to get the niece to sleep with him by telling her that sofa was where Auntie had been laid out, only succeeded in driving her from the house.

But the days of the big parties were over, the evenings of the great restaurant gatherings. When Cosette and Mark went out they went alone together. Without the least element of saturnalia, with no resemblance to those orgiastic parties, there was an atmosphere in the house of high romance. Winter, whatever may be the accepted view, is a more sexual season than summer, a bedroomy season of curtained windows and soft upholstery and artificial heat, of cold shut out and warmth enclosed, of faded, dwindling days and long, long nights. You notice these things more when you have no one of your own, for Robin wasn't my own or much to me then. Had there ever been so many lovers all together in the House of Stairs?

Picture how it was. Gary and Fay, for a start, who having for a long time been no more than fellow-lodgers, had embarked on a stormy, intense relationship. They were always parting for ever and then being marvellously reunited. Diana and Patrick, newly in love, at the touching stage, the ardent eye-contact stage, were apparently unable to bear the rupture that occurred each time flesh was sundered from flesh; Birgitte and her 'cousin', a giggly pair, babes in the wood who had sex as well as cuddles under their leaves; Mervyn and Mimi, a couple with that rare quality, an air of there being no one else in the world who mattered half as much as the other. Of all the lovers I knew then, only they are still together. I saw them a couple of months back, walking down North End Road hand in hand, she holding the hand of a boy of about eight and he of a girl about six. I waved, but they didn't see me.

And, of course, there were Mark and Cosette. If you saw them together you would have taken them to be in love, he with her as much as she with him. They were more decorous than the other couples. They were not to be come upon in corners, rammed almost painfully together, bones bruising flesh, open mouths devouring mouths which themselves ate lips and tongue, fingers prising as if to unearth where and what that essence was which created appetite and produced love. I never saw more than hands touching or a finger laid against a cheek. Their age made dignity harder and they seemed to strive for dignity. *Their* age? Mark was only a year older than Diana's Patrick. But just as Cosette seemed to have grown younger to meet him, so he had aged to meet her; not so much in looks, he retained altogether his handsome, somehow Slavonic appearance, his lean straight figure, but in his bearing, so that without losing any of his grace he appeared more staid and more deliberate.

They weren't lovers in the sense that we use the term. I don't think they were. Of course Cosette went out with him and they were gone for hours and they may not have been in theatres or cinemas or restaurants. They may have been in Mark's flat in Brook Green. But I have, and had, a very strong feeling this wasn't so. At home, in the House of Stairs, Cosette was after a fashion chaperoned by day and night. Naturally, I don't mean anyone would have interfered with what she did, tried to stop her for instance, but they would have known, everyone would have known. It was a curious situation. Here was this house full of lovers, by night everyone a lover except me, love in the air of the place like an all-pervading perfume, languorous and sweet and strangely exhausting, but Cosette, who looked more in love than any of them, whose whole manner, restrained though it was, spoke of a dying for love, remained unfulfilled, remained a kind of reconstituted virgin.

I speculated about it; I couldn't understand why. She had gone to bed readily enough with Ivor and, come to that, with Rimmon, men she had scarcely cared for, men who were stopgaps. Every gesture of hers, every word uttered in and out of his presence, testified to her passion for Mark. And she was no cold woman and no moralist, adhering still to the prejudices of her youth. Love to her, she had said often enough, was something to be consummated as soon as possible. Was it Mark then who hung back? And if he didn't want her, what did he want? Because I was lonely, finding myself in that situation when I wasn't first with anyone in the world, I consoled myself by watching them, how they behaved to each other; discreetly I did it, I hope. Of course I was jealous of Mark. In Cosette's affections he had taken my place as no predecessor of his ever had. So much for those who believe I was myself in love with him . . .

For a long time I had been telling myself he wasn't pursuing Cosette for her money. She happened to have money, a lot of it, but he would have liked her and wanted to be with her whether she had or not. So I believed. Yet who was paying for all these dinners they ate and all these plays they saw? He still had no work. He had no prospect of work. I remembered Ivor asking for money in the restaurant and, on one occasion, a cheque being palmed to Rimmon to spend on acid. Mark seemed beyond all that, having a curious, pure containment, walking tall and keeping himself distant from all these fleshpots.

The position changed and all was altered as openly as on any wedding night in the past when the bride is brought to bed, the bridegroom fetched to her and the guests, barely excluded, are witnesses of a necessary ceremonious rite. It was a few evenings after Christmas. The air was cold and thick with mist and it had been dark since soon after three. With the great feast only a few days past we had all been lazing indolently, no one had got up till late, and it was Walter Admetus who woke me, ringing the door-bell at noon. There was talk of going back to his place for an improvised party and to drink the case of Spanish champagne he had somehow come by. He had a place in Fulham by then, a converted coach-house, and had taken up with Eva Faulkner once more. I didn't want to go, I knew it would be the sort of party it didn't do to be alone at, and I worked on my new book until late in the evening. Gary and Fay went but Cosette and Mark, who were the prizes it seemed Walter was seeking, said they were going out for dinner, just the two of them.

It was very late when they came in. We were all in the drawing room. Those of us not compulsively enraptured by another's body, myself, Mervyn, Mimi and Rimmon, were gathered round Cosette's table drinking wine. The air must have been thick with cigarette smoke in those days, only no one seemed to notice it, or no one seemed to mind. Wrapped in each other, locked together like pieces of a human jigsaw, Diana and Patrick possessed the sofa with a heavy, silent, very nearly unmoving occupancy. Birgitte and Mogens lay side by side, lips sometimes touching, whispers passing, each with a hand on the back of the other's neck. From time to time Mervyn had been playing to us on Gary's ocarina, sometimes accompanying music from the record player. I had never heard him play before and he surprised me. He was good. After a little while he got up and put on an LP of *Carmen*, and when it reached the appropriate passage Perdita, who was there without her husband, who had been sitting in her quiet poised way in the red velvet chair that had been Auntie's, rose and without a word began to dance the *seguidilla*.

It was seldom she would dance for us and when she did I think we all felt privileged that we had had the chance, to see in private, this once-great dancer who had spoiled herself, who had backed down from the last unscaled height of success, for the sake of love, for, if you like, the folly of love. It was flamenco, I suppose, the dance she did. I only know that all of it, the music, the dance, the single lamp and the candlelight, the wine and the warmth and the lovers, was enormously romantic.

She was a little tiny woman, but as straight as a flame, black-haired as Carmen should be, the dress she wore having a flounced skirt of many red frills. She wanted us to clap to the music while she danced but we couldn't, it seemed to interfere with the air of it, the distance of it from us, the otherness. The ancient ceremonial steps, the stylized movements, the slow twirls, followed their prescribed order, and the music its pattern, and Mervyn's instrument made a strange haunting overtone, and the candle flames fluttered with the stirred air. And into it, the door opening very gently, came Mark and Cosette, pausing just inside when they saw what they had interrupted. It was scarcely an interruption, for the dancer didn't pause. And they stood side by side, watching, moving almost imperceptibly closer and closer together until their bodies touched and Mark slid his arm round Cosette's waist.

We all clapped when it was over. I poured a glass of wine for Mark and one for Cosette, who, rarely for her, didn't refuse it. There was no conversation. This wasn't unusual for the House of Stairs, where everybody knew everybody else and knew their views and didn't feel the need to make small talk. It was a place where people sat reading books in company. But that evening, it seemed to me that there was a peculiar wordlessness, as if communication was being made by other means, by touch and sight and music. The lovers were together, absorbed in each other, and we three who were each alone had our own interior worlds in which to lose ourselves. Rimmon was already slipping into that narcosis with its horrible fantasies from which he was never truly to recover, the dancer perhaps had her memories and her sacrifice and I thought of Bell and remembered Felicity saying that, like Carmen, Silas had had nothing left to do and nowhere to go but to die.

The music was changed, replaced by something of Massenet. The doorbell rang and it was the dancer's taxi-driver, come to take her home. I thought Mark would go at the same time, but he only went downstairs to see her into her cab, and although he had no proprietorial air about him, it was the first time, I was sure, that he had behaved in this manner of a host. He returned, but not to his chair. He sat on the arm of Cosette's, drew his hand very softly across her golden head and let his arm rest across her shoulders. She looked up at him, but not smiling; whatever it was they had come to was too serious for that. The music had become gentle and warm and seductive. Instead of returning this long rapt gaze of hers, his eyes ranged the big, warm, candlelit room, passing from the locked jigsaw couple on the sofa to the finger-patting, butterfly-kissing couple on the rug, to Mervyn and Mimi at the table, she with her head on his shoulder and his arm holding her. The light gleamed on the silver streak that banded his brown hair. Mark turned his head and let his eyes meet Cosette's. I could swear that at that moment they might have been the same age. I could have sworn it was a mutual passion.

He bent and kissed her lips, not drawing away but holding the kiss for a little time. You won't believe me if I say I was shocked, but remember it was the first time I had ever seen them kiss. I found myself first staring, then looking away, glad of the wine I had drunk that fuddled me a little, that blurred the hard edges of painful things. Cosette was flushed a rosy red when the kiss was done, proud in that company, the leader of it. She smiled, spoke his name only, 'Mark . . .'

He gave her his hand. 'Time to go,' he said, and pulled her lightly to her feet.

I thought he meant he was going home. She would go to the front door with him if he let her, he didn't always. Sometimes he would shake his head at her and with a movement of his hand indicate to her to stay sitting where she was. She invariably obeyed him. But that night she put her arm into his, for all the world as if they were going out for a sedate walk. And it seemed to me, though this may be hindsight, that the faintest shyness came into her face and made her manner a shade diffident.

But when she said to me, 'See that all the lights are put out, darling,' her voice was steady, and she added in that abstracted way of hers, 'The candles, I mean. You know how I worry about the candles.'

She looked as if she worried about nothing on this earth. She turned her face into Mark's neck and he bent his head, his lips on her forehead, looking like some picture I have seen of Paolo and Francesca.

'Good-night,' she said, and Mark said, 'Good-night.'

They didn't quite close the door behind them. Doors weren't closed much in the House of Stairs except those to bedrooms. I really thought, I still thought, I would hear their footsteps descend the stairs and only one set return. But they mounted. We were all silent in there, listening, even love forgotten, even desire, in the silent press of listening to *know*. Her door shut and no one came down. Mimi released her breath in a long, shuddering sigh.

We were mad, weren't we? This was just a couple breaking the ice of the first time, getting through or over the awkwardness and rapture of a first time that was the more fraught with awe and tension for having been so long postponed. We were insane to make so much of it. But I am telling you how it was and that is how it was, as important somehow as a monarch's wedding night.

I trembled at the thought of Bell, I began immediately to fear for Cosette.

But the fearing and the trembling, the sighs and the awkwardness, were all broken into by the arrival home of Gary and Fay, who banged the front door no more than five minutes after Mark and Cosette departed. They came up the first flight quarrelling bitterly, shouting insults and imprecations at one another, only to be hushed by us, fingers to lips, as they burst into the drawing room, as if upstairs were babies we had at last managed to rock and sing to sleep.

17

To catch Bell and warn her before she saw for herself, seemed to me important. I wasn't sure when she was coming and knew better than to expect her to let us know. She would walk in when she was ready, climb the stairs, all 106 of them, wearily perhaps or energetically and without pausing at the landings, and shut herself into her room. I might only know she had returned by the sound of her movements above my head.

As it happened, I intercepted her quite by chance. It was early and the household was asleep. I went down to pick up the post, expecting a letter from my publisher. Time doesn't mean much to Bell, she knows no regularity in her hours, perhaps because she has never worked for her living, perhaps for other reasons. She is as likely to get up at five as to go to bed at that time. On that particular morning she must have left Thornham at seven in order to be here by nine. It was cold, early January, and she brought a gust of raw, bitter air with her as she unlocked the front door and came in. She had a carpet-bag with her, they were a hippie fashion then, but hers was worn and discoloured, and over her black and brown layers she was wearing a coat of synthetic fox fur which I recognized as an old one of Felicity's. It was plain what had happened. Bell had turned up at Thornham with her usual ragbag of cotton skirts and jumble-sale jumpers and nothing to keep her warm but the shawl which had done duty as a shroud for Silas.

I was standing by the table, reading my letter. We looked at each other and Bell said, falling back perhaps on that perennial staple at moments of awkwardness, the weather, 'Christ, it's bloody freezing.'

Unprepared now that the time had come, I hunted for suitable words. She dropped the carpet-bag, unwound the long grey scarf that wrapped her head and pushed her fingers through that flaxen,

tangled, curly hair. It is a noble face Bell has, Lucrezia Panciatichi's, aristocratic, serene, the proportions of small straight nose
in relation to full folded lips, wide eyes, high forehead, almost
perfect. How can someone like her have a noble face?

She held up her arms. 'What do you reckon?'

'Of the coat? Did Felicity give it to you?'

'I had to have something. She's got so many she won't miss it.
That was what she said, she actually said those words. It's hideous,
isn't it? But beggars can't be choosers. It's not half as warm as the
real thing.'

'Felicity wouldn't wear the real thing, I suppose,' I said, and
then, because I still hoped for something, for love or friendship,
'I'll buy you a coat, Bell.'

'No,' she said. 'No, thanks.' She made things clear. 'If I can't
have something wonderful and wicked, if I can't have snow
leopard, something *you* couldn't afford I mean, I'd rather have
Mrs Thinnesse's cast-offs.'

'That's frank.'

'Well, I am. No point in being otherwise, is there? I'm very
poor – did you know? I don't suppose you ever thought about it.
That money I got from Silas's dad's house, it's not worth what it
was five years ago. What it brings in isn't worth what it was. I've
been talking to Esmond about it. He says going decimal has done
it and it hasn't half begun what it'll do in the next few years.'

It was a muddled way of putting it but I dimly saw what she
meant. 'Talking is pointless,' she said. 'I often think talking about
anything is pointless.' She picked up the bag and walked past me
to the stairs, beginning the climb that with that bag and in that
coat would be a slow, long haul. I followed her, saying, 'Bell . . .'

'What?'

'I thought you might want to know, I mean I don't want it to
be too much of a – a surprise to you.' I nearly said a shock. 'Mark
is up there. In Cosette's room.'

I don't know what I expected, but not what I got: a pleased
smile, the first smile since she had come in, a look of genuine
delight someone might wear when you told her of a friend's good
luck or forthcoming marriage. 'How long has that been going on
then?'

'A week.'

'About time too.'

We began going upstairs together. She took off the mock-fur and I carried it. 'Tell me about it.'

'Tell you what?'

'Well, how it came about, what they did, how you knew, all that. You *know*.'

It was like the old days, when we used to talk and share with each other views and opinions no one else might know. But we were outside Cosette's door and I put one finger to my lips, as we had hushed Gary and Fay that first night. Bell mouthed at me to come on up to her room. The house was as still and silent as other houses would be by night. Even Gary, who nearly always got up early, was sleeping in. We climbed on up to the top. Outside her door I told her how Cosette wouldn't allow anyone else to sleep there while she was away, though we had a house full to overflowing, and Bell only said that was nice of her but she wouldn't have minded. Why should she mind? And when we went in I wondered of course why should she mind, it was such a barren place, with no imprint of its occupant on it, unless Silas's paintings with their backs turned were an imprint. No pictures on the walls, no books, no magazines, no ornaments, no garments scattered, only the bed, a chair, an ashtray as big as a soup bowl, that had once *been* a soup bowl, empty but still smeared with ash, on the bedside cabinet. The air smelt stale and musty, but it was too cold outside to open the window. It presented, from where I stood, a view only of sky, white but veined with grey and shedding a thin, fine drizzle that might have been rain or snow.

I told her about the night of the *seguidilla* and she listened with approval but laughing sometimes, giving whoops of laughter, at places in the account I hadn't found funny. She was unpacking the carpet-bag, throwing aside those unidentifiable lengths of dark cloth, crumpled and faded, in which she dressed herself. Then she locked the door. She came and sat on the bed beside me. She lay on the bed beside me.

'It's all very good, isn't it?'

'For them?'

'For everyone!'

She took me in her arms. It was the first time for months and the last time for ever.

Mark was living in the House of Stairs, though I believe he still kept his flat on. In February, which is about the worst time of the year to do such a thing, though I suppose it doesn't much matter when you're on your honeymoon, he and Cosette went to Paris for a couple of weeks. Cosette must have paid, of course, and they stayed at the George V. I couldn't stop thinking about that aspect of things, I was always thinking of it, how Mark, like the others, had become her kept man, though, without being explicit about it, he had made it plain he never intended to be.

On the subject of the 'others', who should turn up soon after they got back but Ivor Sitwell. He just arrived early one evening without warning. Cosette was too happy for recriminations. He had betrayed her and treated her shamefully, but who cared now she had Mark? It was Fay he had betrayed her with and she had long been good friends with Fay. She seemed delighted to see him and was soon arranging for us all to go out to dinner together. No one could have been in their presence for more than five minutes, not even anyone as insensitive as Ivor, without realizing Mark was Cosette's lover. An outsider might have been with her and Ivor for hours without being aware of the situation, but things were different now. It wasn't just the way she looked at Mark but the way he looked at her. Even I, fearing him bought, corrupt, prostituted, had to admit he looked at her as if money didn't come into it, as if he were passionately in love.

Advance copies of my new book had come and Cosette was looking at the one I had given her when Ivor arrived. She, of course, was being extravagant in her praise and Ivor, taking the copy from her, remarked that I was 'still churning them out'. He was as objectionable as he had ever been, though making no references this time to the Sitwell family. No doubt he had been rumbled, and by others apart from Bell and her informant. He tried to get a flirtation going with her while we were in the restaurant, but you can imagine how far that got him. All the time he was living with Cosette he was never so nice to her as then, when he saw her with another lover.

We were a big party, eleven of us round the table, and by some mischance I had been seated next to Ivor. Bell was on the other side of him, Mark next to her, and Cosette next to him. When Bell had put an end to his compliments and tentative advances with her own brand of devastation ('Why don't you fuck off?') he turned to me and said how nice it was for Cosette to have such a charming 'sweetheart'.

'It's nice for him too,' I said.

'Sure it is. I don't doubt he knows it. What does he do?'

I told him. Ivor said he was sure he must have heard his voice, but it wasn't like being on television, was it? 'Resting at present, I imagine?'

We talked for a while. I didn't have much choice. Bell would have had a choice, she simply wouldn't have replied. She sat isolated, eating, drinking rather a lot of wine, not talking because she had no one to talk to, having rejected Ivor and been rejected by Mark – at least, temporarily deserted by him. He had eyes and conversation for no one but Cosette, had finished his meal and, having twisted round in his chair, was talking to her in a low, loving, intensely intimate voice not much above a whisper. I remember thinking then how alike she and Bell were, like enough at any rate to seem related, Cosette looking far older of course and far less beautiful – that wasn't a mere matter of age – but of the same physical type, with the same fair, northern beauty, a kind of Valhalla goddess cast of face, a Freya or a Brunhild. Her right hand lay on the tablecloth, a plump, white hand not at all like Bell's, and Mark laid his tenderly over it. She made some reply to him and his own response to it the entire table might have heard, a gratified, delighted, ardent, 'Darling!'

Ivor said dryly to me, 'Of course, he's an actor.'

It was cruel, but it was only what I was thinking. And yet, and yet . . . When I was at school and I read Thackeray's *Esmond* I used to wonder how Lady Castlewood who is 'old' and made ugly by smallpox could quite suddenly grow beautiful. Well, Cosette had grown beautiful and no doubt for the same reason. She paid the bill and Mark let her. He didn't have much choice. Cosette told me a little while afterwards that he had recently done some auditioning for television but he didn't photograph well. Perhaps

I should say he didn't film well, which was astonishing with those cheekbones and that mouth.

'He's too beautiful,' she said. 'You see, he couldn't get a big part, I mean he's not a star, and he's too good-looking for supporting parts, he'd steal all the scenes from the stars.'

Perhaps this was true. It sounded a bit like a Hollywood thirties verdict. Mark might just not have been a very good actor and after that, as far as I know, he never worked again. But he was a man of many interests: he read, he walked, he worked out in a gymnasium before this was a fashionable thing to do, he was passionately fond of the stage and he took Cosette to lunchtime theatre and fringe theatre; he cooked, so that those meals of expensive delicatessen became a thing of the past. Strangely enough, he seemed to have no friends of his own, or if he did have friends, none of them came to the House of Stairs. But he became, in a way neither Ivor nor Rimmon had approached becoming, the master of the house.

I don't mean he was domineering or even masterful. He didn't suddenly start dictating to everyone or telling Cosette what she should do. It was nothing like that, rather that when it was a case of making a decision, he made it. And in a way that I know sounds sinister, though it wasn't because Mark himself was about as far from sinister as anyone could be, he began to make it clear that not all the occupants of the House of Stairs were welcome guests.

Gary, for instance, and Fay. 'He asked if I ever in fact cleaned Cosette's car,' Gary said to me. 'That was the arrangement when I first came here, he said.'

'It's not that Gary minds having that sort of thing said to him,' said Fay. 'He's not paranoid. But it's a question actually of who says it. He wouldn't mind if Cosette said it.'

'Except that you can't imagine Cosette saying it. I might have cleaned the bugger sometimes if Cosette hadn't always told me to leave it.'

Birgitte and Mogens he got rid of more easily. How I don't know but I suppose he simply told them to go. They were very young and Mogens was one of those rare Danes who don't speak much English. They had nowhere to go and very little money and Birgitte was actually crying when they left, escorted out of the house by Mark, reminding me of an 'Expulsion from Paradise',

227

Adam downcast, Eve in tears and the avenging angel driving them ahead of him. Cosette knew none of this, he kept it from her, and when she found out she was upset. He told her they wouldn't come to any harm, they could throw themselves on the mercy of the Danish consul.

'All good things come to an end,' he said.

Cosette looked anxiously at him. 'Oh, don't say that!'

'I meant them, not us.'

Since they had only come for a protracted Christmas holiday, Mervyn and Mimi had already gone. Rimmon was rather ill. It wasn't that he was addicted to any particular drug, but rather that he had poisoned himself in some way with all the things he had swallowed and injected over the past two or three years. He was extremely thin and he ate very little, he had no appetite, and he wandered about the house, pale and hollow-eyed, doing absolutely nothing. Mark refused to call him Rimmon but insisted on addressing him by his real name, Peter. Almost anything that was said to him, even mildly critical, upset Rimmon, and when Mark told him he couldn't go on like this, he obviously needed psychiatric treatment, he started crying. Of course Mark was never loud or aggressive, far from it, he was always gentle and with an air of thinking carefully about what he said, but Rimmon cried just the same and couldn't seem to stop, the tears falling in a permanent slow trickle. At last Mark got a doctor to him – naturally, Cosette had her own tame private doctor – and poor Rimmon went into a psychiatric ward, disappearing for ever from our knowledge, at least from mine.

I began wondering who would go next. Gary and Fay were still there, but by then they understood they were there on sufferance, indefinite marching orders had been given them, and the sooner they found a flat or room elsewhere the better. Towards Cosette's friends from outside he reacted very differently. Admetus and Eva Faulkner, who were married a few months afterwards, he made very welcome, as he did Perdita and Luis and the Castles and Cosette's brothers. They were all respectable people, more or less, they had jobs or at any rate they had callings, they didn't use drugs or keep peculiar hours or buy their clothes at jumble sales or make love in public. Sometimes I saw Mark's eyes rest speculatively on

Bell as she lay on Cosette's sofa, chain-smoking, or repaired to the room where the television was, or he encountered her coming upstairs, wrapped in Felicity's synthetic-fur coat. And then I wondered if it wasn't too far-fetched to think her days in the House of Stairs might be numbered.

'They'll get married,' she said to me one evening when we found ourselves alone in the drawing room, Mark and Cosette having gone off to see a play in some suburban theatre. 'You'll see.'

'It's what she wants, I suppose.'

'It's what they both want. You know my views. Marriage is an economic arrangement. You'd realize that if you weren't so sentimental.'

'You mean,' I said, 'that she wants him and he wants her money.'

'That's my kind of blunt speaking,' she said, 'but yes, OK, that's about it. I told you, he'll be nice to her, he'll treat her right.'

'She's nineteen years older than he is. When she's seventy he'll only be a bit over fifty.'

Bell gave me an odd sort of look when I said that. It was as if I had said something incredible, as if I were talking about some contingency not just remote but beyond the bounds of possibility. I didn't understand it then. I thought she was implying something quite different.

'Are you saying that won't matter because he'll have other women?'

'It's not likely he'll stay faithful to her for the rest of their lives, is it?'

'It would kill her.'

'People aren't so easily killed,' said Bell, as if she regretted this. 'It'd solve a lot of problems, wouldn't it, if people died of jealousy or being rejected? Imagine if it was a fatal disease – "She's got terminal jealousy," or, "He won't last long now he's been rejected." '

I didn't ask her what she meant. I thought she was thinking about Silas or even Esmond Thinnesse. But when Mark and Cosette came in a couple of hours later I half-expected them to announce to us their impending marriage. It wouldn't have surprised me if one or the other of them said they had something to tell us and then invited us to Kensington Registry Office on the following Saturday; or, because Cosette was romantic and there was that formal, ceremonious side to Mark's nature, to a marriage service according to the rites of the Church of England at St Michael the Archangel.

Nothing like that happened. The room was full of smoke from our cigarettes and Mark opened the windows on to the balcony. It was April and cold and the wind lifted the red velvet curtains and made them belly and shudder. For someone to do that today wouldn't be exceptional, what would be is such excessive smoking, but it wasn't then, it was normal, everyone in the house smoked, except Mark himself. His gesture, followed by a fanning of himself with his hand, seemed a reproach – more than that, for he looked at Bell with distaste, as if he knew very well that the majority of the cigarettes had been smoked by her. He looked at her as if he wished she weren't there.

Bell returned this look with a classic one of her own, impudent and defiant. It seemed to say, I brought you here, I put you in the way of all this good fortune, and just you remember it. You won't turn me out the way you got rid of Birgitte. Of course all this was in my imagination and in fact I was quite wrong. Bell's look meant a great deal, but not that.

She left the room soon after they came in. I had noticed she didn't like being with them and I had even asked her why she now disliked Cosette. Her reply had a chilling effect.

'I don't dislike her. I'm indifferent to her.'

I ought to have asked her how, this being so, she had the nerve to go on living on Cosette's bounty, but I didn't. I didn't because I loved her, I needed her, to be with, to talk to sometimes, to maintain for myself the illusion she was still my closest friend. And I had begun to be afraid she would leave, either of her own volition or because something would drive her away. Mark would drive her away; I was very afraid of that.

It was soon after this that he asked me to have dinner with him.

The evening he named was one on which Cosette would be at a niece's wedding. This was the niece who had stayed in the House of Stairs and been told by Rimmon she was sleeping on the sofa where Auntie had died. It was to be a big wedding down in Kent with a disco in the evening and Cosette had promised to stay for part of this. Mark hadn't been invited. Leonard and his wife knew him, had met him at the House of Stairs, and Mark had treated them with great courtesy, but I think they found the whole set-up rather awkward. They hadn't liked to ask if he were a friend or a kind of servant-companion or Cosette's 'fiancé' or what. Probably they didn't realize he was living with her. Anyway, he wasn't asked to the wedding. I was very surprised that the first evening he found himself without her he was asking me out. Briefly, I remembered what Bell had said about the unlikelihood of his being faithful to Cosette for the rest of their lives. But I couldn't see myself as a possible candidate, he being, I was sure, as unlikely to fancy me as I was to be attracted by him.

Then of course it occurred to me that this was a party he must be arranging. 'Have you asked Bell?' I said.

Was it my imagination or did the mere mention of her name these days make him, if not quite wince, somehow withdraw himself, brace himself, force a response?

'It will be just you and me,' he said. 'There's something I want to say to you.'

The chances were that this was to be an ultimatum. I was the next member of the household he wanted out. Over an elegant dinner paid for with Cosette's money, I was to be asked, with charm and tact because of my special position and place in her affections, if I didn't think it was time I quitted my two pleasant rooms and looked about for somewhere of my own to live.

You will see that I had come very near to disliking Mark. He was a threat to me, a thief of love, who came between me and Cosette. As they wished me to do, I was seeing everything inside-out.

18

We lived in the same house but we didn't go together. We met in the restaurant. It was a bistro not far from Paddington Station, not at all grand, but not shabby either. For some reason I didn't say anything to Bell about dining with Mark – the reason probably was that I didn't get the chance, I didn't see her – and later on I was glad I hadn't. I took it for granted Cosette didn't know this meeting was going to take place and I was surprised when Mark said to me, it was almost the first thing he said, 'It was Cosette's idea we meet away from the house. You know how it is, you can never be sure if you're overheard.'

His smile and raised eyebrows had a rueful air. All those crowds of people, he seemed to infer, lurking behind doors, listening, sponging. And there was something in what he implied, for Gary and Fay still hadn't moved and to his dismay Diana Castle and her boyfriend had suddenly arrived, begging Cosette to put them up for just a week, it wouldn't be more than a week, and Cosette of course had consented. But this declaration of 'Cosette's idea' made me immediately anxious. I could hardly believe she would depute Mark to turn me out, yet his influence with her was great, was growing greater with every day that passed. She was in thrall to him, and that would not be putting it too strongly.

'What did you want to say to me, Mark?'

'Several things, really.'

He waited. Usually very articulate, he seemed at a loss for how to express himself, and my apprehensiveness grew. It seemed to me that his look had become almost ominous, like that of a messenger come to break bad news. In those moments my expectations changed and in spite of what he had said about our meeting there being Cosette's suggestion, I had a sense that he was going to tell me of a coming breach with her, of his involvement perhaps with someone else, even of his coming marriage to that other woman. His silence was heavy and, unable to bear it any longer, I leant forward and said in the voice one uses to jerk someone from a trance state, 'Mark, what is it?'

He smiled, shook his head. 'Oh, nothing, nothing to look like that about. I find some things hard to say, that's all.'

And then he did say it. It gave me a greater shock than if he had told me he was leaving the House of Stairs, never coming back, going to the other side of the earth. The words came rapidly, almost in a rush.

'I suppose you must realize how much in love with Cosette I am.'

I just looked at him. I didn't say anything.

'It wasn't like that at first,' he said. 'Of course I liked her, I liked her enormously. And then – well, I fell in love.' He laughed a little. 'I couldn't quite believe it at first. It seemed so – improbable.' Why? Because she was so much older? Because he wasn't the falling-in-love kind? He didn't explain, but he forgot his reticence and what might have been embarrassment. 'I tried to stop it, I told myself it was ridiculous. I couldn't stop it. Of course I wouldn't want to stop now – the idea of stopping is impossible, it's laughable. You look surprised. Couldn't you see? I thought it showed in every word I spoke and every way I looked.'

He meant what he said utterly. He was as moved with passion as Cosette herself had been when she told me she loved him so much she would die of it. He leant across the table and gazed at me with an ardour the waiter who came up to us must have thought was meant for me. I was so astonished I just sat there shaking my head. When someone says 'I am in love', we know at once what is meant even though we may find it very hard to define. It isn't the same as 'I love', not just in degree but in kind, it isn't weaker but far stronger than the extravagant expressions, 'I adore', 'I am mad about'. It implies obsessive commitment. It includes thraldom, blindness, total acceptance, absolute fidelity, involuntary exclusiveness. In it lies security. Outside it is the world that cannot get in. When I had got over utter disbelief and into absolute belief, I felt enormously relieved. My relief was for Cosette, that she was safe.

'I don't,' he said, 'actually want it to show.' This was a confession of some significance that I was to appreciate later.

'Is that why you said it was ridiculous?'

Because she's old, I thought, because she was such an obvious pushover. That wasn't what he had meant, as I later found out, but he seemed to have forgotten saying it.

'Did I say that? Ridiculous at my age, I suppose.'

Then what about hers? 'Why are you telling me?'

'Because you're more than just a friend of hers. You're almost an adopted daughter.'

We began eating. I was astonished by what he said and growing more and more pleased by it, yet somehow it had taken away my appetite. I picked at my food. I drank my wine.

'There are things I mean to do,' he said, 'and not to do. I thought it would be right to tell you. What others may think is irrelevant. For one thing, I'm not going to get married.'

So much for Bell, I thought.

'It would seem the absolutely right thing to do when you feel like I do, make a public statement of one's commitment. The reason I'm not going to do it is because Cosette' – he paused for word selection – 'is very wealthy. I don't think it would be quite – well, honourable for me to marry her. Do you understand what I mean?'

I nearly burst out laughing. I knew a lot of people, older people, my father and Cosette's brothers for instance, who thought practically the only honourable thing a man could do by a woman was marry her. Once a woman lived with a man he'd never marry her, was what they would say, he wouldn't make an 'honest woman' of her. And here was Mark telling me that in his philosophy it wouldn't be honourable to marry a rich woman. But I saw what he meant. I even thought it quite admirable and saw him in those moments as a strong-minded, disciplined man.

'Some would think you married her for her money,' I said.

'To put it brutally, yes.' He obviously hadn't liked the way I put it. 'Of course, in the nature of things, if I live with her – and I intend to live with her for as long as she'll have me, for ever I hope – some of her wealth must rub off on me. I must benefit. But at least I won't – have a right to it.' He talked as if the Married

Women's Property Acts had never been passed, but again I knew what he meant. The waiter came over and he asked for another bottle of wine. We were drinking ferociously, to combat emotion I suppose. Mark looked at me and with a quick shiver shed his pomposity, like someone slipping off a cloak. He said simply, 'I'm so happy. I've never been so happy.'

'I can see,' I said.

'The next thing I want to say is that we shan't go on living in Cosette's present house.' He had never called it the House of Stairs. I was suddenly, for the first time, aware of this. 'I've never liked Number Fifteen Archangel Place.' He gave the address a stagey emphasis. The enthusiasm he showed on his first visit was apparently forgotten. 'It's very inconvenient. It costs Cosette a fortune to run – mainly for the benefit of other people, I don't mean you, Elizabeth – and what is it, after all, but a damned great staircase with rooms sprouting out of it? It's a folly, really.'

'Cosette used to love it.'

'It's interesting why Cosette bought it. It was as an antidote to loneliness, the principle being that if you have empty rooms they'll be filled. And they were, they were. Now she wants to be with me just as much, thank God, as I want to be with her.'

'Alone with you?' I was thinking of Bell but he, of course, thought I meant myself. He said quickly, in a cliché to which it would have been hard to find an alternative, 'There will always be a home for you with us, Elizabeth.'

It seemed to put me rather in Auntie's role. I didn't care for the idea of living with these lovebirds. 'Where will you go?' I said.

'A little house in a mews, we thought.'

There would be no room for Bell. And I should lose her once and for all. This would be the rupture and it would be a parting without a promise of reunion, I sensed that. 'Bell will be happy for you,' I said. 'She thought you'd get married, so she wasn't entirely right, but she was right in principle.'

A shadow touched his face. It was as if all the happiness, the glow of it, was cut off by a shutter closing. His gaze had been a room filled with light and happy people celebrating and then the door was shut. 'I wonder if you'd mind not saying anything to Bell just for the moment.'

'About moving, d'you mean?'

'About any of it. It doesn't matter if she thinks we're getting married. I'm not surprised to hear she thinks that.'

'You mean she's one of those people who might think you were marrying for money?'

The lowering of inhibition through drink made me speak like that. It didn't please him. 'I said it was irrelevant what other people think.'

'You don't want me to tell Bell you're in love with Cosette and you're going to live with her and you're not going to get married and you're going to leave the House of Stairs?'

He had to say yes, that was right, but he didn't like it. I had thought of Mark as strong, the way he talked, his peculiar articulacy, his seeming always to know his own mind, his decision-making when Cosette vacillated, but now I understood this wasn't so. He was weak. He was only strong where there was no effort to be made, no barriers to overcome. Cosette was far stronger than he. I had a strange idea. Could it be the vigour of Cosette's love, a love of consuming strength into which she put her whole self, body and soul, could it be that this was so powerful that it had reached out and drawn an answering love from him, ignited a passion where previously there had been no more than a spark? He looked weak as he sat there, he looked young and afraid and curiously wistful, as if he had found what he had been seeking all his life and now feared dreadfully that it would be dashed away. Cosette was a mother to him, of course, and he a son to her, that was part of it and important, but only a small part of the complex whole. That indecisive, apprehensive look passed from his face and it hardened perceptibly. He smiled.

'Of course we'll tell Bell in time. It's just that we'd rather you didn't mention it at present. As a matter of fact, Cosette feels she'll have to make it up to Bell in some way. She's thinking of buying her a flat – well, a studio flat, you know the kind of thing.'

I didn't say any more. I don't think we talked much more about it. We never did have much to say to each other, Mark and I. For the sake of politeness, I suppose, he did his best to be host while we ate our cheese and finished the third bottle of wine. He was no drinker and his voice had thickened as he talked to me about this actor he knew and that actress and some play he had been on tour in and how the author had to cut some scene out so as not to offend the sensibilities of Middlesbrough. Along with the brie and biscuits I digested what he had said, that Cosette would compensate Bell for the loss of her room by buying her a flat. I found it, at first, nearly incredible.

Not incredible that Cosette would do it. That was typical, exactly the kind of thing she would do, if she thought the projected recipient was in need. Remember, after all, Auntie. But someone would have had to put the idea into her head first. Why should she even have supposed it was her duty to compensate a young, healthy woman who was nothing to her, who even disliked her, for the loss of a room for which she had never paid a penny in rent? Had Mark asked her to do it? I felt a momentary gratitude that at least there was no proposal to provide me with some pied-à-terre.

So Bell was not to be told, not to be told any of this, not even, it seemed clear, that the notion of marriage she had got into her head was wrong. She must be allowed to continue in delusion. But when the House of Stairs was sold she would be informed and then fobbed off with the deeds of a bed-sit with kitchen and bathroom in north Kensington. I decided to ask Cosette about it; I wasn't going to be instructed by Mark. Going home alone in a cab – he had gone off in another one to Victoria or Waterloo or somewhere to meet Cosette's train – I found myself making rather wild plans to buy myself a home and ask Bell to share it with me. She would say no, of course, she wouldn't do it. I imagined her disappearing once more, walking out one day and not coming back, and in ten years' time I would go to someone's party and she would walk into the room, heralded perhaps by an Ivor Sitwell look-alike saying the most beautiful woman he had ever seen was about to arrive . . .

I was in error there. I was in error about Cosette and Mark too when I created a picture of them in my mind, living in their shared future. I had even decided on the street they would live in, a little alley of houses like country cottages up north of Westbourne Grove, one of those houses would be right for them, perhaps the one with the great yellow flowering tree growing in its garden.

Since then – a long while afterwards, because for years I stopped myself thinking of any of it – I have sometimes wondered what their life together would have been like.

It would have been a life together, they would have stayed together, of that I am sure. And Mark would have married her, if for no other reason than that she would have come to want it so much. He could never bear to disappoint her. He would have dedicated his life to making her happy, as he had already begun to do. I think it would have been a rather cloistered partnership, one of those of which people say that the couple are 'very wrapped up in each other'. Certainly there would have been no more rent-free tenants, non-paying guests, visitors who came for a night and stayed for a year. There would have been few guests of any sort, myself, Bell of course, Luis Llanos and Perdita Reed, Walter and Eva Admetus perhaps, Cosette's brothers, those friends of Mark's he sometimes mentioned but we never saw. Sometimes they would have been seen, Mark and Cosette, dining alone together at some exclusive restaurant, the Connaught perhaps, or Le Gavroche, celebrating an anniversary, the day they first met, the night they first made love, their wedding day, oblivious of the presence of others, eyes fixed with ardour upon the other's eyes, hands touching, fingers enlaced upon the tablecloth. And by that time it would of course be Mark who paid the bill, went through the motions that is, the signing of the cheque or the presentation of the credit card. For by then she would have become so accustomed to deferring to him in all practical matters, to leaving it all to him, that they would have largely forgotten whose money it had been in the first place.

'Are you really going to buy Bell a flat?' I said to Cosette.

'I'd rather buy you one, darling.'

'I shall manage for myself,' I said. 'Thank you, but I really will. It will be good for me to stand on my own feet, as they say. Time I did. But do you mean to do that for Bell?'

'Well,' she said, 'Mark seems to think it would – soften the blow.'

'What blow?'

'He seems to think she won't like us selling this house and moving. Or I suppose that's what he means. It isn't altogether clear what he means. I think he's rather confused. He seems to think that if Bell were – well, compensated, she wouldn't feel so bad.'

'Why should she feel bad?'

'She'll lose her home, won't she? He's got hold of this idea that she loves this house. Well, I can understand that, I love it, but it was a phase in my life really, something I had to do, and now I'm moving on. It was a kind of dream I had to make come true and the dream I have now is of living alone with Mark in a little house where we have to be close together because there isn't room for us to be apart. Do you think I'm quite mad? You see, he feels exactly the same, and we can't both be mad, can we? And when I think how I said I loved him so much I'd die of it! I love him so much now I want to live for it. Oh, Elizabeth, I'm so lucky, I can't believe it sometimes, I can't believe anyone can be so happy and it can go on and on and he can feel just the same as me.' Cosette, who had seldom talked much about herself, who had always put others before herself, now, transformed by love, deflected every conversation to her own feelings and, of course, to Mark's. She had forgotten Bell.

It wasn't hard for me to do what Mark had asked, for I hardly ever saw Bell. I only heard her, the droning monotone of the television in the ground-floor room, the creak of the 104th stair, her footsteps moving above my head. She avoided me, I think she avoided everyone. I began to make preparations for acquiring a home of my own. I could easily afford to buy somewhere, I was doing well enough out of my books, much better than if I had followed the career I was trained for and become a teacher, better than if I had been a head teacher or taught in a university. Spending a lot of time peering into estate-agents' windows, I graduated at last to getting them to send me details of flats.

The House of Stairs had become a quiet, even decorous place. Sometimes, in the past, when I had been in my room trying to write, I had been exasperated by noise, music, footsteps running up and down, voices calling and voices shouting, doors slamming. So perverse are human beings that now I missed it. Loneliness drove me to Robin (in one of my novels I would have said it drove me into his arms) and to grow closer to him than would naturally have happened, given our very incompatible temperaments. And then Elsa came to stay.

I think I prefer the company of women.

This was something you didn't admit to in the early seventies. If you said you liked being with women it was taken to mean you made a virtue of necessity, you put up with women because you couldn't get a man. Of course things are quite different today and it's acceptable, recognized as perfectly reasonable and indeed intelligent to prefer women's company. I was overjoyed when Elsa came. She had always been my best friend, is still. For the first time I took it upon myself, took advantage of my daughter-of-the-house status, to ask someone to stay without asking Cosette first. It was unimaginable, anyway, that Cosette would say no.

Elsa had been renting a flat while waiting to move into the place she was buying. Things were getting easier, but for a divorced woman on her own to buy a flat on a mortgage wasn't the straightforward operation it usually is today. There were delays and her three months' lease came to an end without the option to renew.

'It might be a month or longer,' she said when I invited her.

'Cosette will hope it's longer – you'll see.'

Mark didn't. He wasn't very pleased. But you could see he was thinking that all this sort of thing would come to an end soon enough, would necessarily come to an end when they had a house without spare rooms. Well, I could see it, but Bell didn't seem to. Bell seemed to be waiting for something to happen, she had an air of biding her time. She watched Mark, but Mark no longer ever looked at her.

We gave Elsa Auntie's old room, on the floor below mine. All Auntie's things were still there, the antimacassars on the chairs, the radio in its veneered wood case. Elsa said to leave them, she liked them, but Perpetua took down the flypaper. I was interested in what was happening in the House of Stairs, I would have liked to talk about it, but Elsa isn't like Bell, people's acts and motivations aren't of much concern to her.

'It doesn't matter, does it?' she would say when asked why she thought someone had said or done what he had said or done. 'I expect he had his reasons.'

Bell was making it plain she no longer wanted to know me. It was as if I had fulfilled some requirement of the moment, served my purpose, and now her needs had changed, I was superfluous. If she passed me on the stairs she would say a casual 'hi'. At the big table down in the dining room she would pass me a plate and ask me if I wanted something. If I addressed her she answered. That was all. My consolation – if consolation it was – was that no one received more from her than I did. When we gathered together in the drawing room, as we still sometimes did, she would never be one of our number. One day she walked into the drawing room while I was there with Elsa and Mark and Cosette, drinking coffee Perpetua had made and brought up to us after lunch.

She said to Cosette, 'Can I take the telly up to my room?'

Down there, in the room where Auntie had died, no one ever watched it. Cosette seemed grateful for the request. I think she was grateful Bell had spoken to her. These cold, laconic people, you can be almost elated by a sign of warmth from them, an ordinary remark even.

'Of course you can, darling, if it will work up there. Will it, Mark?'

'I've no idea,' he said.

'And you mustn't attempt to carry it on your own,' Cosette said. 'Mark will give you a hand with it.'

He didn't refuse but he didn't say he would. His voice sounded strained. 'If you want televison, Bell, why don't you buy a set of your own?'

'I'd like to speak to you,' she said to him. 'In private.'

I thought he would say there was nothing she could say to him she couldn't say in front of Cosette, but he didn't. Elsa and I were there, of course. He hesitated and then he got up and left the room with her.

'It's about having a key to her room,' Cosette said. I was very sure it wasn't. 'She mentioned losing it the other day.'

Elsa helped her carry the television set up those 106 stairs. Later that evening I came upon her in the kitchen going through drawers, supposedly looking for the lost key to her room.

'Why bother?' I said. 'I won't come in.'

It was the only time I ever saw her blush. She left the drawer

241

open, walked past me out of the kitchen and slammed the door. Above me, as I worked, I would hear the television. She had it on at all hours, whenever there were programmes, though luckily for me there weren't nearly so many then as now. Elsa said to me, sitting in my work room, while some cartoon for children chattered and squeaked overhead, 'Mark is a weak sort of character, isn't he?'

It was unlike her to comment on people's natures. 'Why do you say that?'

'For one thing, he's afraid of Bell. He's got someone coming to look at this house tomorrow, to value it, and he doesn't want her to know. He wants me to take her out somewhere so that she's not in when this man comes. He says only I can do it because I'm the only one here that's on good terms with her.'

'He'll have to tell her sooner or later.'

'There's something more than that he'll have to tell her,' said Elsa. 'I don't know what it is but I sense it. She asked me yesterday if I'd heard anything about their marriage plans, but I could only say I didn't know they were getting married.'

'I wish I knew,' I said, 'just what was going on.'

She shrugged. 'Wait a little, said the thorn tree.'

Bell half-guessed. She knew at any rate that something had gone wrong. Aware of people's ways as she was, she must have known his weakness, the sponginess at the core of him, which made him amenable to her suggestions in the first place. She must have known it was this which now held him back from making to her some great revelation. That was what she wanted to talk about to him in private, and at that private conversation I am sure he lost his nerve again and told her only that things were going well, she must be patient. I can't ask her all these things now. I can't. I think she half-guessed and the half she guessed was only that Mark wasn't going to get married. But what she believed was that he was unable to persuade Cosette to marry him. He may even have told her this at their private talk, that she must wait a little, thorn tree-like, while he tried his powers of persuasion.

Imagine, though, what it must have been like for him, poor weak Mark, having to do this and talk like this while loving Cosette with all his heart.

19

'What became of Silas's pictures?' I said.

It was this morning and we were in Bell's room in Kilburn under the railway bridge.

'When I went to prison my solicitor said what would I want to be done about my things and I said burn them, so he did. He said he would, so I expect he did. They would never have been worth anything.'

'I'd have looked after them for you.'

She smiled at me. Sometimes she has this way of looking at me as if I am an eccentric child, given to making artless statements of a charmingly innocent kind. When she was first in prison I got a monthly Visitors' Order and used to go in and see her, but after a while she asked me not to come any more. She didn't want visitors, there was no one she wanted. Well, things have changed and she isn't like that now. She wants me. Irony of ironies, she now wants me. We are here in her room, clearing it out, packing her very small and some would say pathetic quantity of possessions into one of my suitcases. For Bell is moving in. She has told her probation officer and she is coming to live with me, not for a week or two or for months, but for ever. Because she wants to and I don't know how to say no. The past won't let me say no; it would seem like an act of violence done to the past, to my old feelings and vows and desires, to refuse her.

It isn't something I look forward to with relish. If I could afford it I would sell my house and buy a bigger one so that we wouldn't have to live in, as they say, each other's pockets. But I can't afford it. Bell and I will have to live side by side in four rooms. She is destitute and depends solely on me. I haven't yet actually handed cash over to her, I haven't given her pocket-money for her cigarettes, but no doubt that will come. Is she drawing social security benefits? I haven't asked, any more than I asked what happened to the money derived from the sale of Silas's father's house. She told me.

'I spent it on my defence. They wouldn't give me legal aid when they found out I had a private income.'

We began packing her things into my suitcase. Among them I recognized a necklace Cosette once gave her, a long chain of amber beads. I don't suppose they are really amber, they are only amber-coloured, and I have never known Bell to wear them. They were in a box, a long shiny black box that I think is called 'japanned' and which was probably once used for keeping long gloves in. No doubt the beads were in this box when Cosette gave it to her. Also in there, wrapped in one of the remnants of cloth that constitute Bell's garments, was the bloodstone.

The dark green is chalcedony and the red spots are jasper. This gemstone was much in demand by painters in the Middle Ages for flagellation scenes, and to symbolize the blood of martyrs. I sound like Felicity, I probably got that from Felicity. I laid the ring in the palm of my hand, looking closely at it for the first time. The setting is composed of many strands of gold, laid parallel to form the band itself, twisted and plaited where these surround the stone. Examining it, I wondered where it had come from, if it had passed down in our family, perhaps from one afflicted member to another, until it finally came to Douglas's mother, who was my mother's aunt. And I remembered Cosette giving it to Bell for her thirtieth birthday, at the party when Mark came to the House of Stairs for the second time, and how Bell took it indifferently with a muttered word of thanks.

'Have you ever worn it?' I said.

She didn't answer my question, but said to me, 'You can have it. Why don't you have it?'

'All right,' I said. I expect I spoke ungraciously, for I thought of it as Cosette's to give, not hers.

Her action, her words, surprised me. She put the bloodstone on my finger. 'With this ring I thee wed,' she said, and laughed her dry as dust laugh. I don't understand her, I often don't, I don't know what she wants. She can still astonish me. For instance, it always surprised me how little of the paraphernalia of living she needs in order to live. We filled that one suitcase and a single plastic carrier and the room was emptied.

'And think what someone like Felicity has,' I said. 'That great house filled with her things and the flat they have that must be filled with them too.'

'If I can't have the things I want,' Bell said, 'and I can't because I can't afford them, I'd rather have nothing.'

It wasn't the first time I had heard her say that. But the first time I heard it I didn't know what I know now. Someone walked over my grave; I felt a small, cold thrill, but she wasn't looking at me, she had forgotten ever saying it before. She looked round the room with indifference, the indifference I believe she has felt to everywhere she has ever lived. So much for Mark, who tried to make me believe she loved the House of Stairs and would mind leaving it. We went downstairs and out into the street, looking for a taxi. At certain times of the day taxis come down from Cricklewood, making for the West End. This wasn't one of them and we walked southwards along Kilburn High Road, I carrying the suitcase and she the carrier bag, but they weren't heavy and it had been a warm humid day of thick air and hazy sunshine. Even if no taxi came we could have got into the tube at Kilburn Park. It was Bell who, looking down the long slope towards Maida Vale, mentioned the friend we had who lived there.

'Now we're here we could go and see Elsa.'

I was more likely than she to have made this suggestion. Up till today she hasn't spoken of wanting to see anyone from the past, and when Felicity came she was almost violent to her. She has asked about no one, reacts with perhaps natural terror when I speak the names of Cosette and Mark – that I can understand. But Admetus? Eva? Has she no curiosity about the fates of Ivor Sitwell and Gary and the dancers? I had made no reply to her and she said with suppressed violence, 'I should never have come out of there, out of prison. I was best in there. I could cope in there, maybe I ought to go back.'

There is no answer to make. Platitudes and placebos, which I was once quite good at offering, are alien to my present mood. Instead I said, pointing down Carlton Vale, 'Elsa lives down there. Do you want to ring her first?'

'Why, when we're on the doorstep? If she doesn't want us she can tell lies to our faces just as well as on the phone.'

'She won't tell lies to me,' I said. I was aggrieved and glad to be, glad to feel something more than dull indifference. The suitcase suddenly felt heavy and I wondered what I was doing, carrying it. 'Your turn,' I said and I swung it at her, the red sparks in the bloodstone flashing. 'Give me the bag.'

Elsa keeps me informed of things – and people. Certain people I never see any more whom she does see she tells me about, and that is the only way I know. She is my best friend, yet months pass by without our seeing each other. I hadn't even spoken to her on the phone since Bell reappeared in my life. I don't believe there is anyone left but me who still calls her by that school name, Lioness. One of my books is dedicated to her, the one about the safari park: 'To the Lioness, with love.'

She looks like one, strong and lithe and muscular, with amber cat's eyes and a mouth that tilts up at the corners. Of course she must have known Bell was with me, Felicity would have told her, for Felicity is her cousin. Or, rather, Esmond is and as he once gravely told us, 'A cousin's wife is a cousin. Husband and wife are one flesh.' She answered the entryphone and said nothing to my announcement of who it was but 'Come up.' At the top of the first flight of stairs where her flat is she was waiting for us, a towel in her hands and her sandy-orange lion's hair wet from washing. Bell didn't even wait for her to speak a word but said, 'I can see you don't recognize me, I'm so changed. An ugly sight, aren't I?'

For some reason I wanted to hit her. I wanted to scream out. It is a new mood for me and devastating. Of course I did nothing – that is, I said nothing, only made eye contact with Elsa and cast up mine, while a kind of panic hatred of Bell made my whole inner self tremble, though outwardly I was icicle-like, still and stiff and cold. Elsa spoke graciously, reminding me that she was indeed Esmond's cousin, 'It's good to see you, Bell. I hope you and Elizabeth will stay and have lunch with me.'

In this gracious way she spoke to a woman who has done murder and put herself outside the pale of any civilized society. And with aplomb she preceded us into her flat.

*

246

It isn't the same place as the one she was waiting to move into while staying at the House of Stairs. That was a very long way down in Chelsea, practically Fulham, even further west than where the Thinnesses have their pied-à-terre. Since then she has married again and is waiting to be divorced again. She was not particularly interested in people's motivations, but she was interested in sexual relationships. And she loved Cosette, she was pleased to see Cosette happy.

'He doesn't seem to have any friends of his own,' she said to me.

'If he has they don't come here.'

Of course you might have said that Bell had no friends either, but that wouldn't quite be true. The Thinnesses were her friends and the Admetuses, at least she knew them and associated with them; I was her friend and Elsa. But Mark appeared to have no one, nor could I remember his speaking the names of friends in conversation, but only of his referring vaguely to people he knew. He never talked about his past either. He might, for all that was known of his origins, have been born two years ago, aged thirty-six, or been created by Pygmalion-Bell and had life breathed into him specially for me to see him across the room at Global Experience. It was quite a shock for me, though a pleasant one, when researching one day in the British Newspaper Library and looking (for something quite different) through old copies of the *Radio Times*, to find his name among those in the cast list of a play heard five years before. Ibsen, it was, *Rosmersholm*, and Mark Henryson had been cast as Peter Mortensgaard.

He had told me nothing of his past, but why should he? Cosette he had probably told. Cosette very likely knew his whole history from childhood to the present day. How would I know? I was hardly ever alone with her; Mark was always there.

Elsa refused to fall in with Mark's plan to get Bell out of the house while his valuer came, for Elsa is truly honest, truly open. She might – as Bell suggested today – tell a social lie or two, but she wouldn't consent to deceive a friend for an unworthy purpose. She no more believed than I did that Bell was too deeply attached to the House of Stairs to bear the idea of leaving it. By this time I think she had gathered how little Mark had wanted her to come there even for two or three weeks, though she was one of the few of Cosette's visitors who bought food for the house, contributed to the wine stocks and saw to her own laundry. Clearer-sighted than I, fresh of course to the situation, she suspected Mark, and said in a sweet tone that took the sting out of it, 'You'll have to do your own dirty work.'

In the event he did nothing, the valuer when he came didn't want to go into every room and Bell was shut up in hers with the television on. Three days later a man representing a property company – shades of things to come! – came to look at the house with a view to buying it. It was a happy coincidence for Mark that Bell happened to have gone out for one of her long walks, the first she had taken for weeks. Before she came back Mark and Cosette had gone out house-hunting, or I believe they had gone out for this purpose. They made a big secret of this because Bell wasn't supposed to know.

'Short of killing her,' I said to Elsa, 'I don't see how they're going to get out of it.' I was writing a novel in which someone had to be disposed of by murder. It was the only possible way for the life of the book to continue. I suppose I had it on my mind.

'I doubt if they'll do that,' she said.

That night we were all to be taken out to dinner by the dancers. Entertaining Cosette was something they did about once a year, to make up for all the entertainment they received from her. Since they dined with her at least once a week and were taken about by her to plays and concerts and cinemas, it didn't even begin to make up for it, but I expect it eased their consciences. They were resigned to the company of whoever else might be in the house, for Cosette would have contrived, very gently and tactfully, to decline their invitation unless she could take what Ivor had rudely called her 'entourage' with her.

I remember so much, but I don't remember the restaurant we went to. In Soho it may have been, or Charlotte Street. And Luis and Perdita were lucky, for they only had five guests, whereas in the past there might easily have been ten. Bell had consented to come, much to my surprise. It was curious how she had got herself into the position of the odd person out, the third in the two's-company-three's-none situation, almost the spectre at the feast.

We paired naturally into Cosette and Mark, Luis and Perdita, Elsa and me, and then there was Bell. She must have been the worst-dressed woman in that restaurant – she was by far the worst-dressed of our party, a tied-up parcel of layers the colour of brown paper – but heads turned to look at her. They always did. It was the way she walked, so straight and her head so perfectly carried, and that crown of disordered gleaming pale hair and that inde-structible face, the profile carved for a cameo.

It is worth telling you how we were seated. They put three tables together for us and Luis sat at the head of them with Cosette on his left and Bell on his right. Mark was next to Cosette – they always sat like that, they would never be parted – and Elsa next to him. Opposite them, Perdita sat between Bell and me, so that Elsa and I faced each other.

We ate nothing that evening, we none of us reached the point of having dinner. I think Luis actually ate a few pieces of a bread roll and we all had drinks of the aperitif kind. Bell had brandy. It's strange how clearly I remember that. Everyone else had wine or sherry, and Cosette of course had her orange juice, but Bell had brandy, a double brandy which she asked for in a desperate voice as if she were dying for lack of it. Cosette was wearing a new dress of pale yellow lawn with a pattern on it of sprinkled white daisies, and she was looking very nice, her face serene and happy. The dim lights in the restaurant flattered her. Her hair had been done that day and looked as fine and as silky as Bell's. For once she wasn't talking with Mark, behaving, as they so often did, as if no one else existed, but had got into a mild argument with Luis about, of all things, whether Gibraltar should or should not be Spanish.

A waiter came and took our orders, Luis had just finished telling a joke that was going the rounds about Franco having said Britain could keep Gibraltar if she would give him back Torremolinos, when a woman came up behind Mark and touched him on the shoulder. She was about forty, dark, attractive, more convention-ally and conservatively dressed than any of us. He looked round, immediately pushed back his chair and got up. She kissed him on the cheek.

It would somehow be satisfying to say that he turned pale. In the fiction I write all the colour would have drained from his face or he would have flushed 'darkly'. Mark simply locked blank. He said, 'Hallo, Sheila,' and then spoke our names rather slowly and monotonously. It was as if he was struggling to recover from a shock. 'Cosette, Elsa, Elizabeth, Perdita . . .' but she interrupted him with, 'Of course I know Bell!'

She was looking at Bell and smiling. Bell was holding her brandy glass in both hands, just staring ahead of her. By this time it was clear something was very wrong, or something was about to go wrong. At least it was clear to everyone at our table but not to the woman called Sheila who, swivelling her head to the left and to the right, having uttered shrill hallos and how-do-you-dos, said, 'I'm Sheila Henryson, I'm Mark's sister-in-law.'

She turned round and beckoned to a man who was sitting with a party almost as big as ours. He got up and made an excuse to the woman next to him. He wasn't in the least like Mark in feature, and he was much heavier, but as soon as you knew you could see he was Mark's brother. Which meant, didn't it, that he must be Bell's brother too?

Sheila Henryson must be a very insensitive woman. The silence at our table was almost palpable now, but she seemed unaffected by it. Her husband came up, muttered something to Mark and gave him a pat on the back. Isn't it strange that I never learned what Mark's brother's name is and I don't know now? She began making explanations. They lived abroad, Riyadh or Bahrain or somewhere like that, were home for a few weeks' holiday, had tried to write to and then phone Mark but had, as she put it, 'got no joy of that', which wasn't surprising since Mark never went home to Brook Green any more. She began making plans for the two parties to unite, we must all contrive somehow to sit together, the management would fix it, they were with people Mark knew, she said, and who would love to see him again . . .

Cosette was the first of us to speak. She had been looking simply confused. Not unhappy, not that, but bewildered. She interrupted Sheila Henryson's flow in a way quite uncharacteristic of her, and said to Mark's brother, 'Then Bell is your sister?'

'No,' he said. 'What makes you think that?'

I heard Bell make a sound. It wasn't distress but more like exasperation. Cosette didn't turn pale or flush either, but age got hold of her face, she aged before our eyes. She put out a hand as if to touch Mark. He was still standing up, standing quite rigid, with his eyes fixed on a point on the other side of the restaurant. The way he was standing with his brother on one side of him and his sister-in-law on the other, made him look like someone about to be arrested. Cosette put out her hand and withdrew it without touching him. Mark's brother gave a nervous laugh.

'I can tell I've said something I shouldn't,' he said.

It was at this point that a waiter appeared with a plate in each hand, the first of the hors d'oeuvres we had ordered. Cosette looked at the artichoke hearts he placed in front of her, put her hand over her mouth, got up and walked out of the restaurant. She walked fast and clumsily and as if she were blind, bumping into people and pushing chairs out of her path and fumbling with the door and letting it bang behind her.

Everybody began talking at once, Luis and Perdita inquiring what had gone wrong, Elsa casting up her eyes and saying she wished to God she hadn't come, Bell drumming her fists frenetically on the table and saying, 'Fuck, fuck, fuck, fuck – oh, fuck!'

The brother said to Mark, 'But what on earth did I *do*?'

Mark didn't answer. He went after Cosette. I sometimes wondered if poor Luis and Perdita had to pay for that uneaten meal, for I don't think even they ate any of it. I heard Luis say something to the waiter about bad news, about its being impossible to stay. I never saw Perdita again, though Luis I did – but that is another, later story. Murmuring that we were sorry, sorry, that we too must go, I left them there with the brother and his wife now imploring them to explain what had gone wrong, and followed Elsa and Bell. Cosette had disappeared and so had Mark. Elsa said what I hadn't been able to find the words for, 'Why did you say he was your brother?'

Bell heaved up her shoulders in an exaggerated shrug. She cocked a thumb at me. 'It was her idea. She said, is he your brother, and I thought, why not? I thought it'd work better and so it did till that stupid bitch put her spoke in.'

'What do you mean, work better?' I said.

She didn't answer that one. 'He's my lover,' she said.

I think I gasped. 'Since when?' I too had a vested interest – nearly as much as Cosette did.

'Years.'

Cosette and I, then, were in the same boat. When was it I had first seen them together at Global Experience? Three years ago . . .

I said fiercely, 'He's not still your lover.'

'There's had to be' – she paused, in search of a phrase, found one that was wildly unsuitable – 'a temporary suspension of that.'

We were walking along the street, wherever it was. A street of restaurants and clubs and little shops. The weather was warm and sultry and it wasn't anywhere near dark, but high summer and as light as at mid-afternoon. That sort of shock gives you a pain, the kind they call a stitch, that you can get from hard running. I felt as if I had been running. I wanted to sit down and I did. I sat on a doorstep. Elsa stood and looked at me, her face kind and concerned but very puzzled, and Bell stood a little apart. If I had to describe the way she looked I'd say she looked awkward, which was very unusual for her.

'I don't feel equal to this,' she said.

Elsa looked as if she would have liked to hit her. 'Shut up,' she said. 'Why don't you piss off somewhere?'

Which Bell did. She just walked away from us, her head held high. She came to a street that turned off to the right and walked down it, disappearing from view. Elsa and I stayed there for a while, sitting on the step, while I thought about what it meant to me, Mark being Bell's lover, and what it would mean to Cosette, and then we got a taxi and went home in it. The house appeared to be empty. I went outside again to look for Cosette's car. It was still a Volvo, though not the one she had had when she moved there, the successor to the successor of that one. Parking in Archangel Place was getting more and more difficult, but it was always possible to park somewhere down there or in the news. I looked up and down the street and down into the mews but the car wasn't there, and that obscurely made me feel better, it made me think Cosette and Mark must have gone out somewhere in it together. At any rate it made me feel better for Cosette.

Elsa and I got ourselves something to eat and we waited. She asked me no questions but took one of the new novels Cosette had on the table and started reading it. I believe she guessed I had an emotional involvement with Bell quite different from my friendship with herself. But I didn't care then, I didn't care about hiding it. I couldn't read, I could only lie back in my chair and stare at the ornate, complicated ceiling and the cobweb-festooned chandelier and think and think and be wretched. When it got to midnight, I said, 'I have the feeling we'll never see Bell again.'

'Who cares?'

I didn't answer her. She knew very well I cared. 'She won't come back here,' I said. 'She won't bother about her things, they don't matter to her. She'll go to someone, she'll go to her mother.'

'Are you sure she's got a mother?'

'No,' I said. 'No, I'm not,' and then, 'I thought she had a brother.'

Elsa said, 'She told me a long time ago, when I first met her at Thornham, that she had no parents. She had had no parents since she was twelve. I thought it was a bit fishy when you mentioned her mother.'

'What she told you might equally well be a lie.'

'True, but they can't both be.'

'What happened when she was twelve? I mean, did she say her parents were killed in an accident or something? What happened to her?'

'She told me only that she lost her parents. She went into some sort of institution.'

'A children's home, d'you mean?'

Elsa gave me a strange look. 'I don't think it was a children's home, not at that stage, that came later. I don't know what it was.'

As she was speaking, reluctantly, doubtfully, as if the words were dragged out of her, we heard the front door close downstairs. We were sitting in the drawing room and I think we both thought it was Cosette or Mark or, best of all, Cosette *and* Mark. The footsteps, a single set, came up the first flight and passed the door. It must be Bell. We heard her go on up the stairs, walking heavily for her, and because of this we weren't positively sure it was she, and we went out on to the landing to listen. Like personages in a ghost story who have heard some sound that shouldn't be, some unnatural footfall, we stood there clutching each other by the arms and staring upwards. It was absurd, it was hysterical behaviour, but we seemed to be involved in some high drama, and we held our breaths. Even from down there you could hear that 104th stair creak. Her bedroom door closed.

Elsa smiled her crooked ironic smile and broke the tension with, 'She hasn't got a mother.'

In the drawing room again, having no thought of going to bed, though it was past one, we opened the french windows and went out on to the balcony. It was a warm night and very quiet. But after a while of listening you could hear distant music of two sorts, and other sounds, a faint throb of traffic, a light rhythmic hammering as of someone who, because he worked all day, had to build his shelves and cabinets by night. The foliage was as dense as in a country lane, the trees heavy hanging masses of unmoving leaves. On a house opposite a vine grew and grapes dangled from it, gleaming pale green in the lamplight.

It came as a shock to see that the Volvo was there. It filled the space which had been empty when Elsa and I came in. We could see only the roof of it and we had no idea how long it had been there. The notion came to me to go back into the room and put the lights out. Whether this worked or whether the extinguishing of the lights went unnoticed I can't tell, but after a moment or two, the driver's door opened and Mark got out. I nearly gasped, I felt an almost intolerable constriction of the throat. What had become of her? Where was she? It seemed possible he had never found her, that he had come back here only to fetch the car and search for her.

He went round to the passenger door and opened it. I should have remembered his unfailing simple courtesy. Cosette got out without assistance from him, without taking his hand. But they were together, they had returned together. He closed the car door and they stood looking at each other and then, there in the street where anyone could observe them, indifferent perhaps as to whether they were observed or not, they went into each other's arms and pressed their faces together with their cheeks touching.

He put his arm round her waist and led her out of our sight up to the front door and into the house.

*

Elsa is as courteous and friendly towards her as if Bell had done no more than travel on the tube without a ticket. Does she remember that dinner and Bell's flight and my misery? We have all grown decorously into the preliminaries of middle age. After lunch, over coffee, I watched Bell who sat stately and dignified, cool and – harmless. It was absurd what she had said to Elsa about being an ugly sight. Perhaps that was why she had said it, for she has lost years and years since that day I followed her on the tube, since that day I went to see her in her room in Kilburn. She is growing young again, is being rejuvenated, revitalized. I could see Elsa glancing from her face to mine. It may be only conjecture, it may be my imagination, but I fancied Elsa was making comparisons, was thinking, how can Bell look the way she looks after suffering so much and Elizabeth the way she does after so little?

Of course she said nothing and it may be she never thought it. We had talked about everything that was innocuous, we had talked for about two hours, and still I hadn't asked the question I always make a point of asking Elsa when we meet, for I have no other means of finding out the answer. She had told us about her new job and her new man that may be the one she has been waiting for, though she won't marry him, she will never marry again. We spoke of our morning's task and our future plans, our intention perhaps of taking a holiday together. I mentioned my father and his visit. And then Bell got up and asked Elsa where the bathroom was.

'Do you have a bathroom?' was what she asked, as if the chances were that the occupant of this charming and prettily furnished flat had to use a communal lavatory and the public baths.

Elsa smiled at me after she had left the room and I knew the same thought was passing through her mind. Whatever else Bell was, had become, she remained tactless, insensitive and, about such small social niceties, quite uncaring. Quickly, I asked my question.

Elsa seemed to understand. Her eyes went to the closed door. 'Very well, I think. We spoke on the phone a couple of weeks ago.'

'I'm glad,' I said. 'I'm always glad. I don't suppose' – How often I ask this and always so awkwardly! – 'anything is ever said about me?'

That English passive is enormously useful, isn't it? You can thus do without names, should anyone be listening at the door.

'Nothing, Lizzie, I'm sorry.' I nodded a little. 'I get the impression even mentioning you would – cause great pain.'

'Bell hasn't asked,' I said. 'I don't want to say anything until she asks.'

I could hear her coming back, heard her pause outside before bringing her hand to the door handle. She is quite capable of listening. Elsa and I fell silent, looking at each other, waiting for her to come in, awed by her, knowing she stood on the other side of the door in the hope of hearing secrets she was not meant to know.

20

The phone was ringing when we came into my house. That was three days ago, but it seems a lifetime. The widow my father likes but wouldn't marry for fear of depriving me of my inheritance had rung me to tell me he was ill, he had had a stroke. Bell was behaving strangely. She had been quiet, bemused, ever since we left Elsa's. When she heard my father was ill, that I was going immediately down to Worthing where he was in hospital, she said, 'Is he going to die?'

'I suppose so.'

'I shall be all alone here,' she said. 'I shall be alone in the house. I don't know if I'm equal to it.'

'You'll have the cats,' I said.

At present I am staying in my father's house, which is on an estate where the average age of the inhabitants is said to be seventy. I am used to it, I have come down here to stay every year for a week, but in the past I have tried to pick a time when the Arundel Festival is on or there is good theatre at Chichester, so that I have something to do. And once, fourteen years ago, shortly after he had bought it, I lived here with him for a whole month, I and my typewriter, trying to write, trying to seem normal. Poor man, he must have wondered if he was to be saddled with me for years, for a lifetime. I could hardly explain that I had lost my home, my friendships, my life, but I made a convincing enough case for myself with my excuse of not wishing to stay in a place where murder had been done.

Most of each day I spend at the hospital where my father lies half-paralysed and with his face grotesquely twisted. No doubt it is natural to feel as I do when one's father is dying. Just the same, I have never before experienced a depression so deep as to cause physical malaise. A great weariness has taken hold of me and, as was the case with Bell when she first came out of prison, I sleep a lot. I fall asleep in the chair at my father's bedside and, returning to his house in the evening, fall asleep in my armchair in front of the television. But I don't sleep well at night. At night, with my head aching, I lie awake and think about things. And I see figures and shapes form in the darkness whether my eyes are open or closed, I see men and women then that I have never seen before, strange faces like the faces of unknown people we see sometimes in dreams. One of the oddest things, it has always seemed to me, is that our minds can invent people for our dreams. Or are they not invented? Have we seen them all somewhere before and has some camera of the mind photographed them? Between the unknown faces, emerging from a great crowd of them, I sometimes see Cosette's and sometimes Mark's, but they are never together, they are always separated by a multitude of strangers.

That night fourteen years ago I fell asleep quickly, the sleep of relief. But I awoke to understand that though things might come right for Cosette, they couldn't for me. She still had Mark, but I had lost Bell. He had been Bell's lover. When, I asked myself, when was the last time? When was the last time Mark had made love to Bell? And suddenly I knew when it was. It was the night Auntie died, when Cosette begged Mark to stay and I, in my innocence, directed him up to the top of the house, to the room next to Bell's.

That other night, after the scene in the restaurant, while he and Cosette were out in the car, driving and parking and driving again, getting out to walk, sitting on park benches, he told her everything. He had to, he couldn't do less, there was nothing else for it. He laid it all before her, as Bell had conceived it and he, with increasing reluctance, had tried to carry it out. And Cosette forgave him. Why wouldn't she? It isn't hard to forgive someone who tells you he was kept from the ultimate baseness by love of you. But in these instances someone has to be blamed. Not the abject, ardent lover, but the lover's scapegoats. Mark, in those long hours of explanations and excuses, had been obliged (in his methodology) to lay the blame elsewhere, to confess that if some of the

258

action had been his the strategy was not, the original conception was not.

It wasn't in Cosette's nature to send for someone, to seek an interview designed to extract an explanation. She suffered, but in silence. She suffered, but she had Mark, who would mitigate any suffering for her, soften any blow. I was innocent then, unaware that I might be involved in Cosette's immediate trouble. I even felt excluded, an unnecessary presence in the house. That she might have any feelings towards me then beyond an affectionate but abstracted warmth, a mother's feeling for one of her children when, for once, her own concerns have become paramount, never crossed my mind. I had an idea only that when I next encountered her I would hug her and hold her close to me.

The next day, in the early afternoon, I met her on the stairs. There were so many stairs and the staircase was so big in relation to the size of the house that when the place was full meetings took place on the stairs every time you went up or down. There were only five of us now, and Bell had been up in her room ever since she returned in the middle of the night. Elsa was at work and the house was still and silent. I was coming down from my workroom, having finished my morning's stint rather late, and Cosette was coming from the drawing room back to her bedroom. She had a dressing-gown on, it was a Japanese kimono, green with white flowers, and her fair shiny hair hung loose to her shoulders. Her face was pale and drawn and you could see she had been crying, but a long time since, before she slept.

She would have gone past me without a word, without even that look of reproach which itself implies future forgiveness is possible. I put out my hand to touch her arm. You must understand I had no idea then that I could be thought guilty of any offence. If I saw myself as in any way culpable it was only in having been, among others, a witness of that scene on the previous night. She would have passed me without a glance but she was tired, drained of feeling, and when you are as close as she and I, living side by side, mother and child, must there always be greetings, inquiries, signs? Love, as against being 'in love', is about taking for granted. But I spoke to her.

'Are you all right, Cosette?'

She stood there and she looked at me. Behind her head hung that branched and bead-hung chandelier of Murano glass which had been so bright that night when Esmond switched the lights on. She pulled my hand off her arm, plucked it off, the way someone might pluck off a leech. Her eyes looked into mine, but dully, without feeling, without care. If it were possible to use such an expression in connection with Cosette, I would say with indifference.

I rephrased my inquiry. 'What is it, Cosette? What's the matter?'

It's strange, isn't it, that when those you love speak your name, your given name, you know all is well? You know things will be all right. Cosette didn't speak mine, she never spoke it again. She said, 'You brought that woman here.'

'Bell?' I was already cold with fear. 'But I didn't know,' I said. Even then I didn't want to speak of the deception she had practised. 'I didn't know; I was as much taken in as you.'

Cosette moved her shoulders. She was holding quite tightly on to the banisters, and she looked up the staircase, up the winding shaft of it, to the top. Her voice remained gentle, she couldn't change that.

'It was your idea Mark should pose as her brother.' I shook my head but she went on, 'You gave her some book to read.'

'Bell? She's never read a book in her life.'

Cosette said with quiet bitterness, 'She didn't need to read it. You told her the story. You gave her the whole marvellous idea. I suppose you told her what a close parallel there was to the situation here. Only I'm not young and beautiful and I wasn't dying.'

It was a lot to take in, and it took me some seconds to receive it, to begin the process of understanding. While I stood looking at her and she brought her gaze down from that spiralled height, right down, to fix it on her own white hands that side by side clutched the banisters, Mark's voice came from the bedroom above, calling from behind the door that was narrowly open: 'Cosette, where are you?'

She ran to him and let the door slam behind her. I stood where I was for a moment and then I went on slowly down. I had had a shock and knew myself the victim of a great injustice. Perhaps, just because of this, I was even then – so quickly do we rally our forces – sure I could explain, I could make things right. She had had a shock too. Wait a little, as Elsa might have said, wait a little.

Down in the kitchen, where I had been on my way to make myself a late lunch, I sat at the table and thought about what Cosette had said. My appetite had gone but I poured myself some icy-cold white wine that had been opened the day before, a glass drunk from it and the rest left in the fridge overnight. I drank my wine down, poured another glass and thought, you can understand why people take to drink. Mark, of course, had betrayed me – no, not that, for in order to be betrayed in this context I would have had to have done something wrong. Better to say he had shopped me, or borne false witness against me, sold me down the river. Plainly, he had told Cosette I had recommended to Bell that she and he do what the conspirators in *The Wings of the Dove* do, I had advised it as a practical plan. Sitting there with my wine, I remembered Bell picking up the book in my work room and asking what it was about, and I remembered my answer.

'This man and girl are engaged but they can't marry because they haven't any money. There's a young girl called Milly Theale who's terminally ill and enormously rich. James doesn't say what's the matter with her, but he does say it's not what you might think, meaning tuberculosis. I've always thought it must have been leukaemia. The engaged girl proposes to her fiancé that he marry Milly. Then when she dies she'll leave him all her money and he and she can marry and enjoy it.'

Bell had thought Cosette had cancer. Mark would marry her, she would die and he inherit her money. Then he and Bell would live on it. It came into my head how Bell said if she couldn't have nice things she'd rather have nothing. She would have nothing now. It was no wonder, I thought, that she had positively wanted Mark to sleep with Cosette, had been irritated by his delays, had expected him speedily to marry her. But what had her discovery, late in the day, that Cosette didn't have cancer, wouldn't die from natural causes, done to the plan? Not much. Doubtless, she saw herself still Mark's lover after the marriage (or the relationship at any rate resumed) and in that role able to enjoy Cosette's bounty as much as he did. Perhaps that too was part of the plan. Or had she intended to deal with Cosette?

I didn't think of that then. These ideas came to me much later, when I knew what Bell was, when the facts about her sister Susan were known and Silas's suicide came in question. On that summer's day in the House of Stairs I thought only that Bell and Mark had tried to re-live the plot of a novel and it had failed – as indeed the conspiracy in *The Wings of the Dove* fails.

Have I said that it was a very hot day? I don't believe I have. That kitchen, down in the basement, was the coolest place in the house. I went about opening windows, but without making much change in the atmosphere. It seemed only that blocks of hot stuffiness moved in to displace the blocks of hot stuffiness inside. No breath of wind stirred the curtains as the french windows were pushed open to bare the balconies. On the opposite side of the street a man and two girls came out on to the flat roof above the porch, spread out a blanket and lay on it, drinking wine. I had my wine bottle with me in one hand and the glass in the other and as I ascended the staircase, pausing at each open window, I poured myself wine and drank it, a very unusual thing for me to do, very out of character. If you live under the threat of Huntington's chorea you don't do things that will bring about a loss of dexterity, a vagueness, a failure of coordination. The wine began to give me a headache and dry up my mouth, but I wanted more, I thought of starting on another bottle, drinking myself into a stupor.

Cosette and Mark went out together at about three-thirty. I don't think they saw me. I watched them from the drawing-room balcony where I had finally stationed myself, by then with a glass of water. The sun had reached a stage of glare, close and dusty, as if it shone through a sheet of grey gauze. Cosette wore a loose flowing dress, sleeveless, in pastel-flowered voile. Mark was in jeans but with a jacket and a tie. They got into the car, Mark driving as usual. It must have been blazing hot inside the car, for I saw Cosette flap the passenger door back and forth, back and forth, before she closed it and they drove off. Later I found out that they had gone to see the registrar. They were fixing a date for their marriage. He was so weak, Mark, he was as weak as water, unable even to stick to that bold and honourable resolve of his not to marry where it might be thought he had married for money.

After a while I went out into the back garden, hot and dusty and scented by the eucalypt, and looked up at Bell's window. It was wide open, the two sashes pushed up to the top. I thought of calling out to her, but I didn't. I went up instead. By then I had got the idea that my best hope with Cosette was to make Bell explain that none of it was my fault, that I wasn't in on the conspiracy. I must have been drunk to have imagined Bell doing this. I called to her from outside the door. There was a movement from inside, as if she had been lying on the bed and had swung her feet to the ground, but she said nothing and she didn't open the door. I went down again. How many times, I wonder, did I climb and descend the staircase in the House of Stairs that long afternoon? How many times did I retreat to the garden and return to the drawing room? In times of stress I find remaining still very difficult, I need to fidget, to sit down, stand up, pace, wander to windows and gaze out of them.

On the drawing-room balcony, that Ca' Lanier basket, on to which this past year I saw the new occupant come from his red and white streamlined segment of drawing room, I paused, looking down through leaves of plane and laburnum, sycamore and sallow, leaves that flagged in the heat of the day, on to the dusty roadway, car roofs that reflected the sun's dull glare, yellowed grass growing out of splits in the pavement. I felt the heat laid on my arms like a thick soft cloth.

Do you remember in the Old Testament how the sun stood still for Joshua? The sun was stilled upon Gibeon and the moon in the valley. I could see no sun, it was lost in its own white pool of heat, a molten source of burning, but time stood still for me the way it stands still when you long for it to pass. I went back into the neither cooler nor hotter interior, again pointlessly essayed the stairs, and tried the garden that looked to me as grey as mildew. There I sat at the stone table where in days that seemed long past, long gone and lost, I had sat with Cosette and Auntie, and Cosette had been Mariana in the Moated Grange and had asked so plaintively why no one came to visit any more.

As I sat there I understood something. I understood that to

lose Cosette would be the worst of all possible losses, to which separation from Bell would be a mild deprivation, to which my own poor mother's death would be nothing, to which no loss of lover or friend could compare. I could even define it. It would be the heart of loneliness. For Cosette, whatever nonsense I told myself about Bell, it was Cosette I loved, Cosette was this house to me, she was my home, it was she I had chosen to be my mother.

I couldn't lose her. It must be possible to explain to her and make her see. But a kind of panic took hold of me, a primitive fear, closely linked with self-preservation. It was as if, without Cosette, I could not preserve myself, my self. If she had truly been my mother I could never lose her, for no matter what abuses have been heaped on them, what betrayals, insults, neglects, mothers can always be got back, brought round, retrieved. Mothers will always forgive. My terror lay in the fact that Cosette, though chosen, though loved more than any mother, was not my mother and between us there existed no flesh and blood bond of parent and child. The bloodstone, passed down through Douglas's family, had not passed from her to me.

You will see that I was growing hysterical. I returned to the house, went back to the garden, climbed the stairs to the drawing room and the balcony, and still they didn't come back or Bell come down or Elsa return from work. I hung over the balcony in the heat, and what caused this release I don't know, but sweat began to stream off my skin like bath water, as if I had stepped from a bath.

A taxi came down the street. It stopped outside and Luis Llanos got out of it. He had tight white trousers on and a loose white shirt made of some very thin transparent embroidered material and he looked very cool. He also looked, and all he needed to complete the picture was a black hat, like a bullfighter. When he had paid off the taxi he looked up at me and waved, very casual, serene really. Of course I understood he knew nothing, he didn't know the world was coming to an end.

I went down to let him in.

Two days ago, at nine in the morning, my father died. I have done all the necessary things, registered his death, notified the funeral directors, seen his solicitor. And I have done the unnecessary things too, comforted the widow who would like now to be *his* widow, phoned Bell.

I can scarcely imagine what words of sympathy from Bell would be like. What would she say? I shall never know, for now I have no more to lose and the occasion for condolence will never arise. What she said, yesterday afternoon, when I told her my father was dead, was: 'A good thing that didn't drag on.' And then, 'When are you coming back?'

I would have been made very happy once by such an inquiry from her. Now I find it mildly repulsive. Curiously enough, I don't much want to go home, it is quiet here and removed from anything I have ever known, a placid life among the old whose blood is tame and passion spent. We will have the funeral, and I and the widow will attend it and one or two of my father's neighbours, I expect.

It will be the first funeral to come within the scope of my care since that one fourteen years in the past and that I didn't attend. I was told it would be an outrage for me to be there. Bell, of course, was also excluded, but for other reasons. Murderers only attend the funerals of their victims if their crime has yet to be detected, and there was no detection in Bell's story. Surprisingly, that brother and sister-in-law of Mark's who had caused so much of the trouble, were there to show something for him – love or respect or, more likely, accepted behaviour. And Perdita and Luis, both in unrelieved but glamorous black, like participants cast for a dance of death. I saw none of it, I wasn't, as I have said, there. Elsa I think it was who told me, though surely she can't have been among the mourners. Luis Llanos I saw for the last time on that unbearably hot, still, dust-laden afternoon, when he arrived in a taxi to ask after Cosette.

Unfairly, perhaps, I took this inquiry when correctly translated to mean: What was going on last night? Give me all the dirt. Angry with the world, sore with resentment and beginning anyway to feel ill, I tried to force him to say what he really meant.

'Why should there be anything wrong with her?'

'Happy people, people who are having a good time, they are

265

running away out of restaurants in the middle of their dinners? No, Elizabeth, you know they are not.'

Sickness saved me. I said, 'Excuse me, please, Luis, excuse me a minute.'

As I ran from the room I could see him nodding, nodding and smiling, saying with awful complacency, 'Yes, you are throwing up, I think.'

I was throwing up. I had got to the bathroom just in time. Dehydration followed with swift ferocity and, leaving him alone, not caring, I went down to the kitchen to drink glass after glass of water. He had followed me down and was standing in the doorway watching me.

'Where is Cosette now?' he said.

'I haven't the least idea,' and then, because there was no point in being antagonistic, no point in providing the occasion for more explanations, 'Let's go out into the garden. It might be a bit cooler out there by now.'

'Why are you drinking, Elizabeth?'

He meant: why were you drunk? Luis was always, no doubt still is, asking questions. It is something people tend to do when they have a less than perfect command of the language they are obliged to speak. I have done it myself when trying to communicate in French or Italian. Real conversation in English was beyond Luis. He asked questions instead and, I must say in his favour, listened intently to the answers. If one was prepared to give them. I wasn't, not on that afternoon, and I shrugged my shoulders impatiently. I wasn't prepared to make tea for him either or open wine that I was in no fit state to share. Orange juice from a jar was all he was getting. We took it outside on a tray with two glasses.

Thus it was that Luis Llanos was also a kind of witness to the death that was shortly to take place.

By that time the sun had moved enough to leave half the garden in shade and the light in the other half wasn't bright, but hazy and subdued. There was stillness and there was dryness, a scattering of leaves from some pre-autumnal drop lying on the surface of the stone table. Ribbons of silvery bark hung as if flayed from the trunk of the eucalypt. The greyness looked as if it were the result of drought, not a natural property of those leaves, those stems, those effete flowers.

I never remember a single insect in that garden, not even a common cabbage white butterfly, not a bee, nor some bright-bodied blowfly. There must have been birds, if only sparrows, but if there were I have forgotten them. Once I lifted a large, marble-like whitish stone, a giant pebble, and from underneath scuttled away a family of woodlice. But these after all are not insects any more than spiders are. The walls, of brick, of stone, of flints in places, were tall enough to keep out all sight or sign of neighbours except for branches and leaves which showed over the tops of them, their foliage greenish or yellowing. All the grey was inside, grey of flowers and leaves and urns and faded furniture, grey shade and above us a sky of great brightness but a grey sky just the same.

It was the last time I sat there, just as it was almost my last day in the House of Stairs, the last time I spoke to poor, tiresome, irritating Luis with his vanities and his poses, his interminable questioning that had moved on to a series of inquiries as to why Cosette had this garden, kept it like this, had ever bought this house. He gesticulated with his long beautiful hands, naming the House of Stairs as 'an elephant, an absolute elephant', terminology incomprehensible to me until I understood he had omitted the significant adjective.

I hardly listened to him anyway. Looking upwards, I had seen Bell's head appear at her wide open window, appear strangely at floor level, edged out over the sill almost as if not attached to her body, as if it were a decapitated head that had rolled there. It lay, cheek downwards, on the window frame, nest of fair hair outside on the narrow shelf of stone. Of course she was simply lying on the floor, but that was not how it looked from down there. I was to see her again, but not for long and not to speak to – words that seem incongruous, more than absurd, grotesque.

The car returned. I heard it. Luis might have noted a taxi, not the individual engine sound of Cosette's car, a sound familiar to me but not to him. He had reached a point of saying, 'Why aren't you speaking, Elizabeth? Why don't you talk with me?'

I said, 'I'm not feeling well,' and I lay back against the chair and closed my eyes. I was filled with an enormous yearning for

Cosette, for her to come out and tell me it was all a mistake, stupid, she didn't know what had come over her, all was well, would I – would I forgive her? A need for action screamed at me, to move, to leap up and rush indoors, to cast myself upon her. Something told me not to do this, it would be wrong to do it, it would be disastrous. I must make myself wait if I could, if I could.

By now, I thought, they would be in the house. Surely, surely, they would come out here and speak to us? All the windows stood open, the garden doors. Then, of course, I knew nothing of the purpose of their outing, but I sensed it was something momentous. I sensed they had news to impart, perhaps the purchase of a house. And Luis knew nothing. I opened my eyes and saw him looking at me aggrievedly. I said, 'I think Cosette is back. I think I heard the car.'

He asked if she would know he was there. It exasperated me. I felt like asking him if he had left evidence behind, unravelled a ball of string as he passed across the hall and the dining room and out through the french windows. But all I said was, 'Why don't you go and tell her?'

I waited there for Cosette to come back with him, I waited and the sun stood still. Hours passed, five minutes passed. The sickness I felt had nothing to do with wine. I remember throwing my arms out across that table and laying my head in them. And Luis, at last, came back alone.

It seems unlikely that I shall ever return to my father's house. I came home yesterday, having asked his solicitor to see about the sale of it. Incredible the sum I find may be asked for it and probably obtained! Astonishing too the small fortune my father has left, his amassed £20,000, give or take a little.

'Take,' says Bell, when told about it. 'Unless you feel like giving some of it to me.' She laughs, so that I shall know she is joking. But, 'You could buy a bigger house for us now.'

It is an idea. I could buy a house big enough for her to live in one half of it and I in the other. Or I could buy her a flat and put her in it and be rid of her for ever. But this I don't think I shall do. A sense of fatality colours the depression I live in now, colours it grey. I am stuck with Bell for better or for worse. She has abandoned black at last and is dressed in grey herself today, garments in shades of lanata and senecio and eucalypt made of fine knitted cotton, but they don't suit her, they make her look like a witch, one of those beautiful witch-queens or malevolent fairy godmothers.

I am being silly, I am imagining things, for she is very gentle with me today, kinder than perhaps she has ever been. She tells me she has been to see her probation officer, agreed with this woman that she must look for a job, find herself a gainful occupation.

'I said I would. It's easier than giving an outright no.'

The cats have both draped themselves on Bell, the little one reclining in her lap, the big one half on the back of her chair, half on her shoulder. They have taken to her completely and now they prefer her to me. She strokes the big one's head, pushing his face into the curve of her neck.

'Of course I shall never work again. They made us work in the town when I was in the pre-release place – did I ever tell you?'

I shake my head, unbelieving.

'In a hospital, cleaning wards. I got paid. I spent all the money I got on cigarettes.'

I know she is stalling. She is filling up emptiness with talk that will provoke me to question her, so that she may postpone what it is she has to ask. I don't react, I am not to be tempted.

'Don't you want to know what else I did while you were away?'

'I know you want to tell me.'

'Elsa phoned and asked me round and I went. I went for walks, I walked all the way to Archangel Place and looked at the house – there!' She looks at me sideways, lays a hand on each cat as if prepared to spring away, carrying them with her. 'I watched telly. I saw Mark.'

My voice comes all ragged and rough. 'What do you mean, Bell? What do you mean, you saw Mark?'

'I saw Mark on telly.'

'He was hardly on it, only radio, you know that.'

'He made just that one film – don't you remember? Before you knew him. They were doing this Michael Caine season and he had this small part in a Michael Caine film. It was funny seeing him,

269

it was really strange. Do you remember we all once talked about the category of disappointing things? It wasn't much of a film, it was a disappointing film.'

We looked at each other, into each other's eyes. I had this feeling of my thoughts being read or that the force in them was so great as to transmit them into her mind. For I could see another watching that old film – with unchanged love? With indifference? Or in tranquillity?

And for once the thought-reading or the will to have thoughts read has worked.

'Lizzie,' she says, 'Lizzie, what became of Cosette?'

'I wondered when you'd ask.'

'Is she dead?'

'No, she's not dead. She married Maurice Bailey and went back to live in Golders Green.'

21

I have shocked her and she has gone quite pale.

'I thought she was dead, I thought she must be.'

'Why? She's only just seventy.'

'And she married that funny old man?'

'He was only eight years older than she. I believe people thought it very suitable. People like the Castles and Cosette's family must have thought it the best thing that could possibly have happened to her. They must have thought she had come to her senses at last. He was a widower and very comfortably off and he had a house that was even bigger than Garth Manor.'

'Why do you say "must have"? Don't you know?'

'No, I don't know, Bell. I can guess. I can gather things from what Elsa tells me. Elsa keeps in touch with Cosette but I don't, I can't.'

'Why don't you? What do you mean?'

I may as well tell her. I have never told anyone but Elsa. No one has been interested. Why should they be? We fall out with our friends, everyone does, friendships come to an end through disuse and neglect mostly, but sometimes through the violence of a quarrel.

'Cosette hasn't spoken to me since, Bell. She never spoke to me again, she has never forgiven me. She thinks I betrayed her, you see, and that was the one thing she couldn't bear.'

'You could have explained.'

'I didn't get the chance. After it happened, you see, that same evening, she didn't stay in the House of Stairs; her brother Leonard came and took her away to Sevenoaks. I phoned her there and Leonard's wife answered and said Cosette was too ill to speak to anyone. I meant to write but I didn't know what to say. Elsa and

I were still in the House of Stairs, alone there. A solicitor wrote to me on Cosette's behalf . . .'

Suddenly I find it desperately hard to speak of this. I am near tears and my voice is failing. But Bell presses me and Bell has got hold of the wrong end of the stick.

'You mean Cosette got a solicitor to write to you and tell you not to get in touch with her? Did she? I wouldn't have believed it of her!'

'No, Bell, he wrote to tell me Cosette wanted to give me the House of Stairs, she wanted to make it over to me by a sort of deed of gift.'

Her face has changed, it has become greedy, rapacious, the eyes glittering with need. 'She gave it to you? It must have been worth a fortune even then.'

'Don't be silly. Do you imagine I'd have taken it? I wouldn't have dreamed of taking it. She meant it as compensation for herself, for losing her. I understood that. I wrote to the solicitor and told him I didn't want the house or what it would fetch or anything, I didn't want compensation for losing Cosette.'

'And you never got in touch with her again?'

'After your – trial, after that, she went away somewhere and when she came back I couldn't find her, I couldn't find where she was. Perhaps I didn't try very hard. I knew her, you see, I knew how she felt about betrayals. Being betrayed was the only thing she couldn't forgive. Then Elsa told me she'd got married and I got married too and it was all too late.'

When Mark and Cosette came home from the registrar they went straight up to the drawing room, where Luis found them. They told him their news, they had no need to keep it a secret. They were getting married. They had given notice of their marriage to take place three weeks from that day. I don't know what was said, of course, I only know what Luis, coming back into the garden to say goodbye, told me was said, and he had no gift for reportage. But Cosette had referred to the difference in their ages, he told me, and I can imagine her saying, 'We had to put our ages on the form, Luis, and it was a bit humiliating, but not so bad as having to say them out loud.'

Luis, with unusual sensitivity, must have understood his company wasn't exactly the fulfilment of their desires at that moment. Not that Cosette would ever have said so or have failed to press him to stay, go home and fetch Perdita, all go out together and dine. Probably it was Mark who put up no dissuasion when Luis said, half-heartedly, that he must go.

Left alone, the two of them brought to crystallization the flow of doubt, hesitancy, half-decision, which had filled their talk, running between islands of love and love-making and future plans, ever since the night before. Mark must tell Bell. Or they must both tell Bell. Bell must be told.

The thing, the awful thing, was that Cosette never really knew what Mark had to tell Bell. Cosette never knew the magnitude of it, what being told that her lover was truly 'in love' with her would do to Bell. Because, you see, she thought the worst of it was that Bell must be informed of their intention to marry and of the loss of her home, a blow which she had persuaded herself would be much softened by compensating Bell with a substitute. What a one for compensating people with houses Cosette was, incurably generous, undaunted!

But this she saw as the worst of it. Mark, of course, knew better. Mark had some idea of what he faced in confronting Bell. No doubt he was afraid she in her turn would confront Cosette and pour out to her all the early plans she and Mark had made, an intrigue not qualified by loving apologies and excuses (and laying the blame elsewhere) as had been Mark's own policy when confessing to Cosette, but raw and ugly, with every greedy word quoted, every yelp of laughter recalled, every callous aspiration exposed.

You understand that I am guessing, don't you? You understand that I was not there, that Luis was not there, that Elsa wasn't yet home, that he and Cosette were alone? But if I had been there, could I have seen into Mark's heart? No one knows precisely what he thought or what he feared, though what he said when he was in Bell's room, that is known. He was very afraid to go up there. He would have liked to postpone it for ever, to have sat for ever in that close, warm, still drawing room, side by side with Cosette on the sofa, his arm round her and her head on his shoulder, from time to time turning her face to kiss her lips. But for the most part silent, at rest, the awful events, the alarms and excursions of the past twenty-four hours, by a miracle of love – and, yes, of exertion too and passionate hard labour – smoothed into serenity, forgiveness asked and granted, levelled into a kind of rich peace.

But for Bell. But for the task that remained. He probably told Cosette that he was afraid, he wouldn't have minded telling her that, though not precisely what he was afraid of. Wasn't she his mother as well as his lover, the gentle, all-embracing maternal image to whom he could confess anything, admit any terror?

I suppose she told him she would do it and he demurred. He knew Bell wouldn't have believed Cosette. Then she told him it was best to get it over. Procrastination makes things worse. Tell her and get it over. Probably she suggested taking Bell out to dinner. I am exaggerating only slightly when I say there were few things Cosette thought couldn't be ameliorated if not cured by a good dinner in an expensive restaurant.

He went upstairs, up all 106 stairs, or however many there were from the drawing room to the top. He knocked on the door, he called out to her. I don't know if she answered or if he just walked in without being invited. She was there in her room, lying on the floor with her head on the windowsill, the two windowpanes raised up to their fullest extent. A stark, nearly unfurnished room, with boxes of clothes lying about, and clothes on the bed, and Silas's paintings stacked against the walls. He went in and closed the door behind him, but he couldn't lock it. Perhaps he didn't want to lock it. He told Bell he had something to tell her.

After she had done it, some time after but before the police came, she told Elsa and me what had happened. Isn't it strange that, for all her knowledge of people, Bell had never guessed what Mark's true feelings were?

'He said he was in love with her. The fool was standing by the window, the open window, looking out. I knew he was going to marry her, that was part of the plan, that was great, fine. What did I care about the bloody house? I didn't want to live in this house. But he was in love with her? He was going away to live with her, just her, and drop me in the shit? It was him saying he was in love with her, and I knew the fool meant it, that was what did it. He said, "I know what we planned, Bell, I can't forget it,

I wish I could; it makes me feel sick now to remember. I'm in love with Cosette, I love her like I never loved anyone. I have to tell you I just want her and only her for the rest of our lives." And he turned his stupid face and looked at the sky like it was full of angels singing.

'She came in then. She tapped on the door and came in saying she thought she too ought to explain. So I did it. I wanted to do it in front of her. You know what I did. I jumped up and ran at him and pushed him out. I wanted to do it, it was great – until I'd done it, and then I wanted to pull him back out of the air, undo it. Did you hear him scream, Lizzie, did you hear him scream?'

It is something I should like to forget. If someone fell from a height I'd supposed they fell in silence, that the shock stunned them, the empty air. But Mark screamed as he fell, a cry, a roar of terror that split open the still and heavy summer evening. That sound, though, that expulsion of the ultimate expression of fear, was as nothing to the sound his body made as it struck the stone paving of the grey garden, a sound I am unable even now to describe, to convey anything approaching the dreadfulness of both its solidity and its liquidness, the noise of a human being bursting bonds that are its own flesh and bones.

We were inside the house by then, Luis and I, inside the french doors, walking across the dining room. You don't speak or reflect or even pause in these circumstances. You run. Away from or towards. We both ran back into the garden and saw the exploded thing spread like a stain on the grey flagstones, and we whimpered and held each other. We held each other like lovers, and rocked and moaned.

Crying, making these sounds, clutched together, as one we turned away from what lay out there, as we staggered, locked together, towards those open doors, first Elsa came walking across the dining room and then, pushing her aside, uncaring of anyone or anything that might be in her path, Cosette ran through the room and into the garden and cast herself upon Mark's body. She lay on his body until at last they took her away and I saw she was covered with blood, as if she too had been mortally injured.

I have lost track of the times of things. It might have been ten minutes or an hour afterwards that Bell came down and spoke to us. To Elsa and me, that is. Where was Luis? I find I have no idea what became of Luis. Someone phoned the police, but I don't think it was one of us. A neighbour perhaps, a passer-by. Did Mark's terrible cry ring across Notting Hill to summon the little crowd that gathered outside our gate? I heard sirens long before the police came and found out later this wailing came from fire engines rushing to a fire in Westbourne Grove.

It was a police doctor who gently lifted Cosette from Mark's body. Her face was terrible, smeared with blood, distorted into a ferocious ugliness by naked pain. They laid her on the settee downstairs in the television room where Auntie's body had lain the night she died. The doctor gave her a sedative injection, but if she slept it wasn't a deep enough sleep to prevent her going with Leonard when he came for her late in the evening.

I never saw her again.

I heard that she gave evidence at Bell's trial. I didn't, nor did Elsa. Bell told everyone what she had done, the police, the doctor; she seemed proud of it, and I am sure she would have told the Central Criminal Court if her counsel hadn't advised her not to give evidence. There is only one penalty for murder in English law and that is life imprisonment. 'Lifers' usually come out after about ten years unless there is a recommendation from judge or jury that the convicted person serve much longer than that. This happened in Bell's case for, after sentence had been pronounced and it was possible to reveal previous offences to the court, it was revealed that, when she was twelve years old, the middle child of three, the eldest being a boy of fifteen, Bell had killed her infant sister.

Those years of mystery, sometimes hinted at, usually glossed over, had been passed by her in a section of a women's open prison, set aside to receive her and only her. She had had lessons, seldom if ever been entirely alone, and yet her loneliness while there had been intense. When she was sixteen – it was obvious they didn't know what to do with her – she was removed to a children's home and placed in the care of the local authority. Many people, over the years, have told me they tried to kill a younger sibling, the baby brother or sister who, in their eyes, had stolen all the tender exclusive love previously lavished on the potential killer by a parent. Cosette once told me how she tried to kill Oliver by stuffing his mouth and nose with zinc-and-castor-oil cream, but her mother came in in time. Most of these children fail, but through ineptitude or timely discovery, not loss of nerve. Cosette failed because her mother came in. Bell succeeded. If her mother had come into the room two minutes sooner, Bell's strangling of the two-year-old Susan would have been no more than a failed act of violence on the part of a child maddened by jealousy.

But it taught her something none of us should ever learn: that killing, once done, may be done again: *c'est le premier pas qui coûte.*

Bell said to me reflectively, 'Cosette must be fantastically rich now. I mean from what you say the old man's got a lot too and he's bound to go first.'

She doesn't mind what she says, so why should I? 'Would you have killed Cosette?'

One of her sidelong glances. A pursing of the mouth. She looks well and strong, vigorous, her eye on the future. 'I thought she was going to die, didn't I? I wouldn't have had to if she'd got a fatal disease, which I thought she had.' It was a strange look she gave me, speculative, considering, utterly calm. And then, on a different note, 'Seriously, why don't you try and see her?'

'I suppose because I feel it would never be the same. The quarrel, her accusation and my inability to refute it, the silent years – all that would always hang between us.' I knew quite suddenly I wouldn't be able to make Bell understand. The nuances of human intercourse, the subtleties of affection, these are unknown to her. She knows nothing of treading softly, nothing of the kind of innocence Cosette and I had in our long mother-child friendship, which seemed strong but was fragile enough to be destroyed by a single external blow. 'Don't think I fail to appreciate your selfless attempt to secure me a legacy,' I said, 'but don't you think your own presence in my life might be a stumbling block?'

'Not when we've got a big house divided into two,' she said. 'She wouldn't have to see me. Besides' – O, Bell, unchanging, unchangeable, direct, relentless and incorrigibly selfish – 'I've got as much against her as she has against me. She stole my lover, you forget that.'

As if the years had never been. As if Mark had never died or Bell herself passed fourteen years in prison. Cosette had said she would like to steal other women's men, speaking of it as an impossible dream, but she had done it, she had stolen another woman's man, she had succeeded.

'You never told me how you met him,' I said, to deflect Bell from Cosette. 'You never said how long you knew him before you brought him to the House of Stairs.'

She gave me a strange look, sidelong, speculative, as if wondering how I shall take what she has to say – wondering, but not caring too much. 'I met him at that Global Experience.'

'No, that was where I first saw him. Don't you remember? He'd been sitting at a table with you and I said, Is that your brother?'

'You put the idea into my head.' Her smile was so wry, such a sophisticated smile. 'You've been a genius at putting ideas into my head, Lizzie.' Another cigarette, her eyes screwing up as the plume of smoke rises. 'I've got a real brother, you know that, I haven't seen him for a thousand years. When you asked that about Mark it gave me a shock, just a bit of a shock. I thought: It's Alan, but how can it be? I looked and I saw it wasn't. But I said yes when you asked. Alan, my real brother, he's so ugly and stupid, or he was, I expect he still is, but Mark was beautiful, wasn't he? I thought, I'll say he's my brother and then maybe I'll get to know him. Funny, wasn't it? I'd never seen him before, never set eyes on him before.'

I knew she told lies for pure pleasure. My voice sounded in my own ears stone-like, profoundly heavy. 'I don't believe it. It can't be. He'd been at your table.'

'It wasn't my table. I was just there. There weren't enough tables to go round. Those others sitting there, God knows who they were. When he came back – he was on his own, too – I said to him there'd been someone talking to me who asked if he was my brother because we looked alike. Did he think we looked alike? I asked him that. And that was it, Lizzie, that was the beginning of it. That was how it started. We had a drink and then we went

278

back to his place together. He said he was glad he wasn't my brother.

'But it was useful later on. It wouldn't have worked out, him trying to marry Cosette, and her knowing he'd been my lover. It was much better that way. Using both your ideas was really good – and they'd have worked if he hadn't been such a fool!'

So I have been responsible for it all, it all happened because of what I did and what I said, and Cosette has been right to blame me. Perhaps it is the pain in my head that makes it all unreal and any action, any positive step, seem impossible. I have written nothing for weeks, and if the headache is intermittent, the depression is constant. There is something else too, something I have never heard of anyone else having. I go to bed at night and fall asleep but within moments I am awake again and in such a panic of horror, such an indescribable fear of life itself, of reality, of my black-dark surroundings, that my body jerks and twists with it and my eyes, stretched wide open, stare in terror into the empty darkness. It passes, in ten minutes or so it passes, and I return to my customary placid and resigned depression, and eventually to sleep. But what is it? And why does it come?

I told Bell. Telling Bell things like that is useless, but I told her just the same. Put the light on, she said, drink something. Keep a glass of wine there and drink that. I tried it. But the bulb had gone in the bedside lamp, so nothing happened when I pressed the switch, and though I thought I had grasped the wineglass, I succeeded only in knocking it on to the floor. I knocked it to the floor and the other things with it, my watch and the aspirins and the bloodstone ring. So I wear the ring all the time now, I never take it off.

Before we went to see the solicitor, I asked Bell a question. I asked her what she understood love to be. She thought for a while but not for long.

'Being first with someone. It's when you're the most important person in someone's life.'

'What about you?' I said. 'What about when it's you doing the loving?'

She had never thought of that. Love, to her, is something you receive – or don't receive. 'My mother and father, I was first with

279

them till Susan came along. I thought I was first with Mark. No one was first with Silas except maybe Silas.' I could tell she didn't mind talking about it, Bell never minded talking about people, including herself. 'I'll tell you what,' she said, 'it's got to be the person you want wanting you, the rest don't count.'

It seemed safer not to pursue this. And yet do I care at all for her now? Does she care even a little for me? There is another passion in Bell's life which we never talk about and which has never yet been gratified. Isn't that the very heart and essence of frustration? To pursue always through unimaginable suffering yet never to attain? I say we never talk of it, yet in a way it was what our visit to the solicitor was all about.

Bell wouldn't come in, though she came with me as far as the offices, which are in Knightsbridge. The next hour she said she would spend in Harrods where she hadn't been for fourteen years. Among the antiques, the jewellery, the dress materials. The bit of Harrods I like best is the zoo, but Bell looked uncomprehendingly at me when I suggested this.

I went to make my will. It was Bell's suggestion, because I am really quite rich now and if I die intestate, who will it all go to, the two houses and my father's savings? The state? There is literally no one. Cousin Lily is dead now, they are all dead, or for obvious reasons have never been born. I have left everything to Bell, everything except £1,000 to Elsa for being my executor.

'Mrs Sanger is older than you,' the solicitor said.

'Yes, I know.' I didn't say any more and he didn't ask. It hurts my head if I start arguing.

When he has drawn up the will he will send it to me for me to sign in the presence of two witnesses, each to sign in the presence of the other. He said he would get it in the post on Friday, so it should be here by tomorrow. The people next door will be my witnesses. They used to feed the cats while I was away and before Bell came. Occasionally we go in there for a drink with them or they come in here. Their interest in us and the looks they exchange tell me they take us for a lesbian couple and this they find exciting.

I haven't told Bell what else I have done, that I have written to Cosette. I was determined not to do this, but Bell's telling me of her first meeting with Mark has changed my mind. Showing me my guilt, though my involvement was unconscious, has changed things for me. I know how much Cosette has to forgive and I know she will forgive me. Since I talked of her to Bell, I keep seeing her in her old habitat but translated to Maurice Bailey's house, I imagine her planting lilies in the garden. How do I know she is once more a significant presence in the Wellgarth Society, an officer in the Townswomen's Guild, a school governor, a voluntary hospital visitor? I just know. I know she has her grey worsted suits made for her by Maurice Bailey's tailor. I know she has a Volvo and he a Jaguar. Perpetua comes to clean and Jimmy to do the garden and Dawn Castle comes round and tells Cosette what a trouble her grandchildren are but she wouldn't be without them. I dream of Cosette and of these things, I dream of her coming here to rescue me, but from what? From what? After fourteen years I have written to her and now, each time the phone rings, I start and I tremble.

Bell watches me when I tremble. She watches me as if she is weighing things up, calculating her chances. She has been out house-hunting and is full of some house in Notting Dale she wants me to buy and which is so expensive I would have to take out a mortgage and, for safety's sake, cover it with an insurance policy in her favour. I may just do it, to avoid argument. I shall probably give in, though now as I in turn watch her, dressed in silvery-grey and wearing my cats as if they too were part of her clothing, taking and lighting another cigarette, her youth returned to her as when she was happy it returned to Cosette, I think how infinitely I should prefer to do what Cosette herself had in mind and buy her a home of her own.

I have my fantasies about the bloodstone. Some would call them delusions. Sometimes I see it as the bearer of love, as if love were contained inside it, in the pinpoints of jasper perhaps that are embedded in the dark green chalcedony and gleam in its depths. When Bell gave it to me I see her as giving me back Cosette's love, so long suspended. And sometimes it seems to be a carrier of affliction, resting on the fingers of those genetically prone to the disease so many of its wearers died of, passing the others by. It was loose on Bell's finger, is tight on mine, and I pretend to her

281

it won't come off, that unless it is cut off it must stay there for ever.

The phone is ringing. I start, of course I do, and in the seconds that separate its rings, wonder if I can in fact have a happy ending, wonder who will get to me first, Bell, who may be my fate, or Cosette, who would certainly be my salvation. Or will it be that third possibility on which Bell pins her faith . . .

I put out my hand to stop her getting up and I cross the room to answer the phone.

An invitation to

THE BRIMSTONE WEDDING

'*Vine fashions a tender, horrifying mystery ... The story, beautifully written, emerges delicately, yet with shocking, ironic force and breathtaking imagination*' The Times

New in Penguin Paperback **I** £6.99

Also available on Penguin Audiobook **I** Read by Jan Francis **I** £7.99

READ MORE IN PENGUIN

In every corner of the world, on every subject under the sun, Penguin represents quality and variety – the very best in publishing today.

For complete information about books available from Penguin – including Puffins, Penguin Classics and Arkana – and how to order them, write to us at the appropriate address below. Please note that for copyright reasons the selection of books varies from country to country.

In the United Kingdom: Please write to *Dept. EP, Penguin Books Ltd, Bath Road, Harmondsworth, West Drayton, Middlesex UB7 0DA*

In the United States: Please write to *Consumer Sales, Penguin USA, P.O. Box 999, Dept. 17109, Bergenfield, New Jersey 07621-0120*. VISA and MasterCard holders call 1-800-253-6476 to order Penguin titles

In Canada: Please write to *Penguin Books Canada Ltd, 10 Alcorn Avenue, Suite 300, Toronto, Ontario M4V 3B2*

In Australia: Please write to *Penguin Books Australia Ltd, P.O. Box 257, Ringwood, Victoria 3134*

In New Zealand: Please write to *Penguin Books (NZ) Ltd, Private Bag 102902, North Shore Mail Centre, Auckland 10*

In India: Please write to *Penguin Books India Pvt Ltd, 706 Eros Apartments, 56 Nehru Place, New Delhi 110 019*

In the Netherlands: Please write to *Penguin Books Netherlands bv, Postbus 3507, NL-1001 AH Amsterdam*

In Germany: Please write to *Penguin Books Deutschland GmbH, Metzlerstrasse 26, 60594 Frankfurt am Main*

In Spain: Please write to *Penguin Books S. A., Bravo Murillo 19, 1° B, 28015 Madrid*

In Italy: Please write to *Penguin Italia s.r.l., Via Felice Casati 20, I–20124 Milano*

In France: Please write to *Penguin France S. A., 17 rue Lejeune, F–31000 Toulouse*

In Japan: Please write to *Penguin Books Japan, Ishikiribashi Building, 2–5–4, Suido, Bunkyo-ku, Tokyo 112*

In South Africa: Please write to *Longman Penguin Southern Africa (Pty) Ltd, Private Bag X08, Bertsham 2013*

BY THE SAME AUTHOR

King Solomon's Carpet

Winner of the 1991 CWA Gold Dagger Award

'Vine, quite audaciously, deliberately, makes the London Underground the central character of the book ... The tension grows, patiently, hardly noticeably. Suddenly, there is an overwhelming sense of foreboding, of inevitable awfulness. But where from and why and how? Vine is the least predictable of writers, and when the unravelling takes place, it is brilliantly unexpected and original' – Marcel Berlins in *The Times*

'I longed to know what would happen next. Towards the end the tension fairly gets you by the throat' – Andrea Newman in the *Sunday Express*

Gallowglass

'A real valentine from hell' – *Time Out*

'Beautifully composed ... Barbara Vine has cast her fertile imagination into the realm of the fairy tale, and come up with a present-day parallel encompassing obsession, delinquency and romance' – Patricia Craig in *The Times Literary Supplement*

'Barbara Vine deploys her local landscape to evoke fear and build tension. Solid, provoking, well-written' – David Hughes in the *Mail on Sunday*

'Of all living writers, she can enter most convincingly into the criminal, or even pathological, mind' – John Mortimer in the *Sunday Times*

BY THE SAME AUTHOR

A Fatal Inversion

Winner of the 1987 CWA Gold Dagger Award

'Impossible to put down ... she is a very remarkable writer' – Anita Brookner

'No one horrifies as can Ruth Rendell. Writing under the pen-name Barbara Vine ... Rendell turns an East Anglian mansion into a place of terror ... In Rendell at her peak, as this book is, foreboding deters us from turning the page, while the urge to know what comes next forces us to do so. What comes last is a truly devastating pay-off' – *Listener*

'The story is brilliant, the ending a perfect bit of irony ... Barbara Vine has the kind of near-Victorian narrative drive ... that compels a reader to go on turning the pages' – Julian Symons in the *Sunday Times*

A Dark-Adapted Eye

Winner of the Edgar Allan Poe Award

'The writer brilliantly evokes the eerie quality of conventional life when it is invaded by uncontrollable passion – the inconceivability yet also the inevitability of murder among "people like ourselves". I congratulate Ruth Rendell on a fine achievement' – Robertson Davies, author of *What's Bred in the Bone*

'Full of shifts and surprises ... A modern novel with the Victorian virtues of a carefully devised plot unfolded for the reader with the utmost cunning art. Wilkie Collins would have admired it, and so would Dickens' – Julian Symons in the *Sunday Times*

BY THE SAME AUTHOR

No Night is Too Long

In a house by the sea, Tim Cornish is writing his confession of a love he could not resist, for a man he left to die on a distant Alaskan shore. Seductively his tale unfolds in complex layers of self discovery, a life of operatic passion and intrigue.

'A dark, watery masterpiece ... suffused with sexuality, which explores with hypnotic effect the psychological path between passion and murder' – *The Times*

'Storytelling of the highest order, with a narrative that grips like the Ancient Mariner' – *Literary Review*

Asta's Book

Asta and her husband Rasmus have come to East London from Denmark with their two sons: the year is 1905. With Rasmus constantly away on business, Asta keeps loneliness at bay by writing her diary. Published over seventy years later, the diaries reveal themselves to be more than a mere journal. For they seem to hold the key to an unsolved murder, to the location of a missing child and to the enigma surrounding Asta's daughter, Swanny ...

'An absolutely enthralling novel ... Seductive and fathomless, it sets its puzzles and keeps its secrets up to and beyond the final page. Essential reading' – Philip Oakes in the *Literary Review*

King Solomon's Carpet, *read by William Gaminara*, No Night is Too Long, *read by Alan Cumming*, Asta's Book, *read by Jane Lapotaire*, A Dark-Adapted Eye, *read by Sophie Ward, and* The Brimstone Wedding, *read by Jan Francis, are also available as Penguin Audiobooks.*